CRETACEOUS STONES

Jeff Dennis

Nightbird Publishing

Fiction by Jeff Dennis:

The Cretaceous Chronicles

Cretaceous Stones (2022)
Dragons of the Great Divide (2024)
Endangered Species (2026)

The Hobo Duology

King of the Hobos (2012)
Hobo Jingo (2017)

Standalone Books

The Wisdom of Loons (2009)
Daydreams and Night Screams (2013)
To Touch Infinity (2015)

CRETACEOUS STONES

A Sci-Fi Thriller!

JEFF DENNIS

CRETACEOUS STONES

Print ISBN: 978-0-9911871-6-4
ePub ISBN: 978-0-9911871-7-1

Nightbird Publishing
Loganville, Georgia

jeffdennisauthor.com
jeff@jeffdennisauthor.com

Fourth Printing: April 2026

10 9 8 7 6 5 4

One God, one law, one element,
And one far-off divine event,
To which the whole creation moves.

— Tennyson … from *In Memoriam* —

The Sky Is Falling

May 28: Camels Hump Lookout Tower
Lolo National Forest, Montana

GEORGE DANTLEY LOVED this old wooden observation tower perched six stories above Lolo National Forest in the Northern Rockies. Six miles northwest of St. Regis as the crow flies. God's country. Up here on "The Hump," more than a mile above sea level, he could survey 66 square miles of Montana wilderness. The panoramic view always took his breath away. Up top, he felt like a king in his castle lording over his kingdom.

Of course, George was far from royalty. A college student working a summer job for the Montana State Forest Service, he held the title of Forestry Technician GS-04. In government work that meant entry-level fire spotter making $14 an hour. The low pay scale didn't bother him; the responsibilities of the job were ridiculously easy. So easy, in fact, he often felt guilty taking a paycheck. Nothing much to do up here but stroll the catwalk ten minutes every hour, looking for smoke or telltale signs of wildfires, and monitoring the meteorological instruments.

This marked his fourth summer out here. He had just completed his junior year at the University of Montana's W. A. Franke College of Forestry and Conservation in Missoula. He'd arrived two days ago, head still swimming with facts and figures from his recently-completed coursework (Forest Environment Economics, Wood Anatomy, Watershed Hydrology, Fire Management, Timber Harvesting). Forest Service helicopter pilot Peter Lacroix had flown him out here before delivering three other fire lookers to their respective outposts. Saying goodbye to his friend, captain Lacroix, was the last human contact George would have for two weeks, when the allocation chopper brought food, potable water, and necessary supplies. Unless stray hikers showed up, his only contact with civilization would be through the Montana Department of Natural Resources Forest ServiceVHF radio network.

He stood outside the cabin, leaning against the catwalk railing, sipping instant coffee from a tin mug and taking in the beauty of it all. Such a gorgeous landscape! A green blanket of towering red cedar and lodgepole pine rolled out below him, punctuated by snow-capped peaks in the distance. Hiking trails and meandering streams cut through the mountains like brown and blue ribbons. To the north, Flathead Lake glittered in the low-angled sunlight. Closer, the Bitterroot River played hide-and-seek with the greenery.

The early morning chill nipped at his fingers and cheeks. A breeze rustled the treetops with a sibilant whisper. Birds chirped their melodious songs. He took in a deep, satisfying breath of crisp mountain air and thanked his lucky stars that he had landed this job the summer after he'd graduated high school.

He recalled his second interview with the DNRC folks in Helena when he was a wet-behind-the-ears high school graduate three years ago:

The Human Resources interviewer, a middle-aged salt-and-pepper haired woman named Abbie Cromwell, smiled at him skeptically. "Mr. Dantley, I'm sure you are aware this job requires long periods of solitude."

"Yes, I do," he said, wondering if he shouldn't say more.

She nodded, her expression impassive. "Many young people think they can handle the isolation, but it's been our experience that very few can. Are you comfortable working alone? It's a very long summer as I'm sure you know."

"I'm positive I can handle it," he said, hoping he sounded convincing.

She studied him for a long moment, her perusal making him uncomfortable, then said, "I know how you young people love your social media and internet. And many kids just can't bear to part with their cellphones. It's like an additional appendage for them. There is no Wi-Fi connectivity out where you would be stationed. Communications are limited to our radio network. Can you deal with that?"

"It won't be a problem, Ms. Cromwell," he said, surprised at his confidence. "I'm quite familiar with solitude. I've always been a loner. I'm an only child, and frankly, I'm not a fan of social media. I'm not big on cell phones, either. I see way too many people wasting their lives on those things."

She stared at him with a blank expression and he thought maybe he'd gone too far. But then she surprised him by smiling.

"Well, I must say," she said, "I wasn't expecting that. You have a very mature outlook. It's refreshing to hear that from one so young."

George smiled. "I've been told that I'm an old soul."

"Yes, I can see that. You seem like a very self-directed and responsible young man."

"Well, my parents might disagree with your assessment."

Abbie Cromwell laughed knowingly. "Yes, moms and dads can be pretty demanding with their kids." She glanced at her notes. "I see you've been accepted at the university in their forestry program."

"Yes, ma'am."

"Excellent! What do you plan to do with your degree when you graduate?"

He had no idea what he wanted to do after college. That milestone seemed an eternity away. So he told her what he thought she wanted to hear. "I'd like to stay in Montana and work for the Forest Division, maybe specialize in timber management or fire prevention. You know, work my way up to supervisor grade. I feel like this summer job will help me prepare for my career and allow me to accomplish my goals."

He hoped he didn't sound too rehearsed; he really needed this job. Dad had been very direct with him. George was not going to be a lazy couch potato during the summer break. Dad was a stickler for personal responsibility. George would work during summer vacations or else.

She kept her eyes trained on her paperwork, scribbling a few notes as she said, "Anything else you'd like to add, Mr. Dantley?"

He didn't think he'd convinced her of his worthiness. It was time to go for the close. "Yes," he said, "As far as the solitude thing? I have a couple of hobbies that I'm passionate about . . . things that will keep me happy and occupied during slow times in the forest."

"Really? Like what?"

"I love to read. Novels mostly. Thrillers, mysteries, science fiction. I also play guitar. I'm not very good but I enjoy learning new songs."

Abbie Cromwell tucked a curl of hair behind her ear. "I see. So you enjoy solitary pursuits, then?"

He nodded. "I'm really not much of a people person, to be honest."

"That's a good thing as far as this job is concerned." She glanced at the clock on the wall. "Anything else you want to add before we close?"

George felt emboldened. "Yes. Obviously I don't know any of your other candidates, but I believe you won't find a better suited person for this fire looker position than me. When can I start?"

She grinned from ear to ear and stuffed her paperwork into a file folder. Stood from the table and extended her hand to him. "You had the job before we started talking," she said, shaking his hand. "My interview was just a formality. Welcome to the team."

And that was that. The U.S. Department of Natural Resources and Conservation became his new employer. He underwent an extensive physical and a grueling three day training course in Missoula, then was turned loose in the Bitterroot Mountain range here on Camels Hump.

That first summer had been a big adjustment. The coal-dark nights were long and scary with nocturnal animal sounds creeping him out. And being at this high elevation above all the cover, the tower had a tendency to sway in the wind, the old timbers popping and squeaking like the joints of an old man. But he gradually overcame his fears and now loved being up here.

He went inside for more coffee, shutting the sturdy storm door behind him. The one-room cabin was spartan, the living space minimal: small kitchen area with a sink, two cabinets stuffed with canned goods and make-ready meals, a woodstove and a gas oven, a thin mattress laid across a low-rider bedframe near floor-to-ceiling windows, a table and two chairs. Meteorology instruments and the radio console dominated one wall. A lightning chair—a stool with insulated feet to prevent shock in heavy storms—sat near the console. Propane tanks under the reinforced floor fueled the generator that provided the tower with electricity. An antenna extending skyward from the peak of the hip roof provided strong radio reception.

George had just poured his second cup of coffee when he heard the radio belch a loud gasp of static. He looked at the scanner. The green light flashed red on channel 12, indicating an advisory warning. He found this troubling; it was early in the season for a fire.

The static cleared and a calm female voice filled the tiny room:

"Attention. This is an official bulletin directed to all fire looker outposts. Repeat, this is an official bulletin concerning all spotters. We have received authorized word that two meteorites have come down in the Northern Idaho panhandle, near Bonners Ferry. They crashed approximately eight miles apart in difficult terrain, spawning two small wildfires. All Montana fire personnel should be on the lookout for possible meteor showers, with particular attention to meteorite strikes. Our neighbors in Idaho tell us this is probably an isolated incident. However, we must be vigilant. As always, please report any unusual activity in your area immediately. Be careful out there, folks. This is Fire Dispatch signing off."

The channel went silent. George sipped his coffee. *Meteorites?* he thought. *How weird! They didn't teach us anything about that during training. Or at the university.*

The sun had crested the mountain peaks, and a creeping harsh glare began to light up the cabin. He donned his sunglasses and took his coffee out on the catwalk. Scanned the horizon. Wondered what it would be like to see a meteorite come down. Of course he didn't want to see brave men and women risk their lives to contain and vanquish wildfires. But hell, he sure would like to see one of those space rocks crash. It would give him something interesting to write about in his daily journal.

He finished his coffee and went inside to make breakfast. The woodstove remained hot from his coffee prep, so he rehydrated powdered eggs and got out his one and only frying pan, cooked himself an omelette, whistling a tune he'd just learned on guitar as he worked.

He sat at the small table and ate his eggs. As he took his last bite, he heard something strange. A high-pitched whistle, similar to a teapot blowing its spout. He stopped chewing and listened, anxiety growing in his gut.

The whistle became a scream.

He put down his plate, grabbed the binoculars, and rushed out to the catwalk. Scanned the horizon to the north.

And then he saw it, watched in utter disbelief as a small, glowing sphere crashed into the treetops, several miles away. If he had blinked he would have missed it. A few seconds later a muffled boom reached him, the concussion hitting him in his chest. The tower trembled for a horrifying second.

"Holy shit!" he said aloud, his heart racing. He felt a strange mixture of emotions: one part excitement, two parts trepidation.

He thought maybe he should climb down the long, winding staircase and find cover. But his curiosity got the best of him. He continued to glass the area where the meteorite went down. A dark spiral of smoke rose up through the hole in the forest canopy, but he couldn't see any flames. Still, he had to report this.

He went inside to the radio, picked up the handset, announced his discovery in a breathy, angst-ridden voice.

"This is Camels Hump to Dispatch. Come in, Dispatch."

A burst of static, then, *"This is Dispatch. Proceed, Camels Hump. Over."*

George did his best to keep calm. "Reporting a small meteorite strike approximately four miles due north in heavily forested terrain. No sign of fire, but there is a buildup of smoke. Request aerial fire support. Over."

"Request received, Camels Hump. Do you have a read on the

size of the object? Over."

"No. I was only able to catch a quick look before it hit. It was glowing bright red on the way down and had a smoky yellow flame of a tail. Didn't look that big, but I'm a good distance away. I sure did feel the concussion from the strike. It rattled the tower. Over."

"You sound frightened, Camels Hump. Are you okay? Over."

"I'm okay, yes. Just excited. I'm . . ."

He ceased talking as suddenly, an ear-piercing screech racked his eardrums. He dropped the radio mic and brought his hands up to cover his ears, looking around frantically for the source of the noise.

"What is that commotion? Can you read me, Camels Hump? What is that noise? Over."

The meteorite struck The Hump with a deafening impact, about a hundred yards down the side of the north face. The earth shook and the tower tilted precariously, throwing George against the wall, his shoulder taking the brunt of the hit. The windows shattered and two of the walls collapsed, showering him with shards of glass and wood fragments.

"Dispatch to Camels Hump. Can you read me? Over."

He crawled across the crazily slanted floor, struggling as he grabbed the radio handset.

"Mayday! Mayday!" he screamed into the mic. "The Hump's been hit. Send help! I'm . . ."

The tower crumpled and George's world dropped out from under him. The mic ripped from his hand as he felt himself falling, tumbling, rolling. Flying dirt and debris clogged his mouth and nose. The wind was sucked out of him and he struggled to breathe. The woodstove hit him on the way down, hot coals burning his flesh. A chunk of window frame pierced his chest.

The tower broke apart as it skidded down the granite face of The Hump.

George tumbled with it, the pain unbelievable.

Just before he lost consciousness he heard the dispatcher's voice coming out of the rubble.

"Fire Dispatch to George Dantley. Are you there? Can you read me?"

Where There's Smoke There's Fire

May 28: Northern Rockies, Montana

PETER LACROIX HAD BEEN FLYING up north, over Glacier National Park, taking survey photos when he got the distress call. Heliport dispatch in Missoula ordered him to return to Fire Protection HQ to pick up a medevac team. A Lolo Forest fire spotter outpost had been struck by a meteorite. Camels Hump. The tower where he had dropped off his young college friend, George Dantley, just the day before yesterday. Lots of destruction. Potential catastrophic injury.

Worry gripped him as he piloted the Forest Service helicopter south, the rescue team in back. He tried to mentally prepare himself for what lay ahead. Fly in over the remote spot and rescue George, triage his injuries, get him to St. Patrick Hospital.

Or, God forbid, bring back his remains.

Peter had a hard time wrapping his head around it. A meteorite in Montana? He'd lived here for 30 of his 37 years and had never seen a meteor shower, let alone a meteorite strike. Such an absurd notion. He'd asked dispatch to repeat the information. They told him it wasn't just one strike. A second hit had occurred a couple of miles from ground zero. And two more strikes in Idaho had preceded the two in Montana.

What the hell?

"You're awfully quiet, Lacroix," Peter heard in his headset.

He glanced at first officer Martin Fulbright occupying the copilot seat. Fulbright was a large, strapping man in his late forties who had been with Montana Forest Fire Protection for 25 years.

Head shaved to a gleaming shine. Disheveled, bushy red beard veiled much of his face. Fulbright had piloted Forest choppers back in the day, but he had been a fleet helicopter manager the eight-plus years Peter had been flying for the DNRC. They had partnered on many excursions.

"That's my friend out there on The Hump, Marty. George is just a college kid. Really good guy. Very smart. He and I share a love of hockey. We've been to several Missoula Bruins games together."

"We'll get him out safely. Our guys know what they're doing."

The medevac team riding in back consisted of a paramedic and a pair of first responders from Disaster and Emergency Services (DES), who were equipped to handle the challenges of difficult terrain rescue.

This situation with the meteorites was strange enough, but the rack of hazmat suits hanging in the cargo bay added another level of apprehension. When Peter asked about the white Tyvek space suits, he was told they were merely a precaution. A nod to safety protocols. When he asked specific questions about the meteorites, his superiors gave him curt, evasive answers, finally telling him that he and his crew had nothing to worry about. Peter learned a long time ago that when those in authority said not to worry, it was time to start fretting.

Does HQ know something they aren't telling us about these meteorites? Contamination? Extraterrestrial radiation?

Peter spoke loudly into his mic to overcome the rumbling of the rotor blades. "What's your take on this meteorite business, Marty?"

"Sounds like the real deal to me."

"Here? In *Montana*?"

"It could happen. The second largest meteorite strike in United States history is along the Idaho-Montana border—the Beaverhead impact crater."

"Yeah, okay. But wasn't that like six-hundred million years ago?"

"More like *eight-hundred* million."

"So, does that make sense to you, Marty? That out of the blue, after eight-hundred million years, we get four meteorite strikes in this area?"

"Oh, there have been others. In 1999, some amateur geologists found a couple of basketball-size meteorites that weighed in at around a hundred pounds each, right here in the Bitterroot Range. The rocks sold for big money at auction. And there have been many meteor showers in these skies over the years. In fact, the great Lolo Forest fires in summer 2005 were thought to have been started by meteorite strikes."

"Hmmm," Peter mumbled. "I just find it odd."

"Oh, I agree, partner. It's *quite* bizarre. But I was at HQ when your friend's distress call came in. I heard it all. That was either a large jet aircraft or a sizeable meteorite that took down that lookout tower. And we know that no aircraft went down today."

"Jesus," Peter said, thinking the worst. "I pray we're not too late."

"Be cool, Pete. We'll get young Dantley out safely. I have full confidence in our guys in the back."

They approached Bitterroot Ridge. Peter finessed the cyclical pitch stick and let up on the yaw pedal. The craft responded, leaning westward into the turn as they circumvented the craggy cliffs of snow-capped Trapper Peak. The communication console squawked general weather data and intermittent exchanges between Heliport Command and other Forest pilots as the rotor blade droned above.

Peter adjusted his headset, then gently pulled the stick back to the center position. The chopper leveled out. They had cleared Trapper Peak and were now headed northwest over Lolo National Forest. The early afternoon sun brightened the greenery below. They flew over Interstate 90, two long-haul eighteen wheelers charging westward, in route to Seattle.

Peter's mind drifted to Brinshou, his beautiful Kootenai Indian wife of four years. She was in Missoula, taking care of their baby daughter Kimi. He worried about them when he went out on these dangerous missions. Brin had never been comfortable with Peter's line of work, telling him when they first started dating that "If we were meant to soar with the eagles the Supreme Being would have given us feathers and made us flightworthy." At times, her anxiety was off the charts, but Peter had learned how to deal with it, often downplaying the dangers of his profession to calm her. He'd never really lied to his wife outright, but his omission of fact sometimes played with his head.

He worked the collective and pedals, dropping the craft to a lower altitude. When the altimeter read five hundred feet, he leveled off and flew above the treetops.

He squinted into the distance, searching for signs of fire. After five focused minutes, he saw it. "And there she blows," he exclaimed, pointing through the cockpit windshield. "Our first meteorite strike. See that coil of smoke at about one o'clock?"

Fulbright leaned forward. "No, wait a minute . . ." He reached into the side pocket and grabbed high-powered Nikon field glasses. "I've got it now," he said, peering through the binocs. "Wow! It's a flamer. Looks like we've got us an active crown fire. Treetops burning, but it's tough to see much else beyond that." He lowered the field glasses and looked at Peter. "You've got eagle eyes, my friend. No way I could see that without magnification."

They flew toward the burn. As they approached, the wind shifted, and thick plumes of smoke enveloped the chopper. An acrid, charred timber smell filled the cockpit, causing Peter to cough. He switched to instrumentation flight, basically flying blind, to take them out of harm's way.

"Heavy soup." Fulbright said into his headset mic.

"Yep, it's a hot mess. And if it really is a meteorite down there, no telling what kind of toxic fumes we might be inhaling."

Peter punched a button on the Flightcell SATCOM panel to send an update to Missoula. "This is Treetop-Five, pilot Lacroix reporting in. Do you read, Heliport Command? Over."

A baritone male voice sounded in his ear. "*Yes, we read you, Five. Proceed. Over.*"

"Thank you, Command. We have eyes on the prize and are circling. Heavy smoke is obscuring much of the view, but there appears to be a crown fire underneath that is widening in an equidistant circle. Still a lot of deadwood down there this early in the season. Very flammable situation. The area is too dense for smoke-jumpers. Recommend fixed-wing chemical spray treatment. Over."

"Agreed. We have your exact location monitored, Five. I'll get a chem team out there once you have completed your mission. Any sign of the second strike area where our looker went down? Over."

"Not yet. The smoke is seriously limiting our visibility. I don't think we're going to be able to put down at our primary site. I'm searching for another touch-down spot close enough to Camels Hump to hoof it on foot. Over."

"Copy that, Five. Your crew has been briefed on that possibility and are prepared to hike in. Over."

"If I can't find a suitable landing site, my only other recourse is to drop the rescue team with the longline. Over."

He prayed he didn't have to go the longline and cargo net route. Peter knew the risks of trying to keep the chopper stable while offloading personnel into an active fire zone. Knew the dangers to the rescuers.

"We hope you can find a place to park it. Keep us posted. Over."

He was about to sign off when he thought about the meteorites. "I have a question for you, Heliport Command. Over."

"Proceed, Five. Over."

"Before we go heading into the heart of darkness, can you officially confirm that the source of this fire is a meteorite? Over."

"Affirmative. Big Sky Observatory reports meteor showers in the area the past forty-eight hours. Centennial Observatory in Idaho concurs. The areas of meteorite impacts line up precisely with the pattern of meteor shower sightings. Over."

Peter paused, thinking. "Has there been any meteorite hits any-where else? I mean other than Montana and Idaho? Over."

"Negative. The American Astronomical Society in D.C. reports no other meteor shower activity anywhere in the continental U.S. other than here along the Continental Divide. The International Astronomical Union informs us no meteor activity has been seen in any country outside the U.S. the past forty-eight hours. Over."

Peter shook his head. "I guess we're the lucky ones, then. I don't suppose you asked them if these meteorites are radioactive.

Or if they might be riddled with extraterrestrial contamination. Over."

"*You have such limited faith in us, pilot Lacroix. Over.*"

"No disrespect intended, but when I see hazmat suits stowed onboard my aircraft, I get a little nervous. What's the deal? Over."

"*We understand your concerns, Pete, but I'm sure you are aware that this is on a need-to-know basis only. Over.*"

Peter gave his first officer a look of disgust. "Well, Marty and I are the ones flying into this mess. I'd say we have a definite need to know. Over."

Peter waited for a response. The comm unit spewed static. The overhead rotor blade thrummed. Just when he was about to lose patience, the dispatcher came back on.

"*Fair enough. What I can tell you is that we have been in contact with GSA—that's the Geological Society of America—to learn more about meteorites. Most fall into the classification of stony meteorites, which consist of silicates, mainly silicon and oxygen. They also have large concentrations of nickel and iron. So while they burn incredibly hot due to traveling through the Earth's atmosphere, they are absent of extraterrestrial contaminates. We here at Heliport Command have the utmost confidence that no harm will come to you and your crew should you come in close contact with these objects. Over.*"

It sounded to Peter like geology mumbo jumbo. It still didn't answer the need for hazmat suits, but he knew he would be pushing it to inquire further. "Thanks for keeping us in the loop, Command. I'll report back to you once we have a better handle on things. Over."

"*Be safe and Godspeed to you, Treetop-Five. We're with you all the way. Over and out.*"

Peter swung the chopper out wide, reduced the throttle, circled the perimeter of smoke. Peered out his side window, searching for a hollow or bluff with enough clearance in which to safely bring the chopper down.

Found none.

He decided on a different plan of attack. He flew south five miles then doubled back, approaching the back side of Camels Hump. Mercifully, the wind shifted, clearing the smoke. Sunlight brightened the cockpit. He flew in a wide loop. Saw the usual touch-down clearing consumed by leaping flames.

"Well, our primary landing zone is out of the question," he said, pointing to the fiery clearing. "But look. Further up. We might be in luck."

They flew past the rear of the granite ridge known as Camels Hump. Debris from the collapsed tower spread down the steep incline like scattered toothpicks. There was no fire here. It would take monumental heat to burn granite.

Peter cut back on the throttle, coasting slowly past the scene. "You see a body anywhere, Marty?"

Fulbright peered through his Nikon field glasses. "Nope. I see what looks like a guitar case . . . and . . . a twisted up woodstove. But no body."

Peter hit the collective pitch. The craft responded, rising above The Hump, giving them a clear sightline of the summit below.

"Wow, would you look at that!" Fulbright said in a wondrous tone.

Peter saw it too. A large smoldering meteorite had struck the side of The Hump and cracked apart. The impact had gouged a deep fissure in the granite. Three large sections of the meteorite littered the rocky surface below the fissure, steam billowing from each. But the granite surface had prevented wildfires here.

"We can't put down here," Peter said. "The surface isn't flat enough. And we don't really know how stable The Hump is after taking a cataclysmic hit. But we do have a clear sightline and no fire. We're going with the longline basket drop."

"Agreed," Fulbright said. "It's our only option."

Peter alerted his first response team in back to his plans. Asked if any of them had any misgivings. There were none. These guys were prideful, blue chip professionals.

"Okay then. Let's go find George Dantley."

Gilliam's Guidepost

May 28: Heart Butte, Montana

AN EXPLOSIVE THUMP rattled the windows of the old farmhouse. Loretta Gilliam felt the tremor in her chest.

"What was that, Mama?"

Loretta looked across the kitchen table at her seven-year-old daughter, Lianne, who'd been focused on her spelling homework. "Um, that's just thunder, sweetie. Nothing to be afraid of."

"But it's not raining." Fear punctuated her words. "You know it doesn't thunder when it's sunny out, Mama."

Her daughter's terrified expression made Loretta's heart ache. How do you refute a child's resolute logic? Loretta had no idea what they'd just heard. *Possibly an earthquake?* She recalled the 5.8 magnitude earthquake that hit western Montana in 2017. Knocked out their power for 36 hours and cracked the foundation of one of the barns. This didn't feel like that. *Was it a sonic boom?* Malmstrom Air Force Base occasionally tested their supersonic aircraft here above the Blackfeet Indian reservation.

But it's been years since we've heard an aerial boomer.

"You look funny, Mama. I'm scared."

Loretta went to Lianne, stood behind her and massaged her thin shoulders, buying time, thinking. Tried to come up with an answer that would be plausible and nonthreatening.

Finally she had it. "There's nothing to worry about, Lee. It's just heat thunder. Sometimes heat builds up during the day and it causes thunder bumpers."

"But it's not hot out yet. You made me wear my coat to school this morning. It was cold, remember?"

Ah, the snags of dealing with a bright and precocious seven-

year-old.

"Well . . . yes, you're right, darling. It's too cool for—"

She paused, hearing Bryan's creaky Ford pickup rumbling up the front drive, gravel pinging the undercarriage.

"There's your father now, Lee. Maybe he'll know what we heard."

The engine coughed and sputtered and shut down with a lingering rattle. Loretta heard the door slam, her husband's boots crunching through the gravel.

She went to the window, saw Bryan hurrying into the house, his thick brown hair flying away from his face as he hustled up the steps and onto the front porch.

"You won't believe what just happened," he said, barging through the door, out of breath, excitement dancing in his eyes. "Something crashed in the east meadow. Had to have been a plane by the sound of it."

Lianne jumped up, went to Bryan, wrapped her arms around his thigh. "Mama said it was thunder bumpers, Daddy. From the heat."

"A plane, you say, Bry? Did you get a look at it?"

"No. Too far away and beyond the slope. But what I heard could only be a plane crash. We need to get out there right quick and take a look. Somebody could be hurt. Or—"

Loretta gave Bryan a warning stare: *Don't say too much in front of Lianne.*

He nodded his understanding.

"Come on," he urged, gently unwrapping Lianne's arms from his leg and picking her up. "Time's a wasting."

"Are you saying you want me to go with you?" Loretta asked.

"Yeah. I might need some help."

"Can I come, too, Daddy?"

"Sure you can, princess." Bryan kissed his daughter on the cheek and set her down.

Loretta frowned. "Don't you think Lee's too impressionable to tag along, babe?"

"What's *impwess . . . impwesh . . .*" Lianne struggled with the pronunciation. "What does *that* word mean?"

Loretta said, "Impressionable? It means you're too young to see certain things."

Lianne stomped her foot. "But I'm *not* too young! I'm not a baby! I'm seven! I'm big now."

"Yes you are," Bryan said. "You're big enough to come with us. We can't leave you here all alone."

"Why don't we wait for the boys?" Loretta offered. "They could stay here with Lee."

The boys were their two sons: Paul, age 16, and 14-year-old Ethan.

Bryan shook his head. "They won't be home from baseball practice until seven. Coach Watson is working the team overtime, whippin' 'em into shape for the season. No time to wait on our future hall of famers." Bryan shook his keys impatiently. "C'mon, let's get a move on."

Reluctantly, Loretta grabbed a jacket and a sweater for Lianne, followed Bryan out to the truck. She helped Lianne up into the cab then climbed in after her.

"Hold on tight, kiddos," Bryan barked as the truck juddered over deep washboard ruts in the dusty service road leading out to the east grassland.

Bryan and Loretta purchased this 1,285-acre spread on the outskirts of Heart Butte in northwestern Montana 18 years ago, after Bryan returned home from his second tour of duty in Afghanistan. They couldn't believe their good fortune. Fate was surely smiling down on them. They'd been able to close the deal at a rock-bottom price with a highly motivated seller—a rancher's widow who had no interest in keeping the place after her husband's sudden passing. Their purchase package included two dozen quarter horses and a hundred head of cattle.

It should have been The American Dream as imagined by serious aspiring ranchers, but it quickly degenerated into a waking nightmare. By Montana standards, theirs was a small ranch, and both Loretta and Bryan were convinced they could handle the responsibilities that came with it.

How wrong they had been.

Loretta could laugh about their early struggles now. But back then, before children and family duties, there were some dark times. She recalled sleepless nights, fretting over how naive they'd been. She remembered crying herself dry over how quickly their investment disappeared. She and Bryan so erroneously thought they could learn the finer points of ranching and livestock husbandry on the job. But they quickly realized the error of their ways. During the first two years, most of the cattle died off from bacterial infection of the small intestine. The vet had identified the bovine malady as Johne's Disease. She and Bryan had been shocked as they observed their herd shedding poundage, developing bottle jaw, and dropping dead. And then there were the horses, each of which cost upwards of $4,000 a year to feed and stable.

Try as they might, they reluctantly admitted they couldn't pay the bills and raise a family as ranchers. They would have to reinvent themselves.

So Gilliam's Guidepost was born. They converted the largest barn into a 12-room motel and named it Gilliam's Guidepost Inn. During the winter months, at the height of ski season, the cozy cottages were booked solid. Loretta's brother and Bryan's former Army buddy, Jimmy Enright, had helped Bryan build another structure next to the motel, which became Loretta's General Store. Loretta spent much of her time running the store: filling orders, making monthly buying trips to Great Falls, paying vendors, keeping track of inventory. Bryan did his thing by remodeling one of the three barns into a garage equipped with two hydraulic lifts. It's where he worked on tractors, balers, combines, trucks, and passenger vehicles, earning a decent income. Bryan was now known by the farming community around Heart Butte as The Best Damn Mechanic in Western Montana. Bryan also looked after the horses (they still had six of them) and did a thriving business in the summer months giving riding lessons to Blackfoot children from the reservation.

And then there was the doomsday shelter. Bryan's pride and joy. Bryan and Jimmy spent two summers building out the survivalist refuge on the back thirty, modifying a tapped-out zinc mine. Three floors of subterranean living space, outfitted with central air, electric wiring, plumbing, and modern appliances. More than a survival bunker, really, it was a luxurious underground home. The driving force behind it stemmed from the paranoia Bryan and Jimmy brought back with them from Afghanistan.

"Look at that!" Lianne squealed.

Her daughter's shriek snapped Loretta out of her reverie.

Lianne squirmed to the front of the seat and leaned forward, elbows against the dash, face near the windshield, eyes bulging. "Look at the fire! The smoke! What are those black things, Daddy?"

They crossed over the bluff leading to the meadow, dipping down into the bowl of their eastern pastureland. Loretta could see large wedges of smoking black rock jutting out of a deep hole in the earth, a tangle of barbed wire nearby where the fence had been crushed. The columns of rock stood on end, looking like a charred section of Stonehenge. Small fires burned in the prairie shortgrass surrounding the rock segments.

"One thing's for sure," Bryan said, concentrating on his driving. "That's no airplane."

"Nope. It's certainly not like any aircraft I've ever seen," Loretta said while struggling to pull Lianne back into her seat. "Whaddaya think it is, Bry?"

"Don't have a clue, but I aim to find out."

As they pulled closer, Loretta could make out four chunks of glittery black rock standing approximately five feet high, each sending out wavy tendrils of coal-black smoke.

"It looks like a large boulder that's been quartered," Loretta offered.

"That it does," Bryan said, squinting through the windshield, slowing as they got within a hundred yards.

He braked and shut off the ignition. The engine ticked. A crow cawed in the distance. Loretta watched him lean forward to get a better look. He stared, transfixed, at the standing wedges of rock in front of them.

"Whaddaya think it is, babe?" Loretta asked, trying to keep the anxiety she was feeling out of her voice.

"I'll be damned," he said, eyes never leaving the smoking rocks in front of them. "I do believe we're looking at a meteor . . . a meteor that has crashed in our pasture. They're called meteorites when they hit ground. This is *unbelievable*."

"What's a meeteeyite, Daddy?"

Bryan shifted in his seat and smiled at Lianne. "It's a big rock from outer space, baby girl."

"Are there Martians in it?" she said. "Martians come from outer space, y'know."

Loretta let out a nervous snicker.

Bryan said, "No, sweet thing, I don't think this is a Martian meteorite."

Loretta said, "Well, at least there isn't anybody we have to save today."

"No, but we're gonna hafta get somebody out here to tell us what we've got."

Lianne began bouncing up and down on the seat, the springs squeaking. "Can we go see it, Daddy? Can we, can we, CAN WE?"

Loretta answered. "I don't think that's a good idea, Lee. We don't know where this thing came from. There could be a lot of bad things in those rocks. Things that could hurt little girls."

"But Daddy said it came from outer space. Everybody knows about outer space."

Loretta usually found Lianne's vivid imagination and twisty logic entertaining. Now, however, staring at these smoky alien rocks, she felt every nerve in her body tighten. She wished her daughter was not with them witnessing this.

"Your mother is right, Lee," Bryan said. "It might be dangerous. We can't get too close to it."

"That's not fair!" Lianne wailed. "I wanna see it! Right now!"

"No, sweetheart," Bryan said, reaching across her to the glove box to retrieve his cell phone.

"Who're you calling, Bry?"

"Tryin' to call nine-one-one," he said, glaring at his phone. "There's no damn reception out here. I really need to get a new phone."

Lianne continued her outburst, tears now flowing, little hands beating against the seat. "Not fair, not fair, not fair! I wanna see the outer space rock!"

Loretta did her best to quiet her daughter but Lianne was having none of it. Loretta was amazed at how quickly Lianne could change moods, going from absolute fear to out-and-out bravery in a matter of minutes. The boys hadn't been that way when they were Lianne's age, but then, boys were different.

Bryan snapped a few photos of the rock wedges through the windshield with his cell phone, then set the phone down on the seat. "At least this old piece of crap phone is good for something," he said, starting up the truck, the rumble drowning out Lianne's cries of injustice.

"We need to get some experts out here, tell us what we've got," Bryan said, driving them back to the house.

"What about the fire?" Loretta asked.

"It'll burn itself out. Much of the east meadow beyond that meteorite is dirt."

Picking Up the Pieces

May 28: Camels Hump
Lolo National Forest, Montana

A STRONG CROSSWIND buffeted the Bell Huey chopper as they hovered over the wreckage strewn across the eastern slope of Camels Hump. Peter Lacroix muscled the controls, struggling to keep the chopper stable.

"We found him, Pete." Lead emergency tech Jeremy Spang's voice buzzed in his ear.

Peter glanced at the monitor showing the view below. The two DES responders stood near a pile of wreckage, their contamination suits electric-white in the hazy sun. The scene reminded him of Apollo astronauts walking on the moon—the bulbous helmets with dark faceplates, the puffy suits, the oxygen tanks.

"Is he still alive?" he asked.

"Affirmative."

He heaved a sigh of relief and gave first officer Fulbright a thumbs-up.

"It's not great though," came the reply from the ground. "The kid's in bad shape. All mangled up and bleeding. One of the tower walls came down on him. Weak pulse. Respiration the same. BP is flagging. Several broken bones and his back is badly burned. We tried to revive him, but no dice. He's out cold, Pete. It's going to be difficult getting him up there. We could really use your help. We're going to need the board."

"Understood."

The "board" Spang referred to was an ARP, or Aerial Rescue Platform, a high tech stretcher used to lift seriously injured victims into the chopper.

Peter checked the Geiger counter. The needle on the DPS-68 display hadn't budged. Zero radiation inside the aircraft. Same with the area below. He poked Fulbright and pointed to the readout. "It's been fifteen minutes, Marty. You think it's safe now?"

Fulbright leaned in, took a look, then nodded.

Peter flipped a switch on the instrument panel, spoke to his ground crew. "You guys can ditch the monkey suits now. The Hump is clean."

"Hallelujah," Jeremy Spang responded. "Hard to move in these frickin' things."

Peter watched the monitor as the two emergency responders hurriedly stripped off their hazmat suits and returned their attention to the prone George Dantley.

Meteorites, huh? he thought, his hand tensing on the pitch stick, struggling against the buffeting wind. *What a bitch! Well, at least we don't have to battle a fire here.*

Peter looked at Fulbright. "Time for me to join the party," he said into his mic. "This bird is yours for a while, Marty. Sure you can handle it?"

Fulbright scoffed. "I've been handling bigger birds than this since you were in diapers, my friend."

Peter barked out an uneasy chuckle. "That's almost true, old man. But this crosswind is fierce. Been kickin' my ass."

"Yeah, well that's because you're a candy ass. Turn this baby over to me and I'll show you how a *real* pilot does things."

Peter shifted the dual control system to the copilot's seat and uncoupled his harness. "She's all yours, Methuselah," he said with a wink.

Fulbright grabbed the collective stick and pumped the foot pedals, far too focused to offer a witty rejoinder. The chopper rocked a bit on the transfer.

Hovering was one of the more difficult skills a helicopter pilot had to master. A brisk crosswind like they faced today presented real challenges, requiring nerves of steel and pinpoint coordination of the collective pitch and anti-torque pedals. Basically it was akin to anchoring a four-ton aircraft in midair. Peter knew from experience that his first officer was a more-than-capable pilot. No doubt Marty could hover this chopper in a hurricane, if it came to that.

Peter pushed through the canvas curtain and entered the rear cargo bay. He nodded to the paramedic, Nicki Whitlow, an attractive late-20s black woman with tight cornrows and penetrating hazel eyes. She was originally from Georgia, where she'd earned her EMS degree from Emory University. The state forestry job had brought her to western Montana.

"How's it going, Nicki," he said loud enough to be heard over the rattling hum of the rotors. "You ready to receive your patient?"

She gave him a faint smile. "I'm here ready with my A game."

Peter could listen to her lovely Dixie lilt all day long. "Well, we've got to get him up here in one piece before you can do your magic."

"I'll take good care of him," she said, indicating the automated hospital bed, the metal tray holding syringes and assorted medical instruments, the IV bag swinging from a metal hook. A blood pressure cuff lay across the foot of the bed.

Peter went to the open side doors and peered out, the wind whipping at his face. He grabbed hold of the longline frame assembly for support, then looked down to where the basket rested on the rock a hundred feet below. He pulled his head back inside and activated the longline rewind with a foot switch. The hoist motor groaned to life. The pulley mechanism squeaked loudly as the steel cable spooled onto a large wheel, starting the basket on its trip back up top.

Nicki Whitlow watched Peter's back as he stood in the open bay, wind whipping at his hair and pantlegs. "I could have helped them, you know," she yelled over the rushing gusts.

"I know you could, but you know the rules, Nick."

The procedure for air rescue called for the paramedic to remain on board while first responders performed the retrieval. Paramedics were not trained to do risky rescue work. Emergency medics like Nicki Whitlow were there for their medical expertise, not their courage under fire.

He turned, gave her a smile, one that he hoped carried no pity.

"Look, I understand, Nick. You want to do more. I get it. And I certainly appreciate your ambition. I have to tell you, when I was called back to Missoula this morning and briefed on this mission, I asked for the best rescue team possible. They gave me blue chip first responders in Jeremy and Burl Heddison. You? I asked for you by name."

"You did?"

"Absolutely. I was thrilled you were available."

Her face lit up, eyes shining. "Really? You mean that?"

"Absolutely. I want the best medical care possible for my buddy, Georgie."

The longline basket reached the top, the incessant wind banging it against the fuselage. Peter went to it, tugged it inside the bay.

"Time is of the essence," he said. "You heard Jeremy say they need the ARP, right?"

"Yes."

"Do you have it ready?"

"It's ready. They checked it out thoroughly at HQ. Part of the preflight prep."

"I know, but it pays to inspect things two and three times. So check all the straps and buckles and zippers. Last thing we need is to lose our patient on the way up due to faulty equipment."

Today's situation was a harsh reminder of the tragedy that occurred in Peter's first year on the job. Fellow pilot Marv Reichardt was accompanying a rescue team near Twin Peaks when the longline basket broke and dumped the pilot, EMT, and the injured patient. The three fell more than 200 feet to their deaths. Cause of the fatal accident? A pair of rusted buckles, three frayed straps, and a ragged hole in the polymer mesh from a cigarette burn. It had been a huge wakeup call for Peter and other Forest pilots.

He helped her slide the aluminum-and-nylon ARP across the floor, leaning it up against the stretcher. Together they checked all couplings and straps and fasteners. Then, satisfied that all was in proper working order, they carried it to the longline basket and secured it. Pushed the basket out the bay doors where it swung in the wind. Peter reached out, grabbed the basket frame and pulled it back to the side of the chopper, steadying it. Made sure his headset was firmly in place. Climbed in and told Nicki to lower him.

Down he went, his shirt and pants whipping in the gale. The basket swung like a clocktower pendulum. Vertigo paralyzed him momentarily. He could smell smoke. His eyes watered. Just when he thought he would throw up his lunch, the basket touched down. He climbed out, wobbly on his feet. He took a deep breath, trying to clear his head. The air smelled of scorched earth and old wood.

Shakily, he unhitched the ARP, carried it across the rock, carefully sidestepping debris. The going was difficult as he had to haul the stretcher board up an incline to where responders Spang and Heddison worked. The ARP wasn't heavy, but it was awkward in the brisk wind, acting like a sail. Peter finally got to them, winded and exhausted. He didn't like what he saw.

He looked down at his young friend, George Dantley, stretched out on the rocky ledge like a broken rag doll. Blood stained the rock in vivid splashes. His left arm was bent at an impossible angle. His left hip looked crushed and the side of his face was badly burned, the hair on that side of his head gone.

Peter felt empty, and something else—cheated?—as he stared down at his unconscious friend. He whispered a prayer. *Lord, God in heaven, please help Nicki Whitlow perform a miracle today.*

"Swing the board around to this side, Pete," Jeremy Spang said from where he kneeled.

Peter distractedly pulled the ARP around to where the three of them were able to gingerly strap George in. Spang and Heddison each grabbed an end of the stretcher board and began the precarious journey across the rock to the longline basket.

Peter walked with them a ways before he said, "Hey guys. Looks like you have everything under control. HQ wants a report on the meteorite. I'm going to take a look before we lift off."

"Okay, Pete," Jeremy Spang said, grunting with the exertion. "Be safe."

The part about HQ was a lie. It sat in his gut like a bad meal. However, he wasn't about to let this opportunity get away. He just *had* to see this meteorite up close.

He scrambled up the granite facing to the top of Camels Hump, where the fire tower had been anchored. He was shocked to see the damage up here. A crevice a couple of feet wide slashed through the granite mere feet from where the tower had stood. Nothing left of the fire lookout but a slab of busted-up concrete and four frame posts. It looked like the workings of a devastating earthquake.

Georgie, you unlucky soul, you had the misfortune to be in the wrong place at the wrong time.

Flying in, they'd spotted the meteorite at the base of the outcropping on the far side. The western side. Unfortunately, the western side of Camels Hump consisted of a sheer cliff that dropped off 800 feet or more.

Peter carefully worked his way up to the edge and looked down, his dizzying vertigo returning. *Thank God you went down on the other side, Georgie, or we probably would have lost you.*

He peered down the side of the steep granite wall. A two-foot-wide fissure ran from the top all the way to the ground. Far below, at the bottom of the cleft, he could see large black rocks clustered in a smoking heap. Peter realized then how lucky they'd been, with the meteorite striking the rocky face of Camels Hump instead of coming down in the forest. It prevented a massive wildfire like the one four miles away.

But as he surveyed the damage, he couldn't rationalize the devastation. The chaos and destruction all around him boggled his mind.

He felt the cold stab of terror race down his spine.

He turned and glanced back in the direction of the hovering chopper. Nicki Whitlow stood in the open cargo bay working the winch, raising the longline basket. He heard the muffled voices of the two emergency techs as they ascended.

The wind shifted, taking with it the racket of the cranking helicopter rotors.

He heard something. Held his breath and listened.

A most peculiar noise. A deep croaking sound. A chorus of croaks—like an army of bullfrogs.

But not exactly like bullfrogs. Listening more closely, Peter detected a high-pitched chirping in the croaks. More like bullfrogs cross-mated with birds.

What the hell?

The wind changed direction again. A foul odor drifted up from below, making him gag. The putrid stench of rotten eggs.

Marty Fulbright's voice boomed in his headset. "Sightseein' time's up, Pete. We've got a patient badly in need of a hospital."

Peter turned and gave his first officer a wave. "I'm coming."

As he finessed his way down the rocky shelf to the longline basket, he thought: *Something is very wrong with that meteorite.*

Mother Meteorite

June 2: Gilliam's Guidepost
Heart Butte, Montana

BRYAN GILLIAM GRABBED A PICKAXE and a crowbar from his truck bed. Two men flanked him—William Blazenhurst, a scientist from the American Meteor Society, and Greg Dulowski, an eminent geologist who came from a paleontology dig in nearby Choteau. The 24/7 media attention on the meteorites coming down along the Continental Divide had awakened the scientific community. Authorities of all stripes were venturing to meteorite crash sites as fast as they could get there.

"It's over there," Bryan said, pointing the crowbar at the stone wedges.

The two visitors peered across the wide, fallow meadow at the sections of dark boulder, then fell in behind Bryan. The three men tramped toward the mysterious stones, the early-morning dew dampening their shoes.

Bryan was impatient. This meeting had taken far too long to come together. Five long days since he'd brought Loretta and Lianne out here to see the meteorite. The morning after, he had called 9-1-1, told the dispatcher it wasn't an immediate emergency but that a strange event had occurred on his property. He wanted someone in authority to come check it out. That afternoon, a Great Falls police officer made the two-hour drive to Gilliam's Guidepost. Deputy Rob Swanson was a young rookie cop, skittish and edgy, especially near the meteorite sections.

Bryan couldn't blame the young man for being wary; he hadn't wanted to get too close to the cluster of alien rocks either. Something about the fractured meteorite spooked him, as though the wedges of smoking rock harbored dark, otherworldly spirits. And Bryan thought about other unknowns: Poisonous gases? Radioactivity? Biological contamination? He didn't want his family out here near this mess until someone with professional expertise gave the all-clear.

During their earlier inspection, Bryan and Deputy Swanson made a startling discovery. A gelatinous goo glazed the sides of each wedge, puddling along the ground. And the smell—even though they'd maintained a healthy distance—was rancid. They also noticed the way the ebony rocks glittered in the sunlight.

The geologist, Dr. Gregory Dulowski, had arrived last night, too late to go out to the meteorite site. So Bryan had some time to pick his brain. When he asked Dulowski about the sparkly aspect of the space boulder, the geologist told him that 90% of meteorites were comprised of iron and nickel, which would explain the glitter. But what about that goo? And the horrendous smell? The odor wafting from the glazy rocks that made his nasal passages burn? Dulowski had no answers to those questions, and Bryan could see his guest getting excited about the possibilities of new discovery.

"We'll get some photos and rock samples tomorrow," Dulowski had told him last night before retiring to his room at the inn. "But I will tell you something that will ease your mind somewhat, Mr. Gilliam."

"What's that?"

"It is very rare for meteorites to contain any extraterrestrial contamination. From that standpoint, I believe you and your family are safe."

That news helped Bryan sleep better than he had the previous few nights.

When Deputy Swanson left to return to Great Falls, Bryan figured he would never hear from him again. But surprisingly, the young police officer came through. Swanson had contacted the American Astronomical Society (AAS) in Washington D.C. They connected him with William Blazenhurst of the American Meteor Society, a specialized division of the AAS. The deputy called Bryan to update him, saying they'd been lucky to get Blazenhurst to come to Montana, even though there would be a delay of four or five days. Swanson had also enlisted Dr. Dulowski, a geologist working with a Smithsonian paleontology expedition sixty miles south of Heart Butte in Choteau. Dr. Dulowski was quite interested in Bryan's find, though he, too, wouldn't be able to get there for a few days.

Bryan, in spite of his impatience and apprehension of having to deal with this alien intrusion on his property, realized the wheels turn slowly when trying to get top scientific experts out to a far-flung ranch in northwestern Montana. Lots of logistical hoops to jump through. Still, five days is an eternity when your property has been hit by an alien object.

The three men walked the field toward the quartered meteorite. Greg Dulowski recorded the surroundings on his videocam, keeping up a running commentary.

The meteor specialist, Blazenhurst, spoke to Bryan's back, his tone skeptical. "So you say this rock came out of the sky and struck your pasture, Bryan?"

"That's right."

"And you believe it's extraterrestrial in origin?"

"Yessir, I do. I *know* it is."

"Have you ever seen a meteorite?"

Bryan maintained his stride but his anger was rising. Since arriving early this morning, this D.C. elitist had been patronizing at every turn, treating Bryan like he was some dumb hick farmer.

"Of *course* I've never seen a meteorite, but—"

"So how do you know—?"

"Look," Bryan snapped, stopping, turning, peering down into the shorter man's eyes. "With all due respect, sir, I appreciate the fact that you are here. But you've been riding my ass since you pulled into the inn. What's with that?"

"Don't take it personally," Blazenhurst said. "In my experience, many people are convinced they have a small meteorite when, almost always, their finds are terrestrial in composition. Usually dark granite with thick bands of quartz or mica. Dr. Dulowski here could tell you more about that," he said, pointing his elbow in the geologist's direction. "My organization tracks more than five-hundred alleged meteorite strikes around the globe each year. Unfortunately fewer than a dozen are recovered. And of those, only one or two are extraterrestrial in origin. And they are quite small. Nothing like the size of what you have described . . . nowhere near the mass of that grouping across the meadow," he said, pointing at the black rocks. "Ninety-nine percent of all meteors burn up in Earth's heavy atmosphere before they get anywhere near the ground. Surely you can see why I might be skeptical about your find."

Bryan was tired of this man's uppity attitude. "We heard the impact," he said. "It shook the ground, similar to the earthquake we had back in—"

"And then there are those who desperately want to be famous," he said, rudely cutting Bryan off. "Some people do some insane things to attain celebrityhood these days."

Bryan sneered at him. "That's not me at all."

Blazenhurst sighed. "Oh no? Let me be the judge of that."

Bryan had heard enough from this egotistical windbag. "Look, this is no hoax and I resent you judging me!"

Greg Dulowski lowered his videocam and said, "Hey, fellas, what say you quit sniping at each other and let's go have a look."

"Excellent idea," Bryan said, giving Blazenhurst the stink eye, then turning and trudging on.

As they neared the meteorite wedges, Bryan noticed they were no longer steaming hot. They'd cooled. No hazy smoke around the black rocks.

Bryan stopped, and the two scientists pulled up behind him. "From here you can see the glazing," he said. "Looks like varnish."

Bryan cautiously moved forward, ten yards . . . twenty, the pick-axe and crowbar heavy in his hands. Blazenhurst and Dulowski walked beside him.

The smell hit them like an olfactory tsunami.

"Holy mother of Christ!" Dulowski exclaimed, lowering his camera and pinching his nose. "You weren't kidding about the odor, were you, Mr. Gilliam?"

"Nope," Bryan said, thinking the stench was much stronger than it had been four days ago when he was out here with Deputy Swanson.

"Jesus!" William Blazenhurst bellowed. "We need gas masks!"

They inched closer, wariness in their movements.

And then they heard something most bizarre. A raucous chittering that seemed to resonate from inside, or behind, the meteorite rocks. The three men halted their approach in unison, as if their stoppage of movement was a choreographed dance move.

"What the hell is *that*?" Bryan said, on alert, eyes scanning the scene for movement to go with the chirping chorus.

"I don't have the foggiest," Greg Dulowski said, still videotaping with one hand while pinching his nose with the other.

"Well, gentlemen," Blazenhurst said, "It might stink something fierce, but I didn't come all the way from D.C. to examine a meteorite from fifty yards away. Let's move in and see what's what."

The meteor specialist boldly moved forward, leaving Bryan and Dulowski behind.

Bryan fell in behind, saying to Blazenhurst's back, "So do I hear you saying that you now believe me? That it's a meteorite?"

"I'm not convinced yet, but we'll see."

They reached the outer ring of blackened earth where the prairie grass had burned down to crispy ash. The rocks were no more than thirty feet away.

The chittering sounds increased in volume.

The stench was overpowering, like an overflowing sewage system. *Strong enough to strip paint off the walls,* Bryan thought.

He approached the nearest wedge, seeing a wide crevice running from the top to its base. The rock was rooted in a three-foot crater. He jabbed the crowbar into the crack, trying to break it open, and nearly had a heart attack as a tide of the strangest creatures he'd ever seen swarmed out. Like miniature horned lizards, they were. Or maybe direct descendants of the Arizona Gila monster.

They were small but fierce. Squawking. Sharp little teeth.

On the attack.

Bryan took a few futile swings with his crowbar as they came at him, then dropped the heavy bar on top of the pickaxe and ran. Dulowski followed, stumbling backwards attempting to catch the attack on video. William Blazenhurst pulled up the rear.

The three men made it back to Bryan's truck and climbed in the cab, breathing hard, confused about what they had encountered.

"This is some crazy shit," Bryan said after he'd caught his breath.

"Tell me about it," Blazenhurst said, pulling up his pantleg. "One of those little bastards bit me. Leaped right up and snapped me in the shin."

"Wow," Bryan said. He leaned over and looked at the wound. There were three bite marks that had drawn blood. "Let's get you back to the house. Get you fixed up."

Bryan fired up the ignition. "Now do you believe this is an extraterrestrial event?"

William Blazenhurst muttered, "Gilliam, what we just witnessed is way beyond extraterrestrial. It's *madness*."

Relic Hunters

June 3: Smithsonian Expedition,
Choteau, Montana

EXPEDITION LEAD NORA LEMOYNE was in a quandary. Should she go or should she stay?

Her team's geologist, Greg Dulowski, had returned from his trip to the Heart Butte ranch this afternoon with extraordinary video footage. What she saw captivated her, challenged her in ways her scientific mind could not completely comprehend. A meteorite allegedly hatching out extraterrestrial creatures? She wanted to leave the dig site right now and head north to the ranch. However, the Smithsonian Institution was bankrolling this paleontology dig. They were paying her and her team to unearth skeletal remains and fossilized bones. Her paychecks were *not* for galivanting off on some fantastical quest. Sure, she could send other team members to Heart Butte and continue to oversee things here at the Choteau site. But then she might miss out on something big.

Corporate responsibility versus scientific curiosity.

Nora struggled with the conundrum.

Should I go or should I stay?

She could imagine the pitying laughter of the Smithsonian's management as she informed them of the meteorite that purportedly hatched out alien creatures.

They will pull funding and laugh me out of the business.

Nora had worked hard to put this undertaking together. It had taken her years to attain her lofty position, managing an important large dig such as this Smithsonian expedition, leading some of the world's most experienced paleontological minds. After earning her graduate degrees in Paleontology and Evolutionary Biology from the University of Michigan, she'd spent seventeen frustrating years traveling the globe, working on underfunded digs. The travel was fun for a while, but the pay was low and the lack of respect from her male counterparts often made her want to hand in her stone hammers and chisels. Many times through those hard years she contemplated a change of occupation.

She recalled her nine long months politicking the Smithsonian Museum of Natural History board before they finally agreed to underwrite the project. The competition had been stiff, but Nora had impressed the decision makers with her adept organization and recruiting skills. Through Nora's contacts and dogged determination, she built a team consisting of who's-who in the worlds of paleontology, paleozoology, geology, and paleobotany. The eight scientific specialists on the team were considered some of the best and brightest in their fields. Nora was proud of her achievement and equally proud of her team.

She lay in her bunk in her private trailer, thinking about what she had seen on Dulowski's laptop an hour ago. She'd conferred with her lead paleontologist, Hayden Fowler, and together with Dulowski, the three reviewed the shaky video numerous times. Small, aggressive lizard creatures stormed out of cracks in a quartered meteorite. Nora thought her eyes were deceiving her. She watched with alarming fascination as the miniature reptiles tenaciously defended their territory . . .

"Wait, stop it right there, Greg," she'd said, tapping Dulowski's hand.

The geologist freeze-framed the video, getting a closeup of one of the lizards with its small jaws wide open. On the attack.

"What do you think, Hayden?"

Hayden Fowler leaned his beefy frame toward the screen and ran a hand through his beard. "They look a lot like Texas horned lizards. You know, the ones that spit blood. But these things are *not* horned lizards. Their bodies are more streamlined. Their snouts are longer." He leaned in closer and squinted. "And these animals appear to have needle-like teeth, which horned lizards do not."

"So," Nora said, "any thoughts on the species?"

"It's difficult identifying something on video like this. We should let our zoologist have a look. But if I was a betting man I'd put good money on these little guys being of some primordial reptilian genus."

"Could they possibly be dinosaur hatchlings?" Greg Dulowski asked. "That's what the guy from AMS believes."

"You mean the guy in the video who got bit?" Nora asked.

"Yes."

"How's he doing?"

"His shin is torn up," Dulowski replied. "Required stitches. His leg swelled up quite a bit but there wasn't any infection. The rancher, Gilliam, had to take him to the ER in Browning."

Nora watched the video clip. "Does this mean these animals secrete venom when they bite?"

"Not necessarily," Fowler said, eyes intensely focused on the screen. "The swelling could be from torn muscle tissue or internal bleeding. It could be any number of things, really." He looked at Nora with an earnest seriousness. "I won't stake my shining professional reputation on it, but I will say the poor fool with the damaged leg might be close to being correct. Those clicking, chirping sounds we hear is something paleo-scientists have debated for decades. Popular theory now holds that Jurassic and Cretaceous newborns entered the world with loud vocal responses. You know, making those *click-chirp* sounds similar to what we hear on the recording. It's primal vocal articulation, much like human babies that wail when they leave the womb and enter the world. Also, that sticky goop coating the meteorite shards and the awful smell you said you endured, Greg? I believe it all points to a recent hatchout."

Fowler leaned in closer, squinting at the small screen. "It's a little tough to see here, but if you look close, you'll see they have three-toed feet. They look like lizards but they're theropods, like our birds."

"Yes, I see," Nora said. "Most of our terrestrial lizards have five toes."

Fowler nodded. "Correct. And most of our amphibians, like frogs and toads, have four toes on the front feet and five on the back.

Alligators and crocodiles have five digits on the front and four on the back. These creatures have just the three and don't look anything like birds. Also, check out the musculature on their hind legs. Difficult to see here, but their hind quarters are much more powerfully built than their forelimbs. I say these are bipedal creatures. Give them a week or more and they'll be walking and running upright, with those tails giving them balance."

Hayden Fowler turned and glanced first at Dulowski, then at Nora. "All of this considered, I'd say there's a good chance these things are not of this Earth. Not of this time and place. Of course, maybe it's just wishful thinking on my part. It's almost impossible to make a definitive call viewing it on a tiny laptop screen. But I'm excited by what I see here. The possibilities are endless."

"I agree," Nora said.

Fowler added, "The thing that throws me is the meteorite serving as an egg casing. Very peculiar."

"Yeah, I don't understand that either," Dulowski chimed in. "We saw the damage the meteorite did out in that rancher's pasture. Quite the mess. The speed at point of impact was incredible. I don't understand how egg embryos could survive that kind of collision, not to mention the amount of heat generated by entry into the Earth's atmosphere."

Nora removed her glasses and combed the stem through her brunette bob. "If you'll permit me to play devil's advocate here, gentlemen, maybe we're approaching this all wrong. Perhaps these creatures aren't extraterrestrial at all."

"How do you mean?" Dulowski asked.

"Well, think about it. Aside from the enormous impact of meteorite strikes, living biological organisms need oxygen and nutrients to survive. How are they going to get that bundled up in the center of a stone fireball hurtling toward earth at an impossible speed?"

"So what are you saying, Nora?" Fowler asked.

"I'm saying that maybe these lizards—or whatever they are— are subterranean beings indigenous to northern Montana, and are attracted to something in that meteorite that brought them to the surface."

Fowler gave her a haughty look. "That's quite a stretch."

"It's no more ridiculous than what you hypothesized. I mean, meteorites acting as egg housings for alien reptiles? Preposterous!"

"Easy, little lady. No need to get testy about it," Fowler said, his insolence annoying her. "I was just thinking out loud."

"And so was I. *You're* the one who said the possibilities are endless."

Greg Dulowski attempted to ease the friction between his two associates. "Look, we're all just trying to make sense of something complex and mysterious. Something inexplicable."

"Agreed," Nora said, having no desire to make enemies with her lead paleontologist. She steered the conversation back his way. "So I'm trying to understand here, Hayden. You're saying these creatures are not of this Earth . . . that they are not of this time and place. Your words. You say they are bipedal theropod lizards . . . not avian. Creatures of some primordial reptilian genus. Are you suggesting these could be dinosaur hatchlings, then?"

Fowler looked back at the laptop screen and shook his head. "They're obviously immature hatchlings of some unique species. But I would hesitate to call them dinosaurs. Too difficult to make that call from here. Let's get Krause in here to have a look."

"Right," Nora agreed. "Franz might be better able to shed some light on it."

Fowler nodded. "Yes, Krause needs to see this. But I say the best thing would be to take a drive up to that ranch in Heart Butte pronto and see what's going on firsthand."

"I'm with you on that," Dulowski said. "Gilliam's Guidepost will be crawling with media and curiosity seekers once word of this gets out. I know it's ultimately your decision, Nora. But I think we'd be missing a great opportunity if we don't head up there ASAP."

So she had called Franz Krause, the paleozoologist, to her trailer. Krause, a stoic German, showed no emotion as he listened to them repeat their previous observations over the clicking-chirping sounds of the creatures on the short video clip. When the screen went dark, he sat quietly for a few seconds, looking at Nora with an astonished expression fixed on his long, narrow face, then said, "When do we go see this amazing thing?"

Should I go or should I stay?

Nora still struggled with the answer.

She rose from her bunk and went to her desk. Her thoughts strayed to the successes they'd had the expedition's first week at the dig site. They'd hit on some amazing luck. Wednesday they discovered a nest of fossilized Maiasaura eggs. The find also produced a mostly intact Maiasaura skeleton. Maiasauras were duckbilled herbivores of the middle-to-late Cretaceous that grew to be thirty feet long and weighed in at four tons. Of course, Nora was aware the finding of petrified Maiasaura eggs was not a new discovery. Paleontologist John Horner had made the find of Maiasaura hatching mounds in this area back in 1978. She had read much of Horner's groundbreaking work as an undergrad, and footnoted many of his theories in her graduate dissertation. Still, finding this new nest was a thrill and a positive motivation for the entire team. Then yesterday, they unearthed a Triceratops skull near the Maiasaura find. The skull measured seven feet long and she figured it would weigh in at a half-ton or more. Tomorrow they would use a bulldozer and backhoe to begin trenching the area around the skull and Maiasaura frame. Extraction of the Maiasaura skeleton and Triceratops skull would be a delicate, time-consuming effort, probably two weeks or more. Once they carved out the trench, the team would work down in the gutter, chipping rock and sandstone from around the fragile bones. Very tedious, exacting fieldwork, but ultimately rewarding. These finds were a wonderful way to begin the quest. The sponsors were pleased. Nora's first big paleontological dig was going well.

And this *was* a big-scope project—a caravan of seventeen people and several tons of heavy earth-moving equipment. A three-month expedition, beginning here in the low grasslands and gutted gullies outside Choteau and proceeding northward to Glacier National Park just south of the Canadian border. This area of north-western Montana, as well as a large portion of southern Alberta, was known to paleontologists as The Valley of the Dinosaurs. Between

130 million years and 66 million years ago—the Cretaceous Period—this corridor was home to the largest concentration of dinosaurs on Earth. Today, these remote badlands offered remarkable glimpses into the lives of the creatures that roamed these parts over millions of years.

Nora could barely contain her excitement.

Should I go to Heart Butte or stay here?

She went back and forth in her mind.

The Smithsonian brass is happy with our first week's results. Would it hurt to take a day trip up to the meteorite ranch? But what if someone gets hurt in my absence and the Smithsonian board finds out about it?

Nora finally decided it was probably best that she stay here. She could send Hayden Fowler and her paleozoologist, Franz Krause. They would be able to make more sense of the mystery. Maybe send Greg Dulowski with them, too, since he'd already been there, and the meteorite lined up precisely with his expertise.

And then she thought about what she might miss out on if she didn't go.

Oh, the responsibilities of being in charge.

She left her trailer to check on the team's afternoon progress, thinking: *I'm still on the fence with this thing.*

Sickbay Blues

June 4: St. Patrick Hospital
Missoula, Montana

PETER LACROIX GOT THE CALL LAST NIGHT. George Dantley had regained consciousness and had been moved to a private room.

For the past week, he had been unable to get in to see George; only immediate family was allowed into the ICU. So each evening after work he'd called the hospital, and each night he received the same dire message.

"I'm sorry, Mr. Lacroix, but the patient is comatose and on a ventilator. He's been through a great deal of trauma. We're doing everything in our power to help him. I wish I had better news for you."

George had suffered substantial injuries that might have killed an older man outright: a shattered pelvis, three busted ribs, a punctured lung, broken left arm, shattered femur in his left leg, third-degree burns over his back and scalp.

Every night Peter's wife Brin tried to cheer him up by cooking his favorite meals and telling him corny jokes. He loved her for her attempts at levity, but Peter knew it was forced. George had been a dinner guest at their house and Brin liked the college student every bit as much as Peter did. The prognosis was bleak, he'd told her. It was touch and go. Very difficult to find laughter when their young friend was broken and silent.

But now there was hope. George was breathing on his own and talking.

First thing this morning, Peter headed straight to St. Patrick Hospital. Though things had taken a positive turn, Peter still felt nerves as he rode the elevator to George's floor. The door swished open. He walked the bright hallway, checking room numbers. His right knee ached—an old hockey injury that tortured him in times of stress—and he walked with a noticeable limp. He passed rooms with open doors, saw worried visitors gathered around patients' beds, daytime television shows blaring. The corridor smelled of rubbing alcohol, bleach, and sickness. A young nurse passed him pushing a medical cart.

He came to George's room. The door was closed. He took a deep breath and knocked.

"Come on in," George called out in a raspy voice.

He pushed the door open and entered. It took a minute for his eyes to adjust to the dim room.

"Hey there, Pete." George's greeting came out as a strained croak.

Peter moved to the chair facing the bed, took a seat. "Hey, back at ya," he said, trying not to cringe at George's appearance. His left arm was elevated and encased in a thick cast. Bandages swaddled much of his body and one side of his face. A greasy salve coated the blistered burns on top of his scorched head. A dozen wires connected him to beeping machines. An IV bag drip-drip-dripped nourishment and painkiller.

"I'm quite the sight, eh?"

Peter reached over and touched his right hand. "Hell of a way to get out of work, my friend. Brin and I have been worried about you."

George gripped Peter's hand, spoke in a wheezy gasp. "I don't think I'll be going out dancing anytime soon. They tell me I could be in here for a long run."

"I never knew you to be Fred Astaire or Gene Kelly anyway," Peter said.

George laughed weakly. "Now I know . . . you're . . . *old*," he rasped, struggling under heavy sedation to push the words out. "with ref . . . references . . . like that."

Peter smiled. "Okay, how about John Travolta, then?"

"Still old."

Peter emitted a soft laugh. The near-death experience hadn't stolen the young man's sense of humor, though George seemed to be getting more exhausted by the minute. "You just take it easy, Georgie, and get well. I need my sports buddy. Who else am I gonna take to hockey and football games if not you?"

George remained quiet for a beat, then said, "My dad . . . he told me . . . you called the hospital every night . . . to check on me."

"True."

"Thank you."

"You think my service ends with getting you to the hospital? You're stuck with me, buddy."

"Thanks . . . for . . . everything, Pete."

"Now you're getting all sentimental on me."

"Sorry . . ." he said, looking like he wanted to say more but he stopped, his face contorting in a mask of pain.

"You okay? You want me to call the nurse?"

"No . . . no . . ."

Peter didn't know what to say. George's tormented eyes reflected his pain. Nobody should have to suffer like this. Especially not a promising 21-year-old college student with his entire life in front of him.

After several minutes of awkward silence in which George squirmed in discomfort, he spoke in breathy spurts. "So, I have been trying . . . to piece together . . . what happened at . . . The Hump. Last thing . . . I remember was . . . making a . . . mayday call . . ."

Peter squeezed George's hand. "I'll tell you all about it, but you have to lay still and let me do the talking, okay?"

George nodded and listened intently as Peter rambled on about the meteorite hit four miles from Camels Hump that spawned a wildfire. He informed him of the meteorite that felled George's lookout tower and explained that the strike had cracked The Hump wide open down its cliff side. Finally, he walked him through the longline helicopter rescue. Peter didn't mention the bullfrog croaks he'd heard, or the gooey substance glazing the wall of the cliff. No sense trying to explain something he didn't understand.

"And we've been busy this week putting out fires started by meteorite strikes," Peter continued. "Bitterroot Forest got two hits.

Another one up near Flathead Lake. And word is, there has also been a lot of meteorite activity in Idaho. Hundreds—maybe *thousands*—of acres of prime forest burnt to a crisp. All from these weird space boulders."

George said, "So strange . . . meteorites? Whaddaya think . . . about it, Pete?"

"Don't know. It has everyone at HQ bamboozled. They're scrambling to get answers even as we speak. For some unknown reason these meteorites are only targeting Montana and Idaho. Nowhere else. It's crazy to think, but we're international news."

The nurse entered the room, eyeing Peter. "Sorry, sir, but we're going to have to cut this visit short. I need to take the patient's vitals and change out his dressings. Refresh his meds."

"No problem. I understand." Peter said. He released George's hand and stood. "I'll be on my way." To George he said, "You work on getting yourself better, okay? All of the Forestry folks are pulling for you. I'll be back to see you tomorrow, Georgie."

"Thanks for . . . coming, Pete. I . . . I appreciate it," George said, a grimace of pain contorting his face.

Peter retraced his route back to the elevator, a bit of optimism in his step. But mostly he felt a lingering sadness. George's wounds were severe. He could still die. It wasn't fair. Georgie was the nicest, classiest person Peter knew aside from Brin. Someone like him didn't deserve to be broken, crushed, and burned like that. The unjust nature of life had raised its ugly head. Peter hadn't shed a tear in years, but his visit with Georgie brought him close.

He stepped out of the elevator and entered the lobby. It was much more congested than it had been an hour ago, and he wound through the crowd. He passed the Admissions desk and heard a male voice calling his name.

"Pete Lacroix! Hey, Pete, over here!"

He peered in the direction of the voice, spotting George's father, Sam Dantley, and his wife Elizabeth, waving at him. Peter met them last fall when he picked George up to go to a Missoula Bruins hockey game.

He waved and went to them, dread building in him.

What do I say to the parents of a son who is mangled and roasted?

"Hey, Sam, hey, Liz," he said, shaking their hands. Both were in their late forties but looked years younger. He recalled that Sam was a corporate VP for a farm equipment company, and Elizabeth worked as a court stenographer.

Sam said, "I haven't had the opportunity to thank you yet, Pete."

"Ah," Peter said, uncomfortable. "There's no need to—"

"Nonsense, my man! You saved our son's life and we are forever grateful."

"Um, I didn't save George. My crew did. And it was a fairly routine operation."

"That's not the way we heard it," Elizabeth Dantley said.

"Really, I was just the pilot, Liz. The only thing I did was drop my first responder crew down on that rock. They did all the heavy lifting."

"You're far too modest, Pete," Sam said. "We heard you went down the cable and helped save our son. And I also heard there were high winds that day. I asked around and was told it takes a blue-chip pilot to pull off that maneuver. I plan to make sure you are publicly recognized for your courage and skill."

Peter felt a creeping embarrassment. "*Please* don't do that, Sam. I'm pleading with you. I just did my job. All in a day's work, y'know."

"You are too humble. You're a true life hero, Pete. Accept it. The world needs more like you these days."

Does this man not understand that his only child could still die?

Peter left St. Patrick Hospital in a blue funk. He needed to get home to Brin and the baby. As the saying goes, home is where the heart is.

Lianne and Beauregard

June 5: Gilliam's Guidepost
Heart Butte, Montana

LIANNE WOLFED DOWN HER FAVORITE snack—Oreo cookies and a glass of milk. She jammed six more cookies into her jeans pocket and headed out to the stables, her special place. Yesterday was her final day as a second grader at Heart Butte School, and on her first official day of summer vacation, she wanted to spend time with her horse, Beauregard.

The past week she had been preoccupied with the big black space rocks out in the east meadow. The way Mama and Daddy acted all nervous when they talked about the meeteeyite made Lianne wonder if she and her brothers were safe. She didn't get it. How could a bunch of rocks hurt them?

Is it because they're from outer space?

As she made the long walk to the stables, she thought about Mama and Daddy. The way they were acting all bossy and creepy, demanding she not tell anyone at school about the meeteeyite. They also told her she was not to leave the house.

Like I'm a dumb little kid or something.

Not much of a summer vacation if I can't leave the house.

Lianne wanted to tell somebody about the space rocks in the worst way. The whole thing was cool and weird. She'd come close to telling her cousin Marnie Enright. But then, she supposed that Marnie would call her crazy. Or a big fibber. So Lianne had obeyed her parents' first rule and kept the meeteeyite to herself.

But they weren't about to keep her away from the horses. The horse barn was her special place, a magical place. This was her chance. Mama was busy in the store and Daddy was in his garage working on a big tractor. Her brothers were at baseball practice, so she had a couple of hours before supper.

"Here I come, Beau," she yelled out as she skipped along the trail.

Lianne loved the gamy smell of the old barn and the dusty odor of hay overflowing the loft. She didn't even mind the pesky horseflies or the ripe smell of horse dung. That's what Mama called it—*dung*. Daddy called it a bad word that started with s.

She walked down the row of stalls, greeting each horse by name, rubbing their moist noses as she passed. Blackie, Max, Beauregard, Clancy, Roscoe, and Pirate.

She went to where she had propped up two of her dolls against a railing: Patches, her Cabbage Patch doll, and Lyle, her stuffed lion. Lianne usually left them out here to keep the horses company while she was at school.

"Hi, guys," she said, picking the dolls up and hugging them. "Did you miss me?"

Lianne changed her voice to a higher register. "Of course we did, Mama Lee."

She set the dolls on the ground and went to Beauregard, climbed into the stall with him. She kissed him on his snout and rubbed his flank. Beau nickered soft and low.

Lianne had celebrated her seventh birthday three months ago, and Mama and Daddy had given Beau to her as a gift. It was her responsibility to take care of him, but she could not ride him without her parents watching. It made her mad because Paul and Ethan were allowed to ride on their own. So, when she came out here alone in the afternoons, she mounted Beau in the stall and *pretended* to ride him. It wasn't the same as taking him out for a real run, but it was the next best thing. She enjoyed it, and Beau seemed to like it, too.

She threw a blanket on Beau's back and hopped on. Beau neighed appreciatively as she ran her hand through his mane and whispered in his ear, "You're my beautiful boy, Beau, and I love you."

Lianne reached into her pocket and pulled out two cookies. She ate one and fed the other to Beau, keeping her hand flat with the cookie in her palm so that Beau wouldn't accidentally bite her. Daddy had told her a grown horse could easily bite off a finger or two if she tried to feed him treats with her fingers. Daddy had also told her that horses shouldn't eat sweets, that they weren't the same as us humans. But Daddy wasn't here and Beau really liked Oreos.

She pretended they were on the move. In her imagination, Beau was galloping through the meadow and she was spurring him on. But she didn't kick his flanks in here. She knew better. That would make Beau want to run for real. She leaned forward and fed him another cookie, told him he was a good boy.

She had been "riding" Beau for five minutes when she became aware of the other horses snorting and stomping in their stalls. At first she thought it was because they were jealous of all the attention she gave to Beau. But then she heard scrabbling sounds from the corner of the barn. She stopped moving and listened more closely. She heard chirping. Like a bird, but different. With clicks and croaks, much like the spotted toads out in the retention pond.

She swung her leg around and dismounted Beau. Climbed out of the stall. The horses were nervous and frantic, kicking and grunting. The wooden side rails shook as they bucked up against them. Even Beau started acting crazy. Lianne felt a disturbing mixture of fear and curiosity.

What is that sound? she thought, moving cautiously in that direction. *Squirrels? Racoons? Barn rats?*

She pulled up short as she spotted a quick flash along the ground. Too fast to make out any details. Just a greenish-gray streak. And then a second animal appeared, stopping in the dim light of the open area beneath the hayloft. The creature—the size of a small cat—stood its ground and stared at her through heavily lidded, beady red eyes.

Lianne shrieked, remaining motionless, frozen in fear.

It looked like a baby alligator or crocodile, like the ones she'd seen in her zoo books. It sat there, swishing its tiny tail across the dirt floor, gazing at her with those scary eyes. She stood very still and held her breath.

She didn't know what to do.

If I run will it chase me?

Mama had told her often that she was a strong-minded girl. Hearing her mother's voice in her head made her think hard for a way out of this.

And then she had the answer. Slowly, she reached into her pocket and pulled out a cookie.

Surely if Beauregard likes Oreos, then this little guy probably will, too.

Lianne broke the cookie into little pieces and threw them on the ground in front of her. The animal scurried forth, snapping up the first cookie piece with startling quickness. Lianne moved back a few steps, watching as the animal pounced on the remaining pieces, raising its scaly, triangular head back as it gulped them down. It happened so fast she didn't have time to get another cookie out before the little gator-thing charged her, its claws digging into the dirt floor.

She screamed. Turned and ran. Felt a needle-like sting through her jeans leg in her lower calf as it bit her. She cried out in pain as she tumbled. Felt the thing still attached to her leg. She beat at it with both hands until it screeched and ran off into a dark corner.

Terrified and in pain, her leg bleeding, Lianne ran from the barn, leaving the doors wide open. She ran as fast as her hurt leg would allow. When she was halfway down the trail, she heard the horses squealing in fear. She stopped, turned to look back at the stables. Heard wood cracking and loud collisions. It sounded like the horse barn was coming apart.

Panting heavily, she plopped down on the dusty trail and rolled up her pantleg, wiped the blood from her calf. Lianne looked at the tiny teeth marks there and she felt faint. It hurt so bad!

Tears streamed down her cheeks.

Then, shockingly, she watched as Blackie burst through the open barn doors and galloped off in a frightened sprint. Max followed right behind him, and then came Pirate and Roscoe. All sprinted willy-nilly away from the barn, confusion and fear in their startled movements.

But she didn't see Beau. Or Clancy.

I'm in so much trouble, she thought as her tears became sobs. *Mama and Daddy are going to kill me.*

Lianne had one last thought before picking herself up off the ground and going to the house for her punishment.

Oh please, God, don't let that ugly little gator-thing hurt my Beauregard.

Pest Control

June 6: Gilliam's Guidepost
Heart Butte, Montana

BRYAN WAITED FOR THE EXTERMINATOR from Browning Pest Control in the lobby of the inn. He'd put in a call to the company last night, after Loretta and he dealt with their daughter's foolishness.

Lianne had disobeyed their strict orders. She'd pulled rebellious stunts before, but nothing of this risky magnitude. Bryan thought they'd raised their daughter better than that. But then, to be honest, he and Loretta hadn't told her the reason for their concerns. How could they? If they'd let her know about the little reptilian creatures, Lianne would have nightmares for months. *Always a difficult balancing act—how much information to give to the kids to keep them safe and protected.*

Loretta had been shocked when Lianne stormed into the store, her face a rigid mask of terror and panic.

"Help me, Mama, I'm hurt! My leg is bleeding! It hurts so bad, Mama."

Loretta rushed to her, gathered her in her arms, consoled her while freaking out over the severity of the wound. When she asked Lianne what had happened, her daughter spluttered a confused jumble of words.

By the time Bryan arrived, Loretta had dressed the wound with ointment and gauze, and Lianne was coming clean about what she'd done. Bryan listened to his little girl ramble on, her demeanor one of fright and guilt. His heart ached for her, but it didn't diminish his annoyance over her disobeying him.

He knelt and peeled the bandage back, had a look. "We're going to have to take you to a doctor, Lee."

"No! Please, Daddy, no doctor. *Please*."

"Yes, absolutely," he said, securing the bandage and standing. "Your leg might need a stitch or two. At the very least you need a rabies shot. Maybe even a tetanus shot."

Lianne burst out crying.

Loretta said, "Do you have to be so specific, dear?"

"Look Loretta, there's no telling what diseases those animals might be carrying." He turned to his distraught daughter. "Let this be a good lesson for you, Lee. Maybe next time you'll obey your mother and me."

They settled Lianne down and took her to see Doc Parsons, telling him the wound was from a dog bite. The good doctor gave Bryan a curious look, but proceeded to stitch up the wound, followed by rabies and tetanus shots just to be sure. He was good with a needle and possessed a pleasant bedside manner, which put Lianne at ease.

Back home by six. Enough time for Bryan to round up the horses and return them to the stables. But he did so cautiously, armed with his rifle, on alert for the little beasts. Fortunately, they were nowhere to be found during his roundup. The temperature dropped quickly as the sun set, so it was probably too cold for the animals to make a return appearance. Understandably, the horses were still skittish, and he decided to spend the night camped out in the hayloft with his rifle and box of ammunition. He'd remained awake through much of the long, cold night, and thankfully, there had been no further activity in the stables. But the damage done to the stalls depressed him.

He had been touched in a myriad of ways seeing Lianne's dolls laying on the dirt floor of the barn, dirty and rumpled. He and Loretta knew about their daughter's practice of leaving her beloved Patches and Lyle out there so the horses wouldn't be lonely. Lianne possessed a nurturing, loving nature, no doubt inherited from Loretta. The girl had a big heart and an imagination to match. Unfortunately, Lianne also had a reckless, irresponsible side.

That child is so headstrong it hurts.

The exterminator—a young Blackfoot named Joe—entered the lobby and introduced himself. He handed Bryan his business card. Bryan glanced at it and felt a twist in his gut.

Joseph P. Creek
Browning Pest Control, LLC
"If we can't get rid of 'em, they're not of this world!"

"I hear you're having problems with some critters you can't identify, Mr. Gilliam," Creek said. "I've been in the bug business for years and there ain't an animal around who can best Joe Creek. We'll get rid of whatever it is. I give you our money-back guarantee on that."

So young and cocky. I hope he knows what he's doing.

"Don't be so quick to throw your money away," Bryan said. "*My* guarantee is that you've *never* seen any creatures like these."

Bryan sat in the passenger seat of Creek's bug truck, a white Econoline van with a giant plastic cockroach bolted to the roof. He gave the exterminator directions out to the east meadow as Creek drove, jabbering about wild times in the exterminating business.

"Ain't nothin' as dangerous as battling a cellar full of rabid rats, I'll have you know, Mr. Gilliam. Two weeks ago I was called to a condemned building in Dupuyer. Investors wanted to rebuild it, turn it into a restaurant. They didn't want to level it, so they sent me and my partner in to clean out the vermin before they started renovating. You ever seen a rat hiss and foam at the mouth, Mr. Gilliam?"

"No. I haven't had the pleasure. Take a left at that dirt road coming up."

Joe Creek made the left turn. Steel cans containing poisonous chemicals clanked together in the rear of the van as they bounced over the rutted road. "Anyway," he continued, "they started making these high-pitched squeals and their eyes was all flame-red and they went after anything that moved. You wouldn't believe how them suckers can leap. Like little kangaroos they are! My partner on that job, Bryson? They got him in the stomach and he ain't been back to work since."

Man, this guy sure can talk a blue streak.

Bryan said, "See that rock grouping straight ahead?"

"Yeah."

"Head for it. But don't get too close."

"How come?"

"You'll see in a minute. Or I should say you'll *smell* it in a minute."

Creek slowed the vehicle as they approached the meteorite remnants. He made a face. "Oooo-whee! What the hell is that stink?" He stopped the van and looked at Bryan.

"I believe it's extraterrestrial egg yolk."

"Extraterrestrial? You mean like from *outer space*?"

Bryan pointed through the windshield. "Those rocks you see were part of a meteorite that came down here last week." He scanned the ground leading up to the stones. No creatures in sight, which was a good thing. On the other hand, he wanted Joe Creek to get a look at them. Maybe identify them and tell him they were *not* alien creatures.

"I know it sounds crazy," he continued, "but somehow that meteorite is a giant egg casing that hatched out the most bizarre little reptiles I've ever seen. We had a guy here from the American Meteor Society looking into it . . . when they were hatching out. He got bit by one of them. It wasn't pretty. And yesterday my daughter was attacked by one in our horse stables. I have no idea what species these things are, but they're aggressive as hell."

Joe Creek looked at Bryan like he was completely off-the-rails batshit loony tunes. "With all due respect, Mr. Gilliam . . ." He did not finish his thought. He glanced back at the meteorite rocks. "Why didn't you report it that way when you called us?"

"Are you serious?" Bryan said. "Would anyone in your office have believed me if I'd told them what I just told you? Would they have sent you out here?"

"No, probably not. But I will say that we've seen many strange things in this business."

"I guarantee you've never seen anything as strange as this." Bryan opened his door. "C'mon, I'll show you."

Creek got out of the van and opened the rear doors, grabbed a pair of dual cartridge respirators, heavy canvas gloves, and an aluminum pole with a titanium clamp on the end. A snake stick.

"Whew, what a stench!" Creek said, scrunching his narrow face in disgust. He handed Bryan one of the respirators. "Strap this on. It'll cut the smell."

Bryan got his rifle and pointed at the snake stick. "You planning on catching one?"

Creek nodded, strapping the respirator across the top of his head. "If these critters are what you say they are—from outer space—we need to snag us one so we can study it. Can't eradicate pests if we don't know anything about 'em."

Bryan caught the smirk on Creek's face. *The man still doesn't believe me.* Then again, if roles were reversed, Bryan would have tossed off the idea as ludicrous nonsense, the ravings of a madman.

Bryan and Joe Creek positioned their respirators over their noses and mouths, and took tentative steps toward the rock formation. Bryan could see the yolky goop that had been a thick liquid a few days ago had hardened to a thin crust. When they got within touching distance of the rocks, he noticed crushed eggshell fragments near the base of the largest rock wedge.

"Look at this." Bryan said, his voice muffled through the breathing apparatus. He kneeled and picked up a piece of shell. It was thick and leathery. "I think this proves my point. These creatures hatched out here."

Creek examined the piece of shell in Bryan's hand. It had a colorful, swirling bluish-green pattern running through it.

"Interesting, Mr. Gilliam. Definitely something unusual went on out here. But where are the critters?"

Bryan pocketed the eggshell and looked around. He wanted to have something to show the paleontology folks who were coming tomorrow.

"After what I've witnessed," Bryan said, "I'd say we're damn lucky there's no sign of them."

But Bryan worried: *If they're not here, where are they?* He'd seen at least a dozen hatchlings just a few days ago. Now the site seemed deserted.

Joe Creek lifted his mask, said, "Look, Mr. Gilliam. I'm not saying you're wrong, but without seeing any of these things you call alien reptiles, I don't have a job to do."

"Well, let's keep looking then. C'mon, let's check out the other side."

Guardedly, they stepped down into the crater and advanced through the gap between the two largest sections of rock. The opening was just wide enough to accommodate both of them. Bryan led the way, the barrel of his rifle out in front of him. The floor of the crater was littered with vibrantly colored eggshell fragments. Bryan held out a hand, stopping Creek behind him. He didn't want to do any more damage to the eggshells. He wanted the scientists to have the best samples to work with. He knelt and gathered up shell pieces, stuffed them in his pocket, marveling at the vivid colors and distinctive swirling patterns.

Then he noticed something odd about the rock face to their left. He moved in for a closer look, poked at it with his rifle barrel. It appeared to be a small nest of unbroken eggs wedged deep into the rock. He'd almost missed it; a mass of fresh goop enveloped the eggs like a superglued cocoon. Bryan was about to call Joe Creek over for a look when he heard a snarling, *chirp-croak* sound that sent a chill through him.

He turned and saw three creatures charging, their tiny claws scrabbling across the hard-glazed earth. They came at them wild and manic, screeching like little reptilian banshees.

Bryan fired at the lead animal and missed, the gunshot deafening in the close quarters.

A lizard-thing sunk its teeth into his boot leather. Bryan kicked, flinging it off.

He fired again, hitting one. Blowing it apart.

A few more came at them.

Joe Creek moved in with the snake stick, and with surprising quickness and dexterity, clamped one of them around its scaled belly. The tiny creature squealed like a stuck pig. Sensing danger, the other creatures ran off.

Bryan fought to catch his breath through his respirator. Tried to make sense of what just happened. These things were bigger than he remembered them being when he'd first encountered them just a few days ago. These were a foot, maybe two feet, in length. He glanced down at the shredded leather of his boot. "That thing has a heavy bite for something that small," he said.

The exterminator held the snake stick out and away from his body, the creature squirming and shrieking at the end of it. "Oh my god," Joe Creek said, admiring his catch. "I've never seen anything like this. It looks like a baby crocodile, only its front feet are different."

Bryan whipped off his mask and said, "Well, the problem with that is, there's never been crocodiles in Montana. Do you believe my story now?"

"All the way, Mr. Gilliam. All the way."

Bryan looked around warily. The creatures had cleared out.

"Watch my back," he said to Creek. "I'm gonna get those eggs."

"Are you insane?"

"No. I'm just blessed with a relentless curiosity."

Sky Watchers

June 6: Big Sky Observatory
Twin Falls, Idaho

THE SWITCHBOARD LIT UP LIKE THE VEGAS STRIP on a Saturday night. Communications continued to stream in from NASA, the U.S. Naval Observatory, Department of the Interior, Homeland Security, U.S. Geological Survey, the National Weather Service, American Meteor Society, amateur astronomers, and concerned private citizens. The information exchange went on 24/7. And of course there were the inevitable calls from alien invasion conspiracy fanatics.

Big Sky Observatory, being the nearest tracking station, had joined NASA and the Idaho and Montana State Forest Divisions in a four-way information network. NASA and two observatories acted as "eyes in the sky" while the forestry contingents operated as ground crews, fighting fires and attempting to locate meteorite impact sites with their fleets of single-prop planes and helicopters. To date, NASA's Planetary Defense Coordination Office reported fifteen confirmed meteorite strikes along a 300-mile corridor of the Bitterroot Range of the Rockies. Nine in Montana and six in Idaho.

Big Sky Observatory Chief Astrophysicist Dr. Blaine Colton sat in his office, observing the double-tiered bank of computer monitors lining a side wall. The screens displayed satellite views of thousands of square miles along the Rockies and telescope video feeds tracking Near-Earth Objects (NEOs) such as asteroids, comets, fireballs, and meteors. Dr. Colton's eyes followed the scrolling tickers at the bottom of each screen, picking up real-time data that kept him up to date.

Colton saw his encrypted red line light up and heard the

computerized voice announce the caller as Scott Westerly, Geosciences Deputy Director with the National Science Foundation in Alexandria, Virginia. Since the first strike last week, the administration in D.C. demanded frequent updates. The White House and Pentagon were alarmed about the number of multi-ton meteorites raining down along the Continental Divide.

A long beep indicated the connection had been made. The call was now on speakerphone.

"Good afternoon, Scott," Colton said. "How are things in the land of liars and thieves?"

"Probably better than where you are. I sure hope you have good news for me today. Please tell me our national nightmare is coming to an end . . . that things are slowing down."

"No such luck. Three more hits in the past twenty-four hours. All in Montana."

"Big boys, like the others?"

"Yes. The chopper jocks have only been able to get close to a rock they found two days ago. Montana Forestry reports that it's in large segments. They estimate the impact stone was ten to twelve feet in diameter. Very dense, too. Probably weighs in the vicinity of four to five tons."

"Good god! Can you imagine these things coming down in metropolitan areas?"

"I try not to think about that, Scott."

"Most meteorites are only fist size. And those are the largest finds."

"I'm well aware of that, yes."

"What the hell is going on, Blaine?"

"Lord only knows. I wish I knew." Colton thought about the news that came in this morning. Information that any scientist worth their salt would claim to be a hoax. Improbable at best, most likely impossible. He didn't know how he could feasibly brief Westerly without sounding like a conspiracy theorist lunatic.

"You still there, Blaine?" Deputy Director Westerly said.

"Uh, yeah, I uh . . . just got sidetracked with something else. Too much going on around here lately."

"Understood."

Colton decided to ease into the more sensational discoveries of this morning by feeding the Deputy Director known data. "To say that this dire situation in which we find ourselves is most bizarre would be a huge understatement. We've already experienced more meteorite hits the past week than we've charted the previous seven years combined. And we know they're only coming down in this part of the country. Nowhere else in the world are they seeing any meteor showers, let alone meteorite activity. It's just so strange. It's almost like the Continental Divide is a magnet that's pulling in this space debris. And this activity is early. We usually don't see significant meteor showers in these parts until late August. Even then, it doesn't compare to what we're seeing now. Especially the number of them making it to the ground. And the size of these things, Christ almighty!"

"Yes indeed. Very strange astronomical anomaly, I agree. Do you have longs and lats for the three latest strikes?"

"Yes, I'll send them to you while we talk."

"Thanks a bunch."

Colton pulled his iPad off his desk and set it in his lap. He transferred the longitude/latitude coordinates of the three new Montana hits to Westerly. As his fingers moved across the iPad, he struggled with how to best frame the seriously speculative data he had for Westerly. *How can I present it so that the Deputy Director won't think I'm a candidate for a rubber-walled white room?*

"You got any positive news I can pass along?" Westerly said, cutting into his thoughts. "You know our president has zero patience, right? He has his staff pestering us twenty-four-seven. He's ultra-concerned about the safety of the American people. I agree with him on the safety issue. I've gotta get him some answers soon, though. Something positive."

Colton stopped typing. "Well shit, Scott. I'm no miracle worker. I'm just the messenger here."

"I know, I know. Sorry. I'm just supremely frustrated is all. And I'm not above saying I'm fearful of what's going on."

"We all are. How do you think we feel here in the observatory?

We're in the direct line of fire."

"I know, Blaine. Sorry for my selfishness."

"No worries."

Westerly said, "I just got the coordinates. Thanks. Now it's my turn to give you some news . . . some developments."

"Oh?"

"Yeah. We got a briefing from the Pentagon yesterday. They are putting together a large task force team led by the Air Force."

"To do what exactly?"

"To round up these meteorites and take them to a military base for study."

Colton barked out a chuckle. "That's a fool's errand, Scott."

"They don't seem to think so. I spoke with Air Force Secretary Tomlinson this morning. She's working out the logistics as we speak, putting the team together. She wants to be ready to roll in a couple of weeks."

"Isn't that a bit on the ambitious side?" Colton replied. "I mean, an operation like that would take tremendous manpower and lots of aerial equipment. It would be a Herculean effort to get it underway in two weeks. I've never once seen the feds move that fast. The bureaucracy usually jams up the works."

"You're not wrong there, but you know how unique this situation is. Until we know more about the makeup of these meteorites, the American people cannot be considered safe—especially folks living in your area of the country. Teresa Tomlinson is no-nonsense about this. She's cracking the proverbial whip and the Air Force is marching to her orders. The Secretary has also been talking about enlisting your Big Sky Observatory and the observatory at the University of Montana . . . Blue Mountain I believe it's called—"

"Yes, that's correct."

"—and she is for sure going to recruit a few forestry helicopter pilots for the mission, due to their knowledge of the topography. Secretary Tomlinson is one tough cookie. She's a tough leader who always gets what she wants."

"Wow," Colton marveled. "This whole affair started with a few fireballs in the sky and a single meteorite hit. Now we're being bombarded and the Pentagon is getting involved? Unbelievable!"

"I know. How much stranger can it get, right?"

Colton paused, then said, "Well, to be honest, Scott, I have some fresh intel for you. This thing has just hit another level of strange."

"How so?"

"This news just came in a couple of hours ago. The chopper teams found concentrations of a gooey substance on and around one of the meteorites. The searchers were hit with an overpowering smell, a ghastly stench. And here is the real shocker . . . they found pieces of what looks like broken egg shells embedded in the goo."

"What? Eggshells?" What the hell."

"Yeah, and when they checked out the back side of the rock, where the back half had broken off and shattered, they apparently found what they think are fully intact eggs in a nest of ancient foliage."

"Inside the meteorite?"

"I know it sounds crazy, but that's what the report stated."

"Jesus! What have those forestry flyboys been smoking?"

Colton laughed, though there wasn't much levity behind it. "They are putting in a request for federal assistance . . . asking for qualified zoologists and paleobotanists to come out here to try and figure out what's going on."

Deputy Director Westerly whistled, said, "Looks like Idaho and Montana are about to get very crowded. This thing has gone batshit crazy, Blaine."

"You've said a mouthful, partner."

Bones and Booze

June 6: Smithsonian Expedition
Choteau, Montana

THE DISCOVERY OF THE MAIASAURA SKELETON and the Triceratops skull kept Nora Lemoyne in Choteau for two more days. She desperately wanted to make the 60-mile drive north to the Heart Butte ranch where fascinating things were unfolding, but her duties at the field dig site took priority.

The Maiasaura—an herbivore known as *Good Mother Lizard*—presented a serious excavation challenge. Eight feet tall and thirty feet long from duckbill to tail, the operation to carve out a gutter around it had been a delicate, dirty, precise job. The skeleton was embedded in Madison limestone, quartz, and thick argillaceous sandstone, and the team operating the earthmoving machinery had to work slowly and carefully so as not to damage the intact bones. The Triceratops skull near it—weighing in at over half a ton—also tested their resolve.

Mack Renfro and his two heavy equipment operators had worked the backhoe and bulldozer in shifts the past two days to dig out five-foot-wide trenches around the Maiasaura skeleton, its fossilized bed of eggs, and the Triceratops skull. When the trenching was complete, Mack and his team installed scaffolding with a pulley system that would raise and lower workers in the excavation pits. Now at dawn, with the 4,000-watt balloon lights casting an eerie shine across the site, excavators were down in the trenches using picks, shovels, air hammers, stonemason chisels, and pneumatic drills to chip away at the prizes.

Nora beamed with fatigued pride as she walked around the dig, urging her team on, complimenting each digger for their dedication.

She was particularly impressed with the sheer size of the Maiasaura skeleton and the surprising number of fossilized eggs embedded in a bowl-shaped depression next to it. Greg Dulowski counted two-dozen petrified eggs in the nest, laid out in a spiral formation.

Nora knew big numbers of Maiasaura roamed this part of western Montana and southern Canada in herds numbering 10,000 during the Late Cretaceous, more than 66 million years ago. She had a difficult time picturing that scenario, wondering how there could ever be enough vegetation to support those numbers. The Maiasaura find wasn't necessarily momentous; many natural history museums had Maiasaura exhibits. But most of those were composite skeletons cobbled together from many different Good Mother Lizards. The feather in Nora's cap had been this finding of a complete skeleton, buried next to the nest of calcified eggs.

The sponsors were ecstatic. The Smithsonian was opening its new 31,000-square-foot fossil hall this summer, and they assured Nora this Maiasaura find would be given a highly visible presentation. They had shown excitement over the Triceratops skull as well. The three-horned herbivores of the Late Cretaceous were commonly displayed at natural history museums around the globe, but the skull Nora's team had unearthed was much larger than average.

But as successful as the start of this expedition had been, Nora remained troubled about her lead paleontologist, Hayden Fowler, and his serious drinking problem.

Fowler, a world renowned paleontologist from Minnesota, held a Master of Science degree in Vertebrate Paleontology from the University of Chicago, and a PhD in Geosciences from Virginia Tech, considered to be the top paleontological university in the country. He had authored many highly regarded white papers and several bestselling books on prehistoric life, specializing in the Cretaceous Period. His book, *Ancient Life, Final Strife* had become the go-to textbook in the industry for his theories on the Late Cretaceous run-up to the cataclysmic extinction of the dinosaurs. His other bestseller, *Interpreting Cretaceous Fossils*, had won him numerous awards and big-money grants, the most notable from the Paleontological Society. Hayden Fowler was indeed one of the preeminent scholars of Cretaceous vertebrates, and Nora was honored to have that kind of expertise on her team.

However, with that expertise came a veneer of arrogance and ego. Before Nora traveled to Minneapolis to recruit him, she'd heard the rumors. She interviewed others who had worked with him, hearing numerous reports of his womanizing and his three failed marriages, his heavy drinking and dust-ups in bars that led to two arrests for assault and one for public intoxication.

On her recruiting mission, she'd met with him at his house, a spacious, opulent, four-bedroom ranch on a quiet cul-de-sac in Eden Prairie, a well-to-do suburb of Minneapolis. At a beefy six-foot-four with a scruffy beard and graying shoulder-length hair, he cut an imposing figure. She had been intimidated at first by his physical presence, but surprisingly he made her feel welcome during her visit. They exchanged small talk for a while in his bright and airy sunroom before she challenged him on the rumors. He'd been honest with her, but not apologetic. Almost humble. He admitted he'd made many mistakes in his life, but swore he had his drinking under control.

"What about the womanizing?" she'd asked.

Fowler shot her a menacing look. "Wow, you don't mince words, do you?"

"Look, Mr. Fowler—"

"What's with this mister shit?" he said, running his hand through his unkempt, salt-and-pepper beard. "I'm only forty-eight. *Mister* makes me sound like I've got one foot in a nursing home."

"Okay, *Hayden*, then. I'm being direct with you because I've enlisted three young, attractive female grad students. We'll be out for more than two months and I don't need my lead paleontologist acting like a sex-starved tomcat around them."

"Don't worry about it, Nora. I can keep my hands to myself and my middle leg in my pants. This is far from my first paleo road-show."

The man sure has a gruff charm about him.

"So does this mean you'll join my team?"

"Are you kidding? A *Smithsonian* expedition? Wouldn't miss

it for all the beautiful Scandinavian blondes in Minnesota."

"You're not helping your cause with a comment like that."

Fowler leveled his eyes at her. "I'm just toying with you, Nora. Look, I want to be part of this thing in the worst way. I give you my solemn word that my drinking and love of hot young foxes won't get in the way."

"I certainly hope you'll be on your best behavior," she said, not entirely certain of his sincerity. "We need your knowledge on this dig. Nonetheless, first sign of trouble and you're on a plane back home. Got it?"

"Yes, ma'am."

Nora couldn't tell from his neutral expression if he was being sarcastic, so she said, "What's with this *ma'am* shit? I'm only forty-five."

He laughed at that—a booming laugh that filled the room—then directed a warm smile at her. "I believe we're going to get along just fine, Nora."

And they *had* been getting along this first week out. Hayden Fowler was professional, a good team player. Very jovial and personable. Willing to aid and educate the lesser experienced members of the expedition. That is, up until the wee hours of this morning. He was supposed to be overseeing the Triceratops skull dig, but when Nora checked the progress near 1:00 AM, he was nowhere to be found. She asked members of the dig team where he was. No one had seen him since well before midnight.

She was furious. She had stormed to his trailer (Fowler had negotiated his own trailer, among other amenities) and banged on his door. Loud rock music blared inside. She banged harder. Finally the door opened. Hayden Fowler looked down at her, unsteady on his feet, his cheeks and nose a flushed crimson.

"Hey, Nora," he said, the alcohol wafting off of him. "I'm just taking a little break."

She wanted to strangle him. "Your team says you've been AWOL for a couple of hours. When I put you in charge of an operation, I expect you to stay on the job and handle it responsibly."

"Yeah, but I've been out there since noon. I needed to get

something to eat."

"*Everyone else* has been out there since noon, too. And it looks to me like your eats are all of the liquid variety. How much have you had?"

"Just a few belts to get warmed up. It's crazy cold out there."

"Yeah? Well you're from Minnesota. You should be used to the cold. Now I'm going back to my trailer to make some coffee and I want you to join me there pronto. If you're not there in ten minutes, you can consider yourself fired and gone from this expedition."

She turned on her heel and walked away, hearing him plead with her over the thumping music.

The Devil on Brin's Back

June 6: The Lacroix Residence
Missoula Montana

PETER LACROIX ATE A LATE DINNER with his wife. Brinshou had cooked his favorite meal of grilled salmon, steamed vegetables, and sweet camas after putting baby Kimi to bed for the night.

It had been a long 12-hour day and exhaustion sapped him. Wildfires produced by meteorite hits ripped through the forests of northwestern Montana and he'd piloted three flights, delivering smokejumpers to the burn sites. After his shift, he'd gone to visit George Dantley in the hospital. By the time he got home it was 8:30.

"How is Georgie doing?" Brin cut her fish, knife and fork scraping the plate.

"He's doing better since they moved him to a private room. The poor kid's in a lot of pain, but he's hanging tough."

"It's so tragic, Petey. He's just an innocent kid trying to work a summer job. How could something like this happen?"

That's a question Peter had been wrestling with since he'd rescued George from Camels Hump. Fate was a roll of the dice on a rigged craps table.

He glanced up from his meal, saw the skittish, troubled look in his wife's cocoa brown eyes. "Life has never been a fair game, hon. You know that."

Brin, slumped over her plate, nodded with a frown. Resumed eating. He'd seen this nervous posture from her too many times recently.

Please, not tonight.

"Georgie's going to pull through," he said, attempting to calm her. "He's a tough young man. And his parents are good people.

They're behind him all the way. He'll make it out of that hospital bed and back home. He'll be fully rehabilitated. You'll see."

Brin stabbed a camas bulb with her fork, brought it to her mouth. "It's more than Georgie." She chewed the sweet camas root, looking at him. Swallowed. Looked away.

Peter feared where this was heading. "What's wrong, Brin?"

"It's those meteorites. They terrify me. On the news tonight they reported three more strikes today—"

"I told you to stay away from newscasts. That stuff only upsets you."

"I know . . . I *know*," she said, an uneasy catch in her voice. "But I'm here, all day long, just me and Kimi, and I worry about you—being up in the air and those things pelting down like bombs. It makes me crazy . . ."

Peter sighed. "The odds of one of those meteorites hitting my aircraft—*any* aircraft—is negligible. It's just *not* going to happen."

"I'm sure Georgie felt the same way. I'm sure he thought he was safe up in that fire tower."

"That was a freak accident of nature, Brin. A one-in-ten-million chance. I—"

"But it happened, right?" Defiance darkened her eyes.

"Yes . . . yes it did. But—"

"So it could happen to you, too, Petey. That's all I'm saying, love. I'm also worried about you flying above all those fires. All that smoke and heat? It's just so dangerous."

Here we go again. Same old anxiety monster.

Peter pushed his plate aside, his meal half eaten. Put his elbows up on the table, exasperated. "I know you want me to quit my job, Brin. You've made that clear for a while now. And as I keep telling you, I don't know how to do anything else. Except maybe play hockey, but my bum knee and old age rules that out."

"You're not old, Petey."

"Thirty-seven with two knee surgeries makes me ancient by professional hockey standards."

They lapsed into a long silence, chewing their food, taking sips of coffee. The baby monitor on the kitchen counter gave off a low hiss.

Peter's knee throbbed, taking him back to his pro hockey days. It was all the emotional stress and lack of sleep. In his early twenties he'd been a rising star, a high-scoring forward with the Toronto Maple Leafs' top farm team, the Toronto Marlies. He was on a shortlist to be called up to the Leafs when he took a brutal check into the boards that shattered the Plexiglas and blew out his knee. He never again regained his speed and strength after two debilitating surgeries. Hockey career over.

Oh, what might have been.

Brin's voice pulled him out of his reflections. "I'm sorry, Petey. Are you mad at me?"

He gave her a faint smile. "No, just tired and achy and a little frustrated." He was also preoccupied with the news he had to lay on her. It would be difficult to break it to her in her current fragile state, but he had to tell her soon. Preferably tonight.

She said, "You're frustrated with *me*?"

"Oh no . . . not at all, sweetie. I'm just exhausted by life at the moment—Georgie's accident, the meteorites and the wildfires, all the overtime I'm having to put in."

And you're not helping much, Brinshou, he wanted to say, looking at her across the table.

He continued. "Look, I know my work scares you, but you just have to have faith in me. I like my job and I'm really good at it. It's what I've worked hard for. It's what I spent all that money and time to learn at the flight academy in Twin Falls. Besides, how would we pay the bills if I quit? How could we possibly raise Kimi?"

Her face lit up. "My jewelry business is going well. Maybe we could get by on that while you look for something else?"

She never quits.

Brin had done okay with online sales of her Kootenai Native American jewelry. Her seed-bead earrings, silver-and-turquoise bracelets, pendants, and necklaces were popular with online buyers. Peter was glad she had something to offset the stress of raising a baby, something productive to keep her mind off of worrying about his safety in his chosen profession. But it wouldn't pay the bills. Not by a longshot.

"I'm not quitting my job, Brin. That wouldn't work out well for either of us. There's our health insurance to think about. We still owe quite a chunk on our mortgage. Two car payments. Food. Clothes. Diapers and formula . . . it all adds up in a hurry."

Brin sat there, staring down at her plate. "I know," she said quietly. She reached across the table and touched his arm. "I know you think I'm crazy, but—"

"No, I don't think that at all," he said, caressing her fingers. "You just have a difficult time dealing with your anxieties. I sincerely wish I could do more to help you with that. There's always anti-anxiety medications you could take if—"

"No! Absolutely not! You know how I feel about polluting my body with drugs."

Peter stared at Brin across the table. His wife of four years was a striking woman. Lustrous coal-black hair tumbled across delicate shoulders. Tawny, cocoa butter skin soft as satin. Chiseled, high cheekbones—a trait of her Kootenai heritage. Wide mouth with full lips and straight white teeth. Dark, deep-set eyes that hinted at a simmering sensuality and danced with mischief when she was feeling good. Her laugh possessed a musical quality when she was in an up mood. He loved Brinshou with everything he had, but her anxieties made him crazy. It detracted from her beauty and hijacked her personality. These episodes had increased in number since the birth of Kimi fifteen months ago.

Tonight was especially bad. Her usual dazzling eyes were gloomy. He had tried so many times to get her to seek help—medication, therapy, meditation, yoga . . . *something*—but she would have none of it. Tonight he was tired and irritable, in no mood to deal with it. Either through exhausted spite or just wanting to be done with it, he decided to lay his news on her.

"Listen, Brin. There's something I need to tell you . . ."

Panic flashed across her face.

"No, it's nothing bad. It could actually work out quite well for us. Gary pulled me into his office as I was getting ready to leave this afternoon."

"Is he giving you a raise?"

"In a manner of speaking, yes."

She tilted her head, looking at him questioningly.

"I mean, it *is* an increase in income. A hefty one, actually."

"That's fantastic, Petey! For all the great work you've done the past week, I'm sure. Why didn't you tell me this when you first got home?"

He hesitated, and she turned skeptical. "I'm sensing there's a *but* coming."

Peter felt trapped. But he was too far into it to back out now. "Well, it's partly for the work I've done lately. But it's more for what I'm *going* to be doing."

"Oh? And what's that?"

"I've been selected for a special government task force."

"What *kind* of task force?" she said, eyeing him warily.

Here goes nothing.

"To fly along the Rockies and retrieve those meteorites that have been coming down. Take them to an Air Force base in Idaho."

She stared at him, her mouth hanging open.

"Look, Brin, it's an honor. I'll be serving my country, doing my civic duty. And the money will help us erase our credit card debt. Plus the feds will be supplying the Forest Service with a couple of new choppers and a plane. It's a win-win all the way around."

She glanced at the baby monitor. "Why are they so interested in those meteorites?"

Peter thought about the strange bullfrog-croak/bird-chirp sounds he'd heard coming from the base of Camels Hump the day he and his team rescued George Dantley. That overpowering sulfur stench of rotten eggs. Earlier today, he'd asked his boss the very same question that Brin was asking now. Gary had given him no answers.

"I don't really know," Peter said to her, seeing the panic flutter across her face. "But I'll find out soon enough."

She stood from the table, took her dishes to the sink. With her back to him she said, "You say this base is in Idaho. Does that mean you'll be away from me and Kimi?"

"Yes, but it's only for two weeks . . . three at the most."

Her shoulders slumped as she rinsed her plate. "Two or three *weeks*?"

"It'll go by fast."

"You could always turn it down, right?"

"I would be a complete fool to turn this opportunity down, Brin. Surely you can see that."

She put her dishes and silverware into the dishwasher. Turned to face him. "The only thing I see is my husband charging off on a stupidly dangerous mission he really doesn't have to go on. Why do they want you? I mean, why can't it be one of the other pilots?"

"Because the other pilots are all older. And because I know the exact locations of most of these meteorites. I won't be alone in this. There are other helicopter pilots from Idaho doing the work as well. And we'll be accompanied by some very capable National Guardsmen."

Tears glittered in her eyes. "Well, *I'll* be alone. I believe it's time you started thinking more about your wife and baby daughter, Peter. I'm going to bed."

He was left staring at his half-eaten meal. He knew things were serious when she addressed him as Peter rather than Petey.

Dino Might

June 7: Gilliam's Guidepost
Heart Butte Montana

HAYDEN FOWLER WATCHED THE FOOT-LONG juvenile fling itself against the steel slats of the dog crate in a desperate attempt to escape. The other three scientists from the Smithsonian paleo-expedition—Nora Lemoyne, geologist Greg Dulowski, and paleo-zoologist Franz Krause—were grouped around him in the Gilliam utility barn, marveling at the scene. A quiet Bryan Gilliam kept a respectful distance behind them.

Hayden was thrilled that Nora had given him a second chance. He would have regretted missing out on this strangely spectacular event for the rest of his life had she carried through on her threat to send him packing back to Minnesota. They'd shared a brutally honest exchange in her trailer after his drinking episode. Nora had plied him with black coffee while she dressed him down for his unprofessional behavior. The whiskey stirred his anger, and he'd yelled at her. Through it all, Nora maintained her composure, and, as the caffeine kicked in, he began to gain a new respect for her. He realized she was a capable leader and a decent person, interested only in the success of the expedition. Very little ego, not at all high and mighty and hung up on her accomplishments the way he could be at times. He'd acted like a spoiled teenager. This expedition was a career changer for her, and he had tried to step all over it with his irresponsible conduct.

Not good, testing her like that, buckaroo.

Hayden continued to observe the hyperactive animal. When he'd seen Greg Dulowski's murky and jittery video footage a few days ago, he'd had doubts that the hatchlings were dinosaurs. But here in the rancher's barn he became convinced this specimen was an authentic Cretaceous dinosaur.

Incredible.

Awe inspiring.

Observing the creature up close sealed it for him. The way it moved, trying awkwardly to stand on its hind legs. Hopping around on its three-toed feet and back-heel claw. Its aggressiveness as it slammed itself against the metal slats of the cage. The verbal click-chirp-croak noise it produced. And the shell fragments the rancher had collected from around the meteorite also helped to confirm it for him. The pieces were thick and leathery and brightly colored with bluish-green swirls. No other native egg-laying species produced eggs like these. The shell material was even tougher and denser and more durable than eggs laid by terrestrial species such as snakes and crocodiles and tortoises. And the intact eggs Gilliam pulled from the meteorite were more of an elliptical shape rather than spherical. The other scientists excitedly agreed with Hayden, but the exact species of the creature they observed remained under dispute.

Nora Lemoyne's voice carried over the scratching, clawing, cage-slams of the animal. "My guess is it's one of the non-avian protobirds—probably a Velociraptor. See, it's got three toes with the recurved claw on the second toe that it uses to hook onto its prey . . . the longish skull that looks more like a beak than a snout. The stocky breastplate and smallish forelimbs. I think it has to be a raptor."

Hayden thought: *She's close, but not quite right. Careful, Fowler. You're in her doghouse. Use some tact for once.*

"I can see how you would make the raptor call, Nora," he said in a complimentary tone. "Very observant . . . especially about the extended skull and underdeveloped forearms. You're close, but it's not a Velociraptor. I believe it's a near relative—a Dromaeosaurus. They're direct descendants of the flying Archaeopteryx, though they were probably one of the first proto-bird theropods to lose the ability to fly. This little guy doesn't have the feathery plumage of a Velociraptor. You can see he has reptilian scales. He was the dominant small predator during the Campanian phase of the Late Cretaceous. Dromaeosaurus was quick and ran at speeds up to forty miles an hour. They had tremendous leaping ability, and even though this one is a newborn, you can see by its heavily muscled hindlegs how this could be so. They ran alongside their prey and leaped on them, sinking their sickle claws—that extra appendage on each hindfoot—deep, bringing them down and finishing them off with their large, slicing teeth."

Hayden grabbed a push broom leaning against the wall and moved toward the crate. "All of those traits also apply to your Velociraptor, Nora, with the exception of the scales," he said, opening the top of the dog crate and poking at the animal with the broom handle. "But the qualifying tell is in the teeth."

The creature reared up on its hind legs and made a threatening squeal, then attacked the wooden handle. "Notice this guy's serrated teeth. They're small right now, but you can see them when he snaps his jaws. Velociraptors had more conical teeth. And the tail is different, too. Look at his stubby, muscled tail. Not quite as long as a Velociraptor's. Dromaeosaurs used their tails for balance and boost, much like the Australian kangaroo uses his."

Franz Krause spoke. "I believe Dr. Fowler is correct in his assessment. This genus is not well represented in fossil records, but what we do know is that they grew quickly. In a month or so, if this specimen lives and gets enough food, it will reach a length of six feet and stand three feet tall. Smaller than a Velociraptor. Fully mature, it will weigh only fifty pounds or so, but it's all muscle and cartilage. Very strong. It's a vicious carnivore. Its teeth are razor sharp and its jaws exert incredible pressure, as much as three times more crushing power than the Velociraptor's jaws."

Hayden pulled the broomstick out of the cage and closed the top. He turned to Bryan Gilliam. "So you say this creature came out of this meteorite?" He nodded toward the stack of meteorite wedges they'd collected earlier from the east meadow and transported here in Gilliam's pickup.

Bryan cleared his throat. "That's right. The exterminator grabbed it with a snake stick. Had to be pretty quick to snag it."

"I would imagine so. How many of these creatures did you see that day?"

"I don't know for sure. It all happened so fast. I killed one, plus the one here that Joe Creek caught."

"How many others did you actually *see*, Mr. Gilliam?" Nora asked.

"Well, I'd say maybe a half-dozen? Possibly more, I don't know for sure."

Hayden said, "Did they all look like this guy in the cage?"

"Yeah, pretty much."

"What about the first time? When Greg videotaped the hatch-out? When the meteor specialist was attacked? The video was a little shaky . . . hard to get a read on numbers. How many would you say you saw that day?"

"Oh, more than a dozen, for sure."

"And what's the latest count on the number of meteorite hits along the Continental Divide?"

Dulowski said, "The evening news last night reported fifteen total."

"My wife and I have been keeping up with it, too," Bryan said. "Strange thing is, there's never been any mention of creatures hatching out of these space stones."

"Perhaps they don't know it yet," Nora said, pointing at the meteorite wedges lined up on the far wall. "As far as we know, these things have all come down in remote areas. It's difficult terrain to access."

Dulowski said, "Somebody in authority already knows about it. You can be sure of that. The guy from the Meteor Society—Blazenhurst? He's surely let his superiors know. He was attacked. Probably had to fill out a ream of paperwork."

"And obviously Joe Creek from Browning Pest Control has knowledge of these creatures," Bryan said, "since he caught one. He just didn't know what he'd caught."

Nora said, "I'm going to have to let our sponsors know about this new development. I'm sure the Smithsonian will want to send some reps to check it out firsthand."

Hayden nodded. "I'd say our time for having an exclusive on this is running out." He looked at Bryan. "It won't be long until your ranch is overrun by the media and scientists and curiosity seekers."

"That's what I said earlier this week," Dulowski said.

"Yes, you called it earlier, Greg." Nora said. "If we want to stay here and continue our research, we need to make a plan on how to deal with the avalanche of people about to descend on Mr. Gilliam's property. We've got to protect our proprietary rights."

"Absolutely right, Nora," Hayden said. "After all, this is private property. Time to post some No Trespassing signs, Mr. Gilliam. Also time to think about adding an around-the-clock security detail."

"I understand," Bryan said. "The signs I can do. But twenty-four/seven security like that costs money. Loretta and I don't have much."

Nora said, "Maybe I can swing some security through the Smithsonian. I think they'll want to protect their interest in this as well. I'll check on that later when I call them."

No one spoke for an extended time, all lost in their thoughts of what this astonishing event meant. How it would affect their lives now that they knew what they were dealing with, as incredible as it was.

Hayden thought: *Nobody will ever believe this without seeing it for themselves.*

After several long moments of contemplation, Hayden said, "Jesus H! What if all fifteen meteorites are carrying egg clutches that have hatched out? Can you imagine the horror of hundreds—possibly *thousands*—of prehistoric carnivores hunting Montana and Idaho for sustenance? It would be a national disaster unlike anything we've ever experienced."

The atmosphere in the barn turned ominous as they each contemplated that dark thought. The wind picked up and whistled through the eaves.

Krause tried to soften the tension. "Well maybe this meteorite that crashed here is an anomaly," he said hopefully. Maybe it's the only one containing prehistoric life . . . or for some reason, the only one in which life survived the rough landing."

"We can all pray you're right, Franz," Dulowski said. "But logical probabilities say otherwise. The fact that fifteen meteorites have made it through Earth's heavy atmosphere and struck in a three-hundred-square-mile area in a week's time indicates a pattern. I don't think this is random. It's a good bet many, if not all, the other fourteen meteorites contain life. Maybe carrying different species." He picked up an eggshell shard and studied it. "I would love to be able to have a look at some of the other meteorites."

Nora said, "All of this is sheer speculation at this point. As fascinating as all this is, it's just conjecture."

"But we've got proof—both video and firsthand—of a hatchout from the Gilliam meteorite," Hayden said, thinking, almost *hoping*, dare he think it, that other meteorites were loaded with dinosaur eggs, too.

Nora looked at him and he thought he detected worry in her usually calm and in-control manner. "That's true, Hayden. But we can't be sure of anything until we get a look at other meteorites."

"Is there a way we can make that happen?" Dulowski said.

"I don't know, Greg," Nora said. "Maybe our sponsor can provide some muscle to help us get access. The Smithsonian carries a lot of weight."

Hayden nodded. "I'm sure they could help us out. But it'll have to be soon. Hear me out on this. I know you all have a pretty good idea of where this could go very quickly," he said, looking at each of the scientists, one by one. "Let's say they've all hatched out carnivorous dinosaurs. Think of what that would do to this area's ecological balance—hell, this *planet's* ecological balance. We all know about Cretaceous Period dinosaur appetites. Take our much feared friend, Tyrannosaurus Rex. A single fully-grown, eight-ton T-Rex gobbled down more than two-hundred pounds of meat per day . . . a total of a thousand tons of warm-blooded meat over a thirty-year lifetime. Rex could devour a mature cow in a couple of swift bites. Think of the vast ranges of cattle roaming the flatlands east of here."

Krause said. "Hayden's correct. If all these meteorites have hatched out prehistoric life, we're in for some major problems this summer . . . and beyond." He turned to Bryan Gilliam, pointed at the dog crate. "What have you been feeding this guy?"

"Raw hamburger. He ate close to a pound of it this morning. That's up from half a pound yesterday."

Hayden shook his head. "Pretty soon he'll be eating twice his weight. You say you have some horses, Mr. Gilliam?"

"Yes. Six of them. Quarter horses."

"You're going to need to protect them. Even better, *move* them. You have anywhere you can sequester them until we make sure your ranch is safe?"

"Sure . . . yeah. My brother-in-law, Jimmy Enright. He's got a wheat farm about an hour east of here in Shelby. He could take 'em. His horse barn is more secure than ours."

"Good," Hayden said. "I would advise moving them as soon as possible. But even then, depending on how many of these creatures hatched out and scurried off, your horses might not be safe there for long either. Dromaeosaurs had a wide roving range. They could cover a hundred square miles quite easily. It's probably why you haven't seen any more of them around here since the hatchout. You have any other livestock? Pets?"

"No. Just three kids." Bryan glanced at the creature in the cage. "I told you about my seven-year-old daughter being attacked by one of these things in the horse barn."

"Yes," Nora said. "How is she doing?"

"Her leg is still sore. Got a couple of stitches but the swelling is down and there was no infection. No rabies. It's more an emotional thing with Lianne now. The incident scared the crap out of her. Scared the wits out of her mother and me, too."

"I can understand that," Hayden said. "I highly recommend your children and your wife stay indoors until we can sort this out. We can set some traps, bait them with ground beef . . . get them to come to us rather than us trying to hunt them down. Safer too."

Nora sighed, said. "Let's slow down a minute and discuss the real elephant in the barn—the meteorites. Where they come from is one thing, but how is it possible that they contain fertilized

Cretaceous eggs? And how could any eggs survive the heat and stress of Earth's atmosphere, not to mention the explosive impact? It defies all laws of biochemistry and physics."

Greg Dulowski said, "I don't have definite answers to those questions, Nora, but I can throw out some educated possibilities. I've spent much of the afternoon examining these rocks and the goo that varnishes them."

"Let's hear your thoughts."

"Okay. Quick geology lesson. Please stop me if I'm talking down to you . . ."

"Let her rip, Greg," Hayden said.

"Okay, meteorites fall into three classifications: siderites, which consist mostly of iron; aerolites, which are stony meteorites; and siderolites, which contain both stone and concentrations of heavy metals. Siderolites are the most rare of the three. Our meteorite falls into this third category, but it differs from other siderolites in one major way."

"What's that?" Nora asked.

"The metals composition. It contains almost no iron, which is highly unusual. Instead, it is nearly seventy percent iridium, which is a rare, corrosion-resistant, silver-white heavy metal with a melting point of well over four-thousand degrees Fahrenheit. The way the iridium is concentrated throughout the stone suggests a protective firewall around the egg clutches, and might possibly prevent the eggs from frying during flight . . ."

Hayden listened to Dulowski's hypotheses while thinking about the importance of the iridium content. Iridium had special meaning to those who studied the Cretaceous Period and the dinosaur extinction. Toward the end of the Cretaceous, Earth was dusted with a layer of heavy metals, the most prevalent being iridium. He knew from his studies that scientists differ on how the metals got here. One school of thought implied that a great, simultaneous eruption of volcanic activity coupled with tectonic shifts in the Earth's plates caused massive amounts of hot magma to bubble to the surface. As the volcanic lava and magma mixed and cooled, various chemical reactions took place, which formed the metals. Another school of thought was that during the last million years of the Cretaceous, large iridium-filled asteroids impacted with Earth, causing a prehistoric nuclear winter, and consequently, a heavy layer of iridium coated Earth's surface. Hayden knew, regardless of the method of iridium formation, that both the dinosaurs and heavy concentrations of iridium seemed to have disappeared simultaneously 66 million years ago.

He returned his attention to Greg Dulowski's monologue.

". . . and of course we all know now that the goo coating these rocks is the yolk from the eggs that did not survive the impact. Franz put the heat to a sample, returning it to liquid form. You care to enlighten us, Franz?"

Krause stepped forward. "Sure. The yolk contains large amounts of protein and lecithin, which is similar in structure to our own domesticated poultry egg yolks. It also contains some type of alien protoplasm that is a rich nutrient. I believe that unknown protoplasm is what gives off the stench when in its liquid state."

Nora nodded. "Thanks, Doctor."

"Yes. One more thing. Greg and I discovered it while you and Hayden were in town with Mr. Gilliam buying the chicken incubator. It's the most amazing thing of all. Let's walk over to the meteorite and I'll show you."

They moved past the incubator where they had placed the five unhatched eggs Gilliam had retrieved from the east meadow meteorite. The eggs were much larger than chicken eggs, but they fit in the incubator snugly. Hayden hoped the unit would control the temperature and humidity of the colorful prehistoric eggs so they would hatch out a few more Dromaeosaurs.

They all circled the meteorite wedges in the rear of the barn while Dulowski used a hammer and chisel to chip away some of the silvery-white iridium.

Krause spoke. "The center of this meteorite contains long fronds of ancient ferns and palm-like plants. You would expect them to be petrified into plant fossils, but they are not. They are alive. A healthy greenish-yellow. Show them, Greg."

Dulowski worked some vegetation out of the rock with the

chisel, and presented it to the team. Hayden recognized the plant to be primordial, but didn't know the specifics.

Krause continued. "It's simply incredible, the way this plant life has been preserved inside the rock. Looks like it hasn't been out of the ground more than a week."

Dulowski pulled more greenery from the rock. The scientists moved in for a closer look.

"What are they, Franz?" Nora asked.

"Ancient cycads. Last seen in the Late Cretaceous. You can see the leathery, glossy pinnate leaves."

Bryan Gilliam said, "Pinnate leaves?"

"Yes. Feathery leaflets arranged in sets of symmetrical twins on each side of the branch. My early studies exposed me to some ancient flora that thrived during the Cretaceous, and I can tell you the rhizome or stem, the fronds, and sporangia—the chemical reproductive structure—are all indicative of plant life long since vanished from Earth. I have no doubt that these are primitive seed-bearing cycads from more than sixty-million years ago. Sort of a precursor to our contemporary palmettos and ferns. But we'd have to get a paleobotanist out here for a definitive classification. And yet, as I say this, I don't see how this can be possible. I'm completely baffled by this. How can they be so well preserved in the center of a meteorite? How did they get there in the first place?"

Greg Dulowski spoke up. "This egg-bearing meteorite would appear to be inconceivable and quite the conundrum on the surface. But I've been thinking a lot about this since Franz and I made this discovery. I'm only postulating here, but if these meteorites have been traveling in continuous orbit, say as part of a larger asteroid, living organisms could be preserved for extremely long periods of time, due to the existing vacuum and subzero temperatures of deep space. Think of it as nature's cryonics suspension. It's much more feasible for plant life than animals. But eggs could be kept fertile through that type of frozen suspension, just waiting for the necessary heat to hatch out."

Hayden thought about this. "I believe you might have hit on something, Greg." He picked up a leaf of the fern, examined it.

"However, these things look like they were yanked out of the ground yesterday. To clarify, are you saying these plants have been preserved in deep space in this condition for more than sixty-six *million* years? With all due respect, that's a little difficult for me to swallow."

Nora held up a hand, "Greg said it was just a hypothesis."

"Absolutely it could work," Franz Krause said, coming to Dulowski's defense. "Greg and I have been going back and forth on this all afternoon. Cryonics research is still in its infancy, but we know living cells can be suspended indefinitely under the right conditions. For eternity, if environments are right. I'm not an astrophysicist, but I think deep space gives us those perfect conditions. The big question in cryonics is whether the cells are able to resume life when thawed and reinstated to their environment. For example, it is highly doubtful that we could take the frond you are holding and plant it in Mr. Gilliam's field and have it take root. Probably wouldn't happen."

Nora said, "I must say that I share Hayden's skepticism, Franz. The preservation of living things over millions of years is a very difficult concept to comprehend. Even the Egyptian mummies have shown decomposition over a much shorter timeframe."

Krause nodded. "That's true. But we're talking about the perfect climatic conditions of interstellar space . . . a vacuum seal and extremely frigid temperatures necessary to sustain living cells in a suspended state. And since these eggs are not fully matured beings, they require very little oxygen. The ferns seem to provide enough."

"But how would the plants get the carbon dioxide and water needed for photosynthesis?" Nora asked. "What about the necessary sunlight to promote plant growth?" Confined plants couldn't give off the needed oxygen without these other critical elements being in place, right?"

"I don't know. Greg and I are just postulating on our findings of this one meteorite. Just our early thought processes. We'd need to consult with a botanist about the photosynthesis issue. Maybe get the opinions of several astrophysicists to nail down the conditions in deep space."

Dulowski said, "We also need to see a few more of these meteorites before we can reach any kind of conclusions. I found a good bit of volcanic glass in these stone wedges, along with an abundance of Claggett shale, which you all know comes from this part of Montana. We've been referring to this meteorite as extra-terrestrial, but the rock is comprised of ninety percent terrestrial material. The heavy concentration of iridium and the ancient cycads speak volumes to me. I don't know how or why, but I would stake my career and reputation on it that this meteorite is terrestrial in nature. Call me crazy, but I believe it was formed during the Late Cretaceous, right here along this stretch of the Rockies. Unless there is another planet, or an asteroid that is an exact duplicate of Earth in terms of geological and botanical makeup, then this rock came from somewhere nearby approximately sixty-six million years ago. I don't have a clue where it's been over the ages, or why it was delivered to us here and now, but it is truly a marvel of nature's packaging."

The group quieted, staring dumfounded at the Dromaeosaurus hatchling scratching and clawing and screeching in the dog crate.

The chicken incubator hummed.

The wind made a droning sound through the eaves.

Hayden thought about the soon-to-be repercussions of this monumental event, and he felt faint. A quick look at the others told him he wasn't alone.

He needed a drink.

Badly.

The Tully Ranch

June 9: Greenfield, Montana

JOHN TULLY TOSSED AND TURNED through a disturbed sleep, nightmares haunting his dreams. His nocturnal restlessness had become commonplace since Gayle, his wife of 33 years, passed away last year.

Though he had been saddled with bouts of insomnia since Gayle's death, last night's sleep problem was different. Twice in the wee morning hours, he awoke abruptly, hearing wails and frightened lowing from the distant pastures. He knew the Herefords spooked easily and so he dismissed the eerie cries as visits from raccoons or possums, or some other nighttime pest. Two years ago he'd lost a couple of steers to a mountain lion attack, but that night had a different sound and feel to it.

Murky daylight streamed through the bay windows over his bed as he stood in front of the full-length mirror buttoning up his bib overalls. The lack of sleep drained him. His fingers felt clumsy negotiating the small buttonholes. As he looked at his reflection, his image appeared angled and out of proportion, resembling Picasso prints Gayle had framed and hung in the living room. The room seemed to be bathed in a surreal light. Anxiety grabbed him. He became dizzy and he sat on the edge of the bed, shook his head, attempting to chase the sensation.

It's just a dream hangover from last night, he told himself.

Maybe it was time to sell this place and enjoy a comfortable retirement. He'd thought seriously about selling his 2,000-acre ranch after Gayle's sudden stroke, but several factors kept him from putting it on the market. John's daughter, Mindy, had been putting pressure on him to come live with her and his three grandchildren in Great Falls. He couldn't bring himself to do that. John knew he would only be in the way there. And the thought of living in the city unnerved him. He preferred the pastoral simplicity of country living. The smells of dewy pastureland and cow manure worked on him like a rural aphrodisiac. This ranch with its 700 head of Black Angus, Charolais, and Hereford cattle was his peaceful kingdom. This sprawling land of rolling green hills dotted with mirrorlike ponds just north of Greenfield and east of Choteau made him feel like some higher power had selected this homeland just for him.

His thoughts were interrupted by Luther Gaddis yelling from downstairs: "Mr. Tully! Mr. Tully! Come quick! We got us some trouble. Some BIG trouble."

John had never heard his senior ranch hand so agitated. Luther Gaddis, a loyal and dedicated cowpoke who had worked the Tully ranch for twenty years was not a man given to histrionics.

John heard the downstairs kitchen door open, then slam shut. Heard shuffling feet and murmurs of confused voices. Panic made his voice shrill: "I'm coming. I'll be right there, Luther."

His hands trembled as he leaned over and laced up his boots. With trepidation, he made his way down the stairs and into the kitchen, coming upon a very stressed Gaddis standing in front of the other ranch hands, Sonny Rivers and Rory Birdsong.

"What is it, Luther?"

"I—I just c-can't believe it, Mr. Tully," he sputtered, fondling his hat with his big hands, looking down at the floor.

John looked from Gaddis to Rivers to Birdsong, then back to Luther trying to get a read. "Can't believe what?"

Sonny Rivers answered for Gaddis. "I think it would be best if'n we showed you, Mr. Tully."

John slowly scanned the faces of his hired hands, picking up on the despair in their tense body language.

"The squirrely way you're all actin' tells me it must be really bad." When none of them responded, he said, "Okay, show me."

The four of them piled into his battered Jeep. Gaddis told him to drive out to the rear pasture where the Hereford grazed. On the ride, Rory Birdsong repeatedly chanted a Native Nez Perce recitation that John knew loosely translated to *Help us, Great Spirit, for this is the devil's work.* Gaddis and Rivers remained quiet.

John's foreboding grew.

As they neared the rear pasture, John picked up an alarming scent—the coppery smell of blood; the fetid stench of slaughter. He felt his stomach churn. What remained of his spirit plummeted as it dawned on him the shrieks in the night were serious after all.

They rounded the bend, past the thick stands of white pine and cottonwood. And then it came into view. A killing field of evil carnage.

Stunned at the scene spread out before him, John shifted the Jeep into park and shut down the engine. Gaddis, Rivers, and Birdsong climbed out, nervously stealing glances at him, checking out his reaction.

He opened his door slowly, got out and stood on wobbly legs. In a trance, he walked to the barbed wire fence and surveyed the butchery. Most of his prize Hereford cattle had been wiped out. Nothing but bones and stringy, bloody entrails. Breastbones jutted from the ground like calcified plants. Oblong skulls were scattered everywhere. The salt licks had been uprooted and smashed. The wooden water troughs were busted apart. A long section of fencing running along the back, which separated the pasture from the forest, had been trampled.

John felt a lump in his throat. He wiped tears from his eyes. Peculiar thoughts swirled through his mind. *A pack of mountain lions couldn't inflict this much death and destruction in such a short amount of time. Hell, even an army of grizzlies couldn't do this.*

It was unthinkable, but overnight some force of nature far beyond his comprehension had cleaned out a major portion of his livestock.

"Mother of God! Oh dear mother of God!" he mumbled under his breath.

Rory Birdsong was right. *This is indeed the work of the devil.*

A wicked flash of lightning bolted from a dark storm cloud that had rolled in, illuminating the blood-soaked pasture in an eerie phosphorescence, as though the devil was taking a snapshot of his work.

A thunderclap shook the ground.

And then the rains came, a pelting rain that washed away the remnants of the slaughter, like God cleaning up the devil's mess.

The ranch hands scrambled back into the Jeep. John sunk to his knees, weeping as the rain pelted his shoulders and back. His bib overalls clung to him. Bloody mud swirled around his knees.

Between sobs, he thought: *This is something far worse than the devil.*

Conspiracy Theory?

June 10: St. Patrick Hospital
Missoula, Montana

"**SORRY FOR BEING A STRANGER** the past few days," Peter said, talking over the baseball play-by-play announcer blaring from the flat-screen TV in George Dantley's private room. "I've been a little busy putting out fires."

He approached the bed where George sat propped up. His young friend looked bad. The dressing wraps were gone leaving the side of his face and top of his head etched with ugly salve-coated burns that were starting to scab over. Peter wondered if the kid would need plastic surgery and/or skin grafts to repair the damage.

"No need to apologize," George replied, his voice a weak croak. "I know you've got a ton of things on your plate right now."

"Well, I just wish I could get here more often. Brin sends you her love. She wants so much to come with me to visit you, but—"

"She's busy, too, I know. Your wife's a sweetie. How's the baby?"

"Kimi's fine. Growin' so fast. I can't hardly believe she's already sixteen months. Where does the time get away to?"

George gave him a wan smile. "I know what you mean. I'll be a college senior in the fall. That's unreal to me. Feels just like yesterday I was a freshman."

Peter moved to the edge of the bed, touched the thick cast sheathing George's left arm. "I see some people have scribbled love notes on this thing."

"Yeah, some of my college buddies dropped by."

"Mind if I add my thoughts?"

"I'd be honored. There's a pen on the table over there."

Peter leaned over and wrote on the cast, talking as he composed. "You're looking a lot better than the last time I saw you, Georgie," he said, hoping the kid didn't pick up on his lie. "You're talking much better, too." *At least that much is true.*

"Yeah, they took the tube out of my chest yesterday. Thank God! I'm breathing a lot easier now . . . not such a chore. The doctors said my punctured lung didn't require surgery. That nasty tube they stuck in me did its job. It drained the excess air. They say it allowed my injured lung to inflate properly. I'm learning so much about modern medicine being in here."

"Well, I'm happy to see you doing so well, my friend," he said, thinking: *Leave it to the kid to be buoyantly optimistic. His youth and positivity will be what saves him.*

George gave him a lopsided grin, the best he could do with one side of his face scarred up. "Thanks. Tomorrow they're starting me on a physical therapy program. They wanna get the blood flowing, they say."

"That'll be good for you . . . to get up and around again."

Peter finished scratching out his message on the cast and put the pen back on the table. George pulled his arm closer to read it.

Get well soon, my firewatcher friend
The forest needs you!
Peter Lacroix

"Thanks, Pete," he said, his eyes glistening with the hint of tears. "But I think my days as a fire spotter are over."

"Oh? You still want to be a forest ranger, don't you?"

"Oh, yeah, definitely. But only if I don't have to climb back up one of those towers. They couldn't pay me enough."

"That's understandable. After what you've been through I'm quite sure the Forest Service will welcome you and give you a safer position."

"I don't want anyone's sympathy, Pete. I wanna make it on my own merit."

"It *will* be on your own merit. Next year at this time you'll have a Forest Management degree. You'll also have three summers of fire scouting experience. You're a sharp young guy, very personable and responsible. Plus you've got me to vouch for you. You won't have any problem getting a good job with the state. You just need to work with the doctors on getting yourself whole and healthy again."

Tears welled up in George's eyes. His voice turned weepy. "I'm trying. But it's so hard, laying here, dealing with the pain, day after day."

"I know it's difficult," Peter said, pulling up a chair and sitting. "I remember going through both of my knee surgeries. Bein' laid up, thinking I'd never walk again . . . all the negative thoughts running through my mind. Fretting over the end of my hockey career. It can really get to you, I know. But you work at it and it gets better before you know it. You've got strength you're not even aware of. Just stick with it, Georgie. Hang in there and gut it out. You'll be out of here and back to your old tenacious self in no time. Good as new, and you won't be able to keep the girls away."

"Thanks, Pete." He wiped his eyes with his right hand. "I really appreciate your visits. It means a lot to me. I wish the doctors here had half the bedside manner you have."

"Good, I'm glad," Peter said, looking out the window at the pair of ambulances parked by the ER entrance, gleaming in the sunlight. "I'm happy I can do some good for you." A wave of pity overtook him. He regretted what he had to tell him. "However, I'm afraid you're going to have to handle things without me for a while."

"Oh, why's that?"

"I've accepted an offer to be part of a special task force headed up by the Pentagon—"

"Whoa! *The* Pentagon?"

"Yes. *That* Pentagon. The one in Arlington, Virginia. They need pilots who know this area. They want me to assist with recovering those meteorites—or at least pieces of them—and bring them to an Air Force base. I've been sworn to secrecy about the location of the airbase and . . . even I don't know what'll be done with them there. But what I can tell you for sure is that I'll be away for a couple of weeks. Brin is going to try and visit you in my absence."

"Wow," George said, grimacing as he shifted in the bed. "This meteorite thing has become really big, hasn't it? It's all over the news the past week. I even saw the destruction at Camels Hump. Looked like a war zone. I don't know how I ever survived something like that. I've been avoiding the news since I saw that segment. Scared the crap out of me. Have you been keeping up with it?"

Peter shook his head. "No. We don't watch the news in our house these days. It scares Brin too much. Kind of unsettles me, too, if you want the truth. Has anyone from the media approached you?"

"No. Haven't seen any people from the press yet. Security is strict here. They only allow approved family and friends up here during visitation hours."

"I'm surprised. The paparazzi is cunning. And you were the first to encounter a meteorite."

"Well, I didn't really *encounter* it so much as got smashed up by it. They said on the news this morning that there hasn't been any more meteorite sightings the past three days. They said the strike count stands at fifteen."

"That's the last total I heard, too."

"This is all pretty bizarre, Pete. Whaddaya think is going on?"

"Don't know. Maybe we'll have a better idea when we pick up a few of them and haul 'em in for study."

"When do you leave?"

"Thursday. Tomorrow your parents are giving me a hero's luncheon and a grand public sendoff here at the Hilton Garden Inn." Peter made a sour face. "I wish they weren't doing that."

"Why? You *are* a hero. You saved my life."

"No, I didn't. Not really. My emergency rescue *team* saved you. I only got them to the site. My responders—Spang and Heddison— they did the hard physical work. My EMT, Nicki Whitlow? She did all the lifesaving stuff once you were on board the chopper. I just flew the bird."

"Dad told me they would be there. They're gonna be honored along with you, right?"

"They'll be there, yes. I'm just embarrassed by the whole thing, Georgie."

"You're too humble for your own good, old man."

"Who're you callin' *old*?" Peter said, smiling.

George laughed, then groaned in pain. "Don't do that to me, Pete. My face can't take it."

The baseball game on the TV switched abruptly to a breaking news story. Peter and George both looked up at the screen as a national news anchorman's voice echoed in the room.

"This just in from the beleaguered state of Montana. We have reports of more strange goings-on in that Western state. Two nights ago, rancher John Tully of Greenfield lost more than fifty head of cattle to as-yet-to-be-identified marauding predators. The rancher awoke yesterday morning to find one of his pastures littered with the bones and entrails of his Hereford stock. We switch now to our on-the-go correspondent, Kelly Fulcher, who is standing by live with rancher John Tully in Greenfield, Montana. Kelly? . . ."

The scene switched to the Tully ranch. A beautiful young brunette news reporter held a microphone between her and a tall, rugged fiftyish man wearing bib overalls and a brown leather cowboy hat. They stood by a barbed wire fence, behind which Peter could see some of the carnage and destruction.

"Yes, I'm standing here with rancher John Tully at the scene of the slaughter. Just two days ago, this pasture behind me was populated with one-hundred head of mature Hereford cattle. And then, in just hours overnight, more than half of that herd was wiped out by some as-yet-unidentified voracious predators." She turned to the rancher. "Mr. Tully, first let me say I'm so sorry for your loss."

"Thank you. It's been devastating to say the least."

"Do you have any idea what could have caused this kind of destruction and loss of animal life in such a short amount of time?"

"No. Nothin' I've seen over the past twenty-five years could do this. We've had a few serious attacks from wolves and mountain lions, but they couldn't do this. Coyotes are still a problem. They go after my calves. But coyotes are solitary hunters. My neighbors have had a few run-ins with grizzlies, but they've left my cattle alone." The rancher turned and lifted his arm, swept it behind him, indicating the bone-littered field behind them, the camera following the path of his arm, showing panoramic views of the pasture. "No way this was done by wolves or lions. Coyotes or bears neither. It was somethin' that hunts in packs . . . damned hungry sumbitches!" The rancher turned back to the camera, sadness etched on his craggy features, and said, "Nothin' left but bones and blood."

Reporter Kelly Fulcher nodded, a soft breeze blowing strands of hair in her face. "Do you think there might be a connection here to the strange lizard creatures that have been found around the meteorite strikes in Montana and Idaho?"

Rancher Tully shook his head. "I don't know anything about that. We ain't seen any of those meteorites out here."

Lizard creatures? Peter felt a wave of dizziness hit him as he recalled the deep croaking-squealing noises he'd heard coming from near the meteorite crash at the base of Camels Hump that crazy day they'd rescued George. He remembered it sounding like an army of bullfrogs cross-mated with birds. *Could it possibly be?* He shot a glance at George, whose eyes were riveted to the screen and the televised interview.

". . . but do you think it's possible that those creatures were responsible for the decimation of your herd, Mr. Tully?"

"Well, I suppose anything's possible, but I didn't see a single predator during all this. I have no evidence . . . no proof of any kind as to what did this. Hell, it could be some supernatural occurrence for all I know. Stranger thing yet is, whatever it was didn't touch my Black Angus or Charolais cattle. They, um . . . they feasted only on my Herefords."

"Again, I'm sorry for your loss, Mr. Tully." Kelly Fulcher turned and smiled at the camera. "So there you have it. The meteorite mystery continues. Reporting live from Green-field, Montana, I'm Kelly Fulcher with NBC News. Back to you in New York."

Peter swallowed hard and caught George looking at him with an incredulous expression. The New York anchorman, picking up on his field reporter's summation, continued with related stories NBC had reported on earlier in the week.

"This comes on the heels of our reporting earlier this week, in which we heard several wild claims pertaining to the flurry of meteorites coming down along the Continental Divide. Two people we interviewed claim aggressive rep-tilian creatures are hatching out of the extraterrestrial rocks. The most credible of these claims comes from Dr. William Blazenhurst of the American Meteor Society in Washington D.C. Doctor Blazenhurst was a visitor last week at a ranch in Heart Butte, Montana, where one of the fifteen known meteorites struck . . ."

The newscast shifted to a taped interview with the meteor specialist. Peter felt a cold stab of recognition as Blazenhurst described the small reptiles that looked like miniature horned lizards running amok around the shattered meteorite, chittering and screeching and croaking, like something part bird/part frog. Blazen-hurst said they were aggressive with razor-sharp little teeth. He claimed that one of them leaped at him and bit him on the shin, opening a gash that required seven stitches (pulling his pants leg up to show the ragged wound). The scientist went on to describe the awful stench of the gooey substance coating the meteorite pieces. He also said that a geologist who was there that day got it all down on video. Just in case anyone needed proof.

All of this insane testimony hit Peter hard. *That's what I saw and heard at the base of Camels Hump! That's the putrid odor I smelled!*

The newscast moved on to show a clip of a second interview, with a Browning, Montana exterminator who claimed he'd snagged a live specimen at the same meteorite site that William Blazenhurst had visited. He, too, claimed the meteorite had hatched out more than a dozen lizard creatures. He said the specimen was being held at the Heart Butte ranch, someplace called Gilliam's Guidepost.

The news anchor signed off, saying more detailed news about these two extraordinary claims would be forthcoming.

Peter looked at George, whose damaged face was frozen in a stunned, slack-jawed expression.

The TV switched to a commercial break. George said, "Sort of sounds like one of those outrageous conspiracy theories to me."

Peter thought: *I don't think it's a conspiracy at all.*

Hot Librarian Fantasy

June 12: On the Road to Greenfield, Montana

THE DRIVE FROM GILLIAM'S GUIDEPOST to Greenfield took Nora Lemoyne and Hayden Fowler south, down I-89. They got away from Heart Butte early this morning to investigate the scene of the cattle slaughter that occurred at the Tully ranch three nights ago.

Early yesterday geologist Greg Dulowski used his credentials to get through to the NASA Planetary Defense Coordination Office. NPDCO reported two meteorite strikes near Greenfield: one seven miles due southwest, near Fairfield, and a second ten miles east of Greenfield. A follow-up call to the Montana Department of Natural Resources confirmed those coordinates.

"Bingo!" Hayden Fowler had said, excited by the prospects. "We need to get down there ASAP and check this out."

Hayden's enthusiasm was contagious. The meaning of the news was not lost on the four scientists staying at the Gilliam's inn. Nora agreed with her fellow paleo scientists: the possibility of dinosaur hatchlings being the executioners loomed large. She knew Cretaceous carnivores traveled far distances in search of food supplies abundant enough to sustain their high metabolisms and quick growth rates. Newborn hatchouts would be perfectly capable of roaming ten miles or more in search of sustenance. Hayden surmised that was probably why they hadn't seen any more Dromaeosaurs around the Gilliam's property; with the Gilliam horses moved to a safer location, the creatures lacked a plentiful food source.

Nora did, however, have mixed feelings about leaving Heart Butte for the day. With so much going on at Gilliam's Guidepost she found it difficult to tear herself away. The chicken incubator they purchased and installed in the utility barn had hatched out all five of the intact eggs collected from the Gilliam meteorite—five little Dromaeosaur newborns to accompany the larger specimen the exterminator had caught and caged in the dog crate. Nora kept hourly records of their food intake; Greg Dulowski shot frequent videos to track their growth. The four scientists had spent the past few days fascinated by the creatures' aggressive behavior and rapacious appetites. Nora hated to be away even for the day, lest she missed a major development.

But she realized this trip to the Tully ranch could very well pay big dividends. Armed now with the knowledge that a pair of meteorites had hit close to the kill site, she knew a comprehensive inspection of the rancher's pasture could divulge evidence of other prehistoric life forms that possibly hatched out. She was also aware that the violent nature of the attack and high number of livestock lost strongly suggested extraterrestrial involvement. No earthbound animal she or any of her cohorts knew could devour fifty head of mature cattle in such a short time span. Yes, Nora had decided, the 90-minute drive south to Greenfield and visit to John Tully's ranch could provide some clues as to this bizarre cosmic puzzle of meteorites carrying nests of primordial eggs. And Hayden had said if nothing came of inspecting the rancher's pastureland, maybe they could try to find the downed meteorites. The fact that the Choteau expedition dig site was on the route sealed the deal for Nora.

She looked at Hayden now, crouched behind the wheel of the rental car, his seat pushed back to accommodate his bulk and long legs. The windows were open, a stiff breeze blowing through his beard, lifting his hair up off his shoulders. Nora breathed in the fresh air, a heady scent of rawhide, ponderosa pine, and mountain sagebrush. She took in the rolling green grasslands and sprawling farmhouses, eyed the snow-capped Rockies in the distance, and realized just how far she was from her Whitefish Bay, Wisconsin home.

They would hit Choteau an hour into the drive. Nora wanted to check firsthand the progress the team had made with unearthing the Maiasaura skeleton and Triceratops skull. She'd left her heavy equipment manager, Mack Renfro, in charge during their absence. She had been in phone contact with him the past five days and knew he had things well under control. Mack Renfro had the respect of everyone on the team. He was well versed in large-body fossil extraction and she had complete confidence in him. Even so, she wanted to get an in-person look at how things were proceeding there.

Such a control freak, Nora.

She was amused by that thought.

As Hayden drove in silence, her thoughts turned to the FaceTime phone conversation they had with the rancher, John Tully, yesterday. Tully told them the executive director of the Montana Department of Livestock Loss Board reported his team of investigators could not identify specifically what attacked the herd.

"Those jokers spent a full day combing my pasture," the rancher said. "They say they're completely puzzled as to what caused the massacre of my Herefords. They tell me they can't pay up for my loss until they can identify the specific cause. It's an outrage, I tell ya! It shouldn't matter what wiped out my herd. A loss is a loss is a loss! I've paid their high premiums every year. Never entered a claim. And now that I need help, the bastards won't pay up! The insurance biz is a sham, I tell ya!"

After they got Tully to settle down, the rancher went on to give them some facts about the recent history of livestock attacks in Montana. Grizzly bears were the single most destructive predator among cattle ranches in Northwestern Montana. Bears, however, were solo hunters and fed most actively at dawn and dusk, not under the cloak of darkness. Tully told them the insurance examiners considered wolves, too, since they were nocturnal pack hunters. But wolf attacks were down in recent years due to being taken off the endangered species list and allowed to be hunted. The lead investigator told Tully it would take *a well-populated pack of extremely coordinated wolves* to inflict the kind of bloody aftermath they saw at his ranch. The Livestock Loss Board also considered coyotes, since they were night predators. But, like bears and even mountain lions, who were also known to attack mature cattle, coyotes were solo hunters. The significant number of lost cattle ruled out solitary predators. The Livestock Loss Board's conclusion? Some unknown species of pack animal predator was responsible for the bloodshed.

Last night Hayden said to Nora with a frisky gleam in his eyes, "You think maybe vampires have started hunting in packs?"

Nora laughed. "Either that or it was Bigfoot and his cousins."

They both chuckled while Bryan and Loretta Gilliam looked at them like they were crazy mad scientists.

Which maybe we are, Nora thought.

Later last night when they were alone, Nora told Hayden: "Well, I guess if we rule out vampires and Bigfoot at the Tully ranch, we're left with humans and dinosaur hatchlings."

"Humans? You thinkin' insurance fraud?"

"It's possible. We don't know Tully's financial situation. But I do find it puzzling that only one of his pastures was invaded. The way I understand it, none of his Black Angus or Charolais were touched. Don't you find that odd?"

"I do," Hayden agreed. "That very thing crossed my mind earlier. But I think it's too big and too messy for an insurance scam. I mean, we're talkin' fifty to sixty head of mature cattle. It would be a difficult undertaking killing that many big animals. It'd take quite a few hands with black hearts to pull that off. And where did the meat go? Tully told us the bones were picked clean."

"Good point. So that leaves a pack of hungry dinos?"

"Possibly," Hayden said. "There's still the issue of the lack of attack on the other two pastures. You remember Tully offered an explanation of sorts? Said the Hereford stock is a smaller, more docile breed of cattle than Black Angus and Charolais. Said the Charolais are much heftier and have an aggressive temperament, and the Black Angus—especially the bulls—are even meaner."

"True enough," Nora said. "And so, dinosaur newborns, being instinctual hunters, would intuit this and go after the easier prey?"

"Yeah, possibly. This guy Tully is very angry about the whole thing and I can't say I blame him. I have no idea how much fifty to sixty head of Herefords are worth, but I'm sure he could lose his shirt if the insurance board doesn't pay out on the claim. These insurance companies are pretty savvy. Remember, I questioned him about his policy, and he told us it only covers reimbursement due to livestock losses incurred by wolves, mountain lions, and grizzly bears. Very specific."

"And so, if the culprits are dinosaur fledglings, the rancher is SOL?"

"Maybe. Most likely, yeah. We've got a lot to look into tomorrow, Nora," he'd told her late last night just before they'd gone to their rooms at the inn.

Nora stole glances at Hayden as he drove. He had been strangely quiet since they left Heart Butte. She knew he wasn't much of a morning person, but still, he usually was a motormouth. She wondered, not for the first time, why she selected him to accompany her on this day trip. He still made her uncomfortable at times, even though he had cleaned up his act since his drunken outburst last week. He still on occasion showed hints of his male sexist mindset and a smutty attitude. But it was obvious to her that he was trying mightily to stifle his old ways. Twice lately, after displaying his arrogance, he'd apologized, embarrassed, telling her it was "tough for an old hound dog to learn new tricks."

She could just as easily have chosen Greg Dulowski or Franz Krause to accompany her on this trip, leaving Hayden at Gilliam's Guidepost to attend to the hatchlings. That would have been much more comfortable. Easier. It was her call and she'd picked Hayden. Why? Maybe, despite his crude ways, she felt safe with him? Protected? Physically he was a big man and they were headed into an unknown situation. Nora wanted to believe that was the reason for her choice. But if she was being completely honest with herself, she had to admit that Hayden Fowler fascinated her. His breadth of scientific knowledge. His roguish, bad-boy charm. His international fame. The abundant virility that wafted off him like a powerful, scentless cologne. She recalled reading his books and gazing at his author photos on the dust jackets, feeling like an obsessed fan-girl. She remembered interviewing him in his Minneapolis home, thinking she was in the presence of scientific royalty.

Careful, Nora old girl, you've only known him a couple of

weeks.

Whether she wanted to admit it or not, working with him at the Choteau dig awakened something in her that had long been dormant. She couldn't deny his magnetic pull on her. But, at the same time, she remained aware of the cautionary red flags popping up, the way they always did when she found herself interested in a man. Nora had a history of attraction to guys who were completely wrong for her, a flaw that years of psychotherapy had not ironed out of her. While much of her life had been ordered and methodical and intellectual, her romantic involvements had often been sloppy and reckless. Her two failed marriages were testament to that.

Should I heed the warnings or surrender to temptation?

Nora elected to give him a chance. See where it went.

And so, here they were, trucking south on I-89 together.

The two-lane interstate stretched out in front of them. The dull hum of rubber meeting the road made her sleepy. She yawned. She needed coffee in the worst way. She checked her phone GPS, and was about to suggest stopping when Hayden spoke for the first time.

"You want a cuppa joe, right?" he said, keeping his eyes on the road, one big hand on the steering wheel.

She saw the smirk his beard did little to hide. "Yes, how'd you know?"

He smiled in that confident way of his. "I've known you long enough to know you can't go without caffeine much more than an hour." He turned to look at her. "You'd better watch those addictions. They'll grab you by the throat and squeeze the life out of you."

She recognized those words. A word-for-word recitation she'd laid on him last week in her trailer during his drunken incident.

She said, "Look, I—"

"Relax," he said, eyes back on the road, "I want coffee, too. How far to the next cradle of civilization?"

She looked at him for a long moment, then down at the phone in her lap. "Um, we're about fifteen minutes from Pendroy."

"Ah, yes, the booming metropolis of Pendroy, Montana," he said in a faux tour guide voice. "Think it's anything more than a glorified cow crossing?"

"Well, we won't find a Starbucks there, if that's what you mean."

Hayden drove in silence for several long beats, then said, "Anyone special in your life, Nora?"

She stared at him, but he didn't turn to face her. "What kind of question is *that*?"

"A direct one."

"It's a little personal, don't you think?"

He laughed. "Of *course* it's personal, Nora. I'm a person and you're a person . . . hence, a personal question. So, is there? Anyone special?"

She smiled, trying to cover her discomfort. Paused while she thought, then decided on, "Yes. I adore my parents. They're my role models," she said, even though her father had been dead for years and she was estranged from her mother.

"Come on. You *know* that's not what I mean."

"Are you always this direct, Hayden?"

"I try to be. Come on. Out with it. You sleeping with anybody?"

"*What?* Have you forgotten that I'm your boss?"

"No, I haven't forgotten. That fact just increases my interest. I have a thing for intelligent, powerful, take-charge women with bobbed, dark hair who wear glasses. I guess it's my hot librarian fantasy."

Such brash boldness!

A small thrill moved through her. Her skin tingled. She'd never been anyone's fantasy. She did her best to tamp it down. Tried to sound convincing with, "You know I could send you packing with comments like that."

"Yes, you could. But we both know you won't. You would've done it by now if you were going to."

"I warned you last week."

"I know, and I promised to lay off the sauce, which I have. But I never committed to stop sayin' what's on my mind. Life's too short to hold back. We'll all be dead sooner than later, so what the hell. *Let 'er rip* is what I say."

"Wow! Aren't you the life of the party," she said, studying him as he drove. "There's no filter on you, is there?"

"Nope. And something tells me you kinda like that about me," he said, turning and giving her a sly wink.

She felt herself blushing. Hoped it didn't show.

How is it that this man can read me so well?

Nora needed to redirect this conversation before she exposed too much of herself. "Listen, Hayden, I think we need to keep our relationship on a strictly professional level. Okay?"

"Where's the fun in that?" he snorted. "Besides, who said anything about a relationship? We're just talkin' here, one adult to another."

"Well, I, um . . . I don't know about—"

"So tell me," he said, cutting her off, "why is a smart, beautiful, successful woman like you all alone?"

"Who said I'm—"

"I think it's because you're afraid to open up to folks . . . afraid to open up to *me*."

"You don't quit, do you?"

"Nope. Persistence paves the way to success."

Nora couldn't help but laugh. "That is one corny aphorism, Hayden."

"*Aphorism*? I'll have to look that one up in my Webster's."

"I almost said *cliché*, but I didn't want to hurt your feelings."

"Touché. Score a point for pretty Lady Lemoyne. Now quit stallin' and tell me if you've got a friend with benefits."

"Jesus! Why are you pushing me on this?"

"Because I'm interested, okay?"

"And here I thought you were only interested in vacuous young hotties."

"Oh, how you underestimate me, Nora."

"Do I?"

"Yes, you do. Look, you've checked out every corner of my life, but I don't know much of anything about the mysterious Nora Lemoyne, superlative leader of Smithsonian expeditions."

"You mean you haven't googled me?"

"I have, but personal details about you are scarce."

"That's kinda creepy, Hayden."

"What? That I looked you up? Whaddaya think? That I'll agree to a three-month paleo dig with just anybody?"

"Fair enough."

"Why so many walls around you, Nora?"

He had a way of flustering her. "Look, I think it best that we keep things professional here. You want to talk science, I'm fine with that. And just so you know, there are ways to find out things about me that don't include asking me who I'm sleeping with."

"Yeah, but those aren't the *interesting* things."

Her emotions were in a tangle. She tried to come up with something intimate she could tell him without giving too much away, something personal but not *too* intimate. Something that might get him to switch his horn-toad male brain off sex for five minutes and onto something less threatening. Finally she said, "Okay, I'll tell you this: You and I have something big in common."

"Such as?"

"We've both failed at the marriage game. The difference is, you have three strikes while I only have two. You've struck out while I'm still in the batter's box."

"Interesting metaphor," he said. "But it still doesn't answer my question of who might be pleasing you in bed."

"Oooh, you are so aggravating! Is that all you think about?"

He smiled at her. "I don't know anything else that's better to think about."

"You're impossible!" she said, turning to gaze out her window at the passing countryside. "I refuse to listen to any more of your frat-boy seduction talk."

He laughed. "Is that what you think it is? Seduction talk? You need to get out more, Nora. I'd be much more slick if I was trying to seduce you. Let me assure you, you wouldn't be able to resist my advances if—"

"Listen," she cut in, anger overcoming her, "this one-sided conversation is making me really uncomfortable. It's inappropriate and disrespectful. Either talk to me like a grownup or shut the hell up!"

He turned back to the road, rubbed at his beard, obviously taken aback by her outburst. "Sorry," he said meekly. "I have a habit of runnin' my mouth without engaging the ol' noggin. Look, I don't mean to be disrespectful, Nora. I have *immense* respect for you, I really do. I guess I just don't know how to compliment you. I like bein' with you . . . spending time with you. Okay? There, I said it. That's not disrespectful, is it?"

She smiled, feeling her anger fade somewhat. She realized the enormous effort it must have taken him to come out with that. "No. It's kind of nice, actually. Kind of surprising, though."

"What, you think I can't be a gentleman when I want to?"

"I know you *can* be. The question is do you *want* to be?"

"Got it," he said. "I'll work on that."

"And since you're being so honest with me for once, I'll admit that I don't handle compliments very well. You just have an awkward way of dishing them out."

"I'm aware of that. But hey, since this is true confession time, I don't suppose you'd care to tell me anything about your ex-husbands?"

"You suppose correctly. My disastrous marriages are none of your damned business!" Now can we go back to discussing something work related?"

"Sure, if that's what you want," he said, a hint of defeat in his voice. He wrinkled his forehead, reflecting on something. His tone brightened as he said, "Okay, here's somethin' for you. Our little Dromaeosaur friends in the Gilliam's barn are solitary hunters, right?"

"Well, we both know there are differing schools of thought on that," Nora said, relieved that talk was back on a safe plane. "Some of our peers are convinced Dromaeosaurs hunted in groups, but I agree with you—yes. I think they hunted alone."

"So if we find evidence at the Tully ranch that suggests a coordinated attack, my inclination is to go with a creature that was known to hunt in groups. The most ferocious of the carnivores . . . the most populous of all the big meat eaters in the Cretaceous—the tyrant lizard king."

"Surely you're not suggesting—"

"Yes, I am. I think it's quite possible one or both of those meteorites that hit near Greenfield hatched out T-Rex newborns. Tyrannosaurus Rex was the only known carnivorous dino to hunt in packs. At least during the Cretaceous, and I think that's what we're looking at here. Ornithomimids were known to hunt in groups but they were largely herbivorous and would not attack prey larger than them. As you said . . . some of our peers claim raptors hunted in packs, but I say bullshit. That's pure Spielberg Hollywood imagination at work."

Nora felt a growing excitement, albeit a *dreadful* excitement. "T-Rex? You really think so, Hayden?"

"Yeah, I do. A group of T-Rex hatchlings would definitely go after a large number of cattle. And there is a good chance they attacked as an organized group. You know your shit, Nora so I'm sure you're aware of the latest finds about T-Rex."

"Yes, Of course I am."

Nora proceeded to tell him about the Tyrannosaurus Rex bone beds found in Alberta and Utah that changed the world of paleontology. The finds redirected the way scientists thought about T-Rex communal habits. More than a dozen complete Tyrannosaurus Rex frames were discovered together in the Canadian bed. And Alan Titus from the Bureau of Land Management led a team uncovering six intact T-Rex skeletons at the Grand Escalante Staircase national monument in Utah near the scattered bones of a pair of Triceratops. Other recent finds also supported the now-popular hypothesis that Tyrannosaurus Rex was a pack hunter.

"Yeah," Hayden said. "Many herbivores roamed in large herds, like the Maiasauras and Triceratops from our dig site. Maiasauras in particular migrated in huge herds of ten-thousand or more. Hard to believe that many big animals on the move . . ."

"I know," Nora said. "It must have been an amazing sight."

Hayden continued. "Ankylosaurs, Brontosaurs, and other huge planteaters herded as well. But the herbivores were socialized for protection, not hunting. There's no doubt that when Tyrannosaurus

Rex got together with his buddies to hunt, there was terror in the land. I'm pretty sure even a small pack of hungry T-Rex hatchlings could wipe out a herd of cattle in short order."

"I hate to rain on your parade, Hayden, but wasn't T-Rex diurnal?" Nora asked. "They weren't nocturnal."

"As far as we know, yeah. They were most active during daylight. That part throws me a bit. But I think we have to look at newborn hatchlings differently from the adults. The young Tyrannosaurus Rexes must have had insatiable appetites and would need to gorge during feedings. You see how much and how fast our little Dromaeosaurs eat. I imagine a T-Rex baby would gobble down many times what a Dromaeosaur does, based on the differing species sizes at maturity. And as far as the nocturnal attack at Tully's ranch? I think T-Rex hatchlings would be instinctual enough to know it's safer to hunt under cover of darkness. Just a theory, but I like it."

Nora shuddered imagining the devastation roving groups of Tyrannosaurus Rexes could unleash upon Montana and surrounding states. Especially as they grew larger.

"I hope and pray you're wrong about this, Hayden."

He nodded. "Me, too. But the paleontologist side of me would love to see a living, breathing T-Rex. It would answer so many questions we've had about them . . . solve so many mysteries about the fearsome beasts. However, groups of them roaming the countryside? Absolutely not. That's not somethin' I want to witness."

"Well, this is all just speculation at this point," she said.

"Yeah. Let's hope it stays that way. We'll just have to see what shakes out at the Tully ranch." He pointed through the windshield. "This looks like the turnoff for Pendroy. You ready for some coffee?"

"Drive on, Mr. Chauffeur."

Air Force Recruits

June 12: Mount Bennett Air Force Base
Elmore, Idaho

MOUNT BENNETT AIR FORCE BASE sat nestled in the foothills of the Danskin mountains in southwestern Idaho. Peter took a private charter Learjet to Mountain Home Municipal Airport early this morning, then grabbed a cab to the base. Saying goodbye to Brinshou and his baby daughter in the Missoula airport wrenched his heart. It didn't help matters that Brin had become emotional, breaking down and sobbing hysterically, grabbing on to him with a desperation that attracted the attention of early-bird travelers.

He now sat with five other helicopter pilots in the base mess hall, where they ate deli sandwiches and burgers, and listened to Colonel Thaddeus Glick brief them on their upcoming mission. The high-pitched whine and shriek of jet aircraft flying overhead cut through his presentation.

"I officially welcome you forestry folks to Mount Bennett Air Force Base, home of the famous 366th Fighter Wing squadrons. General Charles Ramage, Chief of Staff of the United States Air Force, has personally selected you men for this special task force. You should be proud to be an integral part of this vital undertaking, one that is crucial to our national security . . ."

Peter tuned out the colonel's canned presentation and focused on the man as he paced in front of them. Short with a wiry build. Graying military buzzcut. A too-loud voice and an obvious Napoleonic complex. *He can't be much more than five feet tall.*

Peter had been the last of the chopper pilots to arrive, and immediately upon his arrival, Glick led them on a rushed walking tour of the facility. Peter found the colonel to be borderline comical, the way he strutted like a bantam rooster, his chest thrown out dramatically, his overtly erect posture making him appear to be leaning backward. There was a fraught intensity about him that screamed: *WOULD SOMEBODY PLEASE NOTICE ME AND PROMOTE ME TO GENERAL!*

Peter took in the numerous medals, bars, and ribbons adorning Glick's dress uniform, wondering what the man had done to earn them. The colonel's decorations and serious demeanor painted him as a no-nonsense career officer. Thaddeus Glick obviously relished his power, all but bragging that he directed the 4,500 troops stationed here. His tone was self-congratulatory when talking about overseeing the convoy of 75 F-15 fighter jets and the airmen who flew them. He definitely had a commanding presence about him, a powerful aura. However, in Peter's eyes, his diminutive stature lessened his clout.

Peter had never understood the attraction to military life. He couldn't grasp the rigid regimentation, the blind subservience to sometimes questionable pursuits. The *shit-trickles-down* fraternity-style hazing that rippled through the ranks. What attracted people to an occupation that controlled every aspect of their lives? He didn't think he could handle the no-questions-asked *Yes-sir, no-sir, how high do you want me to jump, sir?* mindset. He already felt out of place here, as though he was an alien visiting a strange new planet.

He glanced the length of the table at the other pilots, who picked at their meals. To a man, they looked as disengaged as he felt. He knew one of them, Larry Bing, whose path he had crossed at Rocky Mountain Rotors Flight School in Twin Falls. The other four pilots flew for the Idaho Forest Department and were strangers to him.

Exhaustion sapped him and he stifled a yawn. The last two weeks had been a whirlwind of activity, what with flying 12-hour shifts transporting smoke-jumpers to and from fire sites, hospital visits to George Dantley, and three A.M. feedings for baby Kimi. Last night, dead on his feet, he was honored in an event sponsored by the Missoula Jaycees. The gathering—organized and promoted by Sam and Elizabeth Dantley—brought nearly a hundred people out to pay tribute to him and his emergency medical team. George's parents wanted to publicly acknowledge them for saving their son's life at the Camels Hump fire lookout tower. Peter appreciated the Dantleys' efforts, especially getting local media recognition for his rescue team. Jeremy Spang, Burl Heddison, and Nicki Whitlow deserved the acclaim much more than he. Peter did his best to show his gratitude to the Dantleys and the Jaycees. But he would much rather have spent the evening at home with Brinshou and the baby.

And then there was the interview he was manipulated into by an aggressive Missoula KECI-TV anchor. The news journalist built him up as if he was a comic book superhero.

Embarrassing.

Draining.

Something Colonel Glick was saying brought him back to the present.

". . . and as you've been informed, the highly classified nature of this operation dictates that your contact with the outside world stops now. While here, you are forbidden to communicate with anyone outside. Nor can you leave the base for any reason, other than to fly your routes. We will be collecting your cell phones, iPads, and laptops tonight."

"Wait, *what?* What kinda horseshit is *that*?" the black pilot sitting to Peter's right yelled out. "What are we, fuckin' pariahs? That's bullshit! We haven't been informed of anything!"

Glick stopped pacing, gave him a death-ray stare. "You will not use that language here, Mr. Williams. You will conduct yourself in a civilized manner within these hallowed halls."

"It's *Curtis*," the pilot answered. "Curtis Williams. What's so goddamned secretive about this thing we can't be part of the outside world? We're just pickin' up a buncha space rocks."

Glick bristled, obviously trying hard to maintain his composure. "General Ramage and the Pentagon brass demand complete secrecy about the work. There's already a great deal of panic in the country over this meteorite madness. The conspiracy fools are heating up Twitter and Facebook with fake news. We don't want to feed into their lunacy. It's best that what happens here remains on the base. It's all for the good of the American people."

One of the Idaho pilots spoke up, Rusty Cavanaugh, ten years younger than Peter with a head full of bright red hair and a sunburned baby face. "With all due respect, we should be allowed to call our loved ones. My wife is due any day now an' I know she's already worried sick about me being away."

Peter could relate. This separation would hit his Brin hard. He doubted his wife could last a day without hearing from him, let alone a few weeks.

Connor Bartholomew, another of the Idaho chopper jocks chimed in, "I agree with Curtis. It's complete bullshit that we can't make calls out. We ain't a sequestered jury on a murder trial, fer Chrissakes."

Glick gave the pilots a malicious smile. "Well, obviously you guys didn't read the fine print on your contracts. Right? Look fellas, this is high-level Pentagon work. Everything's done in a covert manner. Not like the flyin' you do for the forest division. You guys are big shots there. Real hot stuff. Here? You're just grunts carryin' out orders as I dictate them. You're in the United States Air Force, gentlemen. Best you understand that."

Stunned, the pilots regarded one another, their flabbergasted expressions asking the silent question: *Were you aware of that?*

Peter thought about the contract he'd signed. Ten pages of legalese mumbo jumbo he couldn't make much sense of. And the rushed timeframe didn't allow him to hire a lawyer. So he'd skipped over most of it. Signed it. Received a hefty direct deposit sum as a signing bonus. Looking at the others, he was sure they had done the same.

His fatigue and Glick's severe decree had punched a hole in his patience. Peter knew the effect a couple of weeks of silence would have on Brin. On their marriage. He felt an indignant lump form in his throat. A feverish anger.

"That's pretty devious, don't you think, Colonel?" he heard himself say. "It smells like a classic bait and switch tactic to me."

Glick's eyes caught fire. "The hell you say! You've got it all wrong, *whirlyturd*!" He squinted, trying to read Peter's nametag. "What's your name? . . . Lacroix?"

"Yeah. Peter Lacroix," he said, angry at the colonel's snide put-down of his livelihood.

"Well, Peter Lacroix, if you'd checked with an attorney, you'd see that your contract is airtight . . . everything above-board and binding. It's got your signature on it. You're indebted to us for the duration of this operation, however long that might last. You can leave now if the arrangement doesn't sit well with you. I can find a replacement on short notice. Lots of 'copter jocks would love to make this kind of money. You guys are a dime a dozen."

Glick continued to scowl at him.

Peter held the colonel's glare, seething, thinking: *What an arrogant prick!*

"You guys start flyin' out tomorrow at oh-eight-hundred hours," Glick said finally.

"What about training?" Cavanaugh asked. "I mean, we're not flyin' our usual rigs here."

"There's no time for training. You won't need it, anyway. We've got a small fleet of rebuilt Sikorsky S-70s we purchased from the Army. Same make you've been piloting, just an older model. They've been refitted to handle longline heavy cargo pickups, but at the end of the day they're still Sikorskys. Surely you hotshots can adapt quickly."

"We fly Bell 209 Cobras in Idaho," Bartholomew said. "They ain't nothin' like Sikorskys."

"My pilots tell me all helicopters are basically the same."

"Say *what*?" Curtis Williams said. "Your pilots fly *jets*. They're Top Gun mavericks. They couldn't handle a chopper if their lives depended on it."

"I beg to differ," Glick said. "Many of my pilots are certified on rotor wing aircraft. We have the best and the brightest here at Mount Bennett."

Peter, anger building, couldn't hold back. "Then why the hell aren't *they* flying these roundup missions?"

Glick sighed. "Because you guys know the terrain. Your daily work involves low altitude, close-to-the-ground reconnaissance. Pickups and deliveries. My pilots fly high altitude maneuvers . . .

war training exercises." An exasperated look pinched Glick's face. "I don't have to explain my decisions to you, Lacroix."

"I'm not asking you to. But we do need some clarification."

"What's that?" Glick said, impatient.

"The setup for the meteorite roundup. Do you expect us to handle all flight navigation *and* pick up the rocks ourselves?"

"Don't be a moron, Lacroix. I was getting around to that. You guys will fly in teams of two—a pilot and a copilot. Each flight will also include a pair of Air National Guardsmen. They'll be responsible for the meteorite pickups. They're trained on the longline lift apparatus and on-the-ground retrieval. You hotshots only have to fly them to the crash sites and bring back the goods. They'll be doin' all the dirty work."

Larry Bing said, "Shouldn't we be training *with* the Air guardsmen? We'll be working in teams, so—"

"I thought I already made it clear. There's no time for training."

Peter listened to Glick harangue Bing and the rest of them. The briefing had gone sideways quickly. Peter couldn't believe a high ranking officer in the U.S. Air Force would act with such impudence. Would Glick's superiors in the Pentagon approve of this behavior? Would they tolerate the colonel's beat-down of private citizens?

When silence ensued, Peter said, "I think we deserve more respect than what you're showin' us. And I think this whole secrecy thing is nonsense. We're pickin' up rocks, not fighting a war with Russia . . ."

"You know what *I* think, Lacroix? I think you think too much! Now how about you shut your yap and listen to what I have to say. You might learn a thing or two."

Peter felt his anger bubbling up. If he was going to fly for the United States Air Force, Glick was going to have to make some concessions.

"I'll shut my *yap* if and when you lift some of these ridiculous restrictions. We're having to pilot unfamiliar aircraft and fly precision routes over treacherous terrain. It's difficult. And my wife, she—"

"Boo-hoo, Lacroix!" Glick snapped. "I don't wanna hear it. This is no place for whiny pantywaists. You don't like it, you can get yourself a plane ticket back to Missoula pronto. That applies to all of you," he said, leveling his intimidating stare at each of the pilots. "We're payin' you top dollar to fly this operation, so either suck it up and perform at the high level I've been told you can, or hit the road. Your choice."

Peter felt like he'd been slapped. He looked down at his half-eaten burger, pissed off. A jet screamed overhead, the only sound in the cavernous mess hall. None of his fellow pilots dared speak up. Colonel Thaddeus Glick had established his alpha dog superiority. The silence was palpable, awkward.

"Okay then, very good," the colonel said. "Now that we all understand each other, I'll let you in on a few things we have come to learn about these meteorites. Any objections, gentlemen?"

Not a sound from the pilots. Peter stewed. He couldn't look at Glick. He wondered whether he should bow out now. *I'm away from Brin and Kimi for this?*

"Okay," Glick proceeded. "The total count of meteorite strikes is fifteen. Six in Idaho and nine in Montana. Strangely, they haven't hit anywhere else, and thankfully, they've all come down in unpopulated areas. That part we don't understand yet. What we *do* understand is how this whole aberration of nature began. A few weeks back, we saw an unusual abundance of meteor showers. The light show was much greater than usual for this time of year. Astronomers tell us it was caused by a storm of comets that probably came out of the Kuiper Belt, outside of Neptune's orbit. For those of you who don't know, comets are primitive objects left over from the formation of our solar system. They're huge spheres of ice and dirt that orbit the Sun. This group of comets fell out of orbit and collided with the Sun, which caused enormous solar flareups. A once in a millennia occurrence, they tell us. That spectacular solar disturbance caused asteroids in the pathway to take in extreme heat and break apart, kicking off the shower of bright meteors we witnessed. But that wasn't the only blowback from these solar storms. We also experienced heavy gravitational fluctuations here along the Continental Divide. Our pilots were seeing perplexing readouts on their instrument panels. Their training maneuvers were thrown off by unusual magnetic fields, the magnetized pull strong enough to knock F-15 fighter jets off their flight paths . . ."

Peter continued to listen to Glick, interested, but still hot under the collar at the man's condescending, dismissive treatment.

". . . so, the way I understand it, the comets crashing into the Sun and the solar reaction to that huge event caused a vacuum in the Earth's atmosphere that sucked in chunks of those asteroids and pinpointed their descent here in Idaho and Montana. To simplify it, those asteroid chunks are called meteoroids in deep space and meteors when they enter Earth's atmosphere. The fragments that make it to the ground are known as meteorites . . ."

Curtis Williams whispered to Peter. "Uncle Thad must think we're as clueless as his Top Gun flyboys."

Peter couldn't help but laugh.

"Somethin' funny about this to you, Lacroix?" Glick shot him the laser stare again.

"Uh . . . no."

Glick turned his attention to Curtis. "And if you have somethin' to say to the group, Williams, you ask my permission to talk. Got it?"

"Yeah, sure thing," Curtis mumbled, then under his breath so Glick couldn't hear, added "*Thaddeus*."

The sarcastic rebuke brought snickers from Peter and Larry Bing.

Glick sighed and shook his head, as though dealing with children. He waved them off with a sweep of his arm. Continued his talk . . .

"The size of these meteorites is extraordinary. Historically, less than five percent of the original chunk off the meteoroid makes it to the ground. The rest burns up in Earth's protective atmosphere. Prior to this unprecedented event, most found meteorites ranged in size from a small pebble to a fist. These that you'll be rounding up are gargantuan by comparison—six to seven feet tall . . . weighing in at several tons. Of course it's doubtful you'll find any fully intact. We suspect most broke into fragments upon impact. But even the fragments are impressive from what I've been told . . ."

Glick went on to tell them that a report from the U.S. Geological Survey informed them that samples they'd seen thus far contained large amounts of iridium, a heavy metal rarely found in meteorites. The size, weight, structure, and composition of these meteorites made them a geologic oddity. The focused delivery of them within a 600 square-mile area made them an astronomical curiosity. Many astrophysicists, astronomers, and geologists agreed, this directed meteorite bombing along the Continental Divide was a cataclysmic celestial happening, an anomaly of nature that required several divergent galactic events to unfold in a specific sequential order, with the resulting elements falling into place in a timely manner.

". . . and so you can see this is not at all an everyday occurrence, gentlemen. I'm sure you can understand why the utmost secrecy is required. We've got to round these rocks up and get them into our hangar for inspection. Time is of the essence. Any questions?"

Connor Bartholomew said, "What about those reptiles hatchin' outta the meteorites? Why no mention of them?"

Glick shook his head. "Because there's no solid proof of that."

"Bullshit!" Curtis Williams bellowed. "Tell me with a straight face you haven't seen the videos. They're on every newscast now."

"Those videos have been debunked."

"I don't think so," Larry Bing said. "I've seen 'em. We all have. The one from that geologist—his name escapes me—that video is real, all those lizard-lookin' things runnin' around big slabs of that black rock. And the teeth on those things. Yikes!"

"I'm telling you, it's staged," Glick said. The tape has been doctored. It's been discredited."

"No it hasn't," Peter said, thinking about the strange chirping-croaking sounds he'd heard at the Camels Hump meteorite strike, sounds eerily similar to what he'd heard on the video shown on the national news. "That geologist who shot the footage is a bigtime international scientist. He's well respected by his peers from what I understand. His video's been all over the newscasts the past few days. It's authentic. Someone like him would never jeopardize his reputation by doctoring video footage. A scientist of his stature would never distort the truth."

"How do you know, Lacroix? Maybe the guy is going for a book or movie deal. You don't know."

"Oh, but I *do* know, Colonel. Because the audio on that tape matches what I heard near the meteorite I saw . . . the one at the bottom of Camels Hump."

Glick laughed, a sarcastic bark. "Really? You're going *there?* The Montana forests are full of weird noises."

Larry Bing said, "I think Pete's right. I've been watching the newscasts and strange as it is, I believe those lizard creatures are hatchin' out at the meteorite crash sites."

"Yeah, me too," Bartholomew yelped.

"Me three," Curtis Williams said, eyeing Glick with suspicion. "I believe the Colonel knows we're right. I think he knows a lot more than he's lettin' on."

"Yeah," Bartholomew said, "that's the real reason the Air Force hired us. They didn't wanna risk their own pilots on a mission this dangerous. That one video makin' the rounds shows up close footage of the teeth on those suckers. They could take off a finger or a hand . . . maybe your dick if you get too close."

"Wow!" Glick exclaimed. "You hotshot macho chopper jocks are afraid of a few little lizards?"

"Ah, so there it is, guys!" Peter said. "He just admitted the existence of dinosaurs, crazy as that sounds."

Glick was flustered. "You guys have a lot of nerve questioning me. I demand that you upstarts begin walking the straight and narrow right now. My word and my decisions are gospel around here. From here on out what I say goes. Period. You will accept my orders without question. Got it?"

Peter felt the heat of his anger bloom in his face. He left his home life behind for *this*? To be castigated by an out-of-control military officer? Not being able to talk to Brin for several weeks just didn't cut it.

He glanced at the other pilots. All had their heads down, eating and drinking, avoiding Glick's malevolent stare. Someone had to speak up.

He tried to control his runaway emotions and his breathing as he said, "Look, Colonel, I'm fascinated by what's goin' on. We all are. *Unprecedented* is how you referred to it. I want to be involved in this meteorite recovery operation, but your severe restrictions just won't permit me to continue. Now I have a proposition for you that—"

"No way, Lacroix," Glick boomed. "You're not going to dictate how it's going to be. You signed a contract that stipulates—"

"Yeah, we've already been over that, so just hear me out. I don't know how the others feel, but unless you ease up on the no outside contact or activity, I'm willing to walk out now and go home. I'll even return my signing bonus. Bein' held a prisoner at a military installation doesn't work for me."

"Go ahead then, go," Glick said. "You can be replaced."

Peter hesitated, then pushed himself back from the cafeteria table, stood. Looked at Glick, who smiled at him smugly.

Peter turned, started walking to the exit when Larry Bing said, "I'm with Pete. I'm outta here, too, if things don't change."

"Me too. I'd rather be home with my wife when she delivers our baby," Rusty Cavanaugh said evenly.

Peter stopped, turned, saw all five pilots getting up from the table en masse. Heard chair legs scraping the linoleum, voices raised in dissent. One by one, each of them turned their backs on Glick and started walking toward him.

Unbelievable. They've got my back!

Gratitude and a feeling of brotherhood surged through him.

He looked at the colonel, who wore a look of surprised shock.

"Wait," Glick said. "You can't do this. We have a contractual agreement. It's legal and binding."

Peter, feeling bold now, said, "We signed those contracts under duress. Even a first-year law intern could get them declared null and void."

"You're ill informed, Lacroix. Go ahead and quit," Glick said, flapping his arms at them. "Run home with your tails between your legs for all I care. You're all a bunch of feebleminded fools."

Peter walked back toward his fellow pilots, said to Glick, "I don't think your superiors in the Pentagon would think very highly of a base commander who runs off all six helicopter pilots assigned to a highly critical task force. Wouldn't look good in their eyes, no sir, havin' a half dozen highly trained contractors walk off the job. In fact, I believe it might just earn you a demotion. Slap you back down to *Lieutenant* Colonel faster than you can say boo. You can also kiss that promotion to Brigadier General goodbye. Think about it. Who would be the fool then, Colonel?"

He had him. Peter could see the wheels turning in Glick's head, the confusion in his squinty eyes. His career was on the line.

"Whaddaya say, Colonel? I believe I speak for all of us when I say give us the freedom we want while we're here and we'll do a bang-up job for you . . . make you look good. Maybe help you get that promotion. How about it? It'd be a win for all of us."

Glick took a seat at the end of the mess hall table and stared into space, thinking.

Peter noticed the pilots looking at him with newfound respect.

After a long stretch of silence, Glick raised his head and said, "All right. If you guys stay on you can keep your cell phones . . . make calls out."

Curtis Williams said, "What about leavin' the base?"

"I'll give you that, too. But there's going to be some stipulations."

"Like what?"

"No talkin' to the media. And you will keep mum about anything you experience on your roundups. Even to your family and friends. This mission remains highly classified. Got it?"

"You've got yourself a deal, Colonel," Peter said.

Tyrant Lizards

June 12: Tully Ranch
Greenfield, Montana

HAYDEN SAT IN THE SHOTGUN SEAT of John Tully's Jeep, scanning the far reaches of the killing field through binoculars. Tully, slumped behind the steering wheel, watched him with hopeful anticipation. Nora sat in back, quiet. They were parked outside the barbed-wire fence, near the double-gated entrance. The sun baked the mud-caked earth as the midafternoon temperature pushed ninety.

Hayden wiped his brow with his free hand, continuing to glass the pasture with the other. Bleached bones glowed electric-white as far as he could see. Rib racks stood like slatted tombstones. Clumps of prairie grass lay flat, trampled. Long slashes gouged the turf where the Herefords had made their final stand. The stench of rotting meat tainted the hot breeze. An appalling battle had taken place here, an age-old, one-sided clash between predator and prey.

Hayden lowered the binoculars. "Let's get a closer look."

Tully nodded and shut off the ignition. "Sure wish you guys were here a few days ago." He tipped the brim of his Stetson at the pasture. "There was more to see the day after it happened. Rain washed away what the buzzards didn't get." He stepped out of the Jeep and walked toward the gates.

"I believe there's enough here to tell us something," Hayden said, falling in next to Tully.

Nora, walking behind them, said, "The bones and tracks should give us some answers."

They walked to the entrance, the ground spongy underfoot. Tully swung open the gates and entered the pasture. "The insurance people told me the tracks looked like birds," he said, his tone derisive. "I ain't never seen a bird could do this kinda damage."

"That's for sure. No birds did this," Hayden said, eyes down, scanning. The visible animal tracks were partials at best. Rain and insurance investigators had obliterated most prints.

Nora surveyed the field of death. "Yeah, even Hitchcock's birds on their most aggressive day couldn't manage this."

Tully looked baffled. "*Hitchcock's* birds?"

Hayden smiled at Nora, appreciating her attempt at lightening the gloomy mood.

"What?" Tully said, eyes darting between the two of them. "Did I say somethin' funny?"

Nora smiled at Hayden. "No. You're good, Mr. Tully."

"Well, I sure hope you can identify what did this. The insurance weasels won't pay a dime until they get a positive ID. And even then . . ." Tully left the comment hanging.

A cowbell tinkled in the distance, accompanied by a mournful low mooing. Hayden led them thirty feet to the nearest skeleton. Intense heat radiated from the ground and he labored to catch his breath. Sweat trickled down his spine, dampening the back of his shirt. He snapped on a pair of rubber gloves and kneeled to take a closer look at the mound of bones.

Tully spoke. "You told me on the phone you discovered dinosaurs up Heart Butte way. They've been sayin' that on the news, too. I don't believe it for a second. I mean, *really*?"

Nora answered. "I'm afraid it's true, Mr. Tully. We've got six juveniles from the Late Cretaceous. They're Dromaeosaurs. They have been extinct for sixty-six million years."

"Sweet Jesus! How the hell is that even possible?"

"We don't know yet," Hayden said, picking up a leg bone. "There're a lot of theories, but nothing's conclusive yet."

"So you think that's what attacked my herd?"

"It's possible." Hayden scraped dried blood and sticky tissue off the leg bone. "We know for certain our Dromaeosaurs hatched out of a large meteorite at the Gilliam ranch. Two other meteorites came down near here. We think it's probable they were loaded with dinosaur eggs, too."

Tully tugged at the brim of his hat. "That's what the newscasters been sayin', too. I think it's a load of kaka. Eggs hatchin' out of a meteorite? Outrageous! I think it's some kinda prank the government's playin' on us good American people."

"What would the government have to gain by that?"

Tully gave Hayden a sly look. "To instill fear in the public. Keep us scared. Makes us much easier to manipulate and get what they want from us."

Hayden chuckled under his breath. "You're givin' them way too much credit when—"

"Oh, you just don't know the gist of it, sir. The agriculture department screws us ranchers every chance they get. I'm tellin' you, Uncle Sam is up to somethin' with this meteorite scam. Fake news, if'n you ask me."

"That's an interesting theory you've got there, Mr. Tully," Nora said. "But it doesn't hold up. The media is reporting accurately. We've seen the evidence. There're the live specimens at the Gilliam ranch that Hayden told you about. The eggs that hatched out . . . five of them in our incubator. We've been feeding the hatchlings, studying them. And yesterday a report came in from another strike site. Another meteorite bearing eggs. This one in Idaho. Reported by the state police."

"Sweet holy Jesus! Really? *Dinosaurs*? In li'l old Greenfield, Montana? And in Idaho?" He shook his head. "Sorry, with all due respect, missus, I'm still not buyin' it."

Hayden said, "You lost fifty or more head of cattle. They surely didn't kill and eat themselves. Your investigators have ruled out bears and wolves and mountain lions. Our best educated guess is that a group of carnivores did this—*dinosaur* carnivores—and at this point, crazy as it sounds, it looks like we're spot on. Maybe Dromaeosaurs. Probably a different genus."

Hayden moved to another cattle skeleton. A sun-bleached skull lay at the head of the ribcage. Dried blood—black and crusty—coated the ribs. Ragged strips of sinewy muscle clung to the leg bones. The putrid stench of decaying beef was stronger here, bringing bile into his throat. Flies buzzed around his head. He was on the verge of vomiting, but his sheer will held it back.

He took a knee to get a closer look. Though uncomfortable and nauseated, he felt jazzed. Keyed up. Excitement buzzed through him. He just knew dinosaur newborns had done this and he intended to identify the species, no matter how revolting the effort.

His scientific instincts told him another Late Cretaceous creature had caused this carnage. They'd found ancient cycad greenery in the Gilliam meteorite—prehistoric ferns long absent from Earth, identified as being specifically from that pre-extinction geologic period. There was also the heavy concentration of iridium in the meteorite, a heavy metal known to have vanished with the dinosaurs during The Great Extinction. And cocooned within the thick layers of iridium and ancient ferns were Dromaeosaur eggs, hatching out a number of aggressive little beasts. He knew that Dromaeosaurus was the second most prevalent meat eater of the Late Cretaceous in what is now North America.

Number one by a wide margin was Tyrannosaurus Rex, the terrible tyrant lizard king.

He certainly hoped he was wrong this time. But the nature of the destruction here at Tully's farm pointed to T-Rex.

He thought about Dulowski's and Krause's postulation, that these downed meteorites were chunks broken off a large asteroid traveling through deep space, its contents in cryonic stasis until some astronomical event generated the meteor showers. Hayden understood completely why people like John Tully were disbelieving. He would be, too, had he not witnessed what he had. He'd seen the Gilliam meteorite and its strange cargo. He'd seen the live Dromaeosaur specimen the exterminator had caught and the cadaver of the one Bryan Gilliam had killed. He'd experienced the five eggs hatching out. He'd even hand fed the hatchlings. This return of Cretaceous Dromaeosaurs had happened, there was no denying that. But the mystery remained as to *how* it had happened. Hayden questioned the feasibility of his cohorts' thinking. He had a difficult time wrapping his science-trained mind around the *how* and *why* of it all. But he was nearly convinced of one thing: If the Gilliam meteorite carried Late Cretaceous life, then all fifteen of the reported meteorites probably did also. If Greg Dulowski and Franz Krause were right, the downed meteorites would all have to be from the same space and time.

Hayden peered at the gnawed bone in his hand. Looked at it more closely.

An alarm clanged in his head.

He picked up several other loose bones, studied them.

He felt faint. His stomach flip-flopped.

These bones told the story.

This had to be the work of tyrant lizards.

He was fairly certain that the two meteorites striking near the Tully ranch had hatched out the most feared meat eater in all the Late Cretaceous—the tyrant lizard king, Tyrannosaurus Rex.

The human side of him hoped he was wrong, but his scientific instincts told him he was right.

* * *

Nora's stubborn dedication to the Smithsonian expedition made them four hours late for their appointment with John Tully. After the bad coffee they'd picked up in Pendroy, they'd made a planned stop at the expedition dig site in Choteau. Hayden thought it would be a brief stopover to give a shout-out to the team. Nora had other ideas. She felt it necessary to linger. Her procrastination had tested his patience.

Why waste time marveling over prehistoric bones when a monumental quirk of nature has put us at the forefront of the most sensational astronomical event in recorded history?

Why indeed? They now had living, breathing dinosaurs to study. Cretaceous Period Dromaeosaurs. Six of them in the Gilliam barn. And there was a very good chance more hatchlings roamed somewhere near the Tully ranch.

By some curious twist of fate, they were the chosen ones.

They were the beneficiaries of this celestial anomaly that had returned long extinct dinosaurs to Earth.

And Nora thinks it best to spend half the day at the dig site?

According to her, their first obligation was to the expedition. The Smithsonian Institution was signing their paychecks. The Tully ranch could wait. Nora told him she didn't want the team thinking she was ignoring them. She had a responsibility to spend time with the expedition. They both did, she reminded him. He wanted to say something, to get her moving. But he'd held his tongue.

It had eaten away at him, the delay in Choteau. His anxiety ratcheted up with each passing hour they'd spent mingling with the dig team and the two Smithsonian representatives who arrived yesterday. Hayden tried subtly to hurry Nora along, but she would not be rushed. He'd wanted to remind her that unidentified carnivores had decimated fifty head of cattle at the Tully ranch and that's where they should be.

And yet he'd remained silent. Too many people around them in the hot, dusty camp made private conversation difficult. But, the real reason he'd kept quiet? His growing respect for her. Ever since the tongue lashing she'd laid on him in her trailer last week, he found himself appreciating her, wanting more than anything for her to accept him. The last thing he wanted was to disappoint her again. He had to admit to a growing fondness for Nora. This bespectacled cerebral brunette with the pageboy hairstyle and intelligent green eyes had a lot going for her. She was a strong and capable leader. Well educated and intellectually curious. She possessed a dry, quick wit. And Nora was sexy as hell in her own quirky, studious way. *At least for a woman in her mid-forties.* A little old for his tastes, but even so, he found her interesting. A challenge. Dare he admit he'd found his equal? He'd even confessed he liked being with her. Told her it must be his hot librarian fantasy working on him.

What the hell possessed you to say something so lame, Fowler?

Yes, she frustrated him. But he had to give her credit. She was an excellent salesperson, managing to get this huge operation funded. No small feat. He also appreciated that the team she personally handpicked had made significant progress while he and Nora were away. The excavators had chiseled and hammered their way to the bottom of the trenches, down to the Maiasaur's tibia and fibula. The expedition leads and their interns were well trained, practicing meticulous excavation techniques, ensuring they had a complete, intact skeleton. Still a week or two away from the final excavation—lifting the *Good Mother Lizard* frame out of the hole and prepping it for shipment to the museum—but they now knew for certain they had unearthed a remarkable find. The team also did an expert job of digging out the petrified Maiasaur eggs and had made further progress on the Triceratops skull excavation. Enthusiasm ran high throughout the camp and Nora got caught up in the jubilation. She also basked in the adulation from the visiting sponsors.

Hayden was happy for her and for the team. But he'd been bored. Prehistoric skeletons just didn't grab him the way they did a week ago. His head and heart were with the live specimens now.

But he'd played the loyal, dedicated employee, remaining by her side as they made the rounds. He'd joined her down in the cool, gritty Maiasaur and Triceratops trenches to inspect the work. Nora introduced him to the pair of Smithsonian reps, thanking the sponsors profusely for making the long trip. Too profusely, he thought. Hayden understood some sucking up was to be expected for a person in Nora's position. After all, these folks were underwriting the dig. But after a point, he became embarrassed for her. He wanted to tell her she was coming across as fawning and obsequious. But he surprised himself by keeping quiet. It took a Herculean effort on his part, but he'd avoided raining on Nora's parade. She deserved that much from him.

And just when he thought she was finally through and ready to hit the road, she had invited the Smithsonian stuffed suits to her trailer for lunch. They were curious about the living Dromaeosaurs in Heart Butte, and peppered her and Hayden with endless questions. More time crawled by. Lost time, in his view. Nora shared Greg Dulowski's videos with them, and the museum reps watched in openmouthed awe, much in the same way Hayden and Nora had when they first saw the Dromaeosaur videos.

They didn't get away from Choteau until 2:30. The rancher was noticeably annoyed by their tardiness, but Nora put her feminine charm to work and smoothed over Tully's ruffled feathers.

* * *

Hayden sifted through another bone mound. He grabbed a leg bone and turned it over in his gloved hands, examining it from different angles. He reached for a skull, comparing the gnaw marks on it with those on the leg, then held them out for Nora to inspect.

"Put your gloves on and check these out. Look at the striations, the teeth grooves. The bite patterns differ from how our hatchlings latch on. You have to look closely, but the ruts are wider and deeper, more serrated. Our Dromaeosaurs have more conical teeth. Tapered and sharp. They puncture . . . they bite straight down. These animals tear flesh from the bone with a slashing motion. You can see it here." He moved to a new spot and grabbed a few loose bones off the ground, scrutinized them. "Likewise with these. All have the same wide, deep rip-and-scrape patterns."

Nora slipped on her gloves and took the bones from Hayden. "I see. Our predators strip off long pieces of meat and gulp them down. They ingest great quantities rapidly, but aren't mature enough to crush and swallow bones."

"Yeah, you've got it," Hayden said, wondering if she was coming to the same dreadful conclusion he'd arrived at. He stood and looked at her. "By summer's end, these attackers will easily be able to crush thick bones. They'll be devouring every part of their prey— flesh, intestines, bones . . . *everything*. They won't waste their time chewing. Most of it'll go down their gullets whole. Won't be much left for the scavengers to pick over."

"So you're sayin' they're dinosaurs, then?" Tully said, his voice rising.

Nora gave him a slow nod. "It looks that way, yes." She bent and picked up a femur, examined the long thigh bone. "I believe we can rule out Dromaeosaurs though. I agree with you, Hayden. The scrapings on these bones indicate the cattle killers' dental structure and eating behaviors are different from those of our Dromaeosaurs. Our hatchlings are puncture-and-pull chewers. Their teeth are sharp and pointed, designed for biting off smaller chunks of meat they can chew. They're built for masticating their food before swallowing." Nora straightened and faced the rancher. "Your cattle faced a more formidable foe, Mr. Tully. The dinos that did this had bigger, flatter teeth with stronger jaws. They don't puncture and chew but rather rip large chunks of flesh off the bone and swallow the meat whole. Strong neck and throat muscles enable them to throw their heads back and gulp down large amounts without chewing. That's how they were able to decimate your herd so quickly.

"These killers are juveniles, only a couple of weeks old. Even so, they're able to consume many times their weight in meat. If they're what I think they are, they'll gain four-to-five pounds a day, provided they get enough to eat. But until they get closer to maturity, their immature jaws and underdeveloped neck musculature won't allow them to crack through dense bone. And until their digestive tracks develop, they can't break down bone. That's why they left behind these skeletal remains. Hayden is correct. By the end of summer they'll be very efficient eaters, leaving nothing for carrion birds and bears and coyotes to pick over . . ."

Hayden caught her sending him nervous glances from behind her prescription sunglasses. Her calculated looks and body language told him: *I know what did this! Good lord help us, you were right!*

He knew Nora was well versed in Tyrannosaurus Rex facts. Every beginning paleontology student who did their homework knew them. So did the millions of moviegoers who'd seen the *Jurassic Park* films, inaccurate though they were. Tyrannosaurus Rex was the most prevalent of all the big carnivores in the Late Cretaceous. Paleontologists agreed that more than 20,000 adult Tyrannosaurus Rexes roamed North America at extinction, with as many as 15,000 concentrated in a large area of what is now Hell Creek State Park, just 300 miles east of the Tully ranch. T-Rex outnumbered Dromaeosaurs three to one in these parts 66 million years ago. Nora knew those numbers as well as he. She also knew the manner and speed in which rancher Tully's herd was annihilated indicated a vicious predator like Tyrannosaurus Rex.

She knows!

Tully's livestock had been killed and eaten by tyrant lizards.

Tyrannosaurus Rex was back!

He had discussed this with Nora on the drive here, had told her of his strong hunch, and she had doubted him. She didn't doubt him now.

Hayden looked away from her.

An ominous, dark mood grabbed him as he considered the repercussions.

It was all so surreal.

He began walking, taking small, careful steps, shaking his arms, rolling his shoulders, taking deep breaths, trying to shake off a shaky dizziness. He strolled slowly, in ever-widening arcs.

"Are you okay, Hayden?" Nora's voice.

"Yeah . . . yeah, I'm fine . . . just fine."

She leveled a worried look at him before turning back to her conversation with rancher Tully.

Gradually his dizziness passed. But the menacing fear continued to haunt him. He wanted proof. *Needed* proof. Something to convince him they were wrong. Some finding that would refute what they'd discovered with the bones. He moved unhurriedly, head down, searching the mucky ground for tracks or droppings.

He debated the issue in his head, trying to convince himself it wasn't Tyrannosaurus Rexes that had caused this mayhem and destruction. However, every angle he pursued pointed that way.

T-Rex was one of the only Cretaceous carnivores known to hunt in groups.

T-Rex—including juvenile tyrant lizards—possessed insatiable appetites capable of consuming fifty head of cattle overnight.

The gnawed bones indicated T-Rex feeding behavior.

It all added up.

Except for the fact it would have taken great numbers of them.

Would two meteorites produce that many hatchlings? If so, where are they? Why just the one feeding frenzy? Why leave two other pastures of cattle behind?

Some news media types suggested what happened here was due to some kind of supernatural event, something akin to a Bermuda Triangle disappearance. Others cried alien invasion cow snatching.

Hayden didn't buy into the paranormal stuff or the little gray beings from another universe with cattle napping on their minds. He believed in science. Cold, hard facts. Logic.

There's nothing logical about this. Fifty to sixty head of cattle devoured with no sign of the killers? Where are they, Fowler?

He'd meandered fifteen yards when he found a ghosting of prints in the baked earth leading to a wide sweep of wheatgrass. Carefully—for he didn't know what might lurk within—he pulled the curtain of prairie grass aside. Etched into the mud was a jumble of well-preserved tracks running every which way. Their distinctiveness gave him pause. Each footprint was clearly defined, showing three splayed toes out front with a rear claw behind the heel.

Juvenile theropods.

The tracks were small but deep, indicating some weight. The depth of the prints told him these theropods were heavier than the Gilliam hatchlings. Dromaeosaurs had hollowed-out bones that gave them speed and mobility. They were lighter and more agile than T-Rex. The appearance of the rear claw meant they were newborns, not yet coordinated enough to lift the rear claw when walking and running. Every fossilized track he'd seen of adult theropods was absent the trailing claw. He knew it took time for young theropods to learn to keep the deadly claw raised when walking or running, and to relegate use of it only for its intended purpose—hooking and eviscerating their prey.

"You find something, Hayden?"

Nora's voice pulled him out of his musings.

"Yeah. Come take a look."

He peeled back the curtain of wheatgrass to give her a view.

"Theropods," she said. "Youngsters, judging by the trailing claw. But old enough that they're bipedal," she said, meaning they walked upright on their back legs.

Hayden kneeled, ran a finger along the ridge of one of the prints. "They're bigger than our Dromaeosaurs. Heavier. See the depth?"

"Yes."

"Are we on the same page about this, Nora?"

She paused, casting a nervous glance at Tully before answering.

"Yes, I believe we are."

"What? What is it?" Tully asked, joining them.

Hayden stood, his eyes sweeping the pasture as he said to Tully, "Do you have a water source on your property?"

"Yessir. Got a well out in the north pasture."

"No, I mean an *open* water source. Like a pond or a lake."

"Well, yeah. Got a creek that runs between my land and Rich Thaxton's ranch."

"Is it a good size or just a trickle?"

"Oh, Thurston Creek's plenty big. It's wide in some spots, deep in others. Great trout fishin' in most of it. Why're you asking?"

"Because the creatures that did this need water. It's a longshot, I know, since it's been what? Three days since the ambush?"

"Yessir," Tully said, throwing his arm out and checking his wristwatch. "Um . . . eighty-four hours to be exact."

"Is this creek accessible?"

"Most of it is, yeah."

"Take us there."

They returned to the Jeep and Tully drove them down a rutted dirt road. They jounced and bumped, holding on as the rancher swerved to miss gaping potholes. Along the way they passed a sprawling field where Black Angus grazed. Two men wearing cowboy hats and sunglasses cradled rifles. Tully gave them a thumbs-up as they passed, and the men waved at them.

Hayden yelled out to Tully over the rushing wind and groaning engine. "They protecting your investment?"

"Yeah. Two of my hired hands. Been with me a long time. Really good men, both of 'em. Got two more watchin' my Charolais stock."

Could be why there wasn't a second attack here, Hayden thought, reasoning that Tyrannosaurus Rex was a crafty, cautious predator. Even the juveniles would instinctively sense danger in humans with long guns. Tyrannosaurus Rex survived for more than three million years. They didn't last that long by being careless and stupid.

Tully drove through low, flat grasslands, the ride jarring and uncomfortable.

"How much land do you have here, Mr. Tully?" Nora yelled over the road noise.

"Two-thousand acres. More'n fifty years my family's ranched this land. We had a lot more livestock back when my father ran the show, God bless his soul. He was a better rancher than me."

"You plannin' to replace your lost Herefords?" Hayden asked.

"Not if that ripoff insurance company doesn't pay out. I'm seriously considering sellin' the place anyway. My wife passed last year and I ain't gettin' any younger. Ranchin's a young person's work. I love this land, but things are tellin' me it might be time to move on. I've got a daughter in Great Falls . . . three grandkids. Hell, I don't know."

Tully drove over a slight rise, then down into a dale that brought Thurston Creek into view. They rode to the creek and followed it, Hayden thinking it much bigger and wilder than what he would call a creek. A river tributary maybe? Whitewater rushed over smooth stones and fed swirling whirlpools. The stream cut a wide path, as much as thirty yards across in some places. A curtain of tall cotton-woods lined the far bank on what Tully said was his neighbor's land.

Hayden thought those trees might be an ideal refuge for T-Rex hatchlings. Eighty-plus hours since the feeding? Could it be that young Cretaceous carnivores remained dormant for a period of time after gorging themselves? Would they take time to digest their quarry? He knew that large reptiles, like crocodiles and boa con-strictors, could devour a huge meal such as a fully-grown deer and not eat again for days, or even weeks. Pythons were known to consume a warren of rabbits and then lay low for days before their next meal. He'd studied enough zoology to know carnivorous reptiles possessed short guts to efficiently break down meat, and that they were much slower than mammals at digesting food. But did that apply to Cretaceous theropods? Would neonate T-Rexes behave the same? The Dromaeosaurs at Gilliam's Guidepost seemed to be constantly hungry. But they were being fed in cap-tivity. Perhaps infant theropods behaved differently in the wild.

They came to a narrowing in the creek. Upstream, a large

beaver dam redirected the water flow. Hayden instructed Tully to stop. The three of them got out and walked along the bank. The heat was oppressive, the warm breeze doing little to quell Hayden's discomfort. Sweat soaked his shirt. His beard itched.

They came upon a trail of tracks running along the waterline. Dozens of the three-splayed-toes-with-trailing-claw prints.

They've been here! My hunch was right!

He followed the tracks, Nora and Tully close behind, all three commenting on the multitude of footprints leading up the creek bank to the beaver dam. The water was shallow and more placid here. From where he stood, Hayden couldn't see any activity around the dam. He wanted to get a look behind the dam, inside the beaver lodge. He knew he had to exercise caution when approaching the crude construction of small logs, sticks, rocks, and mud.

He stepped in, wading nimbly through shin-deep water, carefully negotiating the smooth stones underfoot, using his outstretched arms to maintain his balance. The coolness felt good against his calves and he stopped, bent down, scooped a handful of water and splashed his face with it. *Sweet relief!*

He legged his way through the water, Nora yelling out for him to be careful. He came to the elevated front edge of the beaver mound and peered over the top, almost expecting what he saw.

A half dozen or more beaver remains floated in the lodge pool.

Their large chisel-like front teeth protruded from skulls that had been stripped clean. Chunks of furred pelts clung to their skeletal frames. Bloody intestines floated in the calm pool.

Something in the water bumped against Hayden's left shin.

Alarmed, he jumped back with a splash.

He looked down upon a drowned dinosaur floating on its back, dead eyes staring up at him.

A Tyrannosaurus Rex juvenile. Approximately three feet long with a bloated belly. Oversized, wide teeth.

He scooped it out of the water, surprised at its weight and the rough texture of its scaly hide.

He held it up for Nora and Tully to see. "We have our proof," he yelled to them over the swishing rush of the burbling brook.

Feeding Time

June 12: Gilliam's Guidepost
Heart Butte, Montana

BRYAN GILLIAM SAT AT THE KITCHEN TABLE eating supper. He chewed his steak slowly, listening to his two sons argue about who was the best baseball player. It was standard dinner table dialogue in the Gilliam household this time of year.

Ethan, fourteen, proclaimed proudly, "We had our first scrimmage game today and I got three hits. Two doubles and a single." He nodded at older brother Paul. "Pauley Poo struck out three times. He swings like a girl."

Paul sneered at his younger brother. "Yeah, well at least I know how to play the field." He turned to Bryan. "Ethan doesn't mention he made three errors that cost us the game. I think he needs a new glove, Dad."

"Up yours, Mister Whiffer," Ethan retorted. "You're just mad cuz coach bats me leadoff. He puts you at the bottom of the lineup where all the guys who can't hit go."

"Oh yeah? That's rich coming from you, Mister Hole-In-Your-Glove! We're never gonna win anything with you at shortstop. Craig Berry ran a marathon in left field chasin' down all the balls you missed."

"Well, maybe if you worked on hittin' a curveball you'd reach first base once in a while."

"All right, that's quite enough, you two," Loretta said. "You should be supporting each other. That's what brothers are supposed to do."

"Yes," Bryan agreed. "That's what good *teammates* do."

Bryan knew all too well that brothers were wired to fight. He saw it as sibling rivalry peppered with pubescent machismo. Loretta didn't understand their sons' macho posturing the way he did. Bryan and his older brother, Bobby, really went at each other when they were kids growing up in Lubbock, Texas. Bobby was gone now, lost to lymphatic cancer twelve years ago. Bryan missed him to this day.

Paul and Ethan played on the same American Legion team, and this one-upmanship went on regularly at the kitchen table. Bryan was grateful for American Legion ball since Montana was one of just three states that did not offer public school baseball. American Legion was a big next-step-up from Little League, where both boys had shined. Ethan was a natural born hitter with a good eye and sweet swing, while older brother Paul, sixteen, was the slick fielder, possessing speed, sure hands, and quick reflexes. One brother's strength was the other's weakness. Baseball had been Bryan's game growing up in Texas, and he was happy both his sons had taken to the sport. It instilled in them self-confidence and the competitiveness they would need later in life.

"Well, the season might not happen, Dad," Paul mumbled through cheeks bulging with food.

"Don't talk with your mouth full," Loretta said. "I'm not in the mood to perform the Heimlich maneuver on you tonight."

"Jesus, Mom!" Paul dramatically spit out a glob of ribeye on his plate.

"Eww!" Lianne yelped from her corner of the table. "That's gross!"

"Yeah, that *is* icky," Loretta said. "Watch your manners, son."

Bryan said to Paul, "Why might the season not happen?"

"There's rumors they might call it off because of the meteorites and those weird reptiles. The guys on the team are freaked about it and I know the coaches are, too."

Lianne whined, "Why do we always hafta talk about stinky old baseball? It's *so* boring."

Bryan held up his hand. "Wait a minute, Lee." He swallowed and patted his mouth with the napkin, then said to Paul, "You haven't talked to anyone about our meteorite have you? Nothing about those creatures out in the barn?"

"Coach Watson asked me an' Ethan tons of questions today. Coach Pelletier, too. We didn't tell 'em anything. At least I didn't. You should ask Ethan. He can't keep secrets for shit."

"Hey," Loretta said. "Watch the trash mouth, Pauley."

Ethan's tone was defensive. "You *know* I didn't say anything. I was too busy gettin' hits and scorin' runs."

"Whatever," Paul said, rolling his eyes and turning to Bryan. "I don't know why you keep denying it, Dad. I mean, come on. We're national news. A lotta people already know about what we have in our barn. That big scientist with the beard—Dr. Fowler?—he told us it would be impossible to keep somethin' like this secret."

"I think your father is aware of that," Loretta interjected. "He's just trying to protect the family . . . trying to preserve our privacy."

"Privacy?" Paul said with a sarcastic snort. "Our privacy ended the day that exterminator dude showed up. We unplugged our land-line because of all the phone calls. The traffic has picked up on Badger Creek Road like I've never seen. Tons of strangers are showin' up, so we've got armed guards at the front entrance. There's no such thing as privacy around here anymore."

"I know that, son," Bryan said. "I'm just trying to keep a lid on it. Something outrageously bizarre like this happens, it brings all the kooks out. We've got enough problems as it is."

"I think it's all pretty cool, myself," Ethan said, prideful. "Somethin' interesting finally happenin' around this dull, one-horse town. Think about it. Tiny ol' Heart Butte bein' talked about on TV. And our place bein' mentioned. How awesome is that?"

Bryan thought it was anything but awesome.

Lianne raised her voice. "I miss my Bobo! I wanna ride my Beauregard again! I want my horses back! I wanna go outside again! It's so boring stayin' in this stupid house all the time."

Loretta reached over and placed her hand on her daughter's. Said calmly, "Now, Lee, you know you're being punished. Even if we had the horses here, you wouldn't be able to ride Beauregard. You know that, right?"

"No! It's not fair! I want my horses back."

Bryan said, "The horses—*your* horses—are much safer at your cousin Marnie's. The Enrights are taking good care of them. And even if you weren't bein' punished, we'd probably still keep you indoors to keep you safe. Until this mess is over."

Lianne persisted. "No fair! Ethan and Paul get to play their stupid baseball and do stuff outside."

"That's because they're grown up, Lee," Loretta intoned. "They're more responsible."

"But I'm re-resp—" she stammered. "I'm grown up, too!"

Bryan could see his daughter working up to one of her loud hissy fits. "You're *not* grown up, Lee," he said sternly. "You did something that upset your mother and me. Something we told you explicitly not to do. Besides, you have a couple stitches in your leg that don't come out for a few more days. We don't want you out runnin' around where you can break that wound open again."

Lianne slammed her fork onto her plate with a clank. Sat back with her arms folded across her chest and thrust her lower lip out in a pout.

Loretta pointed her finger at her. "You sit up and finish your supper, young lady."

"NO!"

"Lianne Grayson Gilliam," Loretta's voice rose, "You finish your steak and green beans quietly or you won't get any dessert. No clean plate means no ice cream."

"NO!"

"I'll tack on another week of indoor grounding."

Ethan got into the act. "Oh boy, little Lee-lee's in the doghouse again," he said in a singsong cadence.

Lianne's eyes darkened in anger. "Shut up, Ethan! You're not so great. I hate you!" She flipped her napkin at him and scooted her chair back from the table snappishly. Stood, eyes on Loretta, and shouted, "I hate all of you!" then burst into tears and ran off to her bedroom.

After an awkward silence, Ethan said, "Well *that* was special."

Bryan shot a look of annoyance at Ethan. "You should know better than to antagonize your sister."

"*What*? I didn't say anything bad to her."

"Lee's goin' through some, uh . . . some *stuff* right now. We all are." Bryan's eyes searched his sons' faces. "Your sister can't take ribbing the way you guys can. You know that."

Ethan looked at his brother and shook his head. "*Girls,*" he said with distaste. "What good are they?"

"I know, right?" Paul said.

"I'll go check on her," Loretta said, getting up from the table and taking her plate to the sink before disappearing down the hall.

The Gilliam men resumed their meals in silence, heads down, knives and forks scraping plates. While he finished his steak, Bryan thought about this crazy situation in which he and his family found themselves. A mere ten days ago their routine lives were upended when a meteorite the size of a compact car came down in the east meadow. And shock of all shocks, the extraterrestrial boulder contained nests of eggs, many of which hatched out aggressive lizard creatures. That out-of-the-blue development caught the interest of the scientific community, and brought a visit from paleontologists working an expedition an hour south of them in Choteau.

The four scientists from the Smithsonian dig—Doctors Hayden Fowler, Nora Lemoyne, Gregory Dulowski, and Franz Krause— had booked individual rooms here at Gilliam's Guidepost Inn. They were captivated by—and obsessed with—the creature Bryan was keeping in the dog crate, the one the exterminator, Joe Creek, had snagged with his snake stick a week ago. Following that, the day after the scientists arrived, the chicken incubator in the barn hatched out all five of the intact eggs Bryan and Loretta had collected from the meteorite. To house the newborn lizards, Bryan and Jimmy Enright made the hour drive to the Big Sky Aquariums and Pet Supply in Cut Bank to pick up a half dozen glass fish tanks.

Bryan thought about the education he'd received in the utility barn after the eggs hatched out. He recalled paleozoologist Franz Krause's clipped German accent. "These little guys are the same as the animal you have in the dog crate. They are Dromaeosaurs, as we discussed, a close relative of the Velociraptor."

Bryan had spoken up, telling the scientists he knew about Velociraptors from the *Jurassic Park* movies, which brought a hardy laugh from the big scientist, Hayden Fowler.

"The *Jurassic Park* books and movies got a lot of things wrong about Velociraptors, Bryan," Fowler explained. "First of all, Velociraptors lived in the Late Cretaceous, not the Jurassic. Nor did they feed their young or hunt in packs. Much of that was pure Michael Crichton imagination and Hollywood bullshit."

The woman scientist, Nora Lemoyne, agreed. "Hayden is right. The raptors in the books and movies were actually Deinonychus, a much larger dinosaur that inhabited North America in the Early Cretaceous Period, around a hundred-and-twenty-five million years ago. They were the terrifying, scaly dinos of movie fame that hunted in packs and used their sickle-shaped claws to disembowel their prey. Velociraptors were smaller—about the size of a wolf—and had feathery plumage rather than scaled hides. They roamed eastern and central Asia around seventy million years ago, in the *Late* Cretaceous. Again they were *not* around during the Jurassic. They evolved from the fierce Deinonychus over the millennia, but it is thought that they were solo hunters and used their sickle claws more as a grabbing device than as a disemboweling tool."

Franz Krause continued the discussion, pointing over the rim of the dog crate at the amped-up creature throwing itself against the wire walls, and the smaller hatchlings scurrying around in the aquarium tanks. "Our harried little friends here will be larger than the Velociraptor. Quicker and more agile. Pound for pound, they will be more fierce than their grandfather genus, Deinonychus. Dromaeosaurus translates to *Swift Running Lizard* in paleo-speak. Fully grown, these little guys will be around sixty pounds and able to run forty miles an hour. As Hayden already pointed out, they'll be capable of leaping like a kangaroo—maybe five to ten feet vertical clearance."

Franz Krause continued. "You can see their hind legs are much more developed than their forelegs—fore*arms,* if you will. Bipedal creatures. It won't be long before they start walking upright, on their hind legs. If they get enough to eat, by late summer they'll grow to six feet in length and stand three feet tall."

Hayden Fowler said, "These guys won't grow anywhere as large as the better known, larger theropods such as Tyrannosaurus Rex. T-Rex also inhabited this part of the world in their time. But mature Dromaeosaurs were every bit as ferocious. Think of them as big track-star kangaroos with teeth and jaws like sharks."

Unbelievable that he, Bryan Gilliam, a 42-year-old mechanic and overseer of a modest Montana ranch, should be dealing with things like meteorites and prehistoric carnivores.

How is any of this even possible? I feel like I'm living in a warped dream.

And now they had six Dromaeosaurs in the barn—the five new hatchlings in the aquarium tanks and the bigger one in the steel dog crate. Yesterday, Nora Lemoyne reimbursed Bryan for the tanks and his gas, but cautioned him that the half dozen Dromaeosaurs would soon outgrow their captive habitats.

"You're going to need larger enclosures for these little guys very soon," she'd said. "Cretaceous carnivores were known to have high metabolisms. They can consume up to four times their weight in meat each day."

Bryan already knew the Dromaeosaur Joe Creek the exterminator had nabbed loved raw hamburger, but the scientists wanted to experiment with the five hatchlings. The hungry creatures gobbled down everything they threw at them. Hayden Fowler started with slices of bologna, which they finished off like nothing more than unfulfilling appetizers. Next he tried minnows purchased by the gallon at Horn Lake Bait and Tackle. But soon the scientists realized Bryan's original choice of Dromaeosaur diet—raw hamburger— was the best choice for the Dromaeosaur newborns. Loretta made two trips to Heart Butte Trading Post to buy out their supply of fresh ground beef. Soon, they'd have to make a longer trip—possibly to Browning or Dupuyer—to find more meat to sustain the baby carnivores.

Bryan recalled watching the creatures devour the thick patties of raw hamburger and worried.

They'll eat four times their weight each day? And they'll need new cages?

Bryan did the math in his head and fretted over the price tag. *We certainly can't afford this.*

As if reading his thoughts, Nora Lemoyne said, "Don't worry about the cost, Mr. Gilliam. Our sponsor will cover it."

"The Smithsonian will pay for it?" he'd said, hoping he hadn't heard wrong. "All of it?"

"Yes, absolutely," Nora said, nodding. "Having an exclusive on this historic event is a windfall for the Smithsonian Institution. Think about it. It's a motherlode of prehistory come to life. Cost is no object for something extraordinary like this. I've already spoken with them and they agreed to foot the bill, provided you give them total access."

"No problem there. I'll welcome them with open arms."

Bryan finished his meal and noticed Paul and Ethan had served themselves dessert while he had been lost in thought. He watched them shovel spoonfuls of chocolate ice cream into their mouths, smacking their lips loudly.

He smiled. *They eat like a couple of growing Dromaeosaurs.*

He wiped his mouth with his napkin, stood, took his plate and glass to the dishwasher. "You guys better slow down," he said over his shoulder. "You'll get the dreaded ice cream freeze-brain head-ache."

"That's the kind of headache we like," Ethan said between swallows.

Bryan checked his watch. Dinosaur feeding time. He went to the refrigerator and pulled out three two-pound slabs of ground beef, preparing to go meet Greg Dulowski and Franz Krause in the barn. The other two scientists, Hayden Fowler and Nora Lemoyne, had gone to Greenfield this morning to investigate the possibility of additional dinosaur hatchouts at the Tully ranch. When Bryan heard about the large number of cattle that had been decimated there, he thanked his lucky stars he and Loretta had given up their livestock years ago.

He checked his watch again. Doctors Fowler and Lemoyne were due back an hour ago. There'd been no communication from them all day, and he wondered what they'd discovered, if anything.

"Time to feed the babies," he said to the boys. "Either of you care to join me?"

"Not me," Paul said. "Those things creep me out."

"I'll go with you, Dad," Ethan said brightly. "Just give me a minute to finish."

"Kiss ass!" Paul said to his brother.

"Chickenshit!" Ethan responded.

"*Language*, boys," Bryan admonished. He set the packs of refrigerated beef on the table next to Ethan. "Here, you take the dino food while I get my rifle."

Curiously there had been no sign of stray creatures from the initial meteorite hatchout. Still, Bryan needed the assurance of a firearm on his walks to and from the utility barn.

One couldn't be too safe these days.

He'd learned that Dromaeosaurs had insatiable appetites and could run like the wind.

Big track-star kangaroos with teeth and jaws like sharks. That's what the bearded paleontologist Fowler had called them.

Christ almighty!

What kind of hell is this?

Breaking News

June 15: The Lacroix Residence
Missoula, Montana

BRINSHOU STABBED THE REMOTE, shutting off the TV. She'd had enough of her afternoon soaps being interrupted by breaking news. Frustrated, she tossed the remote on the coffee table and flopped back into the nest of throw pillows piled on the living room sofa. Since Peter left for Idaho, she'd become a couch potato, lost in a hazy, lonely depression, her world shrinking to the confines of the sofa and the flat-screen television mounted on the wall. Only bathroom breaks, meals, and Kimi's needs pulled her away.

She stared at the dark TV screen, wondering: *Is the situation really as grim as TV news makes it out to be?*

Every newscast painted a hopeless picture of unending despair. Reptilian meteorite creatures, that's the term used by most media outlets. The beasts were everywhere, running rampant, gobbling up all living things in their destructive paths. Every report was delivered with an ominous edge. Reporters focused on the death and mutilation of farm animals. The coverage was graphic, almost gleeful, each story more lurid and shocking than the one before it. TV journalists seemed to be participating in a twisted ratings competition, trying to outdo one another, seeing who could present the most alarming account.

Yes, this meteorite thing was definitely big news. But enough was enough already. Brin didn't need to be bashed over the head with it every ten minutes. They didn't need to cut in on her shows.

The constant barrage of dark images and sounds worked on her like a nauseating virus.

The news reporting reminded her of the children's folk tale of

Henny Penny—better known as Chicken Little—who, when an acorn falls on her head, claims "The sky is falling!" believing that the world is coming to an end.

Before Peter left, he told her it would be best to leave the TV turned off. For her own good, he'd said. But she hadn't done that. She wanted—*needed*—to know what was going on in the outside world. She wished now that she'd followed her husband's advice.

The reports had intensified the past few days. Updates came in fast and furious from around the two-state area. Some channels stayed with it 24/7, preempting regular programming. Three new attacks on livestock had been reported, with 120 head of cattle slaughtered. Ranches had been raided, with dozens of horses killed, their cadavers stripped clean. Farmers reported assaults on their chicken coops and hog pens, the structures demolished and the animals overwhelmed. Yesterday, a sheep farmer in Idaho lost 23 rams and 18 ewes. A Montana farmer, who had 22 of his goats ripped limb-from-limb and devoured, said: "I've never witnessed anything like it . . . like somethin' risin' up outta the depths of hell."

Most of the attacks had taken place at night, so little video evidence existed of the actual raids. Distraught farmers and ranchers recounted in explicit detail what they'd seen and heard. Scenes of devastation and death played over and over in clips showing mangled holding pens and flattened horse stalls and bloody bones and heaps of steamy, half-eaten guts. No human casualties were reported, but that didn't stop the populace from freaking out. The last report Brin saw showed the governors of Montana and Idaho discussing the possibility of activating the national guard.

The world was in pandemonium over this invasion of extra-terrestrial killer reptiles. Local and national networks couldn't get enough. They ate it up and regurgitated it to the public in overly sensationalized, gruesome segments.

Brin thought about her beloved Petey, out there, flying over remote areas where these egg-bearing meteorites had come down. He could very well come in contact with those killing creatures.

Dinosaurs in this day and age? How is that even possible? The whole world has gone mad!

She felt like they were living in one of those monster movies, the ones featuring Godzilla or King Kong. Or maybe *Planet of the Apes* . . . Possibly *Jurassic Park* after the dinosaurs escaped.

Crazy times.

Brin's vivid imagination was her worst enemy. She'd dredged up a nightmarish litany of disasters that could befall her husband. She couldn't help it; she'd always been that way. The world was a perilous place and, more often than not, she expected the worst possible outcome.

Peter did his best to assure her that he was safe. He wasn't involved with on-the-ground pickups, he'd told her. Guardsmen did the groundwork and he remained in the cockpit at all times. The closest he'd come to the ground would be operating the cargo winch longline from inside the chopper. She didn't completely believe him. She loved Peter without question, but he had a habit of sugar-coating things, omitting certain details or stretching the truth to keep her from worrying. She supposed that made her love him even more, protecting her from herself. But there were times when she wanted direct honesty from him, and this was one of those times.

However, even if he was being completely truthful with her, she knew some event occurring outside Petey's control could force him out of the helicopter. What if the air guardsmen were attacked by marauding dinosaurs? He'd have to descend to rescue them, wouldn't he? Or what if, God forbid, his helicopter malfunctioned and they had to make an emergency landing in some remote area, cut off from civilization and surrounded by flesh-eating dinosaurs? What if he crashed and was gravely wounded? Or possibly killed?

Brin knew her husband to be a skilled, experienced pilot; he wouldn't have been selected for this task force if he wasn't one of the best. But she also knew the dangers of helicopters. Choppers weren't the most flightworthy of aircraft. She'd read up on heli-copter safety, and knew the accident statistics for low altitude flying did not paint a positive picture. Add heavy cargo lifting in moun-tainous terrain to the mix and the chances of a helicopter accident tripled. Very dangerous work, Brin knew. It was not *if* a helicopter crash would occur, but *when*. Of course, she'd worried about him every day for the past four years when he left the house and flew his daily routes. But her worries were much greater now that he was in the air with meteorites bombing the countryside and dinosaurs roaming the forests below.

So many what-if scenarios leading to bad ends. She had lounged on the couch these past four days, baby monitor close at hand, her apprehensions and agitated imagination crippling her. She slept out here, catching short winks when exhaustion grabbed her and pulled her down. No way could she sleep in their bed. She tried the first night Peter was gone, lasting only twenty minutes. She'd tossed and turned, finding their king bed too big, too cold, too lonely, his scent wafting from the sheets reminding her how much she missed him.

Peter's absence affected Brin in other ways as well. She hadn't touched her jewelry projects in almost a week. Two overdue custom orders sat half-finished on her work table in the spare bedroom: a First Nations engraved sterling silver bracelet and a hand-beaded medallion necklace-and-earring set. Both would bring in good money, which she knew they needed. But she just couldn't motivate herself to work on them.

Things just aren't the same without Petey around.

Fortunately, she had been able to FaceTime with him. That had been her lifeline the past four days. Had it really only been four days? It felt like four *weeks*!

Peter told her yesterday that she should get out of the house for a while. Maybe take Kimi to the reservation to see her mother. Certainly Kachina would love to see her granddaughter. Brin didn't want to let him know she was afraid to go outside, let alone make the hour-and-a-half drive north to the Flathead reservation with a colicky baby.

Brin's thoughts turned to her parents. Her father, Nashota, made a good living working at the Polson resort and casino on the rez. He came from a long line of proud Salish bison hunters and warriors, and maintained a stubborn connection to many of the old tribal ways. His adherence to indigenous principles wouldn't allow him to accept Peter, about whom he'd said more than once: "This Canuck flyboy kidnapped my daughter off the rez and taught her the ways of American white women." Pure nonsense, of course, but Nash's old school, racist attitude had driven a wedge between Brin and him. Her mother, Kachina, a quiet woman of Kootenai heritage, loved Nash in spite of his obvious flaws, and maintained a quiet subservience when he went into one of his opinionated tirades.

Brinshou loved her mother dearly, and her mother had always reciprocated that love. Mother and daughter had long enjoyed a solid relationship, built on mutual trust and respect. But they had drifted apart over the past four years, ever since Brin married Peter and moved to Missoula. Nash's standoffish snub of Peter had short-circuited Brin and Kachina's close connection. Brin had never seen her father's ugly bigoted side until Peter came into her life. As a little girl, she'd idolized Nash, and even as a teenager never dreamed her father could be so openly hateful. But she now realized that her youthful naivety and life on the Flathead reservation had insulated her from many family realities. As an adult she was able to better see her father's flaws. Her mother's, too. Brin wished she had the courage to tell Kachina to stand up to Nash once in a while. Especially when it came to Peter and baby Kimi, whom Nash thought looked too much like Peter, and was therefore "too pale."

This clash made visits difficult for Brin. Nash's presence made get-togethers tense. Brin still called her mother regularly and they had pleasant, if not superficial, conversations. But her father was always the proverbial elephant in the room. Peter never talked about Nash, never mentioned the man or anything about their differences, for which Brin was grateful. But the fact Peter hadn't accompanied her to the rez since well before Brin's pregnancy told the tale. The last meeting between Peter and her father had been three years ago. It didn't go well, ending with Nash berating Peter for his "white privilege arrogance." Brin wished for more harmony in her family, but her most ardent wishes hadn't made it happen.

Peter's family was different. His parents—Pierre and Janine—were newly retired in Phoenix, and had taken to Brin immediately, inviting her into the Lacroix fold as if she was one of their own. Peter's older sister, Celeste, lived in Quebec and worked as a court stenographer. Though Brin had met her just once, they were close and corresponded regularly. Brin considered Celeste the sister she never had and always wanted.

Her iPad buzzed, startling her. She saw it was Peter on FaceTime, and picked it up, angled it so he could see her.

"Petey!" she said with glee. Her husband's face filled the small screen. "You're calling early today."

"Hi, lovely lady. Yeah, finished up about twenty minutes ago. How's everything on the home front?"

"Okay, I guess." Brin thought he looked tired, then wondered how she must look to him. "I miss you so much, hon."

"Me, too," he said, smiling. "How's our little munchkin doing?"

"Kimi's been a little gassy. She's not getting enough sleep. She misses you. Almost as much as I do."

"I miss her, too. So much."

"Are you okay, Petey? Are you eating right?"

"The food here isn't great. Doesn't compare with your delicious cooking, that's for sure."

"You're so sweet. How's Colonel Prick been treating you guys?" she said, chuckling at the pet name Peter had given the base commander.

Peter laughed along with her. "Uncle Thaddeus is as ornery as ever. He's grounded Curtis and Bart without pay for three days over some unexplained transgression. We were already behind schedule. This'll put us further behind. Curtis Williams and the Glick monster never really hit it off."

"Behind schedule? How far behind?"

She saw Peter scratch his chin, pausing before saying, "Well, we've only rounded up two meteorites the first three days . . . I should say *pieces* of two of the stones. Supposed to have brought in five by now, according to the Pentagon's timetable. It's stupid, Brin. Bureaucrats are sittin' in cubicles in D.C. estimating how long it should take us to do this work. I bet none of 'em have ever been west of the Mississippi."

"That's outrageous. This whole thing is absurd."

"Tell me about it. We might could be moving faster if the Air Force provided us with accurate meteorite locations. Took us all day to find the meteorite sections we picked up today. Their coordinates were off by more than seven miles. We flew around in circles for hours."

"You see any of those dinosaurs yet?"

"No. We picked up some broken eggshells and saw the goop on the rocks, dried to a hard crust. That's the extent of the excitement so far. It's been pretty routine and boring."

"Boring is good, Petey. Safer than excitement. Especially with what's been going on."

"You haven't been watching TV, have you, Brin?"

She could never lie to him. "Yes," she said hesitantly. "Just a little."

She saw him frown. "I told you—"

"I know, I *know*! I'm sorry. I just have to know what's goin' on. That's all."

Peter sighed, shook his head. "Okay, all right. Understood. Have you thought about what I told you? About taking Kimi to see your mother?"

"I don't think it would help. Not really. It might even make things worse right now."

"What about flying down to Phoenix? Stay with Mom and Dad for a while?"

"You know we can't afford that, Peter."

"We can now. We're making good money while I'm flyin' for this task force."

"Maybe so. But I can't be away from my jewelry business. This is making me *so* crazy, honey, bein' apart like this. I can't take this for another week. I'll go out of my gourd."

Peter looked away, as if something was happening offscreen. "Well, I'm afraid it's gonna be longer than another week, babe."

"*What*? How long?"

"I don't know. We're contracted to pick up fifteen meteorites. We've only picked up parts of two. There's a lot of work to be done. I'll know more in a couple of days. You should be happy it's bein' extended. It means more money in our bank account."

"There are things more important than money, Peter."

"I know *that*," he said, exasperation creeping into his voice. "Look, I'm being extra cautious out here. This is a safe operation, Brin. You know I'd never do anything to jeopardize what we have, and—"

"I know, but—"

The baby monitor erupted in caterwauling cries from Kimi's room.

"Ah, there's my girl," Peter said. "Could you put her on? I wanna see my little Kimi girl."

"Sure, just a sec," Brin said, annoyed at the timing.

She stood and picked up the iPad, took it to the baby's room. Held it up over the crib where Kimi could see her father. "There's your daddy, baby doll."

Kimi stopped crying and watched intently as Peter made goofy faces and muttered nonsensical baby talk to her. Kimi reached out to the iPad, giving Peter a big, heartwarming grin. She cooed happily for a few minutes as he continued his patter. When he stopped, she started her bawling again. Louder this time.

Brin turned the iPad towards her, said, "Like I said. She's been gassy."

As she listened to her daughter wail, Brin knew just how Kimi felt. No telling how long she'd have to wait on her beloved Petey to come home.

Her husband had delivered breaking news she could have done without.

Ghost Stories

June 19: Eastern Lewis and Clark National Forest
Little Belt Mountains, Montana

THE BOYS OF GREAT FALLS SCOUT TROOP 279 sat around the campfire eating chicken sausage sandwiches, franks-and-beans, canned corn, and trail mix. Towering trees—Engelmann spruce, Douglas fir, and lodgepole pine—surrounded the campsite like resolute sentries. The low-lying sun peeked through, casting cross-hatched shadows through the clearing. Cool breezes blew, surprising considering how sweltering the day had been. The canvas skins of the ridge tents flapped in the wind. Evening was descending; soon the campsite would be enveloped in darkness.

Scoutmaster Wayne Fahlman sat with assistant scoutmaster, Denny Miaway, watching the twelve- and thirteen-year-olds eat.

"Really good group this year," he said to Denny.

"Yeah, for sure. I just wish everyone could've made it. Our outings are getting smaller each summer."

Wayne nodded. Both scoutmasters accepted this year to be a special case. Only ten boys had made the trip. Seven stayed home, sons of parents worried about the meteorites and dinosaur invasion. Wayne told wary parents the boys needed fresh mountain air and planned activities to give them some structure through the summer months. The boys needed to get away from their video games and cell phones. They needed to exercise their growing bodies, he'd said. This was an opportunity to appreciate the natural world, to learn survival skills in the wild. It was also their one chance to earn their camping merit badge.

Wayne had given this year's campout plenty of thought. At first, he'd been concerned about the meteorite strikes. A very real concern, indeed. But he figured his troop would have a much greater chance of being struck by lightning than by a meteorite. Then came reports of dinosaur hatchouts and attacks on farms and ranches. That certainly gave him pause. However, there had been no reported attacks on humans. And the dinosaur sightings had been a good distance northwest of here. The closest meteorite had struck more than 70 miles away; the closest dinosaur attack, 40 miles. Wayne had gone back and forth on his decision, weighing the risks. He'd finally decided the threat was negligible.

The boys finished their supper. Denny handed out bags of marshmallows. The scouts speared them on sticks and toasted them over the open fire. Wayne watched them stuffing their mouths with charred marshmallows, thinking he and Denny had a good bunch this summer. Good kids, one and all. They were fairly well behaved considering they were in the grip of that confusing and awkward time of prepubescent adolescence, with male hormones raging and their heads full of confusing questions. Wayne's own son, Jason, had hair on his legs, the hint of a mustache, and a voice that seemed to get deeper each day. *Time is passing much too quickly*, he thought achingly.

Wayne was relieved there'd been no incidents over their four days here. He'd been uneasy when they arrived, struck by how deserted the campgrounds were. Usually in early summer, this area south of Neihart was hopping. But none of the neighboring campsites had been occupied. No one else had shown up to pitch a tent. No camper vans were parked in adjoining campsites. The isolation had concerned him. *Could the extreme daytime heat be keeping folks away?* But knew that wasn't it. People were afraid. They didn't want to be out in the wilderness with spotty cell phone service and little chance of medical assistance.

Wayne and his scout troop hadn't seen another human soul as they'd fished for brook trout in Belt Creek. They'd been alone hiking the Memorial Falls Trailhead into the steep-walled canyon, a place graced by two beautiful waterfalls that last year had attracted appreciative crowds. And there'd been no one at the quarry pond where the boys swam. Wayne found the isolation strange. But they hadn't even seen a deer, let alone a bear or dinosaur. So he felt blessed. His only problem at the moment was his aching body.

He said to Denny, "That hike today was brutal. I'm gettin' too old for four-mile slogs in the mountains."

"Yeah, I'm feelin' it, too. That heat was somethin' awful. Thought I was gonna die on that last trail."

They sat side by side on a moss-covered log, drinking coffee from tin cups and observing the scouts, who were now engaged in rowdy hijinks, throwing marshmallows and verbally challenging each other. A couple of boys grappled in the dirt, each trying their mightiest to prove their manhood.

"Oh to be that young again, eh?" Wayne said, a wistfulness in his voice.

"Yeah," Denny said. "If we could bottle that energy and sell it, we'd be Wall Street tycoons."

Denny saw his son, Martin, getting into a playful scrap with Damian Mackelroy. Saw it starting to get more heated. "Cut it out, Marty! You know the rules, son."

"But Damian started it, Dad."

"That doesn't mean you should *end* it."

Wayne laughed. "*Boys*," he said with a sigh, as if that should explain everything.

The scouts finished off the last of their marshmallows as the sun set behind Big Baldy Mountain. Wayne refilled his and Denny's cups with coffee and returned to his seat, handed Denny his coffee.

Denny thanked him, said, "Well, I think it's dark enough now, don't you?"

"Yep. It's showtime, partner. You got a good one for 'em?"

"Yeah, I've got a ghost story that should grab them."

Denny Miaway was a gifted, inventive storyteller. He headed up Story Hour once a week at Great Falls Public Library, where he charmed library patrons with his original tales. His campfire story-telling for the scouts held a decidedly different flavor from the tame fictions he presented to library audiences. Denny gave the boys what they wanted: scary, suspenseful, dark tales that captivated them.

Last night Denny told them about the fearful Mookie, a legendary Bigfoot-like beast that roamed the Montana forests, preying on unsuspecting hikers and campers. When Denny got started with the telling, Wayne thought it might be inappropriate, given the situation. The boys had all been exposed to the televised reports of death and destruction from dinosaur incidents. Kids were impressionable at this age, and Wayne didn't want to inflict any more on them emotionally than what they'd already been through. The first night here, his Jason, as well as several other scouts, had a difficult time getting to sleep. It had been a seemingly endless vigil, with Wayne and Denny standing guard, sitting close to the all-night campfire, sipping coffee, hunting rifles across their laps as the chilly night slowly passed. He'd thought the Mookie story Denny told last night might give them nightmares. But he'd been wrong. The boys ate it up, loving Denny's depiction of Mookie, with his authentic growls and creepy mannerisms bringing the woodsy monster to life. All day today the boys did their impressions of Mookie, trying to scare each other, but ultimately, making each other laugh at the absurdity of it.

And now Denny held the boys spellbound as he told them the story of *The Ghosts of Crow Mountain*. The firelight gleamed in his eyes and he spoke in low, unsettling tones, telling the tale of Crow Indian spirits haunting workers down in the gold mines of Crow Mountain. A hundred years ago, pillaging white settlers flocked to the mountain in a mad gold rush, running the Crow off their land and murdering any of the tribe who elected to stay and fight. Denny painted pictures with his theatrical performance. His descriptions of place were vivid, his sound effects eerie. The boys hung on every word as he told them of miners spooked by "ghostly apparitions that floated through the caves like spirals of smoke, with raven heads and buckskin tunics fringed with elk teeth, snake rattles, and porcupine quills." He told them of unmanned mining equipment running amok, firing up on their own and chasing screaming miners down long, narrow tunnels. He told of miners disappearing without a trace or being buried alive by possessed mechanical drillers and diggers. Denny's audience was mesmerized as he dramatized bizarre noises miners heard echoing through the tunnels, frightening them, driving them to the brink of madness.

Wayne scanned the circle of scouts as they listened. All were wide-eyed. Most stared openmouthed at Denny. A master yarn spinner had them under his spell.

Denny ended the story with a moral, for there was always a lesson to be learned from a Denny Miaway tale. The mining company, suffering many losses and facing lawsuits from miner families for unsafe working conditions, pulled their operations and fled the haunted mountain. The Crow people had regained their land.

The boys stomped and hollered and whistled their approval.

"That was really cool!" Jason Fahlman called out.

"Yeah, that was epic!" Damian Mackelroy shouted.

"Tons better'n the Mookie story, Dad," Marty Miaway said.

Denny took a theatrical bow as the boys continued to show their appreciation for his theatrical tale.

The scouts were worked up and excited. Wayne hated to crash their party, but he had to get them settled down and into their tents. He stood, stretched his legs, and said grudgingly, "Okay, guys. Time to hit the sleeping bags. We've got an early wakeup in the morning. Tomorrow's goin' home day. I don't wanna hear any music and no horsing around."

Amid a chorus of grumbles and a few cusswords, one by one the boys broke from the group, wandering out of the firelight and into the dark perimeter. Wayne watched them lollygag, taking their sweet time, listened to them complain about early bedtime as they aimlessly made their way to the tents. Scattered in the mix he could hear a few comments praising "Mr. Miaway's awesome ghost story."

Wayne patted Denny on the shoulder. "You really captured their imaginations tonight. I tell ya, my friend, Stephen King's got nothin' on you."

"Thanks, Wayne. But you're wrong about that. Steve's got about five-hundred-million dollars on me."

Wayne grinned and slapped his knees, imitating a drum rim-shot. "Touché."

"Well, I'm bushed," Denny said. "Think I'll join the boys and turn in myself. Another long day tomorrow. You stayin' up?"

"Yeah, for a while. Think I'll grab another cup of java and my rifle . . . keep watch 'til the fire burns down."

"We'll be okay. You worry too much, Wayne."

"Don't I know it. I'm worried 'bout those Crow spirits gettin' after me, partner."

"Sweet dreams," Denny said laughingly as he walked away, disappearing between the rows of tents.

Wayne went to his minivan to get his gun, the night mountain air a cool whisper against his cheeks. He propped the gun—his Ruger M77 Magnum he used for deer hunting—against a tree. He always brought the rifle on scouting trips to scare off curious bears or mountain lions. It had come in handy a few years back when his troop encountered a hungry grizzly scavenging for campsite food.

He filled his cup with the last of the coffee. Dumped in two packets of sugar and stirred with a plastic spoon. Returned to his seat on the log near the warmth of the fire. The tin of hot coffee warmed his hands. He breathed in the cool air. The sweet, perfumed pine-woodsy scent blended with the musky campfire smoke, reminding him of the holidays, when he and Joyce and the kids decorated the fresh-cut Christmas tree in the corner of their living room with the yule logs burning in the fireplace.

He sipped his sweet coffee and stared into the flames. Listened to the hiss and crackle of the fire, the swish of the breeze blowing through the treetops. The low murmurs from the tents had died down.

The night was quiet, peaceful.

He tried to get comfortable, but couldn't. Too on edge tonight. They'd made it through three nights without incident, but this return of the dinosaurs still had him a bit nervy. All the attacks on farm animals thus far had occurred after sundown. He knew it was only his head playing games with him, but he still found it daunting. Ever since he was a young scout himself, he loved being out here, camping under the wide, starry sky. But he had to admit, communing with nature was a bit more stressful this trip.

A muffled cry from deep in the woods cut through the silence. Wayne recognized it as the warble of a great horned owl.

He heard high-pitched squeaks overhead, and looked up in time to see a couple of bats swooping low, going after mosquitos, a flash of their webbed wings visible in the firelight.

Silence returned. He finished his coffee, thinking of his family back home. After a time, he yawned and stretched, feeling soreness from the day's activities in his shoulders and legs. He stood, groaning with the effort. Time to turn in.

He was about to douse the fire when he heard a scrabbling sound in the woods near the tents.

He stopped. Remained still. Listened, his senses on alert.

Heard it again. A shuffling across the forest floor.

He grabbed his rifle. Looked to the edge of the woods.

His heart pounded in his throat, thumped in his chest.

The flickering firelight created wavy shadows.

He tried to focus.

The brush moved. Something was in there.

Whatever it was moved again. Heavy footfalls crashed through the thicket, then halted.

Silence.

His adrenaline surged.

His heart galloped. He trained his rifle on the area, unsure whether to shoot.

Another quick movement followed by a guttural growling.

Then silence.

Oh please, God, no! Jesus help us! Ohplease,Godno!

He had visions of being overrun by those Tyrannosaurs he'd heard about.

His hands were shaky on the rifle.

Slowly, eyes never leaving the woods, he backed around the campfire, putting the fire between himself and the noises coming out of the forest.

A shriek—the cry of a badly wounded animal—pierced the night.

Wayne felt the fear all the way down to his testicles.

A vicious growl.

Another animal shriek.

He raised the barrel of his Ruger skyward. He heard laughter coming from the tents.

He pulled the trigger. A deafening explosion. Twigs and pine needles rained down.

A tomblike silence cast a pall over the camp for a long ten seconds. Then Damian Mackelroy and Lenny Greenwood stepped out of the woods and into the clearing "Don't shoot!" Damian cried, hands in the air. "We're just jokin' around."

Wayne lowered his rifle, breathing heavily, trying to slow his rampaging heart. Sharp pain throbbed in his chest. He felt faint.

The rest of the boys emptied out of the tents. There was no laughter now. Many looked embarrassed.

Denny Miaway stumbled out last, confused, obviously pulled out of deep sleep, asking, "You okay, Wayne?"

Wayne tried to collect himself. Arms still shaking, he set the rifle aside. "No, I'm not." He got his wobbly legs working and, with a scowl, walked toward Damian and Lenny. *I could strangle these two delinquents right now. I thought they had more sense than this.* "Do you boys understand you could've been killed with this prank of yours?"

Damian and Lenny nodded in unison, shame clouding their faces. The other eight scouts stood by quietly, eyes lowered.

"I thought you boys were smarter than what you just showed."

Lenny dared to speak up. "We were just havin' some fun . . . just clownin' around is all."

"Oh, is that *all*? How stupid can you guys be? Every last one of you know Mr. Miaway and I have guns. I could have killed both of you." Wayne shook visibly. His voice was strained. "You guys are Boy Scouts. You're supposed to know the wilderness is no place to be reckless. Denny and I have told you over and over again that nature isn't kind to fools."

Heads hung low, both boys apologized for their misconduct. The rest of the scouts stood around, staring at their feet, kicking at the dirt.

Wayne tried to swallow his fury, but couldn't. His tone was acerbic as he said, "You guys are a big disappointment to me right now. Everybody hit the tents. I don't wanna hear a peep out of any of you. We'll talk about this in the morning when I've cooled down."

The boys shuffled off quietly to their sleeping bags.

Wayne and Denny worked silently to douse the fire, then returned to the tent they shared. Denny asked Wayne again if he was okay.

"No, not at all," Wayne said, still shaky as he stretched out on his cot. "I'm most disappointed in Jason and Marty. Our sons should never have let that happen."

"You're absolutely right," Denny said from his cot. "Hopefully this will be a life lesson for them."

"We can hope, Denny, we can only hope."

Three-Ring Circus

June 19: Gilliam's Guidepost
Heart Butte, Montana

THE GUIDEPOST WAS A WHIRLWIND of activity. Used to be, summers in Heart Butte were leisurely and lazy, with the kids home from school, the inn mostly vacant, and business at the general store slow. Summer was a time to relax. But the meteorite that struck three weeks ago had drastically changed their summer. That one inexplicable event had brought dinosaurs, of all things, and an endless stream of intrusive people. Loretta Gilliam found herself yearning for a return to the slower days of summers past.

Last Saturday, Hayden Fowler and Nora Lemoyne returned from their trip to Greenfield, bringing with them the carcass of the ugliest creature Loretta had ever seen. Two feet tall and weighing 70 pounds, the animal was all muscle, with overdeveloped jaws and a deep, shovel mouth full of wicked teeth. A lethal-looking specimen; more intimidating than their Dromaeosaurs. A Tyrannosaurus Rex. A juvenile that had drowned. Even dead, it frightened Loretta. Doctors Fowler and Lemoyne felt certain T-Rex was the species that had attacked the Tully ranch. It was also likely that numbers of T-Rexes had been involved in other attacks on livestock this week across the two-state area.

The evidence of Tyrannosaurus Rex in Greenfield coupled with the Dromaeosaurs here at the Guidepost excited the scientists. Their numbers staying at the inn and at hotels within driving distance had swelled the past week. The Department of the Interior sent an exotic species wildlife biologist along with an evolutionary biologist. They were joined by personnel from the National Security Agency and the Fish and Wildlife Service. Two representatives from the Smithsonian arrived to document the miracle of Dromaeosaurs birthed in captivity and the now credible return of Tyrannosaurus Rex. The 12-room inn was booked to capacity. So were a half-dozen local hotels/motels. The word was out: Gilliam's Guidepost was ground zero for dinosaur study.

Security had become an issue. Television reporters and news journalists hounded them at all hours for interviews and requests to videotape. Rude and unsavory people started showing up. Many were threatening, demanding they be let in. Some of them had guns. Bryan had gotten into heated exchanges with people at the front gate. For two days, the boys—Paul and Ethan, home after cancellation of their baseball season—had patrolled the perimeter armed with rifles. Bryan had taught them gun safety and how to shoot when they were younger, and Loretta knew her sons could handle themselves, but she didn't want them out on the far reaches of their property under these circumstances. Her worries about her sons eased early this week, however. The Smithsonian, realizing the Gilliams and local police could no longer handle the situation, brought in a private Missoula security firm to guard Gilliam's Guidepost 24/7. They wanted to protect what they called their "invaluable assets," meaning the Dromaeosaur hatchlings.

Tuesday afternoon Bryan loaded Lianne's small suitcase in the trunk of the old Pontiac. Bryan and Loretta decided it would be safer and much better for all to have Lianne stay with the Enrights where she could play with her cousin Marnie and ride her horse, Beauregard. Loretta gave her daughter a kiss and a hug, and told her to be good for her Uncle Jimmy and Aunt Olivia. She watched Lianne climb into the front seat hugging her two favorite dolls, Patches and Lyle. The cotton wadding shot out of Lyle the lion in large tufts, and Loretta made a mental note to buy her a new stuffed animal. She'd blinked back tears, feeling a sentimental tug, seeing Lianne waving goodbye through the passenger seat window.

Other big changes had occurred this week. The hatchlings had outgrown the aquarium tanks and needed to be moved. Loretta borrowed five large dog crates from a Blackfoot neighbor who ran a kennel that bred and sold Labs. The scientists very carefully sedated the animals and transferred them to the crates. The growth rates of these reptiles alarmed Loretta. At hatchout two weeks ago, the Dromaeosaurs were eight inches long and crawled on all fours. They now stood two feet tall and walked on their hind legs. *Bipedal theropods* is how the scientists referred to them. The German paleozoologist, Franz Krause, and government wildlife biologist, Barrett Hailey, handled the anesthesia and weighed them every other day. Yesterday's weigh-in revealed the older Dromaeosaur to be 40 pounds, with the five hatchlings at around 30 pounds. They were gaining three to four pounds a day, snarfing down prodigious amounts of raw hamburger. The little beasts were consuming more meat in a day than the entire Gilliam clan ate in a week! Loretta had bought out all available ground beef within driving distance of the Guidepost. She'd also gone to Browning and East Glacier Park Village to pick up raw chicken and beef waste scraps from butchers who wanted to contribute to the cause.

True to her word, Nora Lemoyne reimbursed her for all costs related to their captive dinosaurs. She got the Smithsonian folks to pony up for the care and feeding of these prehistoric wonders. The feds also chipped in, with the Department of the Interior organizing a dinosaur feeding program.

This morning Loretta supervised the first delivery of government-issued Dromaeosaur food. A large refrigerated truck pulled up to the loading dock behind the general store and unloaded frozen 40-pound blocks of compressed beef, chicken, and pork byproducts—slaughterhouse trimmings and waste. "Think of it as dog food for dinosaurs," Nora Lemoyne had told them. A second truck pulled in behind the first, delivering a pair of industrial freezers in which to store the dino food. Loretta was amazed at how fast the feed program came together. Once the feds confirmed the existence of live dinosaurs at Gilliam's Guidepost, they moved posthaste to make the operation a reality. She had stood on the loading platform, directing the delivery men as to where the freezer units should go. A forklift operator removed pallets from the other truck and stacked them in the freezers.

She'd watched the hustle of the men working around her, their voices cutting through the high-pitched whine of the forklift, and thought: *How did our little ranch on the Blackfeet Indian reservation in tiny Heart Butte become the center of the universe?*

Their Dromaeosaurs had become a global phenomenon. With that came new responsibilities. Loretta still wasn't sure they were capable of handling the enormous obligation.

Why us?

She couldn't come up with any answers.

The rapid growth of the Dromaeosaurs dictated a moving target with regards to their environment. The animals would outgrow the dog crates in just a few days. Bryan had a plan to address that. With the Gilliam horses moved to Jimmy and Livvy's place, the stalls in the horse barn now sat empty. Bryan—never one to walk away from a money-making opportunity—negotiated a deal for him and their sons to build habitats to hold the Dromaeosaurs, starting with converting the horse stalls to dinosaur corrals. The feds agreed to pay them for their efforts.

Work in the horse barn began Thursday. Bryan and the boys spent the last three days converting the stalls into escape-proof coops. They replaced old wooden studs with steel posts, and walled each pen with heavy-gauge wire mesh screening. They installed thick tongue-and-groove oak floorboards with undergravel drainage and 15-foot-high ceilings. Hayden Fowler checked the work, saying the stalls would be large enough to hold the animals another month, six weeks at most. Beyond that, they would need a spacious outdoor habitat. Franz Krause agreed, saying they would need a lot of room to run and jump, and an area with a reliable water source.

Bryan started throwing out ideas immediately. They could renovate the east meadow. Plenty of room for the animals to roam out there, he'd told the scientists. And there was a large retention pond on that acreage. He and the boys would reinforce the fencing around the meadow and add a large, colorful entrance gate, with a sign:

GILLIAM'S GLADE
Habitat of the Fearsome Dromaeosaurus
Flesh-Eating Dragons of the Late Cretaceous

The scientists and government officials got a kick out of Bryan's enthusiasm. A couple of them even laughed at his vision. But their snickers didn't deter Loretta's husband. Not in the least. Bryan went on to tell them of his plans of turning the Guidepost into a dinosaur zoo and charging admission prices rivaling those of Disney World.

This was news to Loretta. Her idealist husband was at it again. Stars in his eyes. Envisioning get-rich-quick fantasies. This wasn't the first time he'd dreamed big.

Yesterday afternoon she took sandwiches and lemonade out to the horse barn: lunch break for Bryan and the boys. The barn was hot and stuffy, smelling of hay and sweaty leather and fresh-cut oak. Loretta asked him about the dinosaur zoo idea.

"Well, I've been thinkin' about this extraordinary thing that's fallen in our laps here," he said. "We'd be crazy not to take advantage of the opportunity. We need to start savin' for the kids' college." He glanced at Paul, who guzzled lemonade from a thermos. "Pauley's only two years away and a baseball scholarship is only a hopeful maybe at this point."

"I'll get a free ride," Paul said confidently. He wiped his mouth. "You can count on it, Dad."

"Not if you can't hit a curveball," Ethan said.

Paul scowled at his younger brother.

Bryan continued his pitch. "I've been lookin' at this meteorite-dinosaur thing ass-backwards, Lor . . . seein' it as a detriment when really it could be a windfall for us."

"Maybe so, but I wish you would have discussed it with me before making a public announcement."

Hayden Fowler entered the barn, halting their conversation. "Good afternoon, folks." The big scientist scanned the stalls. "Looks like things are comin' along nicely, Mr. Gilliam."

"Yeah, we should have it finished up tomorrow. Sunday at the latest. Couldn't have done it without my boys."

"I'm impressed," Fowler said, alternating glances at Paul and Ethan, both of whom were wolfing down turkey sandwiches. "You guys are good workers." He turned back to Bryan. "I came by to discuss your dinosaur zoo concept with you."

"That makes two of us," Loretta muttered.

Fowler looked from Bryan to Loretta. "Is this a good time?"

Bryan nodded. "Sure. Good as any, I suppose."

Fowler lifted a leg, put his boot up on the railing and leaned forward. "I've gotta say, your zoo idea is intriguing. We definitely need an expansive area for those creatures. Sooner than later. The way you talk I'm assuming you plan to build it yourself. Am I right?"

"Yeah. Why?"

"Well, you apparently haven't given much thought to what it'll take to enclose that pasture. Your east meadow? That's where the meteorite struck, right?"

"Correct."

"The fencing there is in terrible shape. It's rusted barbed wire. Lots of gaps. Entirely inadequate. In a month those Dromaeosaurs will be able to jump ten feet vertically. You're gonna need fifteen-foot-high fences of heavy grade steel to keep them contained. That's a massive job."

Loretta watched her husband, knowing Bryan was not one to be deterred once he got something in his head.

"Doesn't bother me," Bryan said. "My sons and I can get the job done in a month, weather permitting. The government agreed to pay us for the work, and I'm not too proud to say we really need the money."

"There's no way, Mr. Gilliam," Fowler replied, his expression stern as he tugged at his beard. "You and your sons can't do it. I took some rough measurements and came up with twenty-seven acres. That's over a million square feet, based on how you have it fenced now."

Bryan set his half-eaten sandwich aside. "Yeah. So?"

"So there's no way you and your boys can get that area fenced securely in four weeks. A minimum of fifteen-feet high all the way around? No way. Even six weeks is a pipe dream."

Bryan took a step toward the scientist. "Now wait just a goddamned min—"

"Don't be an idiot, Gilliam. I'm tryin' to help you out here. How much are the feds offering you and your sons?"

"That's *my* business."

"I'll say it again. I want to *help* you. How much?"

Loretta nodded her approval at Bryan. He recited the figures.

Fowler laughed. "They're taking you for a ride, my friend. Trying to take the cheap way out. Those Dromaeosaurs are on your land. You hold all the cards. You can call the shots and name your price. It's one thing for them to pay you to build out these stalls. Quite another to have you construct a large natural habitat. Don't be a fool, Gilliam. Why break your ass slaving in the sun when you can get the feds to spring for it? They should be payin' for a construction company to do the work. Save you and your sons from backbreaking work. A professional construction outfit could knock the job out in a couple of weeks."

"But we need the money."

"I hear ya, Gilliam. But don't you see? They should be payin' you and your wife a hefty monthly rental fee. You guys are providing shelter for these animals. You and Mrs. Gilliam are the landlords. Those Dromaeosaurs are a national treasure. You should be getting paid for leasing out your land."

All eyes were on Bryan, who looked confused. "I can't go back to them now and refuse to do the work . . . demand more money."

"You absolutely *could*," Fowler said. "That's what I came to talk with you about. You're not the negotiating type. I understand that. Lucky for you we've got Doctor Lemoyne on board here. She's a master at fundraising. She has a way of getting people who control the purse strings to shell out money for her ideas. *Lots* of money."

Loretta met Bryan's gaze. "He's right, Bry. You and the boys shouldn't have to break your backs building a habitat. We're entitled to money for our troubles, over and above feed and materials cost. Look at what we've had to go through because of those creatures."

"That's a smart lady you've got there, Bryan," Fowler said. "I'm tellin' you, Nora Lemoyne can move mountains when she wants to. This dinosaur invasion is center stage right now. The spotlight is on you and your ranch and she'll be able to cut you a good deal where you'll make good money without havin' to bust your ass."

"If you think so."

"I *know* so. Just leave it to me. But about your dinosaur zoo—"

"What about it?"

"I've gotta say, you're just asking for trouble letting the public in to view these Dromaeosaurs."

"Why's that?"

"Because they've become public enemy number one. Farmers and ranchers hate them. People in these parts are livin' in fear and I've been hearing there're hunters declaring open season on them. Hunting clubs are putting large bounties on their hides. The news media has painted them up to be killers . . . boogey-monsters that go bump in the night. You think you have security issues now? They've only just begun if you open up a public zoo."

Bryan didn't back down. "We can handle security."

Ethan spoke up. "I think it'd be really cool to have a zoo here. Give people somethin' to do in this boring town."

"Shut up, moron!" Paul said. "Just because you—"

"Stow it, Pauley!" Bryan snarled. "I agree with my Ethan here. I think it'd be cool to have a zoo here at the Guidepost. I say folks will pay top dollar to see these Dromaeosaurs in person. They'll come from far and wide. I just wish we had more than one species. Maybe a few of those T-Rexes."

Fowler shook his head "You have no idea what you're wishin' for. Containing the Dromaeosaurs is one thing. But there isn't any cage or fencing yet manufactured that'll hold a mature T-Rex. You'd probably need a four-foot-thick, twenty-foot-high concrete wall. But Even without T-Rex, I say you'll be opening a huge Pandora's box if you invite the unwashed masses here. I applaud your enthusiasm, I really do. But don't say I didn't warn you."

And so it had been yesterday with Bryan wanting to proceed with his dinosaur zoo. Today, Loretta remained a bit miffed at him. He'd rushed impulsively into an enormous project plan that would affect all of them without consulting her. But she had to admit, he seemed happier and more content than she'd seen him in a long while. And whether she liked it or not, they *were* stuck with raising these Dromaeosaurs. So why not a dinosaur zoo? Why not profit from this extraordinary happening? A *windfall* Bryan had called it. Use the income to fund the kids' college tuitions. Why the hell not?

But tonight, standing before the bathroom mirror brushing her teeth, she reflected on what they had been through the past three weeks. Was it all worth a bump in income? Their privacy was gone. Their daily lives had been derailed. The boys' baseball season had been canceled. They were dealing with endless crowds of bothersome scientists and government officials. They were being harassed by the media and the lunatic fringe. They were caring for dangerous prehistoric animals. Their horses and Lianne were gone to a safer place, and because of it, she was suffering through mother-daughter separation anxiety, feeling the guilt of sending her little girl away for part of the summer.

We deserve a big pile of money for all we've been through.

She put her toothbrush away and rinsed her mouth. Went to the walk-in closet and changed into her nightgown. Climbed into bed and turned on the reading light. Picked up her book, *Untamed* by Glennon Doyle, a memoir that had captivated her the past few nights. She'd read three pages when she heard Bryan clomp up the stairs, then enter the bedroom.

"Holy Christ, I'm tired, Lor." He stripped off his work shirt and threw it in the hamper.

Loretta closed her book, set it aside. "Hey, love. Any word yet about the financing?"

"Fowler just spoke with Nora Lemoyne this afternoon. He told me she agrees the government should pay for the habitat construction and plans to talk with the appropriate people next week . . . both at the Smithsonian and Department of the Interior."

"And the rental fee for use of our property?"

"That too, yes. Fowler guarantees he and Doctor Lemoyne will get that approved. He told me today that the feds don't really have any options other than leaving the Dromaeosaurs here. No conventional zoos will take 'em, and besides, all expert caregivers and paleontology specialists are already assembled here. It only makes sense to maintain the status quo. Even payin' us a boatload of money will be cheaper in the long run."

"That's excellent, Bry."

"You know, that Fowler guy? I didn't care too much for him at first. I found him kinda pushy and arrogant. But he's grown on me, now that I realize he's got our best interests in mind. I didn't really wanna build a crappy fence anyway. I was dreading it."

"Yeah, I know what you mean."

"Listen, not to change the subject, but I got a call today from Mount Bennett Air Force Base. Said they would be here Monday to pick up the meteorite. Asked me about helicopter landing sites. The guy was pretty egotistical—some high-ranking colonel. Said we better not have messed with the meteorite. Like it's his priceless jewel or something."

"Did you tell him this is private property and he needs our permission to take anything?"

"Somethin' to that effect, yeah. He told me it doesn't matter what we think. Said the decree comes directly from the upper echelons of the Pentagon."

"The *Pentagon*? Are you joking?"

"No. He said it falls under eminent domain as part of national security. I checked with that NSA guy who's staying here, and he backed it up. Says it's legit and legal. They have a right to pick it up under eminent domain laws since the government is providing just compensation by paying us to keep and feed those overgrown lizards."

Loretta shook her head, a languid motion of amazement and disgust. "Did you ever think when Jimmy fixed us up on that blind date all those years ago that we'd end up as dinosaur ranchers, Bry?"

He emitted a tired chuckle. "Sounds weird when you put it that way. But no, I could never have imagined any of this."

"So, we're just gonna let the Air Force come and take away our space rock?"

He dropped his jeans and sat on the edge of the bed, bent over to slide his pants over his shins and off. "I guess we have to. But it got me to thinkin' . . . the entire planet is dialed in to this meteorite thing, right?"

"Yeah, so—?"

"So why don't we take some of the meteorite wedges and hide them from the Air Force. We can chisel it down into small pieces, maybe polish the pieces, put them in decorative boxes and sell 'em as good luck talismans. The Air Force has no idea how much of that meteorite we have."

She leaned back against the headboard. "You've got more ideas than an inventors convention, my dear hubby." She gave him a heartfelt smile. "That space rock charm is an interesting idea, but I doubt many people would go for it. Think about it. Pieces of a meteorite that hatched out flesh-eating dinosaurs? Would people really think of them as *good* luck?"

"Okay, maybe not good luck," he said, pausing to think. "You're right, maybe that's the wrong approach. It's all in the marketing, Loretta. Say we package them as magic meteorite rocks that promise to bring strength and good health and long life. After all, these meteorites allegedly preserved dinosaurs for millions of years. We could give them some snazzy name, like—I dunno— maybe *Cretaceous Stones*."

He slipped into a late-night cable TV announcer voice and held an invisible product in his hand. "This miraculous little stone will change your life in ways you never imagined. For only twenty-nine-ninety-five, you can own a piece of the rock, the meteorite that preserved dinosaurs for millions of years. If it did that for prehistoric reptiles, just think what it can do for *you*! Get your Cretaceous Stone today. But hurry! They'll be gone soon."

Loretta laughed. "That's hilarious. You missed your calling, Bry."

"I'm not kidding around, Lor. We could sell these things on Amazon and eBay. People want to own unique things . . . *rarities*. Things don't get much more rare than this." His eyes sparkled. "We could even sell them in the Gilliam dinosaur zoo gift shop. There's no other place in the world anybody can get what we have to offer."

She watched him slip off his underwear and stand naked at the foot of their bed. His broad shoulders, sculpted arms and long, lean torso still did something to her after nearly two decades of marriage.

She crawled across the bed to him, grabbed his hand and pulled him down. "I believe I'm in love with the creator of the magical Cretaceous Stone."

She felt his weight come down on her, heard him whisper in her ear, "Is that love or lust, my gorgeous wife?"

"Take your pick," she whispered. "Either one works for me."

Night Stalkers

June 20: Eastern Lewis and Clark National Forest
Little Belt Mountains, Montana

INSOMNIA PLAGUED WAYNE FAHLMAN. He tossed and turned on his cot in the shadowy tent, trying to find a comfortable position. Dreadful thoughts held him captive. A few hours ago he'd almost killed two boys in his troop. He couldn't erase it from his mind.

If I hadn't shot into the treetops . . . Jesus dear God!

How could I ever forgive myself?

How could I face the parents after a tragedy like that?

His thoughts cycled back to the boys—Damian Mackelroy and Lenny Greenwood—and his distress turned to anger.

What possesses boys to be so reckless? So stupid?

Damian and Lenny weren't the only mischief makers. All the scouts were in on it, including his own son, Jason.

What the hell were they thinking? Were they thinking at all?

A chilly mountain breeze whipped at the tent and he burrowed deeper into his sleeping bag. He listened to Denny's rumbling snores cut through the harmonic hum of katydids and tree crickets. He peered across the dim divide to where Denny slept, saw the outline of his chest rise and fall in loud, rustling breaths.

How can he sleep after what happened?

Wayne fumbled for his cellphone on the cooler next to his cot. 1:27 AM.

No service. This place was too remote for phone service. No internet, either. But he did keep a top-of-the-line satellite phone under his cot. The Boy Scouts of America safety regulations mandated it for scoutmasters. He could call anywhere in the world and that gave him comfort.

He stretched out, yawned. After a time Denny stopped snoring, his breathing quieting and falling into an easy rhythm. Wayne lay in the warm cocoon of his sleeping bag, listening to the night sounds. He thought about the punishment he'd have to give the boys when they got back to Great Falls. Should he deny them their camping merit badges? Ban them from other planned troop activities this summer? Would he—*should* he—inform their parents and let them take appropriate action? He didn't like any of those options, but some punishment was in order. The boys made a serious misstep. They'd had a collective lapse in judgment—a near *fatal* lapse in judgment—and needed to learn that the wilderness was no place for irresponsible shenanigans.

Sleep began to creep in when he heard an odd chirping from deep in the forest. Faint but distinct.

An owl?

No owl he knew chirped like that. He sat up and leaned on an elbow, cocked his head to the side, listened attentively.

The solo chirp grew into a chorus of peeps. Muffled. Far off.

A flock of nighthawks?

If it's those boys again, they'll pay for it!"

The tweeting increased in volume, taking on a warped quality, like wounded birds amplified through steam whistles. Off key and discordant.

The insects went silent.

The eerie chirping continued, louder now.

Wayne thought he could detect faint croaking noises buried in the mix of chirps.

Frogs?

He climbed out of the sleeping bag and sat on the side of the cot, very still, listening, his worry growing.

The chirping and croaking quickly escalated into an unsettling, croaking-grunting-snorting-chirping wall of sound.

Certainly not the boys. Nor are they nighthawks or frogs.

Adrenaline ratcheted up his panic.

His heart raced erratically.

Thoughts of livestock-eating dinosaurs he'd heard about on the news made him feel sick, weak.

Is it possible they're here? How can it be? Please, God NO!

The wall of terrifying sound moved in on the camp, until the surreal noises surrounded their tent. Living things crashed through the brush, grunting and snorting and squealing like wild boars on a rampage.

Animal shrieks, strange as anything Wayne had ever heard.

It chilled his blood.

Denny came awake, startled. "What's that? Our boys actin' up again?"

In one fluid motion Wayne grabbed his flashlight and rifle from under the cot. "Get your gun, Denny! We've got us some serious trouble!" He stood and started toward the tent entrance, colliding with Denny, dropping his flashlight but managing to hold on to his rifle.

Pandemonium erupted in the clearing as screams filled the cool night air.

Raucous growls and snorting.

Snuffling and squealing and the weird chirping.

Canvas ripping, the whoosh of a tent collapsing, aluminum poles clanging against the packed earth.

Running feet thumped through the clearing.

Desperate screams of "HELP!" echoed through the campsite.

Wayne sensed Denny moving behind him, yelling something, but he couldn't decipher it through all the bedlam.

Shock—the unreality of it all—froze Wayne where he stood. The horrific chaos incapacitated him. He couldn't move his arms or legs.

Do something, Fahlman! he chided himself. *You're the scoutmaster! This is on you!*

Heart pounding a frenzied rhythm against his ribs, Wayne willed himself to movement. He bent and retrieved the flashlight and moved to the front of the tent. Pulled the flap open and shined the light out over the campsite. Half-dressed boys ran haphazardly, screaming, horror etched on their faces, attempting to elude a half-dozen or more hard-charging reptilian creatures.

JesusGodJesusGodJesusGodwhatishappening?

The flashlight threw a shaky beam of light across the clearing, giving the scene a flickering, disturbing quality. One boy Wayne couldn't identify struggled to get out from under a collapsed tent as a pair of animals jumped on him, smothering his cries. Another boy—it looked like Ralphie Brewer—was brought down at the edge of the woods, his shouts for help quickly silenced. The creatures were like something out of a satanic menagerie. Three feet tall with scaly hides, running upright on muscled hind legs with stubby tails trailing, long snouts flashing oversized teeth. Exceptionally quick and agile.

JesusGodJesusGodJesusGod... ...

Wayne thought he would be sick, but somehow he willed his sluggish mind to click into survival mode. He stepped out of the tent and fired his rifle into the night sky, once . . . twice . . . three times, trying to scare them off.

The rampaging reptiles continued their assault, unmindful of the gunshots.

He wanted to blow one or two of them away, thinking that might chase them off. He took aim, following the path of one, but he couldn't coordinate the flashlight and rifle and get off a safe shot. The beasts were too quick and he couldn't risk hitting one of the boys.

More gunshots, booming like cannon fire—Denny shooting from the other side of the tents. Didn't bother the animals; they seemed to be impervious to gunfire.

Wayne heard his son screaming, "Help, Dad, HELP!" from up in the trees on the other side of the clearing. Wayne swung the light up in that direction, spotlighting Jason perched on a heavy branch about fifteen feet up in a lodgepole pine. Another boy was with him. It looked like Marty Miaway. A powerful-looking reptile circled the wide base, peering up at them, its mouth dripping saliva.

Please don't let these beasts be tree climbers.

"Stay up there, Jase!" he yelled, struggling for breath. "I'll get us help. Stay there and don't move!"

Gasping, his lungs burning, Wayne rushed back inside the tent, leaned the rifle against the cot, and grabbed the satellite phone. His hands shook as he turned on the handset and punched in 9-1-1, GO.

A female dispatcher answered calmly, *"9-1-1. What's your emergency?"*

"Help! We're under attack! Dinosaurs are mauling my scouts!"

"I'm sorry, sir, but did you say dinosaurs?*"*

"Yes. Hurry! My boys are dying!"

"Okay, I'm here for you, sir. I know it's hard but try to stay calm." The dispatcher kept her voice level. *"Please give me your name, location, and a callback number."*

"I'm Wayne Fahlman, scoutmaster of Boy Scout Troop two-seventy-nine out of Great Falls. We're on a campout in the Little Belt Mountains, ten miles south of Neihart."

"Thank you, Wayne . . . And your callback number?"

He recited his sat phone number and heard her fingers working a keyboard.

"You say you are currently under attack?"

"Yes goddammit! Dinosaurs! Flesh-eating beasts!" He was alarmed at the shrill distress in his voice. "Think I've already lost a few boys. We'll need medical assistance and . . . oh my God, so much more. Please hurry!"

"We're tracking you now, Wayne. Do you have a way to stay safe until we get there?"

He thought he could make a run for his van, maybe scoot along the backside of the tents undetected. "I'll make do," he said into the phone. "Just hurry! Please!" Tears streamed down his cheeks. His shoulders shook as he started crying in great sobs.

"Okay, Wayne. Stay calm. I'm with you all the way. If you can, I want you to stay on the line with me until you can get to a safe place. Okay?"

Suddenly a snarling, growling force hit the side of the tent with the impact of a freight train. The supports broke apart at the connections and came down, slamming into the side of his face. In great pain, he dropped to his knees, losing his grip on the sat phone. The canvas skin came down around him, draping him in a heavy shroud. He fumbled around blindly, trying to locate his rifle or the sat phone.

Somewhere in the entanglement he heard the 9-1-1 dispatcher's professional, even-keeled voice: *"Are you still with me, Wayne?"*

And then two animals pounced on him, slamming the breath from his lungs. Heavy enough to pin him in place under the canvas. He gasped for air, taking in their wild gamy scent. He felt their claws through the heavy fabric and heard their determined snorts. He thought he'd lose it as teeth ripped through the canvas to get at him. He struggled to break free, but couldn't. They were too strong. He yelled out "HELP!" several times, but his pleas were suffocated under the heap of tent canvas.

One of them got through the canvas and snatched his right leg. He felt the bone snap. Lightning jolts of intense pain shot through his body—excruciating burning, electrocution type pain.

He emptied his lungs with a desperate scream.

Wild in the Wheat

June 21: The Enright Farm
Shelby, Montana

THEY RODE SINGLE FILE, STAYING ON the horse path that wound around the central wheat field. Cousin Marnie led the way on her horse, Spirit, with Lianne following on Beauregard and Uncle Jimmy bringing up the rear on his mount, Sugar. Lianne was glad her uncle rode behind her because he smoked those stinky cigarettes. Horrible smell. She wished he wouldn't smoke around her. Her daddy constantly bugged Uncle Jimmy to quit the "cancer sticks" as he called them. Uncle Jimmy would always just say, "You're right, Gilly, I should," then laugh and light up another one.

They were headed back to the barn after an early-morning ride through the open grassland that bordered the Marias River. A stiff breeze whispered through the wheat, offering relief from the rising heat. They cantered along, the horses *clip-clopping* over the hard-packed earth. Lianne focused on her cousin riding in front of her. Marnie's long rust-red hair flowed from under her riding helmet like flames of fire and she sat high and proud in the saddle, as though perching on her throne.

Marnie thinks she's queen of the world.

Lianne liked her cousin, but ever since Marnie's ninth birthday party a month ago, she had become a bossy know-it-all. Earlier in the week, Marnie called Lianne childish for suggesting they play with their dolls. The harsh comment hurt Lianne's feelings and almost made her cry. Marnie had always loved playing with dolls. They'd passed many an hour playing make-believe with Lianne's Lyle and Patches, and Marnie's favorite dolls, Pippina and Twinkle. But Marnie had shocking news for Lianne: she had stuffed Pippina and Twinkle into a cardboard box and shoved them under her bed. "That's little girl stuff, Lee. I've buried Pip and Twink. I'm too grown up for dolls," Marnie had said, eyeing Lianne doubtfully as Lianne lovingly nuzzled Lyle and Patches.

Instead, Marnie talked her into playing dress up with Aunt Olivia's clothes and makeup. Lianne felt ridiculous strapping a bra across her flat chest, parading in front of the full-length mirror, the breast cups collapsed and the straps cutting into her shoulders. She hated the itchy, frilly fabrics of the blouses and cool, slippery feel of the ill-fitting panties. Marnie had also tried to teach her how to swagger like a runway model, saying she'd seen them walk that way on TV. Lianne tried to go along, but ultimately just felt self-conscious, finally turning her ankle trying to walk in high heels. Then Marnie raided Aunt Livvy's makeup table. They'd smeared gobs of smelly creams and powders on their faces. The lipstick tasted icky and the smell of the makeup made Lianne want to throw up. She thought they looked like clowns while Marnie thought they were "cool and ladylike." Finally, afraid Aunt Liv would return early from shopping and catch them messing around in her things, Lianne ran to the bathroom and washed the makeup from her face. Marnie shook her head, disappointed as she watched freshly scrubbed Lianne go to the walk-in closet and change back into her own clothes. "You're no fun anymore, Lee. You're just a big chicken," she'd said.

Marnie was two years older than her, but that didn't give her the right to boss her around. Or call her a chicken. And the way she was trying to act adult was goofy, even though Marnie didn't think so. This new, meanspirited, adult-wannabe Marnie made Lianne want to cry. But she didn't. Lianne was proud that she was able to push back the tears. She was determined not to let her cousin see how much she was hurting her.

But even though the week had turned difficult for Lianne, it began on an upbeat note. When she first arrived, Marnie treated her like she was visiting royalty. She'd wanted to see Lianne's leg wound and begged to hear all about the dinosaur attack that caused it. Lianne, feeling superior with the attention, described the episode in breathless, frightening detail. Lianne saw the respect in Marnie's eyes grow as she related the story. When she finished the telling, Marnie said with a hint of jealousy, "You're famous, Lee. You're the only human being ever to get bit by a dinosaur." Lianne knew that wasn't true—that meeteeyite science man got bit at the Guidepost—but she didn't want to correct her as she was basking in Marnie's attentiveness. "Were you scared?" Lianne told her yes, she was terrified. Even more so when the horses escaped the barn. Lianne wanted to tell her about the nightmares she'd been having, being swarmed by hundreds of creepy reptile things with sharp teeth and unable to escape, but she didn't. Marnie would just call her names. Lianne had kept the disturbing night visions from her parents as well. She didn't want Mama and Daddy to think she was a crybaby.

Marnie had obviously been impressed by the misadventures that had gotten Lianne grounded, and Lianne basked in the specialness she'd felt. But it didn't last. By Wednesday evening, Marnie's hero worship had worn off, calling the dinosaur attack "no big deal" and the bite "just a little cut."

Lianne always looked forward to coming to her aunt and uncle's farm. Jimmy and Olivia's place was very different from her home in Heart Butte. She loved running through the endless wheat fields, letting the silky, golden stalks brush her face as she pretended she was a horse galloping up and down the narrow rows. She loved wading in the river with the squishy mud tickling the soles of her feet. She loved digging up nightcrawlers to catch bass and catfish on bamboo poles. She loved riding horseback through the meadows, which rolled out flat as far as she could see, giving her plenty of space to run her horse full tilt (Uncle Jimmy always let her run her horse full out while her daddy frowned on it). She'd always enjoyed spending time with Marnie doing all these things and more.

Marnie Enright was her only cousin. But really she was more like the sister she'd always wanted. Last fall they'd sworn a sisterly oath, pricking their fingers with one of Aunt Livvy's sewing needles and vowing to be "sisters in blood" forever after touching bloody fingers. But last fall seemed a long time ago now. Marnie's uppity attitude had taken a lot of the fun out of this visit. Over the past few days, Lianne felt a distance growing between them and it made her sad. Several times, Lianne wanted to remind her of the blood sister pact to see if Marnie remembered. But she kept it to herself, fearing Marnie would laugh at her and tell her such rituals were childish, little girl things.

However, overall, coming here had lifted Lianne's spirits. She'd been happy to break free of her indoor punishment at home. She was pleased to be reunited with her horses and able to ride Beau again. She liked getting away from all the weird, overly serious dinosaur people visiting the Guidepost and those scary hatchling creatures in the utility barn. All that was good. But now, after a week away, her joy was fading. She felt a strange ache in the pit of her stomach. She missed Mama more than she ever thought possible. She missed Daddy, too. She was sorry she'd been so mean to them. Thinking back, she was ashamed of how bratty she'd been. She'd told them she hated them. More than once. But she didn't. Not really. She loved them and missed them. It made her feel guilty for saying those hurtful things to them. She realized she missed Paul and Ethan, too, which surprised her, because she still thought her brothers were the biggest dopes in the world. Lianne had FaceTime sessions with her parents every night after supper, but talking with them through a computer screen wasn't the same as being with them. She was homesick and wanted to go home. She needed hugs and kisses and the familiarity of the Guidepost. But she didn't say anything because she thought it might hurt her Uncle Jimmy and Aunt Livvy who were doing so much for her. She didn't want to mess that up on top of everything else she'd already messed up.

Everything was confusing and jumbled up. She wished she could go back to before her encounter with the dinosaur. Then maybe everything would be good again.

They arrived at the stables and Marnie led them to the water trough. They dismounted and Lianne petted Beauregard's snout, whispered next to his ear, "good job, Beau. You're my beautiful baby." Beauregard responded with a clipped snort and swish of his tail. She dug into her pocket, pulled out an Oreo cookie and held it in the palm of her hand, giggling as Beau's slobbery tongue lapped it up.

The horses snorted and whinnied and neighed as they bent their heads to drink. Lianne glanced at the rifle scabbard on Sugar's saddle. Uncle Jimmy's gun reminded her of the new dangers in the world. Daddy carried his rifle everywhere lately, too. Guns scared her. Almost as much as that big black meeteeyite and those nasty dinosaurs.

Jimmy opened the barn doors, saying, "Good ride today, girls. Remember to brush our friends. They like a good grooming after a hard ride." He felt in his pocket for his cigarettes, pulled out the pack and lit one up. "I've got to get on up to the house and make some calls."

"I brush my horses every day, Uncle Jimmy," Lianne said.

"That's good, Lee," Jimmy said, smiling, exhaling a cloud of smoke, "but there's probably not enough time to groom all of them today. Don't dawdle. You girls need to get on back soon. Livvy'll be gettin' lunch ready."

"Okay, Dad," Marnie said, leading Spirit and Sugar inside the barn.

Lianne took Beauregard's reins and followed.

Jimmy turned back to them. "And just a reminder. Stay out of the fields. We just sprayed them and that insecticide ain't no good for a coupla growin' girls."

"Yes, Dad," Marnie said, rolling her eyes and smiling at Lianne. They both had heard the warning repeatedly the past few days.

They removed their riding helmets and led the horses into their stalls. Helped each other remove the bridles and saddles and hang them on racks, grunting with the effort in the warm, musty air. Lianne began grooming Beau while Marnie attended to Spirit in the adjoining stall. Neither spoke as they concentrated on their tasks. Curry combs and dandy brushes swished over backs and flanks, drawing satisfied breathy whinnies from Beau and Spirit. When they finished grooming their horses, Lianne joined Marnie in Sugar's stall, and they brushed Uncle Jimmy's horse together.

When finished, Lianne looked down the row of stables at her

other horses brought here from the Guidepost—Blackie, Max, Clancy, Roscoe, and Pirate—and wished she had time to groom them as well. They looked sad and neglected. "Sorry, guys," she called out to them. "I'll be back later to take care of you."

They closed up the barn and walked the fieldstone path that led to the house. Suddenly, Lianne heard a commotion to their right. A stirring in the wheat, about twenty feet in.

Something flailing around.

"What's that?" Marnie's voice, tense.

A circle of wheat dropped as if being sucked straight down into the earth.

Lianne wanted to scream, but couldn't get a sound out.

More wheat stalks fell.

Weird gruff panting, coming closer.

Lianne was petrified in place.

The thing in the wheat crashed closer.

Raspy grumbling and sniffing.

The wheat parted and a strange looking animal shuffled into the clearing, stopping about six feet from them.

Time stood still. Lianne couldn't breathe, didn't *dare* take a breath. She sensed Marnie next to her, not moving, paralyzed by a mute fear.

Lianne stared at the creature and it stared back. A lizard-looking thing like the one that bit her, but different. This one had a bigger head with a large bony crown and three small horns. Its snout and crown glowed a brilliant, swirling purple, orange, and red. Two feet tall and three feet long, it looked like a baby rhinoceros with a fan-like crown and two extra horns above beady eyes. The creature chewed strands of wheat in its beaky mouth, watching Lianne and Marnie attentively.

Girls and beast observed each other for what felt like an eternity, the lizard blinking and chewing, Lianne and Marnie not moving.

The animal stopped chewing, moved a step forward.

Marnie screamed and took off running for the house, her riding boots slapping against the walkway stones. Lianne hoped she would bring Uncle Jimmy out here fast, because she couldn't move.

The creature advanced cautiously, swinging its thick tail and moving its big bony head side to side, sniffing the air.

Lianne backed up a step but was powerless to move further. She tried to scream but her vocal cords produced only a whispery hiss.

The reptile stopped chewing and moved in next to her. Sniffed her leg. She stood lifeless as a statue, felt warm breaths against her thigh. She was dizzy with fear. The wheat field began to swirl around her. The ground and sky went topsy-turvy on her.

Finally, the creature gulped down its mouthful of wheat, let out a soft squeal, then turned and waddled back into the wheat field.

Lianne took in a deep breath.

Her knees buckled.

On the exhale she fell to the ground in a dead faint.

Piece of the Rock

June 23: Gilliam's Guidepost
Heart Butte, Montana

PETER STEERED THE CHOPPER OVER the southern edge of the Blackfeet Indian reservation. Birch Creek appeared as a thin green ribbon below. A pickup truck motored along the two-lane road that ran parallel. Majestic snow-capped Rocky Mountain peaks loomed to the west. Looking northeast, he could see sunlight reflecting off the mirrored surface of Four Horns Lake. The reservation spanned 3,000 square miles, running north to the Canadian border.

He flew due north, toward the Heart Butte ranch. He and his crew were scheduled to pick up the meteorite that had struck there three weeks ago, the *legendary* meteorite that had astonishingly hatched out the first dinosaurs.

Peter was in a much better frame of mind today. Yesterday had been a colossal waste of time and fuel as he and his team spent hours attempting to locate a ghost meteorite. Astronomers had reported it coming down in the Bitterroot National Forest, near Kent Peak, but Peter and crew couldn't find it. He'd manned the copilot seat handling navigation duties while Larry Bing piloted (a Glick innovation: rotating pilots and navigators to prevent burnout). A pair of guardsmen—Woods and Dietrich—rode in back, chomping at the bit for something to do. Larry Bing and Peter had circled the heavily wooded area most of the afternoon, working their way out from the reported coordinates in ever-widening circles until Peter wanted to scream. Scanning the vast green canopy hour after hour had given him a throbbing headache. There'd been no burn holes in treetops like they'd found on their two successful pickups. No indication that anything had disturbed the natural beauty of the mountainous terrain. Running low on fuel, they returned to Mount Bennett AFB emptyhanded.

Colonel Glick had been irate. Called them rank amateurs. Incompetent. Forest Service failures. He dressed down Peter and Bing publicly, and threatened to replace them with "true aviators," meaning his Air Force pilots. "You're sandbagging it to draw out your time and stay on the payroll," he'd ranted. This scenario had played out many times over the course of the week-and-a-half that the mission dubbed Operation Hot Rocks had been active.

Every one of the helicopter pilots had done their time getting roasted in Glick's hot seat. Peter didn't like being torn apart in front of his peers. He'd come close to punching the little colonel in the mouth, wanting to knock out a couple of those buck teeth of his. But then, he was able to cool his anger when, shortly after, General Ramage—Glick's superior in the Pentagon—made it known the program had been a failure to this point, embarrassing Glick in front of the Operation Hot Rocks crews (so good to see Glick in the hot seat for once). Ten days into the mission and twice as many outings had produced dismal results. They'd recovered just four of the fifteen downed meteorites. And much of that came in pieces that were so badly charred and damaged that government geologists complained of not having enough to work with. They needed a larger sampling to study. At least that's how Glick framed it.

Morale was low.

Tempers were high.

Communication was nonexistent, or at best, a lie.

Glick needed a success to get General Ramage off his back. The pilots knew Glick had been holding onto this easy meteorite pickup as an ace card to play when he needed to report good news.

And so today wouldn't be a repeat of yesterday's frustrations. This was a stress-free flight. It promised to be an easy retrieval. He looked forward to meeting this rancher fellow, Bryan Gilliam, a man he'd seen on the nightly news. And Peter wanted to see the famed dinosaur hatchlings, up close and personal. Such an amazing thing that he would be one of just a handful of people on the planet to get an intimate look at these prehistoric animals.

However, caught up in his enthusiasm, he'd made a huge mistake when talking to Brinshou last night. Not thinking, he'd gloated to his wife that they'd be making this trip today. He knew as soon as the words left his mouth that he'd suffered a lapse in judgment. Brin was well aware there were live dinosaurs at the Gilliam ranch and she didn't want Peter anywhere near them.

Brin had been inconsolable after learning news of the Boy Scout massacre. Eight boys had died, all just twelve- and thirteen-years-old. The two adult scoutmasters were in critical condition in the ICU at Great Falls Clinic Hospital. The head scoutmaster had to have a leg amputated mid-thigh. According to news reports, their sons were the only two to escape unscathed, apparently getting away by climbing trees. The tragedy was shocking, appalling, a terrible loss of young life. They were just boys with their whole lives in front of them. The nation grieved. The *world* grieved.

Dinosaur attacks were happening with greater frequency now. There had been increased assaults on fowl and livestock, with a confrontation between dinosaurs and bison down in Yellowstone just yesterday. Several herds of elk had also been hit, which surprised the naturalists, who thought elk to be less vulnerable due to their quickness and ability to vanish at the first hint of danger. Though there had been no further attacks on humans, biologists claimed it was just a matter of time before another human catastrophe occurred. There were very hungry prehistoric carnivores roaming the Continental Divide. Montanans were in panic mode, screaming for the government or military—*somebody*—to do something to eradicate this growing dinosaur plague.

And no one was more panicked than Brinshou. She had begged and cajoled Peter to please come home. The father of their child shouldn't be out flying such dangerous missions. She didn't want to end up a dinosaur widow, a single mother. She'd cried and claimed she couldn't go on much longer without him. Ten days apart had felt like ten *years*. Her complaints went on and on. Finally, growing exasperated and impatient with her demands, Peter made a second drastic mistake. He told her she was being melodramatic.

"*Melodramatic?* Don't you *dare* belittle me, Peter Lacroix! I'm scared. Can't you see that? I'm really afraid right now. For you. For me. For Kimi . . . for *all* of us."

The anguish in her voice nearly crushed him. He wanted to be with her and the baby more than anything, even if he couldn't convince her of that. He tried, once again, to get her to go to the rez and stay with her parents. Her mother could help out with Kimi, lighten Brin's load. But she stubbornly refused, pleading with him to forget the foolhardy meteorite roundup and come home where he belonged.

Peter understood his wife's fears even if he didn't share them. He knew the chances were extremely slim—*nonexistent* really— that either of them would encounter these prehistoric creatures in the wild. It just wouldn't happen. But no matter how he spun it, he couldn't convince her of it. She kept insisting that those Boy Scouts had thought the same thing, that it would *never* happen to them.

The longer he was away, the more Brin's angst-ridden fragility fed his guilt. After his phone call with her last night, he decided he would ask Glick for a leave of absence. He'd claim a family emergency, which really wasn't far from the truth. A break from this madness and a few days at home would do him and his marriage good. And it just might help save Brin from herself.

"Swing west thirty-eight degrees, Pete." Larry Bing's voice in his headset cut through the rumbling engine and chuffing rotors.

Peter glanced at the GPS display and saw the preprogrammed waypoint of the Gilliam ranch flashing bright blue. He pulled the cyclic stick gently to the left. The chopper responded, veering westward.

"That's good, now even her out."

Peter centered the stick, then pushed it forward. The chopper's front end dipped and coasted toward the ranch. Larry Bing's steady voice continued in his ear, reciting data for airspeed, altitude over range, air temperature, wind speed, wind direction, rate of climb, gyroscopic direction, bank-and-pitch altitude.

Bryan Gilliam had instructed them to land in the east meadow, recognizable by an oblong retention pond and a ten-foot-wide crater of scorched earth where the meteorite had struck.

Peter circled the property, flying over a cluster of wooden buildings with corrugated metal roofs: a small motor inn with several cars angled in front of the units; three large barns studded with ventilation cupolas; a two-story farmhouse; a general store with a delivery truck parked out back. White pine, hemlock, and western larch sectioned off open grasslands. A winding asphalt driveway threaded between the buildings. Two white news vans sat outside one of the barns. A long gravel access drive led out to the main road. A police car, its rack of lights strobing colorfully, sat at the entrance, a pair of uniformed cops standing nearby. A number of people milled around the property.

Peter swung the chopper back around to the east meadow. A pair of Native men in jeans and tank tops stood next to a pickup truck, waving their arms, pointing to the field beyond the fence. He brought the craft down softly, the skids touching down near the perimeter of the meteorite strike pit. He shut off the engine and the rotors wound down.

Peter climbed out, followed by the crew. The afternoon heat slapped him in the face. The two Indians approached the cockpit, long dark braids flapping across their shoulders and down their backs. "Oki, Oki!" they shouted in unison, which Peter knew meant "Hello, welcome!" in Blackfoot.

The elder of the two said "I'm Apisi and my partner here is Chogan." He smiled, showing gaps in a mouth of yellowed teeth. A colorful snake tattoo circled his wiry forearm. "We work for the Gilliams."

Peter introduced himself and his crew. Handshakes and fist bumps all around.

"Mr. Gilliam is expecting you in the utility barn," Apisi said. "He's finishing up a TV interview there. He's quite famous, you know."

"So I've noticed," Peter said.

"I'll drive you there. Chogan will stay and watch your bird."

Peter said to his lead guardsman, Woods, "You and Dietrich stay here."

Apisi laughed a sarcastic laugh. "Don't trust us, huh? If you can't trust Chogan you can't trust anybody."

"I'm sure Chogan is a sweet fella," Peter said. "I'm just follow-ing my mission protocol. We have a very particular boss."

"I understand," Apisi said, laughing again, jovially this time. "Please come with me. *My* very particular boss is waiting."

Apisi drove Peter and Bing to the utility barn. The building was cavernous, larger than it looked from the outside. A musty warmth enveloped Peter as he entered. He breathed in the acrid tang of gaso-line, burnt motor oil, and welded steel. Farm equipment took up most of one wall. Automotive parts, engines, and vehicle chassis in various states of repair cluttered one large corner section. A large John Deere tractor sat with its hood propped open. Greasy work rags were scattered around the work area.

They passed a stack of empty glass aquarium tanks. Half a dozen metal dog crates lined another wall, also empty. Sitting on top of the last crate was a chicken incubator. There were no eggs in the slots of the carousel tray.

This is where the dinosaurs hatched out, Peter thought, an excitement blooming in his chest. *I wonder where they are now.*

Apisi led them to the far end of the barn, where Bryan Gilliam was engaged in a television interview. An elevated commercial lighting rig lit up the area. Two camera operators stood behind tri-pods, focused on Gilliam and the interviewer. KECI-TV appeared in bold script across the sides of the cameras—the NBC affiliate out of Missoula. A large boom microphone hung over the area, out of frame. A group of people, some wearing headphones, stood in a semicircle, looking on in silence. Peter recognized the interviewer, Madison Donnelly, the photogenic, ambitious young newswoman who'd interviewed him in Missoula at the heroes dinner given him by Sam and Elizabeth Dantley two weeks ago. Which reminded him that he'd forgotten all about Georgie. Peter wondered whether his young friend was out of the hospital yet and was ashamed that he'd been negligent in calling him.

"So when can we expect your dinosaur zoo to open, Mr. Gilliam?" Madison Donnelly asked.

Bryan Gilliam scrunched his forehead in thought. "Well, that's hard to say right now, Madison. They're beginning to shut down some public places and events in light of what's happened. I'd open the gates tomorrow if I could, and let the American people see these amazing creatures. But we have a lot of work to do. Got to give our Dromaeosaurs plenty of room to run and still keep things safe."

"So you're saying these Dromo—?

"Dro-*maeosaurs*," Gilliam said, helping her out with the pronunciation.

"Thank you. These Dromaeosaurs are dangerous, then?"

"Yes, absolutely. Doctor Hayden Fowler, the world famous paleontologist staying here at the inn, describes them as big track-star kangaroos with teeth and jaws like sharks."

"They sound deadly."

"They are. Soon they'll be able to run at speeds close to forty miles an hour. And they have voracious appetites."

"That's a scary vision, Mr. Gilliam."

"Please, it's *Bryan*. And yes it is scary . . ."

Peter, Bing, and Apisi stood watching the interview. Peter thought Gilliam looked a few inches shorter in person than he'd appeared to be on television. Heavy pancake makeup and dark eyeliner gave his angular face an artificially tanned, overly alert look.

Peter noticed the shards of scorched black rock leaning against the wall behind Gilliam. Didn't seem to be much there.

Is that all there is of the meteorite? Glick will crucify us if that's all we bring back.

Gilliam was speaking. ". . . this area . . . this reservation is home to the proud Native American people of the Blackfeet Nation. They are destitute and many are living on the edge of starvation. The Blackfeet are a forgotten people. The U.S. government has turned their backs on them and it isn't right. Unemployment is almost forty percent here and nearly sixty percent of the people live in hopeless poverty. My Blackfoot friends need work. They need jobs. My dinosaur zoo will provide many jobs for the Blackfeet Nation. My wife Loretta and I have already hired a few people in need. We'll be hiring many more of my Blackfoot brethren to help build the dinosaur habitat and assist with other projects associated with our

Dromaeosaurs . . ."

Brin would love this guy. The Kootenai and Salish of the Flat-head Indian reservation are a forgotten people, too.

Peter listened to Gilliam go on about the injustices thrust upon the Blackfeet. It was the same sad history that applied to most Native American tribes. Peter had heard similar complaints from Brinshou, and especially her father, Nashota. The government had screwed over their people—the Flathead Nation—stealing much of their best land, using the promise of casinos to bribe them. Peter knew poverty and unemployment were problematic on both the Flathead and Blackfeet reservations; Bryan Gilliam was speaking the truth. Alcoholism and drug abuse existed in frightening numbers, too. But Peter also knew the Blackfeet operated a big casino in Browning, and the Salish and Kootenai profited from their casinos—Gray Wolf Peak Casino in Missoula and the Kwataqnuk Resort Casino in Polson. Kwataqnuk had been Nash's employer since it opened in 1992. Nashota Taleka was one of the lucky few on the Flathead rez, and Peter thought his father-in-law was a hypocrite to complain of unfair treatment by the government. This issue had led to a few verbal jousts between them over the years, a couple coming close to fisticuffs. Peter was all for helping out Native American populations, for they all had problems that stemmed from government theft and corruption. The Native people certainly had legitimate gripes. But he couldn't stand hearing Nash bitch about it when he was lining his pockets with casino money. Peter often thought Brin's father was the most disingenuous man he'd ever known.

As Peter watched Bryan Gilliam field questions, he began to see a touch of Phineas T. Barnum in him. Gilliam possessed a show-manship quality and an impresario spirit he found engaging. Peter observed Apisi as Gilliam spoke of tending to the needs of the Blackfeet Nation, and saw the reverence and respect in the Indian's reactions. Peter flew here thinking he'd be meeting with a hick farmer. Instead, he saw before him a shrewd and savvy master sales-man working the media to his advantage.

Bryan Gilliam shielded his eyes from the bright lights. "Well, I see my guests have arrived," he said, looking in their direction. "Sorry, I'm afraid our time is up, Madison."

Madison Donnelly nodded "That's okay. Are we still on for tomorrow?"

"Absolutely."

"Thank you for speaking with me today, Mr. Gilliam."

"It's been my pleasure."

Gilliam removed his earpiece.

Madison turned to face the camera. "So that wraps up our exclusive interview with Bryan Gilliam, the first human being to encounter Cretaceous Period dinosaurs. Tune in this same time tomorrow when Mr. Gilliam will take us to see the creatures he has penned in another building. You won't want to miss it. This is Madison Donnelly, KECI-TV News, live from Heart Butte, Montana, signing off."

A buzz of chatter erupted as people crowded around Gilliam and the reporter, congratulating them on the well done interview. Peter heard Madison Donnelly telling Gilliam that the segment would be edited and appear in shorter form on tonight's national NBC News broadcast with anchor Lester Holt.

Shortly Gilliam made his way to Peter and Larry Bing. "You guys look like helicopter pilots," he said as a way of greeting.

"And you look like a national celebrity," Peter said, shaking his hand. "Make that *international* celebrity, Mr. Gilliam."

"Please, call me Bryan," he said as he shook hands with Peter and Bing. To Apisi he said, "Thanks, napí. Please meet us in the stables in ten minutes."

When Apisi was gone, Peter said, "I enjoyed what I heard of your interview, Bryan."

"Oh, thanks. I appreciate that. It's not easy when you know it's gonna be on national television."

"I'll bet."

Larry Bing said, "Your interviewer is quite a looker."

"Yeah, Madison's easy on the eyes, that's for sure."

Time to get down to business. Peter said, "She sure asked you a lot of softball questions."

Gilliam blinked a couple of times, looking confused, not quite sure if he was being insulted or not.

"I've got a hardball question for you, Bryan."

"Yeah? What's that?"

Peter pointed to the meteorite fragments. "Is that all you've got for us?"

Gilliam twisted to look behind him at the pile of burnt rock, then slowly turned back around, looked Peter square in the eyes. "Yeah. Why?"

"Please don't bullshit me, Bryan."

"I'm not."

"Come on, man. It'd take a whole lot more rock than this to cause that crater in your meadow."

Larry Bing said, "Pete's right. We saw the videos the geologist shot. That meteorite was a good six feet tall."

"Where's the rest of it, Bryan?"

He hesitated, gazing over Peter's shoulder across the length of the barn. Peter could almost see the wheels turning behind his darkly-lined eyes. Finally he said, "Okay, you guys got me. We've got more of it over in the horse barn. The scientists have more room to work over there. I was gonna take you over there anyway, to see our Dromaeosaurs. Come on," he said, walking toward the exit on the other side of the barn. "Our Cretaceous creatures wait."

Peter and Bing fell in behind him, Peter wondering what Bryan Gilliam was up to.

Impresario spirit indeed! P.T. Barnum is alive and well at Gilliam's Guidepost.

Dinosaur Scouts

June 27: Willingham Farms
Shelby, Montana

"HAVE YOU ACTUALLY SEEN ANY DINOSAURS in your fields?" Nora asked Jay Willingham, weathered-faced proprietor of Willingham Farms, a 9,000-acre wheat and alfalfa farm five miles east of Shelby.

Nora, Hayden, and the farmer were gathered on Willingham's wraparound porch at the back of his rustic, eight-room farmhouse. Nora sat in a white oak Adirondack chair with Hayden across from her on a red cedar porch swing. Willingham perched on the railing facing them.

"Can't say I've seen 'em myself," Willingham responded. "My field hands haven't either. But my neighbors have. Dryden and Culbertson and Enright . . . they've all seen 'em. And their crops are gettin' ate up, just like mine. But that ain't news to you. You've checked out Dana Culbertson's and Jimmy Enright's fields. You've seen the destruction at their farms. And I *know* it's those damned dinosaurs gettin' after my crops, too. Sneaky bastards they are! They eat and run and leave behind huge piles of reeking scat. The hell of it is that this was shapin' up to be our best wheat yield in six years. Best quality, too. Good berry sizes and test weights."

"Test weights?" Hayden said.

"Yeah. Test weights give us the best indication of wheat quality. Higher test weights mean larger milled flour yield, and that's our bottom line. We're scheduled to start harvestin' our winter wheat in a couple weeks. The way it's goin' I fear we won't have much left to reap by then."

The farmer turned away from them and looked out across his

fields. "Jimmy Enright told me you identified these invaders as Triceratops, if I'm sayin' that right. Enright showed me the video you took. Shook me up but good. We're all scared. I'm not embarrassed to admit that."

"All Montanans are afraid, Mr. Willingham," Nora said. "There's a lot of fear in Idaho, too, and even on up into Canada. I can assure you, however, if Triceratops are what we find here, which is highly probable, then there's nothing to be afraid of. They're herbivores . . . plant eaters . . ."

She continued speaking, trying to ease the farmer's mind. Willingham remained turned away from her, scanning his fields, lost in his own thoughts, seemingly disinterested in what she had to say.

Nora and Hayden had visited the Enright farm last week. They'd spoken with the two girls who'd encountered the juvenile Triceratops—Marnie Enright and Lianne Gilliam. Both girls were traumatized, and had trouble describing what they'd seen coming at them from out of the field. The younger girl, Lianne, seemed to be more shaken by the experience. Tears wetting her face, the Gilliam girl had told them in a shaky, breathless voice, "I don't remember much. Just that the lizard thing sniffed my leg. I was scared. It was big and smelly and had a weird shaped head with three horns stickin' out of its face. I didn't wanna get bit again and hafta go to the doctor and get more stitches. Everything got fuzzy then. I remember scrapin' my knee when I fell down and my Uncle Jimmy bein' there when I woke up. That's all I can remember." Lianne had barely been able to get it out before she broke down sobbing. Nora had reached out and pulled the girl to her in a mothering hug, surprising herself with her nurturing gesture. The embrace was awkward, but instinctive and heartfelt. Nora had been overcome with compassion for the Gilliam girl, a seven-year-old who'd already had two close encounters with dinosaurs.

After their talk with the girls, Nora and Hayden explored the Enright fields, armed with a video camera and tranquilizer gun supplied by Barrett Hailey, the government wildlife biologist staying at the Guidepost Inn and working with Franz Krause overseeing the Dromaeosaur hatchlings. She and Hayden had spotted several juveniles easily identifiable as Triceratops rooting through the wheat, but failed to get close enough to capture one. Nora was able to film clear footage of a pair of Triceratops scurrying away from them between rows of trampled wheat. A few days later, they'd visited the Culbertson farm close by, where Hayden videoed four more Triceratops juveniles, all bolting into the wheat at the sight of them. The videos proved to be good source documentation for the Smithsonian folks who were funding these dinosaur scouting jaunts. But Nora was disappointed they hadn't been able to sedate and capture one for further study. Triceratops were proving to be crafty, elusive animals despite their low-slung bulk.

Nora said to Willingham, "I know they look frightening but they're harmless to humans. In fact, we're finding that they seem to fear us. They won't hurt you or your family . . . or your field workers."

Jay Willingham reacted like he'd been slapped. He turned around and rose from the railing, glaring at her. "Won't hurt my family? Do you hear yourself? If they eat up all my winter wheat, they might as well attack me and my family directly. This harvest makes up seventy-five percent of our annual income!"

Nora shrank back in her chair. Striving to calm the man, she ran a hand through her short, dark bob and gave him a conciliatory glance. "We're not trying to downplay your loss, Mr. Willingham. We feel your pain. We've seen the massive damage done to crops around Shelby. I know you and the other farmers in these parts are hurting and I sympathize with you."

"As do I," Hayden said. "It's just unfortunate these animals seem to love wheat."

Willingham leaned against the railing, looking uncomfortable. "Sorry, folks. I'm just angry as hell is all. It's difficult enough running a successful farm without this crap."

"We understand," Nora said.

"Where do they come from, these Triceratops?"

"That's what the world is tryin' to figure out."

"But you're dinosaur scientists, right?"

Hayden nodded. "Yes, paleontologists."

"So, shouldn't you know where they're comin' from?"

Hayden said, "It's not that simple. We're well versed in dinosaur *bones*. Prehistoric *fossils*. But living, breathing primordial organisms? That's a whole different ball game. And where they come from? All we can do is make educated guesses based on the science . . . the bones and skeletons we've studied. We're also learning a lot from the meteorites . . . the type of stone, minerals, metals, and plants that encased the eggs."

"But you still don't know where these things're comin' from?"

"No. Lots of theories. Some of them are way out there. But nothing concrete."

"Well, shit, is there anything you can do to help us out? To save our crops?"

Nora gave Hayden a questioning glance, then said, "Yes, there is, Mr. Willingham. But as scientists, we're in a tough position here. On the one hand we know what a nuisance these animals are, how much devastation and death they can bring. Ranchers see them as livestock serial killers. Farmers like yourself see them as destructive pests. Montanans—especially since the Boy Scout attack—see them as mass murdering beasts. People want to eradicate them, wipe them clean off the face of this Earth. That's an understandable human reaction, I guess. They *are* bad news in so many ways. But on the other hand, the return of these dinosaurs is a gift to science. Especially for us paleontologists. To rid the world of them would be a mistake. Another extinction now would destroy our gift and our chance to learn more about these creatures that roamed this area sixty-six million years ago. They existed on this planet far longer than us humans. As for what's happening here? Triceratops are eating machines. We know that. They'll grow to be bigger than elephants. They'll consume enormous amounts of plant life. I truly feel your misery, Mr. Willingham, but as a scientist, I have to say my wish is that we humans can learn to coexist with the dinosaurs."

"Coexist with them? *Really*? A gift? Give me a friggin' break! You wouldn't be sayin' that if you were a farmer or rancher . . . or a *Boy Scout*."

"She's just being honest, sir," Hayden said, the *sir* having an obvious disrespectful edge to it.

Willingham took offense. "I asked you to come here because I thought you could help. But you tell me you love these dinosaurs that are gobbling up my cash crop? They're a *gift* you say? Outrageous! If you don't have any ideas how to stop it, you can leave now."

"The lady never said we *loved* the dinosaurs," Hayden said. "You're putting words in her mouth."

"She might as well have."

Hayden raised his voice. "Sounds to me like you're blaming us for the dinosaur invasion."

"Well?"

"That's like blaming oncologists for cancer."

Willingham huffed, a belligerent snort. "I think it best that you both get off my property right now."

Hayden stood, his six-foot-four-inch frame an imposing sight. Willingham backed up a step, alarmed.

"Look, Mr. Willingham, we both feel for you and your wheat farmer neighbors. That's no bullshit." Hayden spoke in a calm controlled, placating tone that surprised Nora. "We'll do all we can to help you. But Nora's right. The rebirth of these Cretaceous dinosaurs *is* exciting to us. But that doesn't translate to *love*. Not by any stretch. Yes, we're in awe of them, but we're also extremely sensitive to the dangers they pose. Please settle down so we can figure out what's goin' on and help you. We're not even sure it's Triceratops eating up your wheat. It could be another species entirely."

"Jesus Christ, this is such a bitch!" Willingham said, shoulders slumping. "All right, then."

"No hard feelings?" Nora said.

"No, I reckon not," Willingham said, leaning over and fist bumping both of them. "Sorry, but this whole thing has been a jolt to me."

"You're not alone," Hayden said. "It's been a jolt to all of us. So let's get down to brass tacks. Tell me, how much of your land is planted in wheat?"

"Winter wheat, about five-thousand acres . . . spring wheat, another two-thousand. That comes to around eleven square miles."

"Wow!" Nora exclaimed. "That's a lot of real estate."

"Yeah. We're one of the largest refined flour producers in Montana," he said proudly. "We mill our own wheat here. We take our flour directly to the wholesaler. Cuts out the middle man."

"Smart business move," Hayden said, tapping the side of his head with his forefinger. "How about your alfalfa fields? They been getting hit?"

"Strangely enough, no. But we've seen tracks and scat in both the alfalfa and grass hay fields. They're drawn to the water in the irrigation ditches, but they've left those crops alone."

"Interesting," Nora said. "They love wheat but have no taste for alfalfa. Picky eaters."

Willingham nodded. "Well, the wheat is a lot taller and more bulky."

Hayden said, "Yeah, more enticing for hungry herbivores. Better for hiding as well. How about we go out to your fields and have a look at what's been munching on your wheat. You mind taking us out there?"

"No problem. We'll take one of the combines. More room in the cab and we'll sit higher up. Easier to get into the interior where the damage is the worst. I'll forewarn you it'll be loud, but we do have ear protection."

* * *

They climbed up into the cab, Willingham in the bucket seat behind the wheel, Nora crammed elbow-to-elbow with Hayden on a short bench seat. She was surprised at all the high tech, with several digital display screens arrayed around the steering wheel. They put on their noise-canceling headphones and Willingham fired up the engine. The vibration rattled Nora to her core.

They jounced along a furrowed dirt road, cutting between a field of short green alfalfa on their left, and a long stretch of tall amber wheat on their right. Three steel grain silos gleamed in the distance like rockets aimed for the heavens.

They rode on, the wheat now appearing on both sides of the lane, rolling out as far as Nora could see. Thousands of acres of it. The Willingham farm had much more arable cropland than the other farms she and Hayden had visited in the area.

It would take a hell of a lot of starving herbivores to put a small dent in all this.

Shortly, Willingham took the harvester around a sharp curve. They came to a section of wheat that was leveled flat against the ground. Stalks were scattered across the road like tawny pickup sticks. There had definitely been a feeding here.

Nora made a motion for Willingham to stop. He braked the big, lurching combine to a halt. Shut it down. They all removed their headphones. She jumped down from the cab, followed by Hayden. The sun beat down relentlessly, baking her shoulders and the top of her head. Diesel exhaust floated through the muggy air.

She kicked some of the loose wheat away with the toe of her boot. Bent down for a closer look. Pointed and said, "Look what we have here, Hayden. Hoof prints. Same as we saw at the other farms. Quadrupedal animal. Three hooves on both of the front feet and four hooves each on the back feet. I think the diners here were Triceratopses. No big surprise."

"Yeah," Hayden said, kneeling, peering down, the Pneu-Dart X-2 tranquilizer pistol in his hand. "Ceratopsian. You're correct." He looked around the immediate area, saw the scatter of tracks etching the dirt road. He walked to the side of the road to inspect piles of sunbaked dung. "There were a lot of them here, that's for sure."

Willingham walked up behind them. "I thought you said these things were harmless to humans."

"They are," Nora said.

"Then why is he holdin' that pistol like we're about to be ambushed?"

Hayden eyed the flattened wheat at the edge of the field. "Because I don't wanna miss a chance to capture one and take it back with us to study."

"How're you gonna study a dead one?"

Nora knew dinosaur specimens, whether dead or alive, gave them invaluable scientific data. The young Tyrannosaurus Rex cadaver Hayden had fished out of the creek at the Tully ranch had provided them volumes of useful information.

"These darts don't kill," Hayden said to Willingham, holding up the tranq pistol. "They sedate them. Barrett Hailey—the wildlife biologist who lent me this gun—told me it'll put a juvenile dinosaur out for a couple-to-three hours. Doesn't really hurt them. How about we trek further into this field?"

"Yep. That's what the harvester is for," Willingham said, heading back to the tractor and jumping up into the cab. "The worst of it is a couple hundred yards in."

The harvester plowed through the thick wheat. Willingham kept the thresher unit raised and idle so as not to damage any more of the wheat than he had to. The noisy, lumbering combine moved slowly, flattening everything in its path. Grain dust kicked up into a cloud that swirled through the hot air, mixing with the oily smell of diesel fuel. Nora's eyes itched and watered. Her throat was dry. She had a ticklish sensation in her nose and sneezed a few times.

They crashed through into a wide, bright clearing. An area the size of four football fields had been ravaged. Nora couldn't believe the devastation. The entire area was pockmarked with patches of sickly, small wheat nubbins. It looked to her like this expanse had already been harvested. Just a scraggly patchwork of wheat stubs, everything chewed down to the ground.

Willingham shut off the combine. They removed their noise protectors. The tractor engine ticked. Grasshoppers thrummed all around them. "This is one of the worst spots," he said. "There are at least three others . . . as of yesterday."

They were climbing down out of the cab when Nora spotted them. Three large Triceratops running across the clearing, their bony frilled hoods reflecting vibrant prismatic colors in the sunlight. Juveniles, but bigger than the ones they'd videotaped at the other two farms. Hayden saw them, too, and he took off running, holding the tranquilizer pistol up in a firing position. Two of the animals ran helter-skelter—their thick, heavily muscled legs churning—disappearing impossibly quick into the tall wheat on the far side of the clearing. The third lingered, seemingly confused, frozen in place like a deer caught in the headlights, its oversized head with its three stubby horns raised, sniffing the air with its beaky snout.

Hayden stopped running. Set his feet. Took aim and fired. The tranq pistol emitted a *zinging* sound as the dart left the gun. She watched the barb streak across the clearing, striking the animal in its side. Nora heard a squeal of pain and saw the creature try to turn and run, but the dart caught in a tangle of wheat stubs and trapped it. The animal flopped and shook, braying like a frightened donkey as it tried desperately to break loose. Fifteen seconds of intense struggle and screeching, then the creature collapsed on its side, its thick hind legs flailing and kicking. Another fifteen seconds and there was silence.

The Triceratops lay comatose.

"Well, we finally got us one, Nora," Hayden said, approaching the animal cautiously.

"Good lord, that's a big one," Willingham shouted from the harvester. "That was one helluva shot."

Hayden knelt by his quarry, reached down to touch its scaly hide. "Yeah, I'm public enemy number one amongst the deer popu-lation in Minnesota." He removed the dart from the animal's flank and slid his hands under its body, lifted. "Jesus, this is one big boy, for sure. Probably sixty to seventy pounds. Give me a hand, will ya, Mr. Willingham?"

"Sorry, I ain't goin' near that thing," the farmer said, retreating to the safety of the tractor. "That is one scary beast."

"Are you kidding me?" Nora said in Willingham's direction. "I swear, a woman having to do men's work for them! How embar-rassing for you!" She went to where the animal lay. "Which end do you want me to take, Hayden?"

He pointed his chin at the stubby tail. "I'll take the head since it's heaviest. You take the back end."

They carried the sedated animal to the harvester, huffing and puffing in the heat. Nora could feel the immense strength in the Triceratops' hind quarters. Hard lean muscle packed under a tough, leathery, rhinoceros-like hide. And its bony crown rising up behind its head blazed vibrantly with phosphorescent colors, like bright acrylic paint on porcelain. This went against popular paleontology beliefs that Triceratops—and most dinosaurs for that matter—were dull gray or brown.

They got the animal to the combine and strapped it to the thresher unit. Farmer Willingham kept a safe distance and was no help at all.

* * *

Within twenty minutes they had the sedated Triceratops in the back of the rental van and were on their way back to Gilliam's Guidepost with their prize. Hayden drove while Nora tapped out a report on her laptop. The car smelled of perspiration and a jungle animal odor, similar to what she recalled from her visits to the Milwaukee County Zoo African elephant habitat back home. Distinctive, pungent, wild. Intoxicating to her on some primal level.

As she typed, Nora thought about what had brought them here. The Smithsonian had appointed her and Hayden to fulltime positions as dinosaur trackers, replacing them on the paleontology expedition with two other highly regarded scientists. From Nora's team, geologist Greg Dulowski had been sent back to the expedition while paleozoologist Franz Krause remained at the Guidepost Inn to manage the care of the growing Dromaeosaur juveniles and assist with the habitat being built for them. Dulowski was put in charge of the expedition, which had since fully excavated the Maiasaura skeleton and Triceratops skull in Choteau, ahead of schedule, and moved north to Glacier National Park for the second planned leg of the dig.

Nora had mixed emotions about the switch in responsibilities. The three-month Smithsonian expedition had been her baby, her brainchild. Her *vision*. She had planned the excursion, lobbied for it, sold the idea, and recruited the team. And after all that difficult work, it had been pulled out from under her. Greg Dulowski was a competent and respected scientist. As a renowned geologist, rocks and bones and fossils were definitely his bailiwick. And he had the drive and personality to lead a large paleontology expedition. She knew he'd do a great job, but it still hurt.

Molly Fianola from the Smithsonian told Nora she should see the move to Dinosaur Tracker Lead as a promotion. "Think about it, Nora," Molly had said, "you'll have a lot more autonomy and freedom of travel. You won't be bound to the excavation site. You won't have the headaches of managing a team of very opinionated people. You'll be free of all that. And please know that we wouldn't want just anyone out there doing this. We want you to be our lead dinosaur scout. You and Doctor Fowler are our trackers. But you are officially our lead. I've already made that clear to Hayden, and he's fine with it. You'll be the one filing the reports. You'll be the one calling all the shots—where you go, *when* you'll go. It's very important work. The government has their people out doing the same kind of tracking, but we feel you and Hayden, with your extensive knowledge and experience, can beat them to the punch. You can bring us exclusives, and capture living creatures to bring in for study."

Of course, Molly Fianola and everyone at the Smithsonian had been duly impressed when she and Hayden returned from the Tully ranch with the Tyrannosaurus Rex corpse. And now they had a live Triceratops specimen to show for their efforts. Nora was truly excited about this development. It helped take some of the sting out of losing her leadership role with the paleontology expedition.

"You sure are quiet," she heard Hayden say. "You're a million miles away."

She looked up from her laptop, saw him staring at her questioningly from behind the wheel, aviator shades hiding his eyes. His beard and hair were dusted with grain residue. "Just focused on our report," she said matter of factly. "Our benefactors are gonna be awestruck by what we have in the back."

"The *world* will be stunned by it," he said, looking back at the road. "Quite a day we had today."

"Yes, it was. I just hope we get our animal back to Heart Butte before it wakes up."

"No worries. The dosage I hit that sucker with won't wear off for another couple of hours."

"That was one helluva shot you pulled off back there. I'm impressed."

"You think that was good, you should see me with a rifle."

"You're not lacking confidence. I'll give you that, Hayden."

Nora resumed her typing, but couldn't regain her focus on the report. She thought about how her feelings toward Hayden had changed the past few weeks, how the man himself had changed. He'd stopped his boozing and cleaned himself up. At the start of the expedition he'd let his personal hygiene go. Many were the days when his body odor was quite noticeable and he'd wear smelly, ratty clothes. But since he'd shunned the demon alcohol he took daily showers, sometimes two a day when he knew they were going to be spending time together. He'd even taken to wearing a heady cologne in the evenings and dressing in oxford button-down shirts, freshly pressed khaki slacks, and loafers. Blue blazers on cool evenings. He got a haircut and trimmed his beard. The transformation changed his appearance from wild mountain man to cosmopolitan gent. *Certainly he has to be doing this for me,* she'd thought many times, finding herself wishing, *hoping* that was true. She'd been secretly thrilled when Molly Fianola told her Hayden would be joining her as the other half of this dinosaur tracking team. He was still playfully rascally, and at times, infuriating. But lately he'd been showing her his softer side, more of a gentle kindness toward her that she liked and appreciated. It seemed like he cared for her but didn't know how to show it. What was it he called her? His *hot librarian fantasy?* It should have turned her off, but it did just the opposite. She remembered their conversation in the car more than two weeks ago, when he'd said: *I don't mean to be disrespectful, Nora. I have immense respect for you, I really do. I guess I just don't know how to compliment you. I like bein' with you . . . spending time with you. Okay? There, I said it. That's not disrespectful, is it?*

She smiled inwardly, thinking he was like a teenage boy who felt awkward and uncomfortable around girls.

"What's so funny?" she heard him say, pulling her out of her musing.

"*What?* Nothing. I'm just working on this report."

"Sure you are. You haven't made a keystroke in the last five minutes."

"Just pay attention to your driving, will you?"

She keyed a paragraph, then stopped, looked at him. "Do you enjoy this kind of circus life we're leading?"

"What? You mean this dinosaur tracking thing?" he said.

"I mean all of it. Being paleontologists. Traveling all the time. Being away from home for long stretches. It doesn't make for a very settled life."

Hayden looked at her. "I've had the settled lifestyle. It's overrated if you ask me."

She didn't want to get into the fact that her nomadic career—chasing petrified bones and fossils all over the globe—had cost her two marriages and another serious relationship. She closed the lid on her laptop and set it aside. "I don't know, Hayden," she said. "Sometimes I feel like I'm just bouncing around aimlessly. Like a refugee without a home. I see the kind of life that Gilliam family has, and I feel a bit jealous. Bryan and Loretta Gilliam are so good together. They've built something really special at the Guidepost. Their family, I mean. Lots of love and warmth there. Three great kids. Sometimes I wish I had that . . . hearth and home and all that."

"You're doing important work, Nora. You should be proud of your accomplishments. You should be thankful. Millions of people would love to be in your position."

"You really think so?"

"Come on," he said beseechingly. "You're an excellent scientist and the best damned fundraiser I've ever seen. But I have to disagree with what you said about the Gilliams."

"Oh?"

"I think that Bryan Gilliam fellow is a grifter—a scoundrel and an opportunist. Just a feeling I have, but I don't believe the Gilliam household is as tight and lovey-dovey as you think. You've seen their daughter. We've spoken with her. Lianne needs psychological help, Nora. You know it and I know it. And all good ol' daddy dearest Bryan seems to care about is his idiotic dinosaur zoo and touting it in his TV interviews. I told him his zoo idea would bring him nothing but trouble . . . that he shouldn't do it, but he didn't listen. He's already got trouble in his own family and can't even see it. Or *refuses* to see it. Gilliam is blinded by the dollar signs in his eyes. It hasn't even been built yet and he's already counting his money. He wants to capitalize on the very animals that have terrified his young daughter. That's child abuse, you ask me."

Nora had also found herself thinking a lot about the Gilliam girl since their visit to the Enright farm. Little Lianne had been through so much trauma the past few weeks. No seven-year-old was equipped to handle what she'd endured.

"You're right about the girl," she said. "And I hadn't thought about it much, but I think you might be on to something with Bryan Gilliam. He seems more interested in his celebrity status than his family."

Hayden nodded. "The man's done two tours in Afghanistan. That's got to put some nightmarish shit in your head."

"Even more reason to protect his family. Maybe Lianne isn't the only Gilliam who needs a shrink."

"Well, his wife seems like a strong woman. Maybe Loretta will straighten him out. Maybe she'll get their daughter the help she needs."

"I could talk to Loretta, Hayden."

"No. Don't. This isn't the expedition you're dealing with, Nora. It's their family business. We're just guests staying at their motel."

"Yeah, you're probably right."

She gazed out her window at the passing countryside while he drove in silence. After a while, she said, "That Jay Willingham was a handful. Thanks for having my back today, Hayden."

He glanced at her, a slight grin showing through his beard. "I'd like to have more than your back."

Heat bloomed in her face. Embarrassment or something else, she couldn't tell. She kept her head turned to her window. "Is that the best you can do?" she said drolly. "That line is even more lame than your oncologist crack to Willingham."

"Hey! I *liked* my oncologist line. It broke the ice, didn't it?"

She laughed and turned to face him. "I thought he was going to break your *face*!"

"Nah. Willingham's a coward. He's afraid of an anesthetized dinosaur that's a third his weight. Anyway, I recovered and made nice."

"Yes you did. I was surprised by that."

Hayden slapped the steering wheel. "Damn!" He looked out his side window. "Once again, our gorgeous dinosaur huntress has underestimated her knight in shining white armor!"

Nora laughed again. "You don't look like any knight I've ever seen."

"You've seen a lot of knights, have you?"

"None wearing shining white armor."

Hayden gave her a sidelong glance. "You know, Nora, I really got a kick out of your comment to Willingham."

"Which one?"

"The one about a woman doing a man's work for him, and how he should be embarrassed. It put him in his place. Chalk one up for women's lib."

"Women's lib, my ass! It's the truth. And I swear, Hayden if you say you want my ass, I'll jump out of this car right now!"

"Whoa, easy there, Gloria Steinem," he said with a chuckle. "Yours truly would never be so crass."

"Yeah, *right*," she said, smiling at him.

"You shook up that farmer so much he lost sight of the fact that we left without helping his cause. I, for one, am appreciative."

"Oh, yeah. We were supposed to help him, weren't we?"

"You and I both know the only thing that would save his crops would be laying out poison bait, and I didn't cherish suggesting that."

Nora said, "Unfortunately, I'm afraid that's the next step for farmers and ranchers."

"Well, there's no guarantee these creatures would go for poison traps. I think they might be too smart for that."

He tapped the brake pedal, slowing the vehicle down from its cruising speed to a crawl.

"What're you doing?" she asked.

"I've gotta stop for a minute."

"Where?" she said, noting they were out in the middle of nowhere. Nothing but farmland forever and ever.

"Off to the side of the road here will do," he said.

Gravel pinged the undercarriage of the car as he pulled off the asphalt and onto the shoulder.

"What're you doing, Hayden. You have to pee or something?"

He put the car in Park and leaned across the seat. "If I don't kiss you in the next twenty seconds, I'm going to explode."

"*Hayden*! Uh . . . I'm not sure about—"

And then he stifled her objections with his mouth. His lips met hers and she could no longer resist. She scooted closer and kissed him back with a passion that surprised her. Her tongue danced around his, exploring his mouth as he leaned into her.

They necked and groped and moaned, nestling into each other like a pair of excitable, pheromone-crazed teens.

She giggled as his scratchy beard tickled her face and neck.

A long-haul trucker in an eighteen-wheeler thundered past and honked, two quick, deafening blasts.

Nora didn't flinch. She was lost in the warm cocoon of the big man's strong arms.

Bryan's World

July 1: Gilliam's Guidepost
Heart Butte, Montana

THE CAPTURE OF A LIVING TRICERATOPS in Shelby, Montana was a shot heard around the world. Hayden Fowler and Nora Lemoyne had made history. In addition to the capture, their videos confirmed the three-horned herbivores were the creatures behind the extensive crop damage in western Montana and Idaho.

Bryan Gilliam saw an opportunity he couldn't ignore. He sent out a press release to major news agencies, letting them know there was a new prehistoric attraction at Gilliam's Guidepost. Journalists and camera crews flocked to Heart Butte in staggering numbers. The press couldn't get enough of dinosaur mania. Bryan did interviews on local and national networks, cable news channels, Reuters, and the Associated Press, granting as many as three interviews per hour. That assembly-line kind of scheduling would exhaust most people, but it supercharged Bryan. Each interview segment he did hit him like a shot of adrenaline. At age 42 he was discovering something about himself: He *loved* being on stage. He relished the spotlight.

Now, after a hectic week, he sat on the couch with Loretta in the den watching late-night TV. Oldest son Paul sat in an easy chair, earbuds in, surfing the internet on his laptop. Audience laughter filled the room as Stephen Colbert riffed on self-serving politicians and narcissistic celebrities. The talk show host also included a spot on the dinosaur situation out west, calling the prehistoric beasts "undocumented immigrants that ICE needed to deport." Loretta laughed but Bryan was only halfway listening. He drank from a chilled bottle of Coors, preoccupied with thoughts of his week.

There was the visit from that helicopter pilot, Peter Lacroix. After their initial contentious meeting, Bryan found he liked the man and his chill French-Canadian vibe. So much so that he'd felt guilty at having to scam him and his copilot, Larry Bing. But only a little. Lacroix had presented Bryan with official-looking paperwork complete with a U.S. Air Force embossed seal, explaining in legal terminology the right of the U.S. government to pick up the meteorite via eminent domain laws. To Bryan, rightful ownership of those extraterrestrial rock wedges was questionable at best. The meteorite had struck *his* private property, not public land, and *certainly* not government land, although that was indeed a slippery slope.

Ninety percent of Gilliam's Guidepost was located on the Blackfeet Indian Reservation, that much was true. Bryan also knew the federal government owned all officially-sanctioned tribal land across the country. The feds held Native American real estate in an enormous trust fund spread across hundreds of accounts. The land—56 million acres—was estimated to be worth more than five billion dollars. The Blackfeet rez comprised two million acres of that. Full-blooded Blackfeet living there could not own land and therefore could not build equity. They could only rent from master slumlord Uncle Sam. Of course, that meant no property tax, but that was small consolation when weighed against the way the feds controlled their every move. The Gilliams were one of just a handful of white families living in Heart Butte, and since neither he nor Loretta could claim a drop of American Indian blood, Bryan paid a substantial amount in property tax every year. That made Gilliam's Guidepost private property and *not* the federal government's domain. That made the meteorite *his* property. At least in his not-so-humble opinion.

Uncle Sam can kiss my ass!

Bryan got heated every time he thought about the government's abuse of his Blackfoot neighbors. Anything and everything the Blackfeet wanted to do had to go through the U.S. Department of the Interior, more specifically the Bureau of Indian Affairs (BIA). Adding insult to injury, the BIA doled out monies to the tribe in a miserly fashion. Just one of many reasons why much of the 10,000+ Blackfeet Nation lived in squalor and abject poverty. The government's tightfistedness also contributed to high rates of unemployment, alcoholism, and drug abuse. The roads and infrastructure were a mess (Bryan had lost count of the number of suspension systems and wheels he'd had to replace on reservation vehicles bottoming out in deep potholes). Funding for education on the rez was a joke. It all pissed Bryan off, the way the feds kept Blackfeet Nation on a short leash, micromanaging them on the very land the U.S. government stole from them. It's what he'd been railing about the past couple of weeks, letting the public know just how dire the situation had become.

Like a blessing from heaven, a gift had streaked out of the skies and delivered a prize Bryan had long desired. The meteorite that struck the east meadow had given him instant celebrity status, crazy as that was. He hadn't asked for it. It just fell into his lap, and now he felt it was his responsibility to make the most of it. His newfound fame had brought him a huge television audience, if even just for a few minutes of soundbites on national news channels each day. He was appreciative of the public platform he'd been given. He just hoped people were paying attention. His Blackfoot friends deserved better treatment.

Bryan's blood pressure went through the roof every time he thought about the supreme arrogance of the U.S. government. His two tours of duty in that corrupt hellhole of Afghanistan had taught him many lessons about wealth and the pursuit of power. He'd risked death daily in a war that only served to line the pockets of U.S. defense contractors, American politicians, and connected Afghans. He was overjoyed the U.S. had finally escaped that 20-year, money pit debacle. However, he still harbored a great deal of pent-up anger at how he'd been played, believing the *patriotic duty* bullshit they slung to get him to enlist early on in the conflict.

He wasn't about to let the feds win this time. This was personal. *This meteorite is mine, goddammit!* The certified paperwork that pilot Lacroix delivered included the estimated weight and dimensions of the meteorite (or parcels thereof) as dictated by the

American Astronomical Society. Of course, those numbers far exceeded what Bryan had waiting for Lacroix in the utility barn. Bryan had planned for this eventuality, loading a second batch of meteorite wedges in the horse stables. A backup stash, in case the feds sent somebody intelligent to collect the meteorite. And they had. Peter Lacroix proved to be quite sharp. He'd immediately called Bryan on the scanty quantity of obsidian rock. Bryan wasn't sure he had completely duped the two chopper pilots, but they collected the segments of charred rock from both barns without further complaint, and flew the short load back to the Idaho Air Force base.

Bryan had held back more than half the meteorite for his own purposes. He had used the big tractor rig to drag the remaining three extremely heavy and unwieldly slabs out to the subterranean shelter beyond the west pastureland.

Those meteorite rocks are mine, goddamnit! I'm the one who did all the work, hauling the damned things to the two barns and shelter.

It's MINE!

The half meteorite he'd hidden in the underground shelter was for his Cretaceous Stones merchandising idea. His two ranch hands, Apisi and Chogan, and two Blackfoot women he'd hired, had started on manufacturing. The four of them worked diligently the past week chipping small pieces out of the black rocks and fashioning them into pendants, earrings, bracelets, rings, and novelty items. He'd put Paul and Ethan to work creating a website on which to sell the meteorite trinkets. He'd written the advertising scripts himself, but left the website design and construction to his sons; Paul and Ethan were much more fluent with computer technology than Bryan could ever hope to be.

His Cretaceous Stones vision was coming to life. He couldn't wait to see the reaction they'd get with his sales pitch that would appear on the website home page, with him speaking directly to the camera and holding a golf-ball-size, polished black stone:

"This miraculous little stone will change your life in ways you never imagined. You can now own a piece of the meteorite that

preserved dinosaurs for sixty-six million years. If it did that for prehistoric reptiles, just think what it can do for you! Get your Cretaceous Stone trinkets today. But hurry! There's a limited supply and they'll be gone soon."

This venture was going to make them a fortune, he was sure of it. With the publicity he and Gilliam's Guidepost had already received, these Cretaceous Stone trinkets and jewelry pieces would sell dizzyingly fast. He just wished his Gilliam's Glade prehistoric zoo was ready to open to the public, for those open habitats would be the crowning touch.

And now they had a second dinosaur attraction. A Triceratops, arriving four days ago.

On Monday, Bryan's press release announced this zoo acquisition. He'd stated in the release: "We have acquired a Triceratops, a weirdly-fangled Cretaceous Period reptile that resembles a baby rhinoceros with two extra horns and a crown of bone spurs encircling its head—a true oddity of nature and a must-see attraction."

Wednesday had been media day at the ranch, with local, national, and international journalists flooding into the Gilliam ranch in astonishing numbers. Badger Creek Road had been a bumper-to-bumper snarl most of the day, with many news teams abandoning their vehicles on the side of the road and hoofing it on foot, lugging their bulky equipment in the heat of day. Helicopters circled for hours waiting to land their news teams. The line waiting to get in to the horse stables to see the Dromaeosaurs and Triceratops had stretched around the utility barn, all the way out to the east meadow, where construction of the new dinosaur habitat was underway. Bryan's sore throat and hoarse, froggy voice today was a testament to the dozens of interviews he had given. Paul and Ethan had also been interviewed, and his sons seemed to revel in the media attention. Like father, like sons. Neither boy showed any shyness in front of the cameras. Loretta worked in the store all day. Lianne stayed in the storage room, occupied with her iPad and phone, away from all the strange people, cameras, and microphones. The paleozoologist, Franz Krause, and wildlife biologist, Barrett Hailey, spent the day in the stables, fielding questions from the press.

Hayden Fowler and Nora Lemoyne declined to be interviewed and were nowhere to be seen the entire day. Bryan couldn't understand why they refused to take their bows. Capturing one of these juvenile dinosaurs was a big deal, as illustrated by the huge media turnout. And yet, the two of them treated it as just another day at the office, shying away from any and all publicity.

". . . I don't think you've heard a word I've said, have you, Bry?"

Loretta's voice cut through the commercial that boomed from the TV.

"What? Sorry. Lots on my mind lately."

"Obviously." Loretta gave him a sad smile. "I was talking about yesterday."

"What about it?"

"Just how draining it was. How our property, our *home*, was invaded by hundreds—what felt like *thousands*—of strangers. We've become a public curiosity, Bryan. We're on display. We're under a microscope all the time now. I don't like it. I haven't been comfortable with it since the beginning. But yesterday was the first time I felt threatened. Not by man-eating dinosaurs, but by *people*. There were a lot of very strange folks running around here yesterday. That guy claiming to be Jesus Christ reincarnated? Holy shit, Bry! Are you kidding me?"

He took a pull on his beer and peered at Loretta. She wasn't wrong about that nutcase. It had been a bizarre scene at the front gate. Security had stopped a scrawny, bearded man dressed in a shepherd's robe, ratty sandals, and a crown of thorns on his head. He demanded to see Bryan and Loretta, calling them his *prophets*. Loretta had her hands full in the store so Bryan went to see what the fuss was all about. A large throng of paparazzi had gathered, voices shouting, cameras clicking, the slight man standing tall and proud, pounding his wooden staff into the gravel drive, claiming "I am the second-coming of Jesus Christ, your Lord and Savior! I have returned to meet my prophets who have shepherded our dinosaur flock back into the world . . ."

"It's really getting crazy, Bryan," Loretta said, looking at him sternly, taking a sip of wine. "How long until some lunatic shows up with a gun or a bomb? Someone trying to make their mark? Someone wanting their fifteen minutes of fame at our expense?"

"That's why we have professional security, Lor. And that guy yesterday was harmless. A little off his rocker, but harmless."

"A *little* off his rocker? He needs to be put away in a rubber-walled room! And these media types? They're all pushy and rude. A couple of them were in the store with camera crews, shoving microphones in my face and shouting questions while I was trying to wait on customers. And a fight broke out between two reporters in front of the store. It got pretty heated. I had to call Security to break it up."

"Really?"

Loretta sighed, exasperated. "Yes, Bry. I told you about it last night when we were getting ready for bed, but your mind was on the moon somewhere."

"I was exhausted last night, Lor."

"You think I wasn't? The things I've been saying lately don't seem to register with you, love. I'm worried about you. I like what you're doing for our Blackfoot friends. But I'm worried about what could happen when we open up your damned zoo. If yesterday was any indication of what's to come . . . well, I don't know . . ."

Bryan scooted closer to her on the sofa, placed his hand on hers and rubbed her knuckles. "Things are gonna be fine, Loretta. Trust me. That meteorite was our lucky break. Our *windfall*. Fate with a capital *F* is smilin' down on us. Eighteen years we've lived on the Guidepost, mostly hand-to-mouth, barely scrapin' by. We've got a ranch with no livestock or crops. We've got a twelve-room motel that's occupied only during ski season. There's your general store and my mechanic work, a few scattered horse riding lessons through the summer. Five mouths to feed. It's difficult to stay afloat. I'm tired of livin' the pauper's life, Lor." He nodded at Paul, who was completely oblivious of them, surfing the internet, a muffled voice seeping from his earbuds. "We've got three kids I'd like to put through college. We can knock down the rest of our mortgage. We can live a better life. Just let me manage it, honey. Are you with me on this?"

"We're *not* poor and you damn well know it, Bryan! Every time you get an entrepreneurial itch you paint us as poverty stricken. I'm so over that, baby, I *really* am." She swallowed the last of her wine and set the glass aside. Stood. "I'm tired and a bit tipsy and I don't wanna discuss this anymore tonight. I'm going to bed. We'll talk more in the morning."

Bryan watched her retreat up the stairs.

She stopped at the top of the short walkup, turned and called down to him, "We are *not* paupers, Bryan."

"Yeah," Bryan said. "That's true, but—"

She turned and disappeared into their bedroom. Shut the door quietly.

He felt a crushing disappointment that she wasn't totally with him on his dinosaur zoo idea. Loretta was calling it *his* zoo now. That wasn't lost on him. She saw danger where he perceived a golden opportunity. He saw only the upside—for the Gilliam family, for the Blackfeet Nation, for the Smithsonian Institution and science, for Montanans . . . for the nation and the world.

How is it that Loretta doesn't see that?

He drained the rest of his beer and stood, stretched his legs and yawned. He was headed to the stairs to turn in for the night when he heard Paul's voice.

"Hey, Dad, you have *got* to see this."

"What is it, Pauley?"

Paul turned his laptop around so Bryan could see the screen. "This fool posted a video on YouTube. The guy has some outrageous ideas about where the dinosaurs came from. He mentions us and it's gone massively viral. Already close to a million views. Here, have a look."

Bryan stood next to Paul's chair and watched the video of a young man, maybe early thirties, with close-cropped brown hair, large beaked nose, and jutting chin sitting at a desk. Behind him, a large red banner with white lettering spelled out: *WE ARE WATCHING!* His voice came through deep and rich, with an animated clarity like that of an experienced radio announcer.

"Good evening. I'm Morton Habersham of the Government Watch Action Committee. GWAC for short. My fellow American citizens, I want to make you aware of some startling discoveries GWAC has made concerning the origins of this so-called second-coming of long extinct dinosaurs, these creatures that are roaming the Continental Divide causing mayhem, death, and destruction. The U.S. government and their puppet liberal media would have you believe these prehistoric beasts hatched out of a cluster of meteorites that came down over a three day period. We say that is laughable. In fact, we call *bullshit* to that notion. Oh, the meteorites struck the way we were told. And the dinosaurs do indeed exist. We've seen plenty of proof of their existence. But they didn't hatch out of those meteorites. That's preposterous! So where then are these beasts coming from, you ask?

"Through our persistent digging and reliable sources, we have discovered that these animals are escapees from a top secret military base nestled deep in the mountains of Idaho. For the past five years, the United States government has been cloning these dinosaurs through DNA extracted from dinosaur blood in mosquitos trapped in amber, much in the way it was depicted in the *Jurassic Park* books and films. This practice is part of a biological weapons program the U.S. is developing to combat something China has been working on.

"How these creatures got out is anyone's guess, but the federal government surely has blood on its hands and a lot of explaining to do. We all remember the Boy Scout massacre. Yes, unfortunately we do. It's just a matter of *when*, not *if*, more Americans will lose their lives to these creatures. Ranchers have suffered huge losses of livestock, horses, and other animals. Herds of elk and bison have been cut down. Farmers have lost hundreds, maybe *thousands* of acres of crops. Where will it end? *When* will it end? It's anyone's guess.

"And throughout all this havoc, there is one Montana ranch that seems to be in on it, harboring a half dozen carnivorous dinosaurs. Reptilian *murderers* if you will. This ranch—Gilliam's Guidepost, an out of the way place in Heart Butte—hatched out these evil beasts from eggs supplied to them by government scientists. These people feed them. They *protect* them. We've all seen proprietor Bryan Gilliam echo the government's falsehoods. The rancher is a very effective mouthpiece for the coverup of a program gone awry. He and his brood take care of these man-eaters, if you can believe it! They are even planning a zoo to show off these despicable animals. We at GWAC think—no, let me rephrase that . . . we *know*—this is a cover for the government's ineptitude and gross incompetency for an operation gone horribly wrong. It's an abomination, I tell you. We've even learned of a military helicopter setting down at the Gilliam compound and taking away something from their barn. Very hush-hush, top secret. And we have tracked payments from the government to the Gilliam family! Very mysterious goings-on, folks. Our elected officials are up to something no good, that's for sure. And one ranch in northwestern Montana is in on it and profiting. How many more of these destructive, killing reptiles are they breeding? How many more lives do we have to lose before we say *enough*? How many more crops . . ."

Bryan listened to the imbecile rant. This wasn't the first insane conspiracy theory he'd heard about the dinosaurs. Another popular theory making the rounds was that all the video footage shown on news programs thus far—from the early shots of the Dromaeosaur hatchlings taken by geologist Greg Dulowski to the videos of the dead T-Rex and Triceratops captured by Fowler and Lemoyne—had all taken place on a back lot of a Hollywood soundstage. But that one was tame compared to this biological weaponry idiocy. This was completely off the rails bonkers. It didn't make any rational sense. Sure, Bryan knew several species of animals had been successfully cloned: mice, rabbits, cats, sheep . . . even horses and cattle. But that technology was light years from cloning reptiles that had been extinct for millions of years. And even if the government could clone dinosaurs, what good would that do them against China? Against Russia? What were they going to do with them? Airdrop them into those countries? Ludicrous! Batshit crazy is what it was.

Then again, dinosaurs hatching out of meteorites is pretty out there, too, Bryan ol' buddy.

Yes, but at least he'd witnessed that. He'd seen Dromaeosaur hatchlings scurrying around the still-smoking meteorite. He'd seen the gummy yolk coating the rock and collected pieces of eggshells. He'd killed a hatchling and seen the government scientist, Blazenhurst, get bit by one. He'd seen the results of the attack on his daughter. He'd gathered eggs from the center of that meteorite and hatched Dromaeosaurs in a chicken incubator. It all happened on his watch. He'd seen it and done it.

It was real.

He *did* wonder, however, how they had gotten so close to several truths. The covert military base in Idaho. The Air Force helicopter taking something from their barn. The payments from the government. The hatching out of the Dromaeosaurs. Their facts were off base, but danced around the truth. Was there a leak supplying these half-truths?

Are we being spied on?

But then, how ridiculous were their assumptions? Bryan Gilliam working *with* the U.S. government on a secret weapons program? Absurd! This Government Watch Action Committee bunch didn't know him at all.

"Jesus, Pauley!" he said, reaching down and slapping the lid of Paul's laptop closed.

"Hey, Dad!" Paul protested. "What the—?"

"That clown has read too many bad comic books! That's the most nonsensical drivel I've ever heard. I swear, sometimes I think social media is the assassin that murdered true journalism. Why do you kids waste your time with this garbage?"

Paul reopened his laptop with an angry flourish. "Because it's entertaining, Dad. *Hilarious* actually. I thought you'd like this since you were mentioned in it. You've liked all the other stuff on TV about you—about *us*."

Yeah, but all of that other stuff was positive, Pauley.

Bryan stared at his son for a long time, finally saying, "It's late, son. I'm going to bed and you should, too."

He drained the rest of his beer, picked up the remote and shut off the television. Slowly, he made his way up the stairs.

Paul thinks the YouTube posting is entertaining. Hilarious.

Things were getting out of hand. Maybe Loretta was right.

They were under a microscope all right.

Exposed by a much wider, more powerful lens than he ever thought possible.

The Peter Principle

July 3: Mount Bennett Air Force Base
Elmore, Idaho

"HEY, PETE, I'VE GOT SOME SUPER NEWS!" George Dantley sounded much more vibrant and cheerful than he had when Peter last visited him in the hospital three weeks ago.

Damn! Has it really been three weeks?

Peter stood in the hall outside the base commissary, cell phone to his ear. "Great to hear from you, Georgie. What's cookin'?"

George rambled on with pleasantries, his words lost in the haze of Peter's embarrassment at not having reached out to his young friend in the three weeks he'd been flying for Operation Hot Rocks. Peter had even gone home to Missoula this week on an all too brief, two day leave to be with Brin and the baby, and not once had he thought about Georgie.

The guilt of his negligence hit him hard.

He heard George say, "Your employer is giving me a full ride at the university next year! The DNRC Forest Serviceis giving me an all-expenses paid scholarship my senior year. Tuition. Textbooks. Room and board . . . even monthly spending money. It's so awesome, Pete!"

Peter smiled. "That's incredible. Congrats, my friend. You deserve it. It's great to hear you so upbeat. You sound really good."

"I am, thanks. Your boss, Gary Ralston, and the dean of the university's Forestry and Conservation Department, Frederick Thackery, visited me in the hospital. They came together, as a tag team, and made me the offer. Dean Thackery told me, and I quote: 'Your persistence and toughness is an example all University of Montana students would be wise to follow.' Both said I'm a role model, if you can believe that."

"I *do* believe it, kid. You even inspire a broken-down former hockey player like me."

"There's more. Even better news. Mr. Ralston guaranteed me a job when I graduate next year. The starting salary is epic! I'll be hired in as an entry level Forestry Technician, working with landowners on best practices for managing their acreage and surrounding woodlands. It dovetails nicely with what I've been studying. Of course, I know there'll be a lot of grunt work and office time, probably fetchin' coffee for big shots like you, old man, But hey, I won't have to climb back up in one of those damn fire towers again."

Old man? Georgie is sounding like his healthy self again.

"Wow! You're really excited about this, eh?"

"Come on, Pete. I know you must've had something to do with this. Please don't BS me. Don't tell me this is the first you're hearing of it."

"Truly, this *is* news to me, Georgie. *Great* news, in fact."

"First thing I thought when Mr. Ralston and Dean Thackery made me the offer was that you'd pulled some strings. It seemed like something you would do."

"No, I didn't. I truly wish I *did* have something to do with it, but I didn't. I've been out of touch with Gary since I left for Idaho. This is all on your own merit, and I'm absolutely thrilled for you."

"It's all I've ever wanted. And I get to stay in Missoula, which makes my folks happy."

"That's outstanding, Georgie. I take it you're out of the hospital, then?"

"Yeah. They released me to home care last week. I'm staying with my parents and goin' through physical therapy. It's tough, but I'm managing. The friggin' cast is still on and the itching is driving me crazy but my lung is better. I still need oxygen much of the time and I wheel that tank around like it's a pet on a leash. But at least I can breathe now—short, quick breaths—without it hurting too much. My skin has a lot of scabbing but it doesn't burn and sting the way it did. I still have to slather on the ointments and goopy stuff. Makes me feel like a grease monkey. Can't walk real good yet; I hang on to my walker for dear life and it's exhausting just gettin' to the bathroom and back. But I'm in good hands. The 'rents are takin' good care of me. I'm putting on some weight thanks to Mom's delicious home cooking. I'm livin' the good life. Feelin' blessed."

Peter saw Connor Bartholomew and Blair Minsinger enter the mess hall, the double doors swinging shut behind them. All the other pilots were now inside for the scheduled meeting with Colonel Glick.

"I'm so glad you're on the mend. And a big congratulations on your job offer. I just hope they get this dinosaur thing cleaned up before you start trampin' through Montana forests."

"Yeah, I've been keeping up with that. It's insane, isn't it? Especially what happened to those poor Boy Scouts. You keepin' yourself safe, Pete?"

"So far so good."

"I know you probably can't give me any details, but are you doin' good work for the Pentagon?"

"I'm flying a lot, yeah. Lots of air time. More than usual. But we haven't exactly been hittin' it out of the park. Truth be known, I'd rather be back at my old forestry job."

"You sound kinda down. You okay?"

"Yeah, I am." Peter checked the hallway to be sure nobody was within earshot. "Just tired of workin' for a cranky, ungrateful old coot Air Force base commander."

"Is he elderly like you?"

Peter chuckled. "Listen to the funny guy."

"Well, we're two peas in the same pod right now, Pete . . . Me with my walker and you with your advanced age."

"Last time I checked, there weren't any thirty-seven-year-olds in nursing homes."

George laughed. "All that flyin' for the military has made you sensitive, Pete."

"Speaking of sensitive, I'd be remiss if I didn't apologize for not keeping in touch. I feel really bad that *you* were the one who had to call *me*."

"Stop it right there, old man. No need to apologize to me about anything. I owe you my life."

"Please," Peter said with a tired sigh, "let's not get all mushy again. I got enough of that at the hero's dinner your folks threw for me."

"Okay. We won't go there. But before we sign off here, I have even more good news."

"*More* good news? Man, you must be livin' right, my friend."

"That I am. I scored us two tickets on the fifty-yard-line for the Grizzlies opener against Washington, September fourth."

"What's that you say? The Huskies are nationally ranked! That game's been sold out for months! How'd you swing that?"

"We young dudes have our ways. I plan to walk into that stadium under my own power. No wheelchair. No walker. No crutches. Not even a walking cane. No oxygen tank or mask. Just you and me out in the open air watching Montana upset U of Washington."

"How could I ever resist such an offer? Thank you!"

The double doors leading into the mess hall burst open and Glick appeared. "Goddammit, Lacroix, quit gabbin' like a teeny-bopper girl an' get yer useless ass in here! You're holdin' up the show."

Peter watched Glick turn and go back inside. He said to George, "I guess you heard that."

"I did. He didn't actually say *teenybopper*, did he?"

"That he did."

"Wow! Just how old *is* that dude?"

"Old enough to know better. Did I mention my cranky, ungrateful, old coot boss has a Napoleonic complex?"

"No, I don't recall you tellin' me that."

"Take care of yourself, Georgie. I'll see you soon. I promise."

* * *

The six chopper pilots sat at the long cafeteria table watching Colonel Glick pace in front of them and rant. His monologue carried the same heated message he'd spewed at most briefings since the first week.

"... and here we are three weeks in and you clowns have only collected a little more than half the meteorites. Much less than that if you count the tonnage that was expected. It's a pretty dismal showing, fellas. The total rock weight brought back to the base is absolutely pathetic. Mere pebbles to what actually came down. We hired you because you're supposed to know this terrain. You're supposed to know where these things are. We might as well send the geologists packing because they don't have much to study. Any of you care to share with me why this operation is failing?"

Curtis Williams spoke up. "With all due respect, Colonel, none of us actually saw the meteorites strike. We know the terrain, you're right about that, but we have to rely on longs and lats provided to us by the astronomers and your own Air Force personnel. Let's be truthful here, sir. The coordinates have been way off."

Glick glared at Williams. "Just like a forestry flyboy to pass the blame. I'd say it's *your* incompetence that's holdin' things back."

"Williams is right," Connor Bartholomew said. "We're all expert pilots. But no mission can succeed without accurate intel. The locations of these rocks should be more precise than they've been, what with GPS and satellite imaging at your guys' fingertips. We can only be as effective as their data. Some of these roundups have been off by ten miles or more. It's not us you should be rippin' apart."

Glick's face turned beet red. "You tellin' me how to do my job, Bartholomew?"

"No. I'm just laying out the truth."

Curtis Williams said, "And you say your geologists don't have enough to work with? At least three of those meteorites we've brought back were nearly intact. The wedges fit together tight as a completed jigsaw puzzle. The tonnage is there, too. I say your geologists have plenty to study."

"Yeah," Blair Minsinger said, joining the backlash, "speaking of geologists, why is it we don't hear from them? It might help us to know what they're discovering . . . what they're looking for. Why are we kept in the dark about their findings? I mean, we know dinosaurs hatched out of them. Everybody on the planet knows that by now. But why the secrecy around them? If there's something dangerous about them, we should know about it. We keep askin' about 'em and you keep stonewalling us."

Glick moved in front of Minsinger but addressed all of them. "How many times do we have to go over this, gentlemen? In case it's slipped your pointy little heads, you are hired contractors working for the United States Air Force. Everything here is on a need-to-know basis, and there is nothing you need to know about geological findings. Furthermore . . ."

Glick continued his tirade, shouting the same tired insults Peter had heard ad nauseum for the better part of three weeks. Peter had returned from his short leave yesterday, and his troubling melancholy funk was already back haunting him. After spending two wonderful days with Brinshou and the baby, his depression had come back. Colonel Thaddeus Glick's voice had that effect on him. Everything about this mismanaged operation rankled him. Flying around aimlessly with little to show for it, then being vilified by a crass Air Force colonel was taking its toll on him. He hated this military base, with its rigid regulations and chain of command nonsense. The reek of jet fuel and exhaust hung over the base like a tainted perfume. This commissary, with its bad coffee and greasy, gut-wrenching institutional food gave him intestinal distress. The claustrophobic barracks dorm room, with its drab concrete walls, harsh fluorescent lighting, and tiny window high on the wall reminded Peter of a prison cell. The hard slab of a bed with the lumpy foam rubber mattress and perpetual, susurrating shriek of fighter jets on 24/7 training missions made it impossible for him to get a good night's sleep. And he hated flying the clunky repurposed Army choppers that were so old and rickety he had begun to question their safety. Most of all, he hated working for someone like Colonel Thaddeus Glick.

His two days with Brin and the baby had been a wonderful

escape from this drudgery. Kimi's face lit up with a thousand-watt smile when she first saw her daddy walk through the door, and Peter cherished that vision, a memory he would hold close to his heart forever. The 48 hours at home had rejuvenated him and his marriage. He and Brin had spent most of the time in bed, making love and watching old movies, getting up only to eat and take care of Kimi's needs. The second night he was home, he got a babysitter for Kimi and took Brin out to dinner at Plonk Missoula, an upscale restaurant he knew Brin loved but that they could rarely afford. They'd dined on the rooftop patio, sampling from a cheeseboard and sharing an expensive bottle of French wine before feasting on the main course—Alaskan halibut for her, chicken picatta for him. It had been a beautiful two days. Very restful and reaffirming. Just what the two of them needed. And the more Glick's grating voice droned on, the more Peter longed to be back home with his beautiful wife and their beaming baby daughter. Not for the first time, he thought about quitting this Operation Hot Rocks mess.

You can't do that, fool. You need the money.

He thought about the meteorite pickup at Gilliam's Guidepost. Both he and Larry Bing had fallen under Bryan Gilliam's spell. Or so it seemed. Peter had seen Gilliam on television interviews leading up to the trip, so he thought that might have influenced him in perceiving the man to be bigger than life. Bryan Gilliam definitely had a unique charisma about him, an aura that drew people to him and made them believe in the things he espoused. But that didn't make him an effective liar. Peter knew right away that Gilliam wasn't being totally honest with them. Bryan Gilliam might be a blue-chip salesman, but there was no hiding the fact that he was holding back a large part of that meteorite. Why? Peter had no idea, and neither did Bing. But Peter liked the guy, and especially respected what he was doing for the Blackfeet tribe, and so he didn't press him further. *No skin off my hide,* Peter reasoned. He wasn't particularly motivated on Glick's behalf. It made no difference to Peter how much of the meteorite they hauled back to Idaho. He was tired of Glick's power trip head games and didn't care that he'd surely catch an earful when they returned to the base, which he had.

Bryan Gilliam had charmed them, no doubt about it. Gilliam had taken a lot of time and effort showing them the Dromaeosaurs in the horse stalls, and introducing Peter and Bing to the scientists working at the Guidepost. He took a sincere interest in Peter when he learned Peter's wife was a Kootenai-Salish Indian from the Flathead reservation. Peter had been impressed by the man's depth of knowledge about the Confederated Kootenai-Salish Nation. And it turns out that Gilliam had a deep fascination of helicopters, and Peter—acting spontaneously and against Air Force regulations—took Bryan Gilliam and his two sons up for a quick flyover of the ranch. And getting a closeup look at the dinosaur juveniles had also been a fascinating experience. Peter and Bing had been given an expert tutorial on Cretaceous Period life from the scientist with the German accent, paleozoologist Franz Krause. Peter remembered it as being a very fine day.

Yesterday, out of the blue, Bryan Gilliam called Peter, informing him of the launch of what he was calling his Cretaceous Stones line of jewelry and trinkets. The mystery of the missing Gilliam meteorite wedges was a mystery no more.

"I figured you deserved to be the first to know, Pete," Gilliam said. "At least the first outside my family. I'm pretty sure I didn't convince you that I was turnin' over all of that meteorite. And you were kind enough to not press me too much on it. I hope you didn't catch too much shit from that Air Force commander you told me about."

"Well, yeah, I caught some hell for it. But I could have returned with twenty tons of meteorite and he'd still find somethin' to dress me down about. I figured you had some good use for the rocks. If I brought it back to Idaho, it would have just sat in an airplane hangar while the government geologists bitched about there not bein' enough there for them to do their work. This operation I'm flyin' for is a complete boondoggle."

"Sorry to hear that. But thanks for letting me slide on this."

"No worries, Bryan."

"Well, I'm certainly gonna cut you in on profits we make from this Cretaceous Stones venture. Without you, this wouldn't be happening."

"Oh, thanks, but you really don't need—"

"Nonsense! I want to do this. For you. For your wife, Brinshou. You told me she crafts Native American jewelry, right?"

Peter was amazed Gilliam remembered Brin. He'd only mentioned her in passing. "Yes, she does. Really elegant pieces in the Native Kootenai tradition."

"Outstanding! Send me her website link and a phone number. I'd like to hire her. She could put an exciting spin on our Cretaceous Stone merchandise. We launch tomorrow and we're gonna need all the help we can get to keep up with the demand. And the more tribal our efforts, the more it supports my views."

Peter never saw that coming. When he called Brin last night with the news, she was over the moon excited.

Something Glick just said had angered his fellow pilots, which drew Peter's attention back to the commissary.

"Whaddaya mean Operation Hot Rocks is terminated?" Larry Bing said.

"I told you," Glick said, staring down Peter's chopper partner, "General Ramage has had enough of your ineptitude. He's pulling the plug on the operation, effective immediately."

Peter suddenly felt a huge burden lifting. "So does this mean we can all go home now?" A lilting hopefulness colored his tone.

"What the hell, Lacroix! You just went home to see the wifey. Nobody is going home. All of you will continue flying . . . for the most part, you will be on your same routes. But the mission has changed."

"How so?" Rusty Cavanaugh asked.

"Instead of hunting for meteorites, you'll be searching for dinosaur activity. Your Air Guard personnel have already been briefed. The new objective is seek and destroy. You pilots locate the creatures and your guardsmen target them and gun them down. Where possible, we retrieve the animal carcasses. I'm putting together a second small fleet of my Air Force pilots to supplement your efforts. We cannot fail this time, gentlemen. Training exercises commence tomorrow morning at oh-seven-hundred hours."

Peter felt his ears burning. "That's *insane*, Colonel," he said, trying to keep from losing it entirely. "Our contracts don't contain anything about dinosaur hunting. You have no legal right to—"

"Shut the hell up, Lacroix! The order comes straight from the White House. You all will carry out the mission, or else. I wanna see you in my office right now. The rest of you are dismissed. Get plenty of rest. Tomorrow will be difficult."

Peter fumed as he followed Glick out of the mess hall. He wanted to murder the cocky little bastard.

The Livingston
Roundup Rodeo

July 4: Park County Fairgrounds
Livingston, Montana

HAYDEN LOOKED OUT OVER A SEA of cowboy hats. "I feel underdressed," he said, to Nora, who sat beside him on the top row of bleachers. He combed his fingers through his long, thick hair. "It's a regular Stetson convention out there."

Nora laughed, reached up and fluffed his hair. "You wouldn't look right in one of those hats. They're not Minnesota styling."

"Oh? I'll have you know, cowboy hats are considered haute couture in downtown Minneapolis."

"Somehow I doubt that, Hayden. Viking horns maybe. But not cowboy hats."

"Viking horns, huh? You know that's a fallacy, right? The Norsemen never had horns on their helmets."

She looked at him doubtfully. "Please. Just let me have my fun picturing you wearing a pair of horns, would you?"

"Sounds a bit Freudian to me," he said, smiling.

She slapped his arm playfully. "You're impossible, mister."

He thought she looked fetching today in her Western wear, an eye-catching outfit that emphasized her petite figure. Frilly white silk blouse unbuttoned daringly low, tan leather vest and skinny jeans tucked into a pair of snakeskin cowboy boots. The cowgirl ensemble gave her a youthful, sensual glow; Hayden caught several men checking her out. A few women, too.

The late afternoon sun was setting, casting long shadows across the central corral. The warm day had cooled off. A Garth Brooks song played over the PA, Garth singing about boots and chaps and cowboy hats. Cowpokes busily prepared for the start of the festivities. He breathed in the heady mix of hot leather, horse sweat, suntan oil, barbecued chicken, and roasted corn, all wrapped in a hint of freshly plowed arena dirt and manure. The smell pleased him. *The scent of the fairgrounds.*

More than 5,000 rodeo fans packed the stands for this final day of the annual Livingston Roundup. A full house, which surprised him. He'd thought warnings out of Helena advising against large public gatherings due to the current dinosaur threat would keep people away. Apparently rodeo devotees were a stout breed not easily intimidated. Many more tailgated in the parking lot, eagerly anticipating the Fourth of July fireworks grand finale.

Hayden was thrilled to be treating Nora to this experience. A few weeks back they'd been discussing bucket lists, and Nora mentioned wanting to see a live rodeo. It surprised him. With all the traveling she had done, he'd thought a rodeo would be an easy one to cross off her list. But no, she had never been able to work a rodeo into her busy schedule. He'd thought it a strange want. But then, one of his top wanna-dos was to hang glide off the North Rim of the Grand Canyon, so what the hell did he know. She'd been delighted that he remembered, and even more overjoyed when he told her he was taking her to the final night of the biggest and best known outdoor rodeo in Montana.

The music cut off. The announcer's voice rattled the public address loudspeakers as he introduced the opening event: bareback riding. Across the way, the chute crashed open with a loud crack and a cowboy hung on for dear life as he and his horse burst out of the stall. The bronco bucked furiously, kicking up clods of dirt, the cowpoke's head jerking violently up and down, causing him to lose his hat. Within five seconds, the horse threw the rider a good ten feet, the cowboy tumbling in a cloud of dust. The crowd applauded politely as he got to his feet, retrieved his hat, and dusted himself off. The next couple of bareback riders managed to hang on for the required eight seconds. The judges rated successful eight-second rides on spurring techniques and the degree of bucking difficulty.

Hayden learned this from the printed program. He also learned that bareback riders could be eliminated for *marking out*, which meant the cowboy didn't have both spurs touching the bronc's shoulders coming out of the chute. Marking out had disqualified one of the riders. Another rider was eliminated for using a second hand to grip the rigging. The crowd was well versed in rodeo rules and roared in appreciation with each successful ride.

"Isn't it exciting, Hayden? All the energy and pageantry?"

He looked at her. Saw the happiness brightening her striking green eyes that peered at him from behind her jade-colored designer frames. She bounced and clapped where she sat, enthusiastically showing her appreciation for the cowboys' performances. Her uninhibited joy touched him. He leaned over and kissed her, felt her hand snake around the back of his neck to pull him closer.

The past week had been hectic and they both needed this break. The dinosaur invasion had erupted into a full scale outbreak. Reports from remote locations in Idaho and Montana were coming in so fast there was no way they could keep up. It was physically impossible to cover every incident in Montana, let alone Idaho. The hatchling juveniles were fanning out and he and Nora were putting many miles on their rental van. The past week had taken them hundreds of miles away from Heart Butte, first to Little Belt Mountain south of Great Falls to check out the Boy Scout camping tragedy (they confirmed the attack was carried out by a small group of Tyrannosaurus Rexes), then on to Helena and finally to Bozeman, where they stayed the past two nights. The past week had seen them investigating three more T-Rex assaults on farm animals and two incidents of elk slaughters by Dromaeosaurs. They'd also visited a half dozen crop farmers who had lost substantial portions of their winter wheat to Triceratops. They had shot hours of video footage to accompany Nora's reports to their Smithsonian sponsors, but unfortunately hadn't been able to snag another live specimen.

The week had taught them a great deal. They'd learned that Triceratops were diurnal creatures that grazed in small groups and used hardwood trees as rubs for their horns, much like deer used them for their antlers. Nora thought Triceratops rubs were for marking their foraging territories. They had learned Dromaeosaurs and Tyrannosaurs were largely nocturnal. They had confirmed that Dromaeosaurs were solo predators while Tyrannosaurus Rexes hunted in packs. All the Triceratops they'd seen had brightly colored heads and crowns rather than the gray appearance depicted in most paleontological illustrations. These discoveries went against most current scientific thinking. And since there had been just the one attack on humans thus far by the carnivores, Hayden surmised that the meat eaters might harbor some primeval, intuitive fear of human beings.

The past week had been exhausting and stressful, dealing with ticked off ranchers and farmers and documenting the grisly aftermath of dinosaur attacks. He and Nora had even spent two long nights in tree stands scanning fields of cattle with night vision binoculars and an infrared camcorder. They had seen quite a few nocturnal creatures—bats, great horned owls, flying squirrels, red foxes, coyotes—but none of the dinosaur variety.

As hard as the past week had been, Hayden welcomed leaving Gilliam's Guidepost Inn behind. The Gilliam ranch had become overly crowded with government bureaucrats, security dicks, and television and print journalists, both legitimate and tabloid. Too many people milling around who cramped his style. His and Nora's stay there had become too invasive. They had no privacy there, with all the gawkers and media types harassing them with their idiotic questions and requests for interviews. He blamed it all on Bryan Gilliam, a guy who put his wife and kids second to fame and fortune. A guy who never met a TV camera he didn't like.

A meteorite comes down in his pasture and suddenly he thinks he's a big television star. The man is a publicity hound fool!

The bareback riding event had concluded and the announcer's voice blared over the PA that the second event—bull riding—would begin in five minutes. More music filled the arena: "Rhinestone Cowboy" by Glen Campbell.

"Are you ever going to write another book, Hayden?"

The question surprised him. "Where did *that* come from?"

Nora shrugged. "I just thought with all we've been through—

all the amazing things we've seen and done the past month—it might inspire you to write again. There's certainly no shortage of great material."

"Don't tell me you actually *liked* that crap I wrote back in my youth."

"Please, don't do that. False modesty isn't your thing."

Hayden shook his head. "Twenty-five years ago they were calling me the paleontology whiz kid. That's a lot to live up to. I was just doing something I loved. Still am. All those accolades were a little much. Blatant media hype to sell books is all that was. I look at my early writings now and I think: How unsophisticated."

"Don't be absurd. Your book *Ancient Life, Final Strife* is still considered one of the preeminent texts among scholars of the Cretaceous-Paleogene extinction event. I referenced it quite liberally when writing my dissertation. I was quite a fan-girl of yours in grad school, Hayden. I don't mind admitting that now."

"Really?" he said, a warm glow blooming in his chest. "That's quite a confession."

"I mean it. The world needs more of your work. Especially now."

"Ah, Jesus!" He swept his hand through the air, brushing off her comment. Kept his eyes on the action in the corral.

"So, are you?"

"Am I what?"

"Are you going to write another book?"

He turned to face her. "Only if you write it with me."

She looked befuddled. "Don't tease me, Hayden."

"Who's teasing? We've been going through this incredible journey together from the beginning. You've contributed many informed perceptions. And I've read your Smithsonian reports. You're one hell of a writer."

"Are you serious right now? Sometimes I can't tell with you."

"I've never been more serious, Nora." He leaned in and whispered in her ear, "But you have to promise not to write about the things we've done in bed the past two nights! I have to draw the line there, my sweets."

She let out a joyful giggle. "Ooh, you are such a naughty man!"

"You seemed to enjoy that side of me last night."

"Stop it," she said, grinning and gently slapping at his forearm. "You mean you would actually coauthor a book with me?"

"Absolutely. You don't think I'd go out on a promotional book tour without you, do you?"

"Wow. I don't know what to say."

"No need to say anything, love." Hayden smiled and reached for her hand. "Besides, it'll give me a good excuse to continue seein' you after all this tracking business is over."

"You don't need an excuse, Hayden." She kissed him tenderly on the lips.

The bull riding event was about to get underway. Three rodeo clowns sprinted into the arena, honking air horns and throwing rubber chickens at each other. One of them had a microphone headset. He made funny noises and told bad cowboy jokes as he rolled a heavily padded barrel into the center of the corral. The crowd loved their antics, roaring their approval at each joke and pratfall. Hayden thought their routines were cheesy, but Nora was enjoying herself so he laughed and clapped along with her.

The first bull roared out of the chute with the rider on its back. The clowns waved their arms and shouted, antagonizing the bucking beast into going after them. The rider hung on for a few long seconds before being thrown, the clowns moving in to distract the bull. The clown with the microphone waved his arms and screamed silly insults at the bull until the animal charged him. Hayden felt Nora grab his arm as the bull ran at the clown, who turned and dashed in a comical zig-zag to the barrel. The bull lumbered after him, gaining on him, nipping at his heels, trying to stick him with its horns. The clown—continuing to yell insults at both the bull and announcer—leaped into the barrel at the last possible second before the bull lowered his head and struck the barrel with a devastating impact, rolling the barrel a good thirty feet, the clown inside never pausing his commentary.

This same scenario played out a number of times before the announcer called the winner. The next event up was steer wrestling, also known as bulldogging. Hayden liked this event, which called for two cowboys on horseback going at full speed, working in tandem, one riding parallel to a full-grown steer to keep it running in a straight line, the other leaping from his saddle to grab the steer by the horns to wrestle it to the ground. He thought these guys were completely nuts. *Redneck daredevils.* That's how he thought of them. He couldn't picture himself participating in such an insane stunt. His bucket list want of hang gliding off the North Rim of the Grand Canyon seemed tame by comparison.

Tie-down calf roping came next. These cowpokes were almost as crazy as the steer wrestlers. A calf tore out of the chute followed by a cowboy on horseback, swinging a lariat high over his head while in hot pursuit. The rider closed in and hurled the rope, lasso-ing the calf around its neck, bringing it to an abrupt, jerking halt, then jumping off his mount, slamming the calf on its side and tying three legs together with the tie-down rope. The 'poke raised his arms exultantly and the crowd cheered. The cowboy grinned and doffed his hat, acknowledging his fans. After a few more roping runs, Hayden became bored with the mechanical sameness, and his interest waned.

A gentle breeze brought a whiff of Nora's perfume, a Versace brand that smelled of rose and magnolia and some other aphrodisiac ingredient that drove him absolutely wild. The fragrance awakened his longing for her, reminding him of their lovemaking the past couple of nights in their Bozeman motel room. He'd been surprised by her eagerness and inquisitive nature in bed, her seemingly unquenchable desire to please him. And he knew from her reactions that he pleased her as well. She was much more vocal than he thought she'd be, directing him without inhibition as to what she wanted. She'd even uttered a few F-bombs in the midst of her passion. And she had introduced him to tantric sex, schooling him in the finer points of slowed-down, meditative sex that prolonged orgasm to a point of delicious bliss. This studious, intellectual woman continued to mesmerize and fascinate him, surprising him daily with her deep intellect and thinly veiled sensuality. He was getting hard again just thinking about being with her.

She leaned into him and talked close to his ear to be heard over the announcer's booming voice. "I guess I never realized how cruel rodeos are to the animals. Those poor calves could have their necks broken . . . their spines dislocated. I'm not sure I like this as much as I thought I would."

"I understand. But you wanna stay for the fireworks, right? What's the Fourth without a fireworks show, right?"

"Sure, but I can't take any more of this roping. I'm going to the ladies room and get some coffee. You want anything?"

"No, I'm good, thanks."

He watched her leave as the tie-down roping champ was announced. That left two more events—team roping and barrel racing—before the winner of the Miss Livingston Pageant would be announced. Then would come the fireworks show, which for Hayden, held an even bigger allure than the rodeo.

He'd loved fireworks since he was a boy growing up in the suburbs of Indianapolis. His late father, Max, had been a fireworks fanatic and never let an Independence Day go by without throwing a huge neighborhood bash, spending extravagant sums of money on advanced pyrotechnics to honor the holiday. Fourth of July fireworks shows always reminded Hayden of his dad, who passed down his explosive passion to him, starting Hayden off at a young age with sparklers, pinwheels, and fountains, then working up to black cats and M-80s and cherry bombs when he was older. Finally, the adult Hayden graduated to bottle rockets, Roman candles, whistlers and screamers, then on to more sophisticated, high tech sky displays.

Hayden held precious, vivid memories of those Fourth of July parties in the vast field behind their house on Flagler Hills Lane. Preparing for those gatherings had brought him and his father closer. Max taught him how to plan a show and set up effective sequencing to get impressive displays. Max had also taught him to respect fireworks, that they were potentially dangerous and not to be used recklessly. No matter where Hayden happened to be in the world, he'd always made it a point to come home to celebrate the Fourth with Max. He'd never missed getting home for the holiday.

That is, up until eight years ago, when Max died from a massive coronary in May of that year. What followed was the saddest year of Hayden's life. There had been no party or fireworks at the house since. His mother still lived there, and Hayden had tried to convince her that another Fourth of July bash would honor Max and bring the neighborhood together. But Miranda Fowler wouldn't hear of it. She had become reclusive and much less outgoing with Max's passing. Fireworks would only make her weepy and emotional, she'd told him. But for Hayden, every flash of light and percussive boom reminded him of his late, lamented pyrotechnic wizard dad in positive ways, sure that Max could see the night displays from where he lounged in heaven.

Dusk was gobbling up the remaining sunlight and the stadium lights flicked on, bathing the corral in milky, artificial light. The air had turned crisp and cool.

Nora returned and took her seat beside him.

He said, "*There* she is. I thought I was gonna have to come fish you out of the toilet."

"The lines at the concession stands are long and service is slow," she said, blowing steam off her large plastic cup of coffee. "What'd I miss?"

"Just more calf abuse. Nothin' you wanted to see."

The last of the rodeo events—barrel racing—ended. Darkness descended and Hayden could no longer see cars in the parking lot behind the bleachers. Two rangy cowboys wheeled a small wooden platform to the center of the arena. A young, pretty cowgirl walked to the makeshift stage, decked out in a silver ten-gallon hat, leopard-print blouse, jeans and spurred boots, waving to the crowd, smiling ear-to-ear, her bright white teeth gleaming in the stadium lights.

"Let's have a big cowpoke welcome for our new Miss Livingston Roundup Rodeo queen, the beautiful and talented Amy Lynn Beckett." The announcer waited for the scattered cheering and whistling to die down before continuing. "Amy Lynn resides in Bozeman and is currently a junior at Montana State University. She beat out dozens of other talented cowgirls with her poise in the saddle and her advanced horsemanship skills. As is our custom here at the Roundup, Miss Amy Lynn will demonstrate her riding prowess before kicking off our fireworks extravaganza."

The new queen mounted her horse and circled the arena in a freestyle trot, then showed off her horse-handling ability in a slalom run where she expertly zig-zagged the horse around a set of flags. At the finish she sat high in the saddle and waved to the appreciative crowd before pulling a six-shooter from her hip and firing blanks into the air. She then rode to the presenter's booth. The announcer handed her his microphone and she shouted enthusiastically, "Let the fireworks begin!"

On cue, the arena went dark and the skies lit up in showers of multicolored streaks, the crowd oohing with each new burst. Thunderous blasts rattled the bleachers. Hayden recognized some of the patterns and works that he and his father had displayed on Flagler Hill Lane—a peony sequence followed by a long, arching Girandola tracer; a bright spattering chrysanthemum burst with fading trails; a flying fish of colorful stars; a branching willow; a brilliant orange-purple Crossette splitting in two at its apex.

Nora cuddled up next to him, pulling his arm into her, the pulses of light reflecting off the lenses of her glasses.

"It's beautiful, isn't it?" she said, her head tilted back, taking it all in with a childlike sense of wonder.

Hayden nodded. "It absolutely is. These guys really know what they're doing."

His thoughts turned to his father.

I'm sure you're enjoying this as much as I am, Dad. Wish you were here with us and that you could have met Nora. I think you'd like her.

He looked at her, her head tilted back, hypnotized by the light show above, a soft smile on her lips. He glanced out across the darkened arena, saw the faint outlines of cowboys moving animals to the trailers outside, saw the faint light coming from the announcer's booth, where an AV crew was packing up.

Five minutes passed. Whistling rockets illuminated the sky. Concussive explosions rocked the grandstands. Then, during an impressive pyrotechnic routine Hayden knew as umbrella blooms interspersed with aerial repeats, he heard screams.

He turned his head and saw Nora staring at him, a worried frown pinching her face.

More screams. Distinct now. Coming from the parking lot.

Horns honking. Car headlights flashing on.

Gunshots.

Gunshots or fireworks?

Chaos.

"What's happening, Hayden?"

"Don't know."

They both stood. He hugged her close to him, wrapping his arms around her protectively. Looked out over the parking lot, saw people running, their bodies flickering through hazy headlight beams.

Concerned murmurs rippled through the stands, then quickly escalated into shouts of fear. People seated near them started gathering up their things and scrambling down the rows of bleacher seats.

Mass confusion.

The exodus quickly turned into a panicked mob, the horde tripping over each other, pushing and shoving and knocking others down in their haste to escape. A woman cried out as she tumbled over the aluminum benches and landed hard on the cement floor. Nobody stopped to check on her.

Hayden tried to make sense of what was happening.

The fireworks ceased.

Gunshots punctuated strident car horns. *Definitely gunshots.*

Shouts and screams chilled him where he stood.

The arena lights flashed on and he saw the source of the commotion.

Oh, NO! Jesus fucking Christ, NO! It can't be!

Tyrannosaurs! Near the entrance gate.

Hayden couldn't believe the size of them. More than five feet tall. Probably 250 pounds.

They're as big as a grown man!

Rodeo fans poured out of the arena running for their lives, many getting pulled under the onrushing crowd. Hayden watched in horror as several T-Rexes brought down people from behind, sinking their disemboweling claws into them, slashing them, ripping them open. He fought the urge to vomit as he watched the beasts dip their oversized heads to feast on the steaming innards of their human prey.

Frightened people slammed up against the chain-link fence that separated the parking lot from the corrals, trying to get out, bringing down a section, trapping and injuring more rodeo fans. In the parking lot, he saw a man attempt to shoot another onrushing creature and missed, hitting and wounding—perhaps *killing*—a man and a woman with his errant shots.

Nora tucked her head into him. "Oh my god! I can't watch this."

He stood rigid, on the top riser of the stands, cradling a terrified Nora against his body, her glasses digging into his side. He could feel her tears wetting his shirt, her body shaking with each sob.

Three creatures stormed into the arena over the downed fence. People scattered wildly. A woman tripped and fell. A Tyrannosaur pounced on her, tearing her limb from limb. Another animal leaped at a man feet-first, like a kickboxer, gutting him with one lethal swipe of its claw.

The horrific sights and sounds surrounded him. The scene was a surreal tapestry, the soundtrack of his darkest nightmares.

How many of them are there?

Hayden wished he had a weapon. The tranquilizer gun even. But then he'd seen the damage guns had done in the chaos of the parking lot.

He felt utterly helpless, knowing their best bet was to remain up here, high in the stands, behind the wall of protective chain-link that separated the stands from the corrals.

But people are being slaughtered down below!

He felt like a coward. The big dinosaur expert cowering in fear as his fellow human beings were dying.

Hayden hugged Nora tighter. He closed his eyes, taking in the cacophony of screams and honking horns and random gunshots.

"I've got you," he said to her. "Just hang on. It'll be over soon."

Sirens wailed in the distance, a discordant, heartbreaking sound.

Family Matters

July 6: Flathead Indian Reservation
Polson, Montana

BRINSHOU COULDN'T ESCAPE THE NEWS being reported from Livingston. A large group of Tyrannosaurus Rexes had invaded the outdoor rodeo, leaving 16 people dead and another 21 seriously injured. The wounded had been transported to Bozeman Health Deaconess Hospital. Rodeo livestock and horses had also been killed in the onslaught. A pair of the marauding Tyrannosaurs were shot and killed. The news reports, attempting to put some kind of positive spin on things, informed viewers that it could have been far worse—the ear-piercing sirens coupled with gunfire had interrupted the pack's feeding frenzy, sending the creatures scurrying into the Custer-Gallatin National Forest.

The Livingston rodeo disaster dominated news cycles the past two days. Brin had taken baby Kimi 75 miles north to her parents' house on the reservation, as if the rez was hermetically sealed to keep out horrible news. Foolish thinking. News of the dinosaur attack was everywhere—TV, radio, internet, newspapers. Coverage even extended here to the Salish Kootenai College cable channel, KSKC TV.

The Tyrannosaurus Rex rodeo attacks normally would have sent Brin spiraling downward into another angst-ridden, black hole depression. Yes, the appalling news *did* affect her, as it did millions of Americans. But on a personal level she felt reborn. Things were looking up. The phone call from Bryan Gilliam offering her a job crafting jewelry from meteorite rocks had started her on the road to emotional recovery. It took her mind off worries about her beloved husband and his dangerous profession. She had been a little star-struck on the call at first, having seen Gilliam on television. She didn't know what to say to somebody famous like him. But he'd put her at ease and seemed to be a very nice man. And he was doing so much to help her brothers and sisters of the Blackfeet tribe. So after speaking with him for a few minutes, she felt a genuine kinship, and thought him to be someone she could trust.

She would be leaving for Gilliam's Guidepost tomorrow to get started on the Cretaceous Stones project. At first the thought of going to Heart Butte gave her the jitters. She knew—the entire *world* knew—the Gilliams were housing live dinosaurs there. But Peter had been to the Guidepost and he reassured her the dinosaurs were securely contained. He'd explained to her the lay of the land there, that the Gilliam ranch was like Grand Central Station—with scientists and press and government types coming and going—but that it would be a safe haven for doing her jewelry work. She would have to leave Kimi with her mother for a week or more, which gave her a bit of separation anxiety. But Brin knew her mother to be a loving, competent grandmother to Kimi.

Peter's surprise two day leave added to her emotional turn-around. Petey had returned home for two glorious days and nights, and they'd shared some of the most intimate and memorable times in recent memory. Her husband's presence lifted her, and instilled some of the strength and self-esteem she'd lost in recent months.

Brin hadn't known what to expect when she and Kimi arrived at her parents' home this afternoon. Her father, Nashota, had a way of ruining visits. He was the sole reason Brin and Peter stayed away. Peter hadn't been back to the rez since before Brin was pregnant. Almost three years now. Her father had never accepted Peter, primarily because Peter was "not of the tribe." Nash went out of his way to denigrate him for his "lack of quality ancestry." Fortunately Nash was still at work at the casino when they pulled in, and Kachina was all easygoing smiles and hugs. Brin loved seeing her mother so upbeat and happy, watching her face light up upon seeing Kimi, Kachina taking her granddaughter in her arms and smothering Kimi with kisses.

Brin put Kimi down for a nap shortly after they arrived and she and Kachina enjoyed a long overdue mother-daughter gabfest session at the kitchen table. They shared a bottle of L'acadie Blanc, a popular local wine, both becoming more animated as the alcohol took effect. Brin talked about her jewelry business and her excitement of going to work for "that famous dinosaur guy" Bryan Gilliam. She also offered up cute anecdotes about Kimi while Kachina filled her in on the latest rez gossip. Brin was surprised to hear that Chayton Erling—the young man Brin was seeing before she met Peter—was engaged to be married. Her father thought Chayton was the perfect mate for his daughter, and Nash did everything in his power to get him into the family. Chayton was tall and handsome and charismatic, and more importantly to Nash, one-hundred percent Salish blood. But after more than two years of serious dating, Brin knew it could never work out. It took a while, seeing as how Chayton was so secretive, but she eventually learned of his tomcatting ways. He was a runaround. A lying, two-faced ladies' man. Brin had broken it off after she caught him in yet another of his long line of improprieties. Chayton Erling wasn't cut out for a wife and kids and financial responsibilities. He went through as many women as he did jobs.

"Who's the *lucky* lady?" she asked her mother, putting air quotes around *lucky*.

"Tala Koostmin."

"Koostmin? Do I know her?"

"No, I don't think so. Her family moved here from Spokane last year. Her father is a detention officer. Her mother works in home care for the elderly. Tala is their only child."

This was all very intriguing to Brin. "How do you know so much about Chayton's future in-laws?"

"Your father has kept in touch with him."

"Oh, well, of *course* he has," Brin said, shaking her head. "For her sake, I hope the marriage lasts. Is Chayton even employed?"

"He's at SKC, studying Business Administration. Her family is putting him through."

Brin laughed. "I hope they get a return on their investment."

She hadn't thought about Chayton Erling in years. Everything changed when Peter Lacroix drifted into her life. Almost seven years ago now she was working as a waitress at a barbecue joint on the eastern shore of Flathead Lake—the Shoreline Smoke House—when Peter came in for lunch with three of his fellow pilots. She noticed him right away, and slyly checked him out as the group perused their menus. Brin didn't believe in love at first sight, thinking the concept to be the stuff of bad romance novels. But she fully believed in *interesting at first sight*. And Peter Lacroix *was* interesting—the most intriguing man she had laid eyes on in quite some time. A little over six feet tall. Athletic build and self-assured way of carrying himself despite a slight limp. A small scar across his cheek and cute dimple in his chin that lent character to his boyish face. Alert, liquid brown eyes and shock of thick black hair that kept falling across his forehead. An easygoing smile and boisterous laugh. A confident, take-charge attitude. She decided right then and there—her shyness be damned—she *had* to get to know this man.

The pilots were seated in Donna's section so Brin asked her if she would trade out tables with her. Donna gave her a knowing look and said, "Go get him, girl!" This was so unlike Brin, being immediately attracted to someone and then taking action. She was nervous and approached the table with great trepidation, hoping her generous smile camouflaged her fear. She stammered badly reciting the day's specials and dropped her pencil twice taking their orders. She eyed the other three pilots but couldn't bring herself to look directly at Peter for fear of revealing her emotions.

She turned to take their lunch orders to the kitchen when Peter, looking at her nametag, said, "Brinshou? Are you a Blackfoot?"

She found her voice. "No, um . . . I, um . . . I'm a Kootenai. From here on the rez."

"Well, Brinshou is a beautiful name. A *gorgeous* name, in fact." He looked directly into her eyes and said, "Almost as gorgeous as its owner."

A rush of heat flared across her cheeks and forehead. She glanced down at her order pad, hoping her blush didn't show.

The other pilots groaned and razzed Peter for his hackneyed come-on. One of them told her, "Pete's a single guy. He's somehow got it in his head that he's an *eligible* bachelor."

Another pilot said, "And with lines like his, he'll *always* be a bachelor!"

Peter's fellow pilots laughed and slapped the table.

"Don't listen to them, Brinshou. They're a jealous bunch. I'm Peter," he said, extending his hand. "Peter Lacroix. From Canada originally. Living in Missoula now."

Brin stared at his proffered hand. She didn't care how lame his introduction was, she thought he was cute and sweet. She felt airborne, giddy, as if lifted on a thick cloud of helium. *Is it possible he's interested in me?* She reached out, slid her hand into his. Felt the callouses on his palm as his hand swallowed up hers. Felt the power of his grip and something akin to an electric current in his touch. Brin was momentarily paralyzed, locking eyes with him, caught up in the moment. She stood there, order pad in one hand, Peter Lacroix's hand in the other.

Finally, she pulled her hand away, feeling awkward, another flush of embarrassment heating her face. "I, uh . . . I'd better get your lunch orders in before you guys starve."

She bustled to the kitchen, thinking: *Did I make a fool of myself? Don't get your hopes up, girly! He's got to be eight to ten years older and probably has a harem of sophisticated women waiting for him down in Missoula.*

Thankfully, she was more composed on her next few trips to the table. She discovered they were helicopter pilots working for the Montana State Forest Division, here doing training exercises, learning how to pull water from Flathead Lake to douse forest fires. Peter gave her that dazzling smile each time she approached. When Peter's group left, Brin felt an inexplicable emptiness. That is, until she picked up the check. Peter had left an overly generous tip and had scribbled on the receipt, *I really enjoyed meeting you, Brinshou. I will definitely be back.*

He returned for lunch twice that week, solo both times. She discovered through a series of subtle questions that Peter Lacroix didn't have any women waiting for him. In Missoula or anywhere else. She believed him. He wasn't a *player* with a little black book of conquests like Chayton Erling. He was older, more mature. A cultured man of the world. A *pilot*. A real man with a responsible profession. Seven years older than her. And most important, she gathered he was sincerely interested in her.

And so started Brin's love affair with the dashing helicopter pilot from Missoula by way of Quebec. The 75 miles that separated them was no barrier as Peter had access to a chopper, and could come pick her up within twenty minutes. With her fear of flying, she hadn't been real crazy about helicopter dates. But she'd put on her brave face and would have endured almost *anything* to be with him. Of course, they'd had to plan dates around her father's work schedule to hide the relationship from him. Brin knew Nashota would go through the roof when he discovered she was getting serious with an older white man. She'd told her mother about Peter and even introduced him to her after they'd been seeing each other a while. Kachina loved Peter immediately. He was polite and gentlemanly, always bringing Kachina small gifts when picking up Brin. Kachina thought he was a good match for her daughter. Predictably, Nash pitched a fit when he found out. He still thought Chayton was the right man for Brin. Both Brin and her mother paid dearly for months while Nash threw his tantrums, her father even threatening to disown Brin and divorce Kachina.

Brinshou's relationship with Peter drove a wedge between Brin and her father. Nash's vindictiveness hurt Brin, but she wasn't his little girl anymore. She was 23 years old when she began dating Peter and very much her own woman, making her own decisions. And if her father didn't like it, that was his problem, not hers. She loved Peter. He made her happy. She didn't really care about the nature of Petey's ancestry the way "his improper bloodline" affected Nash. The final indignity to Nash was when Peter came to take Brin to Missoula for good. Before marrying, they lived together in a tiny rental house on Grove Street.

Brin had fond memories of their two years in that Grove Street bungalow. She loved hearing him talk about his days as a professional hockey player prior to getting his pilot's license. That's where he'd picked up the scarred cheek and the gimpy knee that resulted in multiple surgeries and ended his playing career. He had shared his love of the game with her and took her to several of the now defunct Missoula Maulers games. Brin had never been exposed to ice hockey before Peter, and he had patiently explained the game to her, answering her dumb questions about blueline offsides and faceoffs, and mysterious penalties like roughing and boarding. Brin developed a fondness for the game and they watched a lot of NHL games on TV together. Her favorite team was the Chicago Black-hawks while Peter rooted for his old organization, the Toronto Maple Leafs.

Their third year together saw them get married in a Missoula courthouse, attended by Kachina and Peter's parents, Pierre and Janine. Peter's sister, Celeste, flew down from Quebec City for the occasion. Nash couldn't be bothered. He'd called the wedding a farce and stayed home in Polson on the big day.

One of Brin's secret fears was that Peter would leave her due to Nash's hateful nature. She'd never voiced that fear but it was certainly put to the test the last time Peter accompanied her to the rez. Nash had too much to drink and went into one of his drunken tirades, insulting Peter with every derogatory barb in his ugly repertoire. Peter kept his cool and tried to calm him down, but Nash would not quit. It turned ugly. Peter, who normally had the patience of Job and the serenity of a Buddhist monk, lost his self-control and got right up in Nash's face, both of them red-faced and jawing at each other, the spittle flying. The confrontation scared Brin. Finally, before things could degenerate into fisticuffs, Peter wisely walked away, telling Brin to get their things and meet him in the car, that they were cutting the visit short. In the car headed home, Peter, still angry, huffed, "I love you and your mother dearly, Brin, but I refuse to put up with *that*! That's the closest I've come to decking some-body since my hockey playing days."

As if reading her mind, Kachina spoke. "Your father will be home soon. We need to finish this bottle and hide it. He doesn't like me drinking during the day."

Brin watched her mother across the table, nervously twirling her wineglass and fidgeting with the saltshaker. Kachina kept glancing up at the wall clock like a death row inmate counting down the minutes of her final hours, worry creasing her forehead as she gulped back big swallows of wine. This image of her mother saddened Brin. Kachina Taleka was the living, breathing textbook example of a browbeaten wife.

"Why do you let him bully you, Mother?"

"Nashota doesn't *bully* me, dear. Sure, he has his strong opinions. His peculiar ways. We must remember he's Salish. He's got warrior blood in him. He's not refined like us Kootenai."

"Oh, that's a load of hoo-ha, and I'm tired of hearing it."

"Well, he always has our best interests at heart." Kachina reached across the table and emptied the bottle in Brin's wineglass.

"Does he?" Brin asked, taking a careful sip.

"Yes. He's a wonderful provider. Nashota works hard. That's why we live in this nice house and have so many beautiful things. I tell him sometimes that he needs to slow down some, but he won't have it. And he loves me. He loves you, too, Brinshou."

"He has a strange way of showing it. The way he goes on about my Petey is despicable and nasty. And he ignores Kimi when I bring her here. Like my baby has a communicable disease or something."

"He's not comfortable around children. He never has been."

"No, Mother. I've listened to that line of reasoning long enough. He doesn't like her looks. Peter's either. He's a racist."

Kachina gasped. "Don't say that about your father. It's hateful."

"It's *true*. And *he's* the one who's hateful. I'm tired of dancing around it. We can't have a decent family get-together because of him. In fact, I'm beginning to have second thoughts about leaving Kimi here for the week."

Kachina looked shocked. "Oh, Brinshou, how could you *ever* doubt me?

"Oh, I'm not doubting you, Mother. I know you'll take good care of Kimi. It's your husband I'm worried about."

"My *husband*? Don't you mean your *father*?"

"No. I mean your husband." Brin hadn't referred to Nash in fatherly endearments for four years. Ever since he hadn't shown up for her wedding and had referred to her marriage as a farce. The father she had known and loved through childhood and her teen years didn't exist anymore.

"You should have respect for your elders, Brinshou."

"Respect has to be earned," she snapped. "He hasn't earned a bit of it. The way he treats Peter is deplorable . . . the way he treats you, too, Mother."

Kachina started sniffling, softly at first, then breaking into a full-throated crying jag. Brin got up from the table and went to her, draped her arms around her from behind.

"I'm sorry, Mother," Brin whispered into her ear. "But I just can't take it anymore."

"Me either," her mother said between sobs. "All I've ever wanted is a nice happy family. But you talk that way about Nashota and then you say you might not feel comfortable leaving Kimi with me and I . . . well, it just feels like my whole world is falling apart."

Brin, crying now herself, got Kachina to stand, and she hugged her tightly. "I love you so much," she said. "Please believe that."

"I do," Kachina said, stepping back to look at Brin, her chest heaving, her face streaked with tears. "And I love you, too. You have to believe that your father would never do anything to harm little Kimi. I will give her all the love in my heart while you're away and he'll just ignore her the way he always has. Besides he's been working a lot of overtime lately and isn't home much."

Brin heard the garage door squeak open and Nash's car pull in. The motor shut off. A car door slammed. A look of alarm crossed Kachina's face as she stiffened and wiped her eyes. She hurriedly disposed of the empty wine bottle and tucked their glasses in the dishwasher, then returned to the table, her motions stiff and apprehensive. Brin felt herself tensing up, too. So sad her father had that effect on them.

Nash entered the kitchen from the garage. Stopped and stared at his wife and daughter. "Well aren't you two a sight for sore eyes. Why so weepy?" he said, tossing his keys on the table, a judgmental grin on his face. "Did somebody die?"

Brin looked at him standing there, dressed in his work uniform of starched white shirt, dark vest, black pants, and black bowtie. The tie was unraveled around his neck. She remained silent.

"Antisocial, are you?" He grabbed a bottle of beer from the fridge and took a seat at the table, twisted off the cap and took a swig. Looked at Brin. "When did you get in?"

"Around two o'clock."

"I hear that useless boyfriend of yours is out chasin' dragons."

Indignation burned Brin's insides. Any chance that this would be a smoother and more civil visit than previous trips was gone. "Peter is my *husband* and a very good one! I'd appreciate you calling him that, no matter how much it pains you." She was immediately glad she'd be leaving in the morning.

"He's a chickenshit Canuck who's afraid to face me like a man."

"Good to see you, *too*, Daddy dearest," Brin said spitefully.

Nash slammed the beer down on the table, making her jump. "Don't you *dare* speak to me with that kind of disrespect, young lady! I won't have it in my house."

Kachina got up from the table and went to the sink, keeping her back to them. "It's my house, too, Nashota," she said, gazing out the window over the sink.

"What did you say to me, woman?" He stood, moved behind her.

Surprisingly, Kachina turned to face him. "I said, it's my house, too. And it's *you*, not Brinshou, who is disrespectful."

I don't believe it. She's actually standing up to him! Brin was pleasantly shocked at her mother's courage. Kachina had never shown this kind of grit before.

Brin saw the veins pulsing in the side of Nash's neck, saw him clenching his fists. She scooted back in her chair, prepared to jump into the fray if it came to that.

"You're drunk, aren't you, Kachina?" He looked over his shoulder at Brin. "Both of you are loaded!" He moved in closer to Kachina, so that she was pinned in against the sink. "I bust my ass six days a week and my pathetic wife spends the afternoon getting plastered. I've had one helluva shitty day at work and when I get home there's no supper on the table. That's not too much to ask, is it, woman? That you have my evening meal ready when I get home?"

He grabbed at her and Kachina squirmed away, giving her enough distance to let loose with a wicked roundhouse slap, the force of which knocked Nash back a few steps. Surprised and angry, he went for her, his closed-fist punch connecting with the side of her face in a crunching blow. Kachina's head whipped back, slamming against the wall, a trail of blood following her down as she crumpled onto the linoleum floor.

Nash jumped on Kachina, straddling her, yelling obscenities as he punched her face, Kachina's head rocking back and forth with each vicious thump.

Brin bolted out of her chair and jumped on Nash, wrapping her arms around his neck and pinning him in a stranglehold. She squeezed and yanked and cursed him, cutting off his air. Nash struggled to breathe. She was insane with red-hot, pent-up rage. Adrenaline fueled her, giving her a superhuman strength that surprised her. She wanted to kill him, to crush the life out of his hateful, misogynist, racist neck. He pleaded for her to let go, his voice a raspy cry. His hands desperately grabbed at her arms, trying to peel her off of him. But she only squeezed tighter, on fire with her loathing. It was only when she felt his body starting to go limp that she came to her senses and let go. She heard Kachina moaning in the corner. Brin rolled off of Nash, leaving him splayed out on the floor, coughing and sputtering and gasping, and went to help her mother.

Kachina's face was a bloody mess. Broken nose at the very least. Possible shattered cheekbone. She grabbed two washcloths from under the sink, went to the fridge and wrapped a cloth around ice cubes and used the other to clean her mother's face, all the while keeping an eye on Nash, who remained down, disoriented and wheezing.

She placed the cold compress against the wound.

"Here, hold this against your cheek to keep the swelling down. You okay?"

Kachina nodded.

Her mother was being very brave. Brin could tell Kachina was in great pain. "Deep breaths in and out, Mother. Try to relax. I'm going to get you some help."

Brin stepped over Nash and retrieved her purse from under the table. Pulled out her cellphone and called the Tribal Police.

"Sorry to hear that Mr. Taleka is acting out again," the dispatcher said. "We'll get a patrol car out there right away."

"Thank you," Brin said, ending the call. She angrily tossed the phone in her purse.

Nash had crawled into a sitting position and was leaning back against the cabinets, groaning hoarsely and massaging his neck.

"It seems you've got quite a reputation around here," she said, unable to look at him.

"Jesus, Brinshou. You . . . you could have . . . killed me," he whined in a strained voice.

"I probably should have. Would've done the world a favor. And you wonder why my husband doesn't want to come see you. Pathetic!"

Habitats for the Homeless

July 8: Gilliam's Guidepost
Heart Butte, Montana

LORETTA STOOD PEERING THROUGH the chain-link fence. Bryan was on her left with Jimmy Enright standing on his far side sucking on a cigarette. Two of the scientists—paleozoologist Franz Krause, and wildlife biologist, Barrett Hailey—were flanked to her right. All eyes were riveted on the six Dromaeosaurs that had been moved from the horse stables to the new outdoor habitat this morning. The potentially dangerous transfer went smoothly due to the precautions taken; the animals were tranquilized and muzzled, and their clawed feet bound together tightly in heavy canvas wraps.

The Dromaeosaurs had come out of their sedation just an hour ago, which excited the throng of news media in attendance. News teams spanned the fence, angling to get the best perspective on the happening. They knew the importance of the event, knew they were recording history in the making, and that their clips would be seen by millions of viewers.

The Dromaeosaurs seemed to be adapting quickly to their new environs, sprinting from one end of the spacious enclosure to the other, exercising their heavily muscled legs after being cooped up in cramped horse stalls for three weeks. And they loved to jump. The theropods possessed superior leaping abilities, hopping around the enclosure like reptilian kangaroos, bounding five feet or more with each jump. Loretta heard Franz Krause remark that jumping seemed to be a competition with them. Two of the larger animals attempted to scale the 15 foot high fence but soon learned that 8,000 volts of electricity was a convincing deterrent.

"They're fast and lightning quick," Barrett Hailey said. "Look how they turn on a dime."

Franz Krause nodded. "Fully grown, they'll reach speeds of thirty-five miles per hour." He watched two of them zip across the meadow with reckless abandon, clawed toes kicking out chunks of soil in their wake. "They look like they're racing each other. Interesting how competitive they seem to be."

"I can't believe how big these things have gotten," Bryan said. "And so quickly."

Dr. Krause said, "Dromaeosaurs have exceptional growth rates. Our Triceratops friend, too. We expected that from these animals. And from what we've seen, Tyrannosaurs grow even faster."

Jimmy tossed his cigarette butt on the ground and stomped it out. "How big will these guys get?"

Dr. Krause looked down the fence line at Jimmy. "They're pretty close to maturity now—four feet tall—but they still have some filling out to do. We were a bit off when we were analyzing this species at hatchout. There were dozens of Dromaeosaurid genera at the end of the Cretaceous, so determining the precise species is a bit difficult. We thought they'd max out at sixty pounds, but the heaviest one this morning weighed in at seventy-two pounds. We believe our Dromaeosaurs are close descendants of Deinonychus, which was one of the larger of the raptors. We now think these guys will get somewhere between eighty and a hundred pounds."

Loretta remembered them being small enough to keep in aquarium tanks just a month ago.

Bryan said, "They look like large birds the way they hop around and run."

"They *are* birds, actually," Dr. Krause responded. "Some of the earliest, preflight birds. You can see the feathery downs along the top of their heads and across their backs. Their long snouts are like beaks. They are bipedal and their three-toed, talon feet are similar to the birds we know—birds of prey like hawks and eagles and owls. Our Dromaeosaurs have the three toes pointing forward and one hind claw. The middle toe and hind toe are strong claws, used for gripping their prey, while the outside toes are used for balance when walking or perching. Same foot anatomy as our present day raptors. And you're right, Bryan, their movements are very birdlike. All they lack are the necessary wings for flight. Of course, you all probably know of Pterodactyls, the flying dinosaurs of the Late Cretaceous. Pterodactyls were smaller and lighter, built for flight." Krause lifted his chin at the Dromaeosaurs behind the fence. "Thankfully, these fellows can't fly. Can you imagine trying to put a roof over this enclosure strong enough to contain them?" He glanced at Bryan. "How big did you say this habitat is?"

"Twenty-seven acres," Bryan said.

Loretta looked at Bryan and thought: *Your dinosaur zoo is nearing completion, Bry. I hope this makes you happy because it's surely been a drain on me and the kids.*

Challenging to family life though it had been, she did have to admit to being impressed with her husband. With input from the scientists, Bryan designed this habitat, naming it *Gilliam's Glade*. Bryan and the scientists had directed two construction companies in the building of it. The quick conversion of part of the east meadow into this space amazed Loretta every bit as much as did the rapid growth of the Dromaeosaurs. In a little more than three weeks, crews had installed two miles of 8-gauge industrial chain-link fencing around the pasture. Engineers had wired the inside of the fence with electric fence insulators, which generated high-voltage electric current around the interior of the enclosure but did not zap anyone coming in contact with the exterior of the fence. A three foot deep concrete foundation all the way around prevented the animals from digging their way out. Steel posts embedded every fifteen feet gave the fence a rigid stability to stand up against the enormous strength of the creatures. A large, open-air shed had been constructed at the rear of the stockade to give the animals overhead shelter from the elements. The retention pond provided drinking and bathing water. Light towers were erected for night viewing. Aluminum bleachers were positioned along two sides of the enclosure with a seating capacity of 500. Two long picnic tables sat near the bleachers. A wooden observation tower overlooking the facility had been erected, equipped with an electrical control panel that operated the lights and sound system.

A small area of the pasture had been sectioned off to isolate the Triceratops, the lone herbivore. Loretta understood why the Triceratops had to be segregated, but she felt bad for him. He looked lonely laying in the shade of a stand of hemlock trees, idly watching the six Dromaeosaurs roam their new space while ignoring the bales of hay and fresh greenery strewn across his enclosure.

The rows of aluminum benches sat mostly empty. After the Livingston rodeo tragedy two nights ago, the Montana and Idaho governors had issued a joint mandate that prohibited public gatherings of more than 25 people. Violation of the order brought stiff fines and possible jailtime. Today was to have been a big promotional unveiling of Bryan's dinosaur zoo. He'd wanted to offer an open invitation to the public to witness the introduction of the animals to their new habitats and for the masses to get a closeup look at the first outdoor group feeding. But that had to be changed at the last minute. Bryan was reduced to inviting select news teams to cover the events, which was okay (the news would still get out to the world) but it lacked the impact the day would have had could he have invited large crowds to see his new attraction.

As it stood, other than the media, only a handful of people sat in the stands, the two most noticeable being the two roving paleontologists, Doctors Hayden Fowler and Nora Lemoyne. They had returned yesterday from Livingston to attend today's proceedings. Both were uncharacteristically speechless and spiritually haunted. Loretta had been stunned to learn the two scientists had actually been at the rodeo, witnessing first-hand the terrible T-Rex attacks the rest of them had only seen on TV. Dr. Lemoyne seemed especially affected. Loretta couldn't possibly conceive of the weight of their torment.

News teams were now gathering on the bleachers in a section Bryan had designated for the press, getting prepared for the second big event of the day—the first outdoor habitat group feeding. It would mark the first time the media—and the world—would witness a dinosaur feeding. The anticipatory buzz in the air was palpable.

Loretta nudged Bryan and spoke in a hushed tone. "I'm a little nervous about this feeding, Bry. Are you sure Paul and Ethan are ready for this? Are they gonna be safe out there?"

"Relax, honey. They've got this. The boys *wanted* to do this. They're going to be outside the fence at all times. It's just a matter of manipulating the loader. We've practiced this. Plus, Pauley and Ethan have been feeding the animals in the barn the past week. They'll be fine. You'll see. Just relax."

Just relax, he says. Like this is baling hay or picking straw-berries.

Suddenly the loudspeakers on the light towers blasted the opening of the soundtrack music to *2001: A Space Odyssey.*

Bryan grinned at her. "Like my opening?" he shouted over the blaring classical piece. "The media folks will eat this up!" He scanned the empty sections of the bleachers. "I sure wish we had a full house. Regardless, it's showtime," he said with a gleam in his eye.

I should have expected as much, she thought, a thin smile on her lips.

She heard a vehicle approaching up on the service road leading to the habitat. She turned and saw Apisi behind the wheel of the old Ford pickup rumbling down the winding road, the long flatbed trailer squeaking and clanking along behind it. The bed of the truck was loaded down with large blocks of compressed meat byproduct, as was the forward section of the trailer. A John Deere backhoe loader was anchored to the rear end. Paul and Ethan clung to the backhoe, attempting to keep their balance as the trailer bounced over the ruts in the road.

Apisi backed the pickup in so that the rear of the trailer and backhoe bucket were nearest the fence. The animals clustered together and charged the fence aggressively, getting jolted back by the electric shock. They focused solely on the blocks of raw meat as they ran at the fence again and again, salivating and snarling, jostling for position, drool dripping from their maws. The Triceratops remained uninterested, not budging from his spot in the shade.

Apisi shut down the pickup, got out and hopped up on the

trailer. Paul pulled himself up into the cab of the backhoe and settled in the bucket seat, fired up the engine with a loud blast of exhaust. Apisi and Ethan grabbed pitchforks and stabbed one of the 40-pound meat blocks, working together to maneuver it into the loader bucket, then went back for another. When they had four meat cubes stacked in the bucket, Ethan whistled at his brother and gave him a thumbs-up. Paul worked the joystick. The loader arm rose with the bucket of meat blocks, producing a winding, grinding sound that competed with the *Space Odyssey* music. Paul toggled the stick, raising the loader bucket up, up, up . . . clearing the top of the fence and dumping 160 pounds of raw meat into the habitat with a thundering thump.

The gluttonous carnivores tore into the meat blocks in a violent ballet of clawing, ripping, shredding, and gorging. Loretta and the others watched in silence, transfixed, obscenely fascinated by the primal dance of predator mastication, watching the animals use their claws to rip out chunks of meat, then snatch it in their heavy jaws and throw back their heads, shaking their bodies as they gobbled it down their gullets, then insatiably attacking the meat block for more. Loretta trembled, imagining what it must have been like for those Boy Scouts and rodeo fans who were attacked by even bigger and more deadly Tyrannosaurs. She shivered, though the afternoon was quite warm.

Barrett Hailey pointed across the way, to the Triceratops enclosure. "It's interesting how the herbivore is keeping his distance from them. He's remaining on the far side of his pen."

"Yes," Dr. Krause said, nodding. "He instinctively knows he'd be a gourmet meal for them. I must say, I'm quite surprised these Dromaeosaurs eat so well in captivity. They are raptors, natural born hunters, and I thought initially they wouldn't be interested in anything but live prey."

"I'm not really all that surprised, Franz," Barrett Hailey chimed in, "wild animals—especially large reptiles—have deeply primal survival instincts. Same with sharks and other marine predators. They'll eat almost anything to stay alive." He pointed to a pair of Dromaeosaurs that were scrapping with each other, battling over a chunk of meat. "I'm sure these guys would prefer to track down and eat warm prey, but they are governed by their high metabolic rates. As long as it's meat and protein, whether warm or cold, moving or stationary, they'll gobble it down. I'm sure, however, they'd love to get at us warm-blooded humans."

Heads turned to look at the wildlife biologist, who responded with an uncomfortable "Hey, I'm just being factual."

The press photographers and videographers had moved off the bleachers and positioned themselves along the fence to capture the moment. Journalists chattered into their microphones excitedly, using the backdrop of the Dromaeosaur feeding to present their exclusive onsite reports. Paul, Ethan, and Apisi watched from the flatbed trailer as the Dromaeosaurs devoured the four meat blocks in less than five minutes. The boys and Apisi loaded up a second bucket and dumped another 160 pounds of meat into the habitat. Loretta shook her head, astonished at how much these creatures could consume.

Franz Krause said in his thick Germanic inflection, "Barrett is correct. These animals have a very fast metabolism, so they need a lot of protein. But unlike most mammals and reptiles today, they need to eat the equivalent of their weight each day.

"You mean each of them eats sixty pounds of meat a day?" Jimmy Enright said.

"That's right. They need it to maintain their weight. They burn it off quickly."

"Wow! How often are they fed?"

"We've been feeding them just once a day," Barrett Hailey responded, not taking his eyes off the feast. "But that was feeding them solo, and indoors. This first outdoor group feed is a big experiment. In a group feed, the smaller animals might not get their share."

"Barrett's right," Dr. Krause said. "We might have to go to two or three smaller feedings each day to ensure equitable food distribution. So far, so good. But we'll see."

Loretta's cell phone buzzed and she saw it was Mitena, the young Blackfoot woman who worked the front desk at the inn. Loretta picked up, walking away from the group and plugging her other ear to shut out the *Space Odyssey* music.

"Hi, Mitena. What's up?"

"Sorry to bother you, Mrs. Gilliam, but Mrs. Lacroix has arrived."

"Oh, good. She's a day late, but we're still holding a room for her, right?"

"Yes, but—"

"Go ahead and check her in and show her to her room."

"Well, I would but . . . well, there's a problem. Could you please come?"

"What kind of problem, Mitena?" Loretta heard a baby crying in the background.

"It's too complicated to go into on the phone," Mitena shouted over the baby's wailing. "Could you please come to the office? I need your help."

"Okay," Loretta responded, wondering what could possibly be wrong. Mitena was a confident and competent young lady. The way everything else was going recently, Loretta feared the worst. "I'll be there in five."

Bryan said, "Problem?"

"Don't know, but I need to head up the hill. Your new jewelry maker finally arrived."

"Brinshou Lacroix?"

"Yes."

"Oh, good."

She held out her hand, palm up. "Keys please."

"Can't Mitena handle it?"

"Apparently not. Give me the keys."

Loretta drove their old Pontiac up the dirt road, the orchestral music fading away behind her. She parked in front of the inn and entered the lobby. The large reception area was in chaos. A crimson-faced baby strapped into a stroller bawled loudly. A young Indian woman, seated on the sofa and looking distraught, held the hand of an older Indian woman whose face was battered and bruised, looking like she'd been on the losing end of a street fight. Loretta did her best to hide her shock at the older woman's appearance. One side of the Indian woman's face was discolored in deep shades of purple and yellow. Her nose was askew and one eye was swollen shut. Mitena stood behind the counter, worry tightening her face.

The young woman stood, her look of despair turning hopeful. "Mrs. Gilliam?"

"Yes, I'm Loretta Gilliam. Are you Brinshou Lacroix?"

"Yes. I'm sorry about having to delay my arrival. Thank you for holding my room for me." She pointed to the beaten woman on the sofa. "This is my mother, Kachina. We ran into a bit of trouble, I'm afraid."

"So I see," Loretta said, going to the woman and taking a seat beside her. She reached out to touch Kachina's face but the woman pulled away from her. "What happened?"

Brinshou's voice was shaky. "A domestic problem. My father, he, um . . . well he—"

"That's okay, darlin'," Loretta said, her heart aching for these two women. "Say no more." She looked over the woman's wounds. "Are you hurting, dear?"

Kachina nodded with a grimace. The baby continued to bawl.

"You should go to the hospital, dear."

"She can't," Brinshou said. "She doesn't have any health insurance. Well, she does, but the deductible is so high she'd have to pay out of pocket, and there's no way she can afford it. Peter and I could maybe help some, but we're pretty strapped, too." She looked at Mitena. "I was inquiring about getting a second room for my mother, but she said you're all filled up. No vacancies."

"I'm afraid that's true, Mrs. Lacroix . . ."

"Please, call me Brin," she said, going to the stroller, trying unsuccessfully to quiet the baby.

"Will do, Brin," Loretta said, walking behind the front desk. She stood next to Mitena and shuffled through a stack of papers to give herself time to think and assess the messy situation. She thought about taking the woman to the house, but Olivia Enright was there, watching Lianne and Marnie while the unveiling of the dinosaur habitat was going on. Loretta didn't want her young daughter to be exposed to this. Lianne was already experiencing nightmares from her dinosaur encounters and Loretta had started taking her to a child psychologist on Tuesdays and Thursdays. Those sessions were going well and Loretta didn't want to pile more psychological damage on her Lee-lee. Finally, she said, "Could you please excuse me for a few minutes, Brin?"

"Of course."

Loretta went into the back room and called Olivia's cell.

"Hey Loretta," Olivia said.

Loretta could hear the girls giggling in the background. "Hi, Livvy."

"Everything all right at—what did Bryan name it?—Gilliam's Glade?"

"Yeah, everything went well. The media got quite the spectacle, just as Bry had hoped. Listen, I hate to ask this of you and Jimmy because you've done so much for us already, but—"

"Just name it, girl, and consider it done. Whatchya need?"

"Something has come up at the inn. Could you guys take Lianne again for a few days?"

"Absolutely. We love having Lee with us. So does Marnie."

"You're a godsend, Liv. Thanks a million!"

"Don't mention it, sis. What's goin' on?"

"Just something that I'd prefer Lee not to witness right now. She's been through enough. I'll call you later and give you the full scoop."

"Sounds good. I'll help Lianne get packed."

Loretta ended the call and returned to the lobby. Said to Brin, "I tell you what. We have a spare bedroom at the house. Your mother can stay with us while you're here working for my husband." She turned to Kachina. "We have medical supplies at the house. I'm not a nurse, but I'll do my best."

"You'd do that for us?" Brin said in surprise.

"Yes. Absolutely. I couldn't live with myself if I didn't."

"Oh, thank you, thank you, thank you!" Brin gushed as she went to Loretta and hugged her. "You're an angel, Mrs. Gilliam."

"I don't know about an angel," Loretta said, feeling awkward in the embrace, "but I can't ignore somebody in need." She broke free of Brin and offered her hand to Kachina. "Come with me, dear. I'll take you up to the house and get you fixed up. Mitena, please show Brin and her baby to their room."

As Loretta left the lobby with Kachina, she thought: *The dinosaurs aren't the only creatures in need of a new home.*

Lethal Legalities and
Aerial Masturbation

July 11: Mount Bennett Air Force Base
Elmore, Idaho

PETER SAT IN THE BASE COMMISSARY eating lunch with fellow helicopter pilots Larry Bing, Curtis Williams, and Connor Bartholomew. Uniformed airmen surrounded them, spread out at other tables in the spacious cafeteria. The smell of flame-grilled meat and onions hung heavy in the air. A clattering of pots and pans and spatulas slapping the griddle drifted out from the kitchen.

Conversation was minimal as the diners took interest in the Idaho *News at Noon* program showing on multiple TV screens. The dapper male newscaster announced a big breaking story—the wrongful death lawsuits being brought against the Boy Scouts of America, and scoutmasters Wayne Fahlman and Dennis Miaway of Troop 279 in Great Falls, Montana. Parents of three of the scouts killed by rampaging dinosaurs at the Belt Creek campsite had thrown in together to pursue civil suits. Peter thought the settlement compensation bordered on the ludicrous: two million against the Boy Scouts of America organization and nearly as high against the two scoutmasters. The prosecuting attorney handling the cases briefly outlined the legal reasons for moving forward with the litigation, stating that the scoutmasters had ignored very specific government warnings pertaining to the dangers of the dinosaur invasion.

Harold T. Montgomery, Wayne Fahlman's slick defense lawyer, then gave his rebuttal, stating: "This loss of young life is certainly tragic and I feel a deep sense of sorrow and sympathy for the families of the eight victims. However, with all due respect, under no circumstance should the boys' deaths be ruled anything but accidental. There is no legal basis for holding my client liable for gross misconduct or negligence, the twin pillars of all wrongful death suits. These lawsuits cannot, and *will* not, be proved by any jury in any court of law, here in Montana, or any other state. It saddens me to have to say this, but what happened at that campsite the night of June twentieth was an unfortunate accident that occurred in the natural world, no different really than scouts being mauled by a bear or dying from snakebites. Think about it. A lifeguard is not held accountable if a swimmer or surfer dies in a shark attack. So why should a Boy Scout leader be held liable for something so far out of his control? Why should an organization like the Boy Scouts of America, which does so many good things for our nation's youth, be on the line for *two million dollars*? It's an outrage! Let's be clear. What happened that night was an *accident*. A very unjust and untimely accident, but an accident nonetheless. It was the result of an historic anomaly . . . a bizarre twist of nature. And let it be known that my client, Mr. Wayne Fahlman, did everything humanly possible to save those boys, losing a leg and nearly costing him his life in the process . . ."

Peter thought the lawyer was thoroughly convincing, if not a little too over-the-top dramatic for a brief local television segment. He thought Harold T. Montgomery might be rehearsing for his day in court, trying out a few defense angles before presenting his case to the judge and jury.

Both attorneys agreed it would be a landmark case, seeing that similar lawsuits were sure to follow after the Livingston Rodeo disaster.

Peter really couldn't grasp losing a child or loved one that way—being devoured by flesh-eating dinosaurs. It was a scenario too horrible to contemplate. *Is any child really ever safe in this world?* he wondered, thinking of his baby daughter, Kimi. She was so tiny. Vulnerable and impressionable. The past few days he'd been consumed with what she might have witnessed during the dustup between Brin's parents on the rez. Peter was livid when Brin called him and told him about Nash's attack on her mother. Then when she told him of her participation—the way she'd damn near strangled her father trying to protect Kachina—Peter had wanted to fly up to the rez and murder the cowardly bully himself. But Brin calmed him down, telling him they were safe with the Gilliams now and that Nash was in the custody of the Flathead Tribal Police, taken in for his third domestic assault charge in six months.

Three assault arrests? Good god, Kachina, how can you stay with that animal?

Brin deserved a better father. Kachina deserved a better husband. Kimi deserved a better grandfather (thank God she had one loving grandfather in Peter's father, Pierre).

Peter had spent the last three days bogged down in guilt. *I should have been there to protect the women I love. I never should have pushed Brin to take the baby to the rez. I should have known it wasn't a safe place with Nash there.*

Three assaults in six months? Peter knew Nashota Taleka to be a misogynist and a Neanderthal tyrant, but this news was a surprising shock to him. *Why do women stay with brutal men who abuse them?*

Brin assured him that Loretta Gilliam was taking good care of Kachina, even taking her to their family doctor for professional care of her broken nose and shattered cheekbone. Peter believed the way he could be most helpful would be to convince Kachina she needed to get far away from Nash and help her navigate the legalities of getting a divorce from her monstrous husband. When he made her an offer to come live with them in Missoula, Kachina told him she appreciated his kindness but that she'd have to think it over.

Sweet Jesus! What is there to contemplate, Kachina?

He could hear Brin's mother's voice in his head: "Nash can't help it. He's got Salish warrior blood in him, that's all."

Oh, the excuses we make for people's cruel behavior.

There was a baby involved! His daughter!

How much did Kimi see? How much did she hear?

Brin had told him simply that Kimi slept through the whole sordid affair, and was barely awake when they left the rez.

The reporter's resonant voice pulled him back to the newscast. "Scoutmaster Wayne Fahlman lost his right leg three weeks ago in the Tyrannosaurus Rex attack that cost the lives of eight boys. Mr. Fahlman is now wearing a temporary prosthetic leg while waiting to be fitted with his permanent appendage, which he expects next week. Today he speaks publicly for the first time about the attack and the pending lawsuit against him. Mr. Fahlman is joined by his wife, Joyce, and attorney, Harold Montgomery, from his home in Great Falls."

The newscaster turned and looked behind him at a widescreen monitor on the wall. "Good afternoon, Mr. Fahlman. This is James Franklemeyer here with KTVB in Boise. Thank you for agreeing to speak with us today."

"Thanks for having me on." The man, in his early forties, was slumped in a wheelchair. Round, sickly pale face. Thinning brown hair with a widow's peak above a protruding forehead. Lifeless eyes and a glazed expression. He looked troubled, wincing with discomfort as he repositioned himself in the chair. "Please, call me Wayne."

"Okay, Wayne. Let's start off with a question about your health. How have you been feeling?"

"Emotionally or physically?"

"Both."

"Well, physically I've been in a lot of pain. Surgeons had to remove the lower part of my thigh bone, then shave down what was left to prepare a connective base for the prosthetic. Not able to sleep much. I hate to think what it'd be like without painkillers."

"And emotionally? How's that been for you?"

"Oh man, that's been much worse than the physical part of it. Those murdering reptiles will forever haunt me and Denny . . . my son Jason, too. The way they moved. The way they sounded with their snorting and growling and the weird screeching and chirping. Their aggression . . . the way they attacked with all-out abandon, leading with those teeth and jaws—my god, those *teeth*! Sharp as butcher knives. N-no-nobody . . . should have to . . . y'know . . . go through . . . well, an experience like that. I wouldn't wish it on my worst enemy."

The man was close to breaking down. Tears welled in his haunted eyes.

James Franklemeyer said, "I'm sure it was a frightful night, Wayne. But I suppose you know the public opinion about this . . . that your son and the other scoutmaster's son were the only two boys to survive that night. How do you explain that? Were you not looking out for *all* the scouts in your troop?"

Wayne Fahlman shook his head, disconsolate. "Yes, every one of those boys was my responsibility. But the attack by those ferocious beasts came out of nowhere in the middle of the night. Surprised us all out of deep sleep. We didn't have time to think. We all just reacted the best we could. My son, Jason—and Denny's son, Marty—had the presence of mind to climb high up into the trees and wait it out. It's just unfortunate that the other scouts weren't able to get away."

"Is that how you see it, Wayne? As *unfortunate*?"

"Yes, I do," he said shakily. "I want to say to the parents of all eight lost boys that I'm sorry. I apologize that I . . . I wasn't able to do more. I loved those boys, every last one of them and they are in my thoughts every waking minute. They even appear in my dreams. *Nightmares* I should say. You have to believe that every minute since that terrifying night, I have wished those, um . . . those Tyrannosaurs had, um . . . taken me and spared the boys. If there was any kind of justice, that's what would've happened . . ." Tears streamed down Wayne Fahlman's cheeks now. "But it didn't happen that way, and . . . and . . ." he was full-on crying now, his bottom lip quivering, his shoulders shaking with each sob. "I'm so sorry . . ."

Curtis Williams said from across the table, "Nuthin' like kickin' a man when he's down. Poor bastard. He gets his leg chomped off and then is sued by distraught parents, most of whom probably didn't have time for their kids when they were alive. And now he's takin' the finger of blame from this shitweasel reporter."

Peter didn't know how to respond to that, or even if he should.

Wayne Fahlman's wife, Joyce, replaced him on the screen. "As you can see, my husband is going through a living hell and I beg you . . . I *implore* you scouting families to please drop the lawsuits. Betty? Joanne? Rachel? We've been friends for years. Please, have some compassion for us. *Please*. Have some mercy. We're hurting. Our medical bills are astronomical. Your lawsuit will ruin us."

James Franklemeyer said, "At least you and your husband and son are alive. Eight dead Boy Scouts and their families don't have that luxury."

"Okay, that's it," Harold Montgomery, said, nudging Joyce Fahlman offscreen. "This interview is over. Your tone is biased and offensive, Mr. Franklemeyer. My clients have nothing more to say."

Somebody mercifully changed the channel to a daytime soap.

"TV journalism sure ain't what it used to be," Larry Bing said.

"Welcome to the age of performance journalism," Connor Bartholomew said. "All these young reporters think attack mode is the direct route to a Pulitzer or Peabody, or some other prestigious TV journalism award. Maybe a way out of backwoods local coverage to a major market. I'm surprised anybody who knows of their reputation wants to talk with them."

The pilots continued to eat and discuss the shortcomings of television news reporting while Peter retreated into himself. The situation with Brin's family and his ongoing dissatisfaction with this job flying for the U.S. Air Force weighed heavily on him. It was times like this that he wondered what his life would have been like had his professional hockey career not ended with a blown-out knee. He frequently fantasized about skating as a winger for the Toronto Maple Leafs, his blazing speed sending him flying up and down the ice, scoring goals at a record pace, the enormous arena crowds cheering his every move. He would be on television, the name Peter Lacroix known by millions of fans. People would buy his replica jersey. He'd be making the big bucks and could afford a much nicer house than the cramped two bedroom Missoula matchbox they lived in now. He could give Brin and Kimi a much better life than he could afford as a Montana Forest Service chopper pilot. But then, if he'd continued playing hockey he probably would not have met Brinshou.

This life is a series of tradeoffs.

"You're awfully sphinxlike today, Pete," he heard Connor Bartholomew say. "Somethin' on your mind?"

"Just some family stuff going on. It's got me thinking about what we're doing here."

"Whaddaya mean?" Bing asked.

"Well, we're not doin' any better huntin' dinosaurs than we did retrieving meteorites. Worse even. We haven't nabbed a single animal since we changed the focus of this operation. We've all seen a few, but only briefly. They're too quick and they've got lots of cover. We don't even have approximate coordinates the way we did with the meteorites. Glick has us looking in heavily forested areas. Can't see shit for all the trees. Every day we go out flying willy-nilly all over the Continental Divide without any results. It's all just starting to feel like a huge waste of time and energy. Are you guys happy doing this day in and day out?"

"I love the money," Bartholomew said.

"I second that emotion," Williams said. "If the government wants to pay me primo dollars for aerial masturbation, so be it."

Bartholomew laughed. "*Aerial masturbation,* Curtis? I've been wondering about that wiggling motion you've been doing in the pilot's seat!"

Peter smiled, but he wasn't laughing with the other three. When they calmed down, he said, "I don't know, guys. I'm not real happy working for an idiot like Glick. I don't like flyin' out each day searching for ghosts, returning emptyhanded. I especially hate flyin' these rickety old Sikorskys—these repurposed Army hand-me-downs. I really want to get back to my forestry job. At least there I feel like I'm accomplishing something."

Williams said, "Lighten up, Pete. You take things too seriously. Just take their goddammed money and fly around in circles. Fill out their dumb reports. Make shit up if you have to. I do. Don't punch a gift horse in the muzzle."

"Yeah," Bartholomew said. "I don't know about you, but I'm glad we haven't been able to bag any of those creatures. I'm with Curtis on this—go through the motions and take their money. For me, these paychecks are goin' toward a new bass boat. I've had my eye on a Bass Cat Puma—twenty-three feet of streamlined beauty. Another coupla weeks of this, um, aerial masturbation, and she's mine!"

Peter was about to respond when he heard Colonel Glick enter the commissary.

"All right, idle time is over," Glick announced loudly. "We have a red alarm search and rescue emergency. We have a missing helicopter. Two missing chopper pilots and two air guardsmen. I need all hands in aircraft on the main tarmac in twenty minutes. Your pararescue teams are being assembled there."

Men jumped up from their seats, leaving their lunches unfinished. Glick continued shouting as they scrambled past him out the doors. "Pilots Minsinger and Cavanaugh fell off our radar an hour ago and we can't pick up any trace of them through radio communication . . ."

Peter moved slowly, every movement of his limbs a struggle, as though he was underwater, fighting a strong undercurrent.

Blair Minsinger and Rusty Cavanaugh missing?

Did they crash? Problem with their electronics? Did they cut communications on purpose? Were they on the ground facing off against flesh-eating dinosaurs?

His mind was in a jumble as he made his way to his dorm room to pick up his flight gear. Rusty Cavanaugh's wife just delivered her baby last week. Their first child.

Peter was determined to find Rusty and Blair.

Hopefully alive.

Moths to a Flame

July 12: Vinson Farms
Conrad, Montana

A WEEK HAD PASSED SINCE THE LIVINGSTON rodeo disaster and Nora still struggled with the sights and sounds of that awful night. She sat cross-legged on a plywood plank high in a cottonwood tree overlooking a long stretch of barley fields at Vinson Farms, a large conglomerate co-op in Conrad, an hour drive east of Heart Butte. The massive agri-compound spanned more than two-thousand acres, and produced wheat, canola, hemp, and barley—all crops that necessitated abundant irrigation, which attracted wild animals. Hayden sat next to her, scoping the fields through binoculars. Both had tranquilizer air rifles, ready for action.

Yesterday they had captured another Triceratops here, and had taken it back to the Gilliam ranch. They had also spotted three T-Rexes roaming the adjoining canola fields, marking the first time they'd seen carnivores in the same space as herbivores. Hayden thought that was significant. The Tyrannosaurus Rexes here could indicate the carnivores were hunting Triceratops. It was a well-known fact among Cretaceous scholars that Triceratops was the prey of choice for Tyrannosaurus Rex. So, much to Nora's displeasure, they had returned to attempt to capture a T-Rex specimen.

It was a tall order. Especially the way she was feeling.

Nora would rather be anywhere but here, but she wasn't about to let Hayden know that.

Since the T-Rex rodeo attacks, there had been more than a dozen dinosaur sightings across Montana and Idaho. T-Rexes, Dromaeosaurs, and Triceratops were making their presence known in bigger numbers than Nora thought possible. They had even briefly spotted what they thought was a pair of Ankylosaurs, the bulky, low-slung quadruped herbivores with bony armor that were prevalent in these parts during the Late Cretaceous. The prehistoric animals were spotted in woodlands and fields, from southernmost Boise through western Montana and eastern Idaho, all along the base of the Rockies up to the Canadian border. Small herds of elk, bison, and cattle had been hit, but mercifully there had been no new clashes with humans. Triceratops were munching their way through acres of wheat, barley, alfalfa, and canola. Farmers and ranchers, trying to protect their crops and livestock, had taken potshots at the primordial intruders, but the animals were fleet and crafty, evading rifle fire and disappearing into forestland or scurrying into caves and fissures in rocks on higher ground.

Nora and Hayden followed up on as many incidents as they could get to. Covering so much geography by car, however, limited their reach. And the nature of their work frustrated Nora. They were reduced to playing zoological pathologists, arriving well after the fact, examining prey carcasses and missing out on the predators that had done the damage. Usually the only evidence of the attackers were tracks and droppings. They had managed to collect a handful of broken teeth from juvenile T-Rexes at one of the elk kill sites, which told them that the young carnivores could replenish teeth as needed. But they hadn't been able to collect much data to help them better understand Tyrannosaurs. They had two T-Rex carcasses they were studying at Gilliam's Guidepost—the water bloated cadaver retrieved from the beaver dam on Thurston Creek on John Tully's property, and the body of a Tyrannosaur killed at the Boy Scout camp. Authorities at the Livingston rodeo wouldn't allow them access to the kill site as it was still being investigated and processed. That was just fine with Nora. She never wanted to revisit the Park County Fairgrounds in Livingston as long as she lived.

Hayden, on the other hand, seemed to be on an obsessive quest to bag a live Tyrannosaurus Rex. Nora knew the importance of nabbing a living specimen. Their research would be greatly enhanced with a living, breathing animal. Capturing one would allow them to understand so much more about the Tyrannosaurid genus. The Dromaeosaurs and Triceratops they had in captivity had revealed a wealth of information they could never glean solely from remains. They'd learned that contrary to previous theories, the creatures were warm-blooded like current day mammals and birds, not cold-blooded like reptiles. Their body temperatures averaged just over 100 degrees, which contributed to their fast metabolic rates and constant need for nourishment. Capturing a living Tyranno-saurus Rex would be a big research win for them.

Still, the idea of getting anywhere near these terrifying beasts sent jolts of panic through her. She had seen enough T-Rex carnage a week ago to last her a lifetime. She shuddered every time she recalled the blood spilled on the parking lot pavement, glistening like oil slicks under the sodium vapor lights; the screams and keen-ing of the dying; the gunshots; the mournful sound of sirens in the distance. She wasn't sleeping well; she'd been gripped by a couple of panic attacks during long, sleepless nights, fortunately able to keep them hidden from a sleeping Hayden. She was exhausted and not eating right due to abdominal pain she suspicioned might be the beginnings of an ulcer.

Despite this, Nora was doing her very best to hold it together, to present a brave face to Hayden. They were supposed to be pro-fessional researchers, scientists trained to handle what the laws of nature delivered. She understood this. They had to soldier on. Fight the good fight for the benefit of accumulating valuable zoological data. That seemed to be Hayden's stance and she went along with it, not wanting to show weakness. They really hadn't discussed it the past week, much as she wanted to. They just danced around the subject of the Livingston Roundup like it never happened. The tainted rodeo outing was the silent wedge that had subtly worked its way between them. Their intimacy and passion—so intense and comforting in the beginning—had been dampened. Even their lovemaking had taken a hit. Just a week ago their couplings had been explosive, adventurous, inventive. They still had regular sex in their motel rooms as they traveled this week, but to Nora, their bed relations felt more mechanical and obligatory. Perfunctory. No pizzazz like before.

Maybe this relationship is moving too fast.

We're together all the time.

Maybe we need a break from each other.

She was no longer sure about many things.

Nora Jane Lemoyne, voted "Most Likely to Succeed" by her classmates senior year at Woodbury High School, was at a crossroads, and having a difficult time dealing with it. A little more than a month ago she was leading a prestigious paleontology dig in Choteau, successfully finding and unearthing an intact Maiasaura skeleton and a Triceratops skull. Now she sat twenty feet up in a tree casing out a field of wet barley. She sure wasn't feeling very successful at the moment.

The Vinson Farm proprietors had sent an SOS message with photos of the creatures that were rapidly consuming their crops, and Hayden and Nora answered the call. Yesterday had been a success, adding a second Triceratops to the Gilliam menagerie. Today, feeling the need for more firepower and muscle to snare a T-Rex, Hayden had recruited government wildlife biologist Barrett Hailey and one of his employees. The two feds were camped out in a pickup truck Nora could see across the way, partially concealed behind tall shoots of barley straw, armed with long range air rifles fitted with tranquilizer darts that carried a bigger punch than the Pneu-Dart tranq pistol Hayden had used on both of the captured Triceratops.

Dusk approached. The sun played peek-a-boo behind the craggy summits of the Rockies to the west. Irrigation sprinklers hissed, shooting out long arcs of water, the low-angled sunlight creating prismatic rainbows in the spray. She shifted her position on the hard plywood and glanced at Hayden. They had been perched in this tree quietly for several hours and had seen no activity. By this time yesterday, they had a sedated Triceratops in the back of their van and were on their way back to Heart Butte.

Nora was exhausted and bored. Her back hurt and her legs were cramping up. Her eyes burned. Staring at the symmetrical rows of barley was bringing on a dizzying headache. She'd had enough of this nonsense.

"This is a waste of time," she said, her voice alarmingly loud after hours of nothing but hissing sprinklers. "We might as well be trying to capture Sasquatch."

"Have some patience, love," he said, continuing to peer through the binoculars, glassing the far perimeter of the barley fields. "My well-honed instincts are telling me this will pay off. I believe they are close by. I can *feel* them."

"This is madness. I've seen quite enough of Tyrannosaurus Rex the past week. Let's leave now while we still can."

Hayden lowered the binoculars and looked at her. "We knew it was going to end up like this, Nora. As soon as we had that first confirmation that T-Rexes hatched out, we knew they'd be trouble. We need to bring in a live one to further our studies. Surely you can see the importance of what we're doing here."

"Of *course* I see that, Hayden," she said, more snappishly than intended. "It's just that I'm feeling way out of my comfort zone here. What happened in Livingston last week really messed me up. And sitting for hours casing farmers' fields, and . . ." she raised the long gun from her lap, "clutching this rifle like I'm a modern-day Calamity Jane or something. It's absurd. I'm a paleontologist, not a cowgirl. Or a poacher."

"*Poacher*? You think that's what we're doing? Poaching?"

"Well . . . no. Not really. It's just that . . . um, you seem all gung-ho for meeting up with these beasts again. You don't seem nearly as affected by what we experienced at that rodeo. I can't un-see what I saw there. I can't un-hear what I heard. I hate to break it to you, but I've been seriously traumatized by it. But you? You're like one of those moths that's attracted to a flame, not realizing the flame can burn you. But, Hayden, honey, I'll have you know what we're doing here is tempting fate. What we're doing here can burn you—burn *us*— very badly, like we saw at that rodeo."

"What? You're talking nonsense."

"Am I? We haven't discussed this, and I need to."

He reached across and took her hand in his, caressed her knuckles affectionately. She could see compassion softening his eyes, could hear the kindness in his voice as he said, "I'm well aware the effect that rodeo experience has had on you, Nora. I'm sorry you had to go through that . . . that *we* had to go through it. It sucks and I wish there was something I could do to make it all disappear. There's nothing I want more than to make things better for you. But I can't. I love you so much, my lovely Lady Lemoyne. But you've been so wrapped up in yourself lately, I don't know how to reach you. You know you can talk to me about anything."

"I know that, but—"

"Believe it or not, that dreadful night spooked me, too. Yes, I know I could get burned getting too close . . . that *we* could get burned. We're flirting with danger here. Every day. But I see it as the price we pay for being scientists on the cutting edge of something spectacular. But look, I see your pain. I feel it, too. I just show it in different ways. I love you madly, Nora. I really do. So please, if you want to talk about it, I'm all ears. I can be a good listener. I *want* to hear what you're thinking . . . what you're *feeling*."

His fingers rubbing her hand sent a warm glow through her. His look was honest and heartfelt, open and vulnerable. She felt some of their AWOL intimacy returning, sensed a welcoming closeness in that moment. Even so, she had come to some stark realizations about what she needed to do to save herself. He wasn't going to easily accept what she had to tell him. But now was the time. She was unsure just how to start such a difficult conversation. After a few long moments of deliberation, she decided to just let it out. Nora knew she shouldn't hold back any longer.

"I've been doing a lot of thinking," she said, gently pulling her hand away from his.

"Oh-oh," he said, glancing at his empty hand. "That doesn't sound good."

She looked away from him, out over the fields. "I'm not sure I'm cut out for this . . . this dinosaur hunting thing. I think I want to go back to the paleo expedition."

"Wait. *What?*"

"I know. Not what you expected, right?"

"Well, it *is* a little abrupt, I must say."

"Oh, Hayden. This is so hard for me. I spoke with Greg Dulow-ski last night when you were in the shower. They're having great success with the dig. He told me they found an intact Troodon Formosus skeleton on top of a nest of unbroken fossilized eggs. Up near Two Medicine in Glacier National Park. I really miss that sense of discovery. I miss the team."

"You don't think what we've been doing is *discovery*?"

"I do, yes. And parts of it are fascinating and challenging. But it's just a little too violent for my tastes. You can't take back what we witnessed in Livingston. Fossils and bones don't attack and eat humans. They tell a quiet story—an intriguing story minus the savagery. I'm finding out that's more my speed."

Hayden tugged on his beard, a habit she had learned he resorted to when nervous. He said, "You can't return to the expedition, Nora."

"Why not?"

"Because Dulowski is running the show now. You'd be seen as a meddler. Take heed in what Thomas Wolfe wrote: You can't go home again."

"I was hoping to convince you to come with me."

He shook his head. "No way. From a work standpoint, that would be foolish. That excursion only lasts another month. This gig we've got now is a permanent job, as long as the dinosaurs stick around. It gives us authenticity for the book we talked about writing. Don't you realize how incredibly lucky we are to have been put in this position? We're in the driver's seat of one of the greatest scientific events in recorded history. We're being paid good money to track down and study these creatures *before* they become bones and fossils. It's a blessing, love, and we should embrace it."

"Yes, I'll give you that. But after the Livingston rodeo, this feels more like a curse than a blessing. This is not what I signed up for, Hayden. That's *my* dig team up there in Glacier National Park. I recruited every one of them. Spent the better part of a year putting it all together, only to have it pulled out from under me. That's where I should be. That's where I belong."

Hayden combed his fingers through his hair. "What about us?"

"What *about* us?"

"I can't do this without you, Nora. I *won't* do this without you."

"Then come with me."

"I can't. Returning to rocks and bones would bore the hell out of me after working with living animals. It'd be too static for me now. Besides, you know as well as I do most of that team would have problems with the fact we're sleeping together."

She studied him in the dying light, her heart hurting, sensing an end to something that had moved swiftly and flashed brightly, like the meteor showers that had launched the strange situation in which they now found themselves. Their relationship was beautiful and life-affirming, a magical moment in a bizarre time. The emptiness she was feeling told her that she really did love this man. She wanted to be with him. She didn't want to lose him. And yet, she had to be true to herself. She had to *save* herself.

"Well, I guess we're at an impasse then," she said with regret.

"Please don't do this, Nora."

"We both have to do what's best for ourselves."

"Hmmm," he said, pulling at his beard again, thinking for a long beat. Finally he said, "Would you consider a compromise?"

"Compromise? Sure. I'm listening."

"How about sticking it out until we can capture a Rex? Then we walk away from it. We resign our dinosaur scout positions and retire to the Gilliam ranch to write our book. We'll have three species of Cretaceous animals in captivity to study. We'll be safe there. No more of this trucking hundreds of miles chugging bad coffee and staying in shitty roadside motels. No more taking chances on encountering deadly beasts in the wild. No more moths to the flame."

"How is that a compromise? Didn't you hear me? I told you I want to return to the expedition team."

"The paleo-expedition ship has sailed, Nora. It's Greg's baby now. You have to accept that. Let it go and move forward."

"Easy for you to say. You're not interested in paleontology anymore."

"You're wrong. I *am* interested in paleontology. Just a different branch of it. Paleo*zoology* is a more active, intriguing science." He scooted closer to her, draped an arm across her shoulders. "Jesus, Nora. Don't you realize what a gift it is we've been given?"

She looked away, focusing on the hood of Barrett Hailey's government truck. She couldn't look at Hayden. Her emotions were bubbling up. Her eyes became heavy with tears. Her voice warbled as she said, "I love you, Hayden Fowler. I really do. I'm just . . . just really confused right now." She turned her head to look at him, their faces close. "I'm suffering an identity crisis, I guess. I don't know who I am anymore . . . who I'm supposed to be." Her tears streamed. She removed her glasses to dab at her eyes. "God, I feel so silly. Weeping like a little girl. This is *so* not me."

"I know," he said, using his thumb to wipe her cheeks. "You've been through a lot, sweetheart. We both have. It's been a tough week and I understand. I really do. No need to feel silly. We all need a good cry now and then."

They sat there, Hayden holding her close, stroking her shoulder while she sobbed. After a while he said, "You know, that's the first time you've said those words to me, Nora. That you love me. Do you really mean that?"

She came out of her funk, letting out a little giggle, slapped his side playfully. "Of *course* I mean it, you big dumb oaf! Jesus, I never thought you, of all people, could ever be insecure."

"Insecure? Naw. It's just that I haven't heard those words very often from someone I care about. It makes me feel incredible."

"You mean, none of those bedroom Barbies you've slept with uttered words of enduring love to you? I'm shocked."

"Ouch! Foul ball, my Lady Lemoyne."

She laughed. "You just invite it sometimes, Hayden. I can't help myself."

"Yeah, well, I'll have you know I'm not the Barbie type," he said. "Barbie isn't anatomically correct."

She laughed again, louder this time. "I really don't know why I put up with you."

He grinned and kissed the side of her face. "You put up with me because I'm the one man who can make you laugh."

"You think that's why I'm attracted to you?"

"One of *many* reasons, yeah. I'm willing to bet your exes were both sticks in the mud."

"You don't know a damned thing about my ex-husbands."

"I know I don't. Because you won't talk about them. When I ask you about them, you retreat into your shell. I'm beginning to think they might be white collar criminals or something. Maybe even serial killers."

She tried to come up with a snappy comeback but couldn't. "Well I will tell you this. I haven't said those words—told a man I loved him—since my second husband, Marcus. And that was six years ago."

"Six *years*? Jesus! No wonder you're so hot in the sack. Makin' up for lost time."

"You wish! I didn't say it was the last time I had sex before you. Not even close."

"Say what you will. God knows how much I love you, Nora. Please stay with me so I can prove it to you."

"The point I'm trying to make is that those words don't come easy for me, Hayden. It scares the hell out of me to put myself out there like this. I'm afraid of being hurt . . . afraid of losing every-thing again. I can't go through all that again. You've bragged about your stud playboy past and that scares me."

"Okay, okay. I see the problem now," he said. "I told you about my not-so-honorable dating past as a way of opening up an honest conversation between us. Most of those 'bedroom Barbies' as you call them were just warm bodies to scratch my restless biological itch. *Biology*, not emotional *love*. Nothing real and lasting. I need a lot more than one-night stands now that I'm older and wiser. Some-thing with substance . . . something durable. I need what I feel when I'm with you, Nora. I would *never* think of hurting you. You've made me a better man. I want to make your life as wonderful as you make me feel."

"That's nice to hear. But I've heard that kind of promise from men before. Too many times to count."

"Wow. *That's* your response? That's cold."

"Sorry," she said, leaning over and kissing him on the mouth. The kiss went on for a drawn-out, impassioned minute or more. "Is that warmer?" she said when she pulled back from him.

"Much," he said, hugging her close. "Look, I know you've been hurt pretty bad in the past. I understand that. I guess time is the only way I can get you to trust me, to let you know that I love you . . . that I admire you like I've never admired anyone before. I think I actually fell in love with you the day you came to interview me in Minneapolis."

"Really?"

"Truly. After talking with you for five minutes I knew you were special. You hit me with a feeling I never felt with any of my three wives."

"But I was pretty hard on you during that interview."

"Yeah, you were. But I was attracted to your strength, of your innate intelligence. All that talent and smarts wrapped up in a gorgeous package. I don't know what the hell was wrong with your exes, but they were fools for letting you get away."

Nora hoped he couldn't see her blushing. "Both of my marriages were complicated."

"Aren't they all? Look, I know my words are just that to you right now—*words*. But I want to prove to you there are authentic feelings behind those words. I can't do that if we're separated. How about trying things my way for a while so I can prove it to you?"

"You mean *your* version of compromise?"

He snickered. "Yeah, *my* version. It could turn into *our* version if you'd give it a chance."

Suddenly loud caterwauling shrieks pierced the stillness— raucous, screeching animal sounds. Protracted, high-pitched whinnies, like a horse in distress. Nora looked out to see a Triceratops bolting wildly through the barley, zig-zagging, trying to flee a couple of brawny Tyrannosaurs in hot pursuit.

"Ah-ha! I *knew* they'd come!" Hayden barked excitedly, sliding across the plywood and grabbing his rifle.

The Triceratops—built lower to the ground—was slowed by the thick barley. It snorted and shrieked, trying desperately to crash through to open ground in an adjoining field. The Tyrannosaurs growled fiercely as they pursued, bounding over and through the barley. They worked in tandem, one going for the Triceratops' stubby legs, the other jumping on the herbivore's back, bringing it down with a loud thump that shook the tree stand.

The Tyrannosaurs pounced and began to feed, viciously ripping chunks of flesh from their prey.

The downed Triceratops' cries went from strident braying to a mewling whimper.

The feasting Tyrannosaurs gulped and slurped.

Nora heard twin firecracker pops followed by compressed-air *ping-whooshes*. The two government wildlife biologists stood erect in the bed of their pickup on the far side of the fields, firing their tranquilizer rifles. The first two darts sailed high and they quickly reloaded, launching two more darts, one hitting the T-Rex nearest them, a solid stick into the side of the neck. The carnivore roared, annoyed at being struck, the sedation dart flopping wildly as the animal flailed its scraggly forearms, trying in vain to knock the dart free. The beast raised its head and turned, a lump of Triceratops meat in its dripping maw, its malevolent, blood-red eyes searching for the deliverer of the pain. The animal stared at the government pickup truck and the two shooters pointing long guns in his direction. He stopped chewing, seeming to be momentarily in a quandary on whether to attack the human shooters. But then, just as quickly, decided his hunger was more important and lowered his head, plunging back into his Triceratops feast.

"Wow, good shootin', fellas," Hayden said, kneeling and taking a shooting position on the platform. "One for the money, two for the show, as they say." Nora watched him bring the rifle barrel up, focus on the second T-Rex through the telescopic sight.

He hesitated for so long she wondered what he was doing.

"What are you waiting for, Hayden?"

"Waiting until the second one comes up for air," he said. Hayden breathed evenly, held the rifle steady, eye never leaving the scope. "He's gotta stand upright to be able to shake and shimmy that meat down his gullet. He'll present an easy target any minute now."

The sedated Tyrannosaur stood, erect, a bloody leg bone clutched in its jaws, dazed, walking unsteadily in circles, eyes wildly unfocused. It took four wobbly steps toward Barrett Hailey and his charge before collapsing in a heap on its side. Nora heard a cheer go up from the government biologists.

The second Tyrannosaur rose up out of the barley, exposing its full body. Ropy intestines filled the animal's shovel mouth. It shook its head ferociously from side to side, trying to get the bloody mass to slide down its long neck.

Hayden fired. An explosive pop and sharp *ping-whoosh* as the dart ejected, gliding across the field with a low whistle and plunging into the middle of the Tyrannosaur's broad chest. The impact stunned the creature momentarily.

Nora was impressed. "You're a regular Daniel Boone."

"Thanks. That should be enough to take him down," Hayden said, watching the creature quickly lose his bearings. "How big would you estimate they are?"

"Bigger than the ones we saw at the rodeo," she said. "I don't know, probably six feet tall judging by the height of the barley. Maybe three-hundred pounds. Just a guess, mind you. It's a little hard to tell from this distance."

"And they're just juveniles. They're all muscle and jaws and teeth," Hayden said in an awed tone of wonder. "Eating machines. Did you see how they worked as a team to bring down that Triceratops?"

"I did, yes."

"We could never learn that studying bones and fossils."

"I get it, Hayden. No need to rub it in."

She watched the second Tyrannosaur stumble around the mound of the fallen Triceratops, struggling to maintain his balance and obviously confused by his loss of control, then falling into the wet barley next to the other T-Rex. Nora was amazed that a relatively small tranquilizer dart could incapacitate a large animal so quickly.

Hayden stood and looked at his air rifle. "Too bad we didn't have these things at the rodeo, huh?"

"Yeah, too bad," she said, looking out across the field, seeing the two government biologists carefully approaching the mutilated Triceratops and two anesthetized Tyrannosaurs.

Hayden strapped the rifle over his shoulder and started to traverse the rope ladder down the tree. "Time to collect our new zoo additions."

Nora shook her head. "I'm not going anywhere near those things."

"I didn't expect you to, sweets. I think the three of us can get the animals up into Barrett's truck. I'll meet you in the van in a little while."

She regarded the two T-Rexes laying in the barley. "Are you sure they're out of commission?"

He climbed back up on the tree stand and kissed her. "You worry too much, Nora."

She threw her arms around him and kissed him back. "It's only because I love you, you big dumb fool. Please be careful."

Skeletons in a Tomb

July 14: River of No Return Wilderness Area
Central Idaho

AFTER THREE ARDUOUS DAYS OF SEARCH over and through remote wilderness, the missing helicopter was located. U.S. Air Force and Army search and rescue teams had traversed thousands of square miles of Idaho's rugged backcountry for the chopper that had mysteriously gone silent. Mount Bennett AFB Air Traffic Control had lost radio communications with helicopter pilots Blair Minsinger and Russell Cavanaugh thirty minutes before the aircraft disappeared from flight radar. The two civilian pilots and two Air Force guardsmen had been incommunicado for 76 hours.

An Air Force jet pilot spotted the wreckage partially hidden under the rocky overhang of a sheer cliff in one of the most isolated places in the continental United States—the Frank Church River of No Return Wilderness in central Idaho. The area was two-and-a-half million acres of rugged mountain ranges, plunging canyons, dense highland forests, and the mighty Salmon River. It was an inhospitable no-man's land, a federally protected wildlife area untouched by human hands, and home to large populations of mountain lions, grey wolves, black bears, bighorn sheep, and feral goats.

Peter Lacroix's pararescue team had been sent to the crash site to rescue any survivors, attend to the injured, and/or bring back bodies of the dead. They'd also been instructed to retrieve the black box flight data recorder to analyze the cause of the crash. Colonel Glick selected Lacroix to pilot the mission because he was the most experienced of the Mount Bennett helicopter pilots at flying medevac rescue and longline lift operations. The team consisted of Lacroix, copilot Larry Bing, and the on-the-ground rescue crew of three Air National Guard pararescue medics attached to the Mount Bennett Air Force Base 366th Fighter Wing squadron. Combat Rescue Officer (CRO) Chad Powell led pararescue medics Melvin Ryhoffer and Eric Blanchard on this assignment. The three men were members of a special operations squad cross-trained for military combat and emergency medical rescue. They carried M4 carbines as well as emergency trauma equipment, and were trained to be prepared for anything. Their bulky gear added an extra eighty pounds to their burden. All three were also highly trained parachute jumpers, often referred to as PJs.

The crash site along the wall of the steep rocky precipice ruled out the possibility of parachuting in. The rugged topography called for a helicopter longline. The PJs had been lowered, one at a time, from the rescue chopper in a longline basket onto the 20-foot-wide shelf of rock that protruded from the side of the peak. The rescue helicopter hovered a hundred feet above, pilots Lacroix and Bing working the sticks to hold the chopper steady against stiff headwinds.

The pararescue team scanned their surroundings, gusts of cold wind whipping at their fatigues. Chad Powell cautiously peered out over the vast chasm. The thousand-foot drop sucked the breath from his lungs. Far below, the meandering Salmon River wound through rocky gorges, looking like a shiny ribbon. He moved along the cliff wall, to the mouth of a small cave, where large sections of the downed aircraft had broken apart on impact and scattered. Much of the chopper's fuselage was jammed up into the cave. It appeared as though the aircraft had clipped the outcropping with the main rotor blade and twisted around before slamming into the granite face.

Why were they flying so near the cliff?

Gale force winds?

Mechanical failure?

Amazingly, the crash hadn't caused an explosion. There was no evidence of a fire.

Were the fuel tanks spared direct collision?

Did they run out of fuel?

Pieces of the rotor blade lay in the dirt in front of the cave amongst a scattering of bolts and screws and bearings and dented metal panels. Chunks of rock littered the area. Deep gouges scarred the stony shelf above the cave opening. The smell of aviation grease and crankcase oil was strong, as was a hint of kerosene. Approaching the cave entrance, Powell caught a whiff of more ominous smells: the bright, metallic scent of blood and the gassy putrescent reek of decomposition.

He glanced at Ryhoffer and Blanchard questioningly as he made his way around the detritus and entered the cave. The two medics quietly fell in behind him. A cloud of black flies swarmed around their heads. The men sputtered and coughed and waved their arms, batting the flies away as they worked their way around the framework of the wrecked Sikorsky.

Powell saw that the centrifugal force of the collision had whirled the aircraft around, so that the tail section had smashed into the cave first. The cockpit was jammed up against a boulder on the near side with the windshield facing out. The Plexiglas was shattered, spider-webbed so finely Powell couldn't see inside.

He heard Peter Lacroix's voice in his ear buds. "What are you seeing down there, Chad?"

"The aircraft—what's left of it—is jammed up inside a small cave, Pete," Powell said into his shoulder mic. "It went in tail first, so retrieving the black box could be problematic."

"Find any bodies?"

"Not yet. The cockpit is pretty smashed up and difficult to get at. We're looking for an access point now."

"Got it. Keep us posted."

"Roger that."

Powell walked around the huge boulder that hid the wreck, to the opposite side where he thought there was clear access to the cockpit. He pulled a heavy duty flashlight from his backpack and climbed piles of loose rocks to get a view down into the small pocket of open space where the wrecked chopper was wedged. The stench of rotting flesh hit him in a wave and made him gag. He grabbed a face mask out of his pack, put it on. The flies buzzed around his head, and he had to repeatedly swat them away to get a clear look. He aimed the flashlight down into the area.

Death and destruction spread out below him.

The helicopter doors and windows had blown out in the crash. The side of the fuselage was sprayed with blotches of dark blood.

He saw bodies. Three of them.

Or what were once human bodies.

Three skeletal remains, each with missing bones.

Lumps of gooey organs and muscle tissue glistened under the flashlight beam.

Chad Powell shivered.

"It's hell in here, Pete," he radioed up to the rescue chopper.

He moved the flashlight beam over a body that hung from the pilot's chair, the badly frayed shoulder harness clinging to what was little more than a skull, ribs, and hip bones with strips of bloody flesh hanging from them. Two other skeletal corpses and gristly bones were strewn across the blood-soaked dirt floor.

Three mutilated bodies that he could see. There were four onboard when the craft went missing. He called out for Ryhoffer and Blanchard to join him.

Can carrion scavengers work that quickly?

Not much left to identify them by, Powell thought. *The crash alone didn't do this to them.*

The three pararescue medics investigated the grim scene. In addition to bones and intestines, they found torn and shredded pieces of the Air Force guardsmen's uniforms: two ragged boonie hats, swaths of camouflage-patterned trousers and blouses, a military rigger belt. A pair of sage green combat boots, one with the stump of a foot still inside.

Chad Powell kept up a running commentary with Lacroix and Bing up in the chopper, keeping them informed of their progress. He reported they could account for only three of the missing four airmen. They were able to identify the two Air Force guardsmen from their name and service patches embroidered in midnight blue on their combat shirts. The chopper pilots were civilians and carried no such identifying marks, so it was a wild guess which one had died. Colonel Glick informed them in their preflight briefing that Blair Minsinger was the assigned pilot with Russell Cavanaugh handling copilot duties.

Lacroix's voice hummed in his ear. "Any idea which pilot you've got there?"

Powell spoke into his shoulder mic. "It's a real mess in here, Pete. We believe it's Minsinger. But only because what's left of the body is still strapped in to the pilot's chair. There's no other way to make ID."

Peter Lacroix said, "That leaves Rusty—Rusty *Cavanaugh*—as missing and unaccounted for. Any sign of him leaving the scene? Any footprints leading away from the crash? Any blood trails?"

"No, Pete. We've canvassed the entire area around the cockpit and fuselage. No indication of a fourth body . . . dead or alive."

"You say the three dead men are, um . . . torn apart and stripped clean?"

"Pretty much, yeah. There's a lot of blood. Some connective tissue and intestines. But we're pretty much looking at three frag-mented skeletons. A crash of this force would certainly break bones and cause all kinds of havoc on a body. But no way did the crash cause this kind of damage."

Lacroix was slow to respond. "You don't think—?"

"Hey, Chad," Ryhoffer called from near the tail section. "Come take a look at this."

"Hold on a minute, Pete," Powell said, walking around the demolished aircraft. "Ry might have found something . . ."

Powell walked further into the cave, the beam of his flashlight leading the way. Ryhoffer and Blanchard stood thirty yards behind the wreck, leaning over what looked like the carcass of a black bear.

"Somethin' ate the guts clean outta this bear." Blanchard's muffled voice echoed off the cave walls as Powell approached.

Chad Powell kneeled and examined the downed beast. The flies were thick here, the smell of blood more pungent than at the crash site. This was a fresh kill. Much of the torso, arms, and legs had been eaten away, leaving clawed paws and feet, and a head with glassy eyes staring up at the cave ceiling. Powell thought its dead eyes bore the look of terror.

He stood and shined the flashlight along the ground, saw the tracks leading away from the bear, deeper into the cave. Tracks he'd been schooled to recognize. Three toes with a trailing hind claw.

Dozens of them.

He leaned into his shoulder mic, said, "Hey, Pete. It looks like our late chopper team had the misfortune of running into hungry dinosaurs."

"Oh no!"

"Yeah. I think the impact of the crash killed them—at least three of them—which might be a blessing for them in this case, based on the bloodshed. It looks like a dinosaur feeding frenzy took place here. We've also got the body of a mature black bear—six foot, probably close to four-hundred pounds—picked apart like a post-dinner Thanksgiving turkey. Distinctive dinosaur tracks, more than one, leading away, down the tunnel, further into the cave." He took a knee to study one of the tracks. "Whatever kind of dinosaurs they are, they look to be big based on the depth of the prints."

"How the hell could dinosaurs get up into a high-country cave like this, Chad?"

"Don't know," he said, raising the flash and illuminating the near section of the cave. "My guess would be there's an opening on the other side of this mountain. Maybe a sheep or mountain goat trail leading up to it."

Blanchard, walking along the far wall, yelled out that he'd discovered boot prints. Powell went to investigate.

"Hey, Pete," he said into his mic while following the human footprints along the wall, "we've got boot prints heading deeper into the cave. Can't tell if they came before or after the dinos arrived. There's no blood trail. So unless we missed something, it looks like Cavanaugh might have survived."

"Well, at least that's a bit of positive news we can hang our hopes on."

"Yeah," Powell said, looking down the wide tunnel into the dark maw of the cave interior. He pulled his M4 rifle off his shoulder. "I'm taking Ry with me to follow these prints, and sending Blanch to retrieve the flight data recorder."

"Are you sure that's wise?" Lacroix questioned. "Splitting up? We need to get the remains and flight recorder back to the base."

Chad Powell looked at Ryhoffer and shook his head, as though amused. "You civilians are obviously not familiar with our Air Force Pararescue doctrine, are you, Pete?"

"Uh . . . no I'm not . . . Neither is Bing. What is it?"

"*These Things We Do, That Others May Live.* As long as there's a possibility that we can save one of them, then that's our priority. Not to be crass, but the other three aren't going anywhere anytime soon."

"Well, okay. I think I understand. I'd appreciate it if you'd keep communications open and stay in constant touch. And you're gonna have to hustle. Remember, we have our fuel level to consider. We burn twice as hot while hovering."

"Got it. No worries, Pete. This is a walk in the park for us. How much time can you give us?"

"An hour . . . ninety minutes, max."

"Check. We'll see you soon."

"I certainly hope so. Godspeed, Chad. Be safe."

Stones in the Cellar

July 17: Gilliam's Guidepost
Heart Butte, Montana

"LIFE IS LIKE A CREAKY OLD ELEVATOR. It rumbles up and down, never remaining at one level for long. It makes a lot of strange noises along the way, but it's dependable. Just enjoy the ride and appreciate the view at each stop."

Advice from Dr. Elias Richardson, the VA therapist Bryan Gilliam had worked with when he returned stateside from Afghanistan. Nineteen years ago, Bryan thought the analogy was ridiculous. He'd thought the good doctor was full of shit. Told him if that was the kind of thing they taught in Yale graduate clinical psych programs, he should ask for a tuition refund. Told the man it was nothing more than cheap emotional calisthenics.

Bryan had been full of himself back then. Chip on his shoulder as big as Montana. Truth was, Bryan Richard Gilliam was an abysmal mess. Part brash wiseass know-it-all, mostly wounded warrior. Elias Richardson, Ph.D./Psy.D., recognized it and did not take the insults personally. He'd seen and heard it all before in his work with returning vets. Gradually, through months of counseling sessions, the psychologist gained Bryan's respect and trust. Their talks went a long way in repairing the faulty wiring in Bryan's war-wrecked brain. But that elevator metaphor? For many years after, Bryan continued to laugh at it. Thought of it as simplistic and inane. A cheap head doctor trick. Funny thing, however. As silly as he thought the elevator adage to be, he never forgot it. It stuck in his head like a catchy song. As the years passed, he came to understand and accept the fundamental wisdom behind Doc Richardson's message—that optimism paid better dividends than pessimism. Look for the positive at every stop while navigating the serpentine journey of life. Most days Bryan followed that path of positivity. It made things easier. He'd adopted it as his personal dogma.

He'd done his best to maintain that optimism through the bizarre and inexplicable events the Gilliams had experienced the past seven weeks. Through it all, he heard Doc Richardson's even-toned voice in his ear, the doctor's elevator analogy playing in his head in a persistent mantra.

The strangeness of this summer kicked off with the meteorite. Initially he saw the extraterrestrial boulder that crashed in the east meadow to be a call for alarm. However, the cratered rock turned out to be a financial windfall, now generating a lucrative revenue stream from the sale of his Cretaceous Stone line of merchandise. The meteorite Bryan cursed in the beginning had also hatched out baby Dromaeosaurs and transformed Gilliam's Guidepost into Dinosaur Central. Almost overnight, the Gilliams were catapulted into the pantheon of celebrity. They had become household names. The dinosaur hatchlings brought a steady flood of media types from all over the globe. He had also welcomed some of the best and brightest minds from diverse fields of scientific study—geology, paleontology, zoology, biology, wildlife ecosystems. Government officials from many of the alphabet agencies came to Gilliam's Guidepost. Representatives from the private sector came—the Smithsonian Institution, American Meteor Society, and American Astronomical Society—as well as head zookeepers from big-city zoos. The heavy daily foot traffic created booming business for the Gilliams and led to the buildout of his cherished dinosaur zoo, with its half dozen Dromaeosaurs, two Triceratops, and the newly acquired pair of Tyrannosaurus Rex juveniles.

The meteorite hatchout and subsequent dinosaur habitat led to a positive outcome for Bryan's in-laws, too. Jimmy and Olivia Enright were profiting greatly from the deal paleontologist Nora Lemoyne had brokered with the U.S. Department of Agriculture. She had negotiated for meat byproducts (the 40-pound blocks of compressed wastage from meat processing plants) to be shipped to

Gilliam's Guidepost to feed the Dromaeosaurs. It was a stroke of genius to Bryan's way of thinking. But what to do for the herbivores—the two Triceratops they had now? The solo Triceratops they'd had in captivity for more than three weeks had not been eating well. Last week, Hayden Fowler and Nora Lemoyne captured a second Triceratops, giving the animal a herding partner, and now the two of them were packing away enormous amounts of shrubs and leaves and assorted vegetation. Whatever the handlers could find and drag into the habitat, the creatures devoured. The growing beasts were eating machines. So much so the scientists had named them *Glut* and *Grub* for their prodigious appetites.

But still, no one cherished having to work "vegetation detail," which consisted of foraging through the outlying forest with chainsaws and hatchets, hauling the greenery back to the Glade. Bryan just happened to be in the barn when the scientists were discussing dinosaur feeding programs, and he knew Jimmy and Liv had lots of wheat straw baled up and sitting in their fields going to waste. Seeing as how the herbivores seemed to thrive on wheat, and thinking *byproduct*, which wheat straw was, Bryan suggested his brother-in-law Jimmy's farm as the primary herbivore feed supplier. The Enrights could easily provide enough feed to sustain (at that time) the single Triceratops they had in captivity. And the Enright farm was in Shelby, only an hour drive away, so delivery costs would be minimal. After a couple of successful test feeds, the Enrights signed the deal with the USDA to be the sole provider of wheat straw feed for the Gilliam's Glade Prehistoric Zoo.

Jimmy and Olivia were ecstatic.

And now, with a pair of Triceratops in captivity, the Enrights' profits had doubled.

Things were on a positive track. Lucrative.

We're on the top floor of Doc Richardson's fabled elevator.

So why can't Loretta see that?

Deep down, Bryan knew the answer. His wife of eighteen years was a realist to his dreamer. He knew that just like an elevator, what goes up must eventually come down. But he elected to ignore it. There *were* some negatives. Loretta was right. Many downsides, if he was being truthful. The Gilliams' newly minted celebrity status had brought them a loss of their once cherished privacy. They were in the public eye now, and quite often exposure of this magnitude brought out the crazies. Visits from lunatic fringe elements had called for beefed-up security. This, and the threat of dinosaur attack, had family members on guard, constantly looking over their shoulders for trouble. He and Loretta had increased worries over their children's safety. They'd had to move the horses to Jimmy and Livvy's stables. But the most problematic of all was their daughter's anxiety issues: Lianne getting attacked by a Dromaeosaur hatchling; her encounter with a Triceratops in the Enright wheat field; her nightmares of being eaten by hungry dinosaurs; Lianne's sessions with Dr. Krickstad, the family psychologist in Browning.

Yes, Loretta, it certainly hasn't all been a top floor view.

Bryan knew a thing or two about night terrors. He'd suffered a long stretch of them through the first two years of his marriage. Back before Paul and Ethan and Lianne came along. He'd spent many a night waking up shrieking, thrashing, drenched in sweaty sheets. The sandman turned evil on him, clips of vivid scenes projected on the inside of his eyelids, transporting him back to the horrors of Afghanistan. So real. So *intense.* Squatting inside the rubble of a bombed-out school in a kill zone, taking on a Taliban attack, bullets zinging over his head and past his ears like insane mosquitos, spraying the wall behind him. The fear ratcheting up in him like a metastasizing demon. He could hear the *rat-a-tat-tat* of machine gun fire, the thumps of bombs exploding in the distance. Could hear the cries of anguish and pain coming at him in quadraphonic sound. The *whip-wop-wop whip-wop-wop* of the Black Hawk helicopters, the low growl of Humvees on the move. Dreams so real he could smell the desert dust tinged with the gassy odors of the burn pits and feel the sting of sweat and smoke in his eyes. Nightmares so authentic he suffered through a startling recurring dream of two men in his platoon getting fatally shot within an arm's length as he looked on helplessly. Another recurring dream vision was of innocent Afghan schoolgirls being gunned down by the Taliban. More than two dozen of them. The bursts of automatic rifle fire. The girls' screams as their classmates were executed, the blood-soaked burqas of the dead bodies sprawled in the sand. Young girls, not much older than Lianne, a disturbing scene he'd witnessed near Yakawlang that, nearly twenty years later, he had not been able to expunge from his mind's eye.

Doc Richardson had done his Yale educated best to cleanse Bryan of these awful visions. The VA therapist had helped him in many ways but it took more than psychological counseling to chase his PTSD nightmares. Loretta provided that extra layer of calm that finally got him through. Bless her soul, she helped him through those most difficult of times. She was a strong woman. His best friend, his best medicine. Still was. Most lesser women would have run for the safety of a more sane man. But Loretta stuck with him. To this day he still had no clue why she had. He'd been a human wreck. He despised the world. Hated the military. Detested himself for enlisting a week after 9/11 happened like tens of thousands of other naive young men hellbent on revenge. Hated the U.S. government for the way they used the hijacked planes and crumpled twin towers as a patriotic ploy to get him to rush into something he didn't understand. Something he would *never* understand. Many nights he'd awaken from a fitful sleep after one of the debilitating dreams, screaming in abject fear, flailing his arms and kicking his feet wildly until Loretta could get him under control. Afterward, he would sob hysterically—a grown man *crying?* How frickin' embarrassing!— until Loretta could talk him down. It got to the point where he feared falling asleep, and would try to stay awake for days at a time. But Doc Richardson cured him of that, convincing him the insomnia was doing more damage to his health than the nightmares. Eventually Loretta's calming influence on him won out. She was the perfect elixir. Always had been. Loretta was stronger than him. Still was.

Every wounded dreamer needs a patient pragmatist. Thank God she stuck with me. I love you, Lor.

But at least he'd come through it without getting hooked on drugs the way so many of his fellow vets had. That was something, at least. He knew of many survivors of the Afghanistan and Iraqi wars that were hamstrung by another war when they returned home—addiction to heroin and methamphetamines. His own brother-in-law, Jimmy, brought his crystal meth habit home with him and amped up his usage his first year on his family ranch before he got help. Maybe that was why Loretta had stuck with Bryan through his darkest days and nights—she'd had a good bit of experience helping her brother kick his demons.

Bryan's experience with night terrors made him sympathetic to Lianne's sleep issues. When their daughter had a bad night and burst into their bedroom crying, wanting to crawl in bed between him and Loretta, he understood and took her in. He'd been twenty-three when he'd gone through his nocturnal heebie-jeebies. He couldn't imagine what it must be like for a seven-year-old girl who'd had two frightening close encounters with dinosaurs.

After the fourth straight night of Lianne making a beeline for their bedroom bawling for her mama and daddy, Bryan had sat with her on the edge of the bed. Loretta was stretched out behind them, leaning back against the headboard, listening.

"You know, Lee, there was a time when I had bad dreams, too," he said in a soft, accommodating whisper. He rubbed her shoulder, looking into her frightened eyes. "They scared me. A lot."

"*You*, Daddy?" she said, disbelieving. "Were you little then?"

"No. I was an adult, sweetie."

"But you're big and strong and . . . *old*."

Bryan turned and exchanged smiles with Loretta. He looked back at Lianne, wiped the tears from her cheek, pulled her close to him in a side hug. "Yes, I am old, I guess. I was younger when I had the dreams that upset me, but a lot older than you. I dreamed about bad people trying to hurt me. I was a soldier in a war thousands of miles from home and everywhere I went there were bad people trying to hurt me. When I finally came home, those memories came with me. It made me not sleep right. So you see? You're not alone, Lee. I went through the same thing you're going through."

"I didn't think big people had bad dreams."

"Oh, but they do, darling. Yes, indeed, we *can* and we *do*."

"How did you make them stop?"

"Well, your mother helped me. So did a very wise doctor."

"Just like me, huh?"

"Yeah, sweet pea. Just like you."

Lianne paused for a long moment, thinking, then said, "Why is there bad things in the world, Daddy?"

"It's just the way it is sometimes. The best thing is to shut out thoughts of those bad things that bother you. Don't think about them. Concentrate on the things that make you happy."

"You mean like riding Beauregard and playin' with Patches and Lyle?"

"That's *exactly* what I mean, yes."

"That's what Doctor Helen says, too."

"Your Doctor Helen sounds like a very smart lady."

Lianne grinned. "She is. I like her. She's my friend." Another hesitation, then, "Doctor Helen is a better friend than Marnie. Marnie's mean to me sometimes. She makes fun of me. She hates me, I think."

Loretta spoke up from behind them. "Your cousin is going through some things, Lee. Just like you. She doesn't hate you, baby. She loves you, but just doesn't know how to show it. Marnie will come around. You'll see."

"I have something to give you, sweetcakes," Bryan said, standing and going to his dresser in the corner. He opened the top drawer and pulled out a silver necklace with a polished black stone pendant, brought it to Lianne. "This is the first piece of Cretaceous Stone jewelry to roll off our production line. I can't think of anyone more deserving to wear it than you, Lee." He held it out in his palms for her to see. "Do you like it?"

"Yes, it's pretty, Daddy. Really shiny and smooth."

He draped it around her neck, reached around her to secure the clasp. "This necklace has special powers. When you wear it, nothing will harm you. No bad people. No bad animals. No more bad dreams. Does that sound good?"

She looked at him doubtfully. "But it's from the rock the dinosaurs came in. The meeteeyite."

Smart girl.

"Yes, it is, but that meteorite protected the dinosaurs for millions of years. Until they landed here. It keeps all the bad things away that could hurt you. Just like it did for them."

Lianne looked down at the pendant laying against her nightgown. She fondled the smooth stone in her hands, her eyes alight with joy. "It's *beautiful*, Daddy. I love it. I'm gonna wear it all the time. I can't wait to show it to Marnie. She doesn't have anything this nice. She'll be jealous."

"I'm sure she will be, Lee," he said, standing, holding out his hand. "C'mon now. Let's get you back in your bed so we can all get some sleep."

She grabbed his finger and jumped down off the bed, let Bryan guide her from the bedroom. At the door, she pulled to a stop. "You know, I've been thinkin'. Where did those creepy dinosaurs come from?" she asked.

"I don't know, Lee-lee. That's a question a lot of people are trying to figure out right now."

She looked up at him, the overhead bedroom light reflecting in her eyes. "But I thought old people knew everything."

Bryan laughed, turning and winking at Loretta. He looked back at his daughter. "A lot of old people just *think* they know everything. But what I know for sure is that when you're wearing that necklace, those creepy dinosaurs won't haunt your dreams anymore."

"Okay. Thank you for giving me the necklace. I love you, Daddy." She peeked around Bryan's leg. "You, too, Mama."

"We love you, too, Lee," Loretta said before she yawned and pulled the covers up over her, rolled over to go back to sleep.

That had been ten days ago and Lianne had not woken up with a nightmare since. Granted, their daughter had spent three of those nights with the Enrights, but Olivia told them there had been no problems, and that Lianne had slept straight through each night. The girl and her Cretaceous Stone necklace were inseparable. She wore it all day long and slept with it on, even though Loretta initially worried it might choke her in her sleep. But a call to Dr. Krickstad convinced her there was no harm in Lianne sleeping with the necklace on. If it kept the night frights away from their little girl, it was a good thing.

He smiled as he recalled that conversation.

You are the luckiest man on the planet, Bryan.

But still. Loretta's reservations?

He had to admit there were some negatives he conveniently looked past while enjoying the glow of his newfound fame. With Loretta's constant reminders, it was beginning to dawn on him that things had maybe gotten out of hand around Gilliam's Guidepost. With hundreds of strangers coming and going, and with living, breathing prehistoric carnivores boarded onsite, a palpable air of danger hung over the ranch.

What could possibly go wrong, right, Bry?

Listen to your wife, you fool. She's usually right on target.

But what was he supposed to do at this point? How could he stop this runaway freight train of flesh-eating dinosaurs and curious humanity? For some mysterious reason, the Gilliams had been chosen to host this return of Cretaceous beasts. Where he thought he'd been making the most of an extraordinary happening, Loretta glimpsed the dark side. Try as he might, he was at a loss to understand what he could have done differently to keep his family out of harm's way.

But even with Loretta's doubts, his dreamer/entrepreneurial side continued to rule. He just couldn't part with that side of himself. He reasoned that it was baked into his DNA.

His thoughts swirled back to Doc Richardson's mythical elevator as he rode a real elevator down into The Cellar, the doomsday shelter he and Jimmy Enright had converted from a hundred-year-old tapped out zinc mine at the rear of Gilliam's Guidepost. He and Jimmy had built the hideaway during the time when their post-war service paranoia was at its peak. Returning from Afghanistan, they both had been convinced it would not be long until the power-mad loons running the world would launch the missiles of Armageddon. He and Jimmy put everything they had into the project over two summers, believing nuclear holocaust was inevitable.

Dark days, indeed.

They had done a thorough construction job. The subterranean

refuge had all the modern amenities: central heating and air, filtered tap water, indoor plumbing and electricity, a fully stocked kitchen with modern appliances, four bedrooms, and even Wi-Fi connectivity. Bryan was proud of the engineering skills they'd employed building out The Cellar. He was pleased with the architectural artistry he and Jimmy had designed into the place. He referred to it as his *subterranean castle*. He had personally built the general store and utility barn from the ground up in the years since, and had overhauled/refurbished the inn, farmhouse, and horse stables, but none of those projects gave him the feeling of accomplishment the way The Cellar did.

And The Cellar would never have been possible without Loretta. It had been her money that enabled them to make a down payment on their property and get started with their ranching fantasy. It was her money that allowed him to take on all the construction and remodeling work. Her money that let him and her brother Jimmy build out The Cellar.

Bryan met Jimmy Enright in basic training at Fort Sill, Oklahoma in the spring of 2002. They instantly hit it off. Jimmy replaced the brother that Bryan lost to cancer and Bryan was the brother Jimmy never had. As fate would have it, they shipped out together and were soldiers in the same unit—U.S. Army 187th Infantry Regiment—on their first deployment to Afghanistan. They took part in the early Operation Enduring Freedom campaign, battling al-Qaeda and Taliban forces. Many nights in the bush, Jimmy would talk about his sister, Loretta, younger by two years, and how, if and when they got back home, he'd introduce Bryan to her. Jimmy talked about her a lot, said they'd be perfect for each other. Gave Bryan photos of her, which he kept in his combat helmet to bring him good luck.

Bryan became obsessed with Loretta Enright long before he ever met her in person. They started corresponding, writing letters to each other. Bryan cut that off when he discovered Army Intelligence was redacting much of his communications. They tried e-mail with the same results. The few times Bryan was in a safe zone near city cell towers, he spoke with Loretta through FaceTime. He liked being able to see her when they talked, but he couldn't quite relax and be himself knowing every word he wrote or spoke was being observed.

This cornfed, milk-skinned Midwestern farm girl with plump kissable lips and locks of caramel colored hair cascading over her shoulders dominated his thoughts day and night, helping him get through his first tour.

Turns out, the Enrights were well off. Jimmy's parents owned and operated a thriving wheat farm in Shelby, Montana that had been in the family for three generations. Jimmy talked about returning to Shelby to take over the farm from his ailing parents. Jimmy's father had recently undergone quadruple bypass surgery and his mother was battling breast cancer. Jimmy was anxious to get back home before he lost them both. Meanwhile, a couple of uncles and a few farmhands ran the business while Loretta helped out the best a 19-year-old girl could on a large farm. Bryan, having lost his older brother Bobby to cancer, could certainly sympathize. Jimmy told Bryan he'd love to have him come work the wheat fields with him when they broke free of this nasty war. To a longtime Texan like Bryan, the lure of Montana farming held a motivating appeal. The promise of meeting Loretta face-to-face was icing on the cake.

Bryan visited the Shelby farm when he and Jimmy took their first leave. When he met Loretta in person, he felt like he'd known her his entire young life. When they kissed that first time, out by a hay baler under the big Montana night sky after their introductory dinner with the senior Enrights, Bryan knew he had met his life partner. They were inseparable during his two week leave and he feared going back overseas for his obligatory second tour. He envisioned getting his ass killed and losing out on what might have been the best thing that ever happened to him. But he made it through the torturous eight months safely and returned to Shelby to marry Jimmy's sister. Loretta Enright became Loretta Gilliam in June of that year.

The big freight elevator jerked to a halt three levels down in The Cellar. Bryan slid open the accordion gate and walked out into a large airy room with a high ceiling. This was the manufacturing hub of his Cretaceous Stone jewelry and trinket operation. He had dubbed it *Cretaceous Cavern* because in his hyperactive marketing mind, everything needed a snappy name. It delighted him to see it bustling with activity. An assembly line of proficiency. Staffed with nine Blackfoot workers and his newest employee, the helicopter pilot's wife, Brinshou Lacroix, the young Kootenai woman. Brin turned out to be a wonderful addition—an experienced jeweler who had immediately taken on a leadership role. She was an effective trainer, showing the three younger Blackfoot women how to achieve a better quality product while working faster. The three women quickly took to Brin for her skills and engaging personality. Bryan thought she would be a good fit, and was happy to see it working out.

The buzz of low volume conversation filled the chamber as the workers went about their business. A cheerful young woman— Nadie—sat at a desktop computer taking orders by phone and through the website. One of his ranch hands, Chogan, sat in a corner near the wedges of meteorite, chiseling off small pieces of the black, sparkly rock. Bryan's lead ranch hand, Apisi, worked a grinder, sizing and shaping the stones. An older Blackfoot man, Mingan, operated a buffer machine, polishing the raw stones into a dark shine. The three female Blackfoot jewelers sat with Brin Lacroix at a long table, using tweezers and fine-tipped pliers, doing the detail work of setting the finished stones in their mountings. One end of the table was laden with a wide array of finished Cretaceous Stone products: necklaces, bracelets, rings, earrings, chokers, bolo ties, pins, anklets, brooches. Bryan smiled as he spied several Cretaceous Stone "eggs" in the mix, which were small elliptical meteorite stones with tiny imitation dinosaur claws poking out of cracks, as though the rock was hatching out baby dinosaurs. Packaged as they were in beds of straw and boxed in shiny black lacquered cases, the Cretaceous Stone Egg had quickly become their most popular item and biggest moneymaker. At the end of the production line, two young Blackfoot boys pulled items from the table and packed orders for shipment.

Bryan walked around and chatted with each of his employees,

complimenting them on their work. They were in the third week of selling Cretaceous Stone merchandise and sales had exceeded his wildest expectations. He'd started out with a team of just four workers. By the third day he could see that the small team wouldn't be able to keep up with the demand, and he'd doubled the staff. Seems everybody, from all over the globe, wanted a piece of the infamous space rock that had hatched out dinosaurs. His boys—Paul and Ethan—had done a bang-up job creating the flashy website and getting the word out on social media. And he liked to think his video commercial had rocketed sales into the stratosphere.

Each time he ventured down here he laughed about the marketing angle he'd taken with that video come-on ad. It was absurd really. But the multitudes were buying it, no matter the cost. And the price on most of these items was exorbitant

The words of his sales pitch resounded in his head:

"This miraculous little stone will change your life in ways you never imagined. You can now own a piece of the meteorite that preserved dinosaurs for sixty-six million years. If it did that for prehistoric reptiles, just think what it can do for you! Get your Cretaceous Stone trinkets today. But hurry! There's a limited supply and they'll be gone soon."

They were selling the merchandise faster than they could produce it, and last week he'd added two more workers. He was proud to be able to offer employment to the people of the Blackfeet Nation. Competition for work at Gilliam's Guidepost was fierce among the Blackfeet as Bryan paid a much higher wage than did the few available jobs on the reservation. However, he knew this project was temporary due to the limited supply of meteorite base stock. He dreaded the day in the near future when he'd have to lay off everyone but Apisi and Chogan. Every day that sales boomed and his supply of meteorite rock diminished, he regretted that he'd handed so much of the rock over to Peter Lacroix.

Bryan went to where Chogan was working with a small jeweler's hammer and chisel, pinging pieces of varying sizes off a large wedge of rock. Bryan walked around the slabs of meteorite and inspected the quantity on hand, estimating they had enough to get them into August. Two weeks, maybe three.

He admonished himself. *I lost my chance to finagle more meteorite rock from Peter Lacroix now that the pilot has left that Air Force gig. Should've moved on it sooner. Lacroix would have worked with me, I just know it. Especially since I've employed his wife. You blew it, Gilly old boy!*

He stopped at the long work table to chat with the help. He'd long held a deep affinity for the Blackfeet people. The tribe referred to themselves as the *Niitsitapi*—the real people—a most accurate description. They were genuine, warmhearted folks despite their initial reticence in new social situations. Bryan enjoyed conversing with the three Blackfoot women, Nuna, Tahki, and Koko. They were dedicated and hardworking, personable and easygoing.

"How's everything going, ladies?"

"Just fine, Mr. Gilliam," Koko said, focusing on her work.

"It's *Bryan*, remember?"

"Oh, yeah," the young woman said with an embarrassed smile. "Sorry, Mr. Bryan."

Bryan laughed. "Good one, Koko." He glanced around the table. "You all are doing excellent work. You'll be getting a nice bonus in this week's pay."

"Thank you, Mr. Bryan!" the women said in unison.

He smiled. "You all are quite the team." He looked at Brin, who was concentrating on crafting a brooch, fingers moving nimbly, eyes focused behind her jeweler's loupe. "How is your mother, Brin? Does she like her accommodations?"

Brin looked up. "She's doing better. And our rooms are so nice. Thank you for putting us up."

"You're very welcome," he replied. Bryan was astonished at the condition Brin's mother had been in when they first showed up at the inn. Her pretty face had been beaten to a pulp. He had offered up two of the four bedrooms here in The Cellar so Kachina could mend, and Brin and her baby could relax away from the daily bustle on the Gilliam Guidepost grounds. That also allowed Bryan to hire another Blackfoot woman, Luna, to provide daycare for Brin's baby while Brin worked long hours here in Cretaceous Cavern.

"You've been so nice to us, Bryan. I don't think I can ever repay you for your kindness. Ms. Loretta's, too."

"You already have. By coming to work for me. Is your husband still planning on coming in tonight?"

"Yes. You know Peter quit that awful Air Force job after the helicopter crash, don't you?"

Bryan nodded. "I heard that, yeah."

"I'm so relieved. He's going back to flying for the Forest Service next week. He'll be in later tonight. I'm so happy I'll have my Petey back again. Safe and sound . . ." She paused, thinking. "Well, not totally safe. He'll still be flying one of those damned egg-beaters."

"I take it you're not too thrilled with helicopters."

"They're dangerous. I mean, that crash that killed Peter's pilot friends? It shook up my Petey something fierce. I wish he could find another line of work."

Bryan said, "He's a very skilled pilot from what I've seen."

Brin nodded, the magnifying loupe sliding down her forehead. She reached up to reposition it. "Yes, he is. Flying is in his blood. Sometimes I think he's part bird. I'm surprised sometimes that he hasn't sprouted feathers."

Bryan chuckled in surprise. *This Kootenai woman has a sense of humor.* "You might be right about that." He glanced around the spacious room. "I've been too busy to keep up with the news. Have they found the missing pilot yet?"

"No. Lots of search parties have gone out, but there's no sign of Russell Cavanaugh. I never met Rusty, but Petey says I would like him. He's been missing a week. I don't think there's much hope. It's such a shame. His wife just delivered their first child."

"There's always hope, Brin. We have to believe that."

"You think so?"

"Yes. Absolutely."

Doctor Elias Richardson, psychologist extraordinaire, says so.

Scribes In the Subterranean World

July 22: Gilliam's Guidepost
Heart Butte, Montana

HAYDEN LIKED THEIR NEW RESIDENCE. Bryan Gilliam had comped him and Nora a suite in The Cellar, the luxurious underground shelter on the Guidepost back acres. Gilliam offered them free lodging for as long as they wanted to stay. Bryan said the free rent offer was thanks for Hayden and Nora supplying the dinosaur zoo with the pair of Triceratops and two T-Rexes. But Hayden knew the Gilliams' generosity was mainly for Nora Lemoyne's negotiating skills in getting the Smithsonian and federal government to fund the dinosaur feeding programs, the buildout of the zoo habitats, and property security.

All things considered, Hayden considered Bryan Gilliam to be a bit of a flake. The man could go on and on about the most ridiculous things if you let him. And Gilliam's penchant for assigning exotic alliterative names to places and things bordered on pretentious, i.e., *Cretaceous Cavern, Gilliam's Guidepost, Gilliam's Glade*. But there was also a generous big-heartedness about the rancher-turned-mechanic that he appreciated.

Hayden and Nora's living area was the largest of four suites on the second level of this amazing subterranean structure. High vaulted ceiling. Central heating and air. A well-appointed *boudoir* (Gilliam's description that gave Hayden a reluctant smile every time he heard it) with three smaller adjoining rooms. Branching off the airy bedroom was a bathroom with shower, hot tub, sink, and toilet, an office alcove with a desk and recliner, and a kitchenette complete with refrigerator-freezer, microwave, sink and stove. The bedroom, er, *boudoir,* had a comfortable king bed, sofa and matching loveseat, credenza desk with hutch, a dresser topped with a wide oval mirror, and a flat-screen TV. "Only the best for my paleontologist friends who put Gilliam's Guidepost on the map," he'd told Hayden. These quarters were so nice Hayden wondered why Gilliam and his family elected to live in the weathered two story farmhouse up on the hill. Plenty of elbow room for him and Nora to dig in and do their thing. He laughed every time he thought about *digging in*, being that they were entrenched deep below the back pastureland in a subterranean chamber. Nora got a kick out of it, too. She'd laughed along with him and called it ironic. Just one of many reasons Hayden loved Nora—she shared his nerdy sense of humor.

Staying in this underground retreat beat the hell out of the cramped rooms at the inn where they'd first stayed when this dinosaur thing happened. This arrangement wasn't without a few nagging problems, however. The Canuck helicopter pilot, Lacroix, and his fine looking Indian wife had moved into the suite next door. They seemed okay, but their baby cried at all hours. The tot was a major-league bawler. Hayden was amazed parents could keep their sanity with such harsh cacophony going on all the time. Made him glad he'd never produced any offspring. He knew he wouldn't be able to stand ten minutes of an infant's yowling. Lacroix's mother-in-law was staying in another unit across the hall. Hayden had caught several quick glimpses of her when the Lacroix clan first arrived. The woman had a dark beauty that she'd obviously passed on to her daughter. But she was beatdown and defeated, hunched over, one side of her face mashed into a purplish pulp, like she'd come out on the wrong end of a TKO boxing match with Mike Tyson. He didn't know what her deal was and asked no questions.

A lesser issue was the muffled pounding and whine of machinery drifting up from below, where Gilliam's team of Indian employees were churning out jewelry crafted from meteorite rock. Gilliam crowed that his Cretaceous Stone items were "selling like food to the famished," necessitating round-the-clock production. *Food for the famished?* Gilliam working his flowery alliteration again. Hayden wondered why he couldn't speak in plain English. It seemed everything that came out of the man's mouth was overly colorful and/or steeped in simile or metaphor, as though he was always selling something. The guy missed his calling—he could have had a bang-up career on Madison Avenue writing ad copy. Hayden had caught Loretta—Gilliam's very practical, down-to-earth wife—roll her eyes at him after a few of his more flamboyant pronouncements. The man possessed an ingratiating charm tinged with a grifter's showmanship, which played well on television. Much of it was annoying, albeit harmless. But Hayden gave the man credit where it was due. This underground utopia Gilliam had built with his brother-in-law was impressive. Hayden couldn't have accomplished this in two lifetimes.

This subterranean wonderland provided the perfect refuge for Nora and him to work on the book they were coauthoring. Here they could focus on the task at hand, shielded from the day-to-day madness aboveground, free of the daily media circus that the ranch had become. Each day Hayden rode the elevator up one flight and walked the quarter mile out to the Glade to meet with Franz Krause and Barrett Hailey and the small group of government wildlife biologists and veterinarians who were running tests and tracking results.

Nora elected to stay in the suite most of the time. After the rodeo from hell, she had become skittish around the dinosaurs penned at Gilliam's Glade. Their presence—especially the T-Rexes—frightened her, and instantly flooded her with memories of that tragic night. Her first visit to the Glade after they captured the two Tyrannosaurs caused Nora to suffer a panic attack so drastic Hayden and Franz Krause had to help her back to The Cellar. Luckily it was more embarrassing than serious, happening as it did in front of a small throng of assembled media. The episode had scared Hayden, who feared she might be in the throes of a heart attack. They both agreed it best that Nora stay clear of Gilliam's Glade for a while.

So they worked out a deal. She would stay camped at the

computer, grinding out the early sections of the first draft while he would be her connection to the outside world, spending hours up at the Glade, amassing zoological and biological data for the book and occasionally leaving the Guidepost to do follow-up fieldwork when dinosaur sightings came in. He also shopped for groceries and supplies when needed, and prepared most of their meals. He was far from a gourmet chef, but he did okay by downloading recipes from the internet. Nora seemed to appreciate his efforts. At least she ate what he put in front of her without complaint. It was an efficient, symbiotic arrangement at first, but Hayden worried she was becoming agoraphobic. Nora hadn't left their Cellar suite once in the past five days.

She sat at the desk in the office alcove, hunched over her laptop, fingers racing over the keyboard, lost in the process of recording Hayden's notes from the past few days. Stacks of paper surrounded her—colorful graphs, datasheets, sketches of various dinosaur species with anatomical charts. Multicolored flash drives were scattered across the desktop. Hayden's reference notebook was propped up on an easel beside her, his scribblings prominently displayed, her ever-present steaming cup of coffee plated on a saucer near her mouse hand.

He moved in behind her, reached down and massaged her shoulders, kissed the top of her head. She smelled intoxicating and he felt himself responding down below.

"Aren't you getting burned out on that stuff, my lovely?"

"Not really," she said, head down, continuing to type.

"You've been going at it all day. C'mon, how about taking a break."

"I'm in a groove, Hayden. If I don't get this down now, I might lose the thread."

"That's what you said last night. And the two nights before that. You know what they say about all work and no play." He continued kneading her shoulders, lowering his head next to her ear and whispering, "C'mon, just fifteen minutes and you can come back to it fresh."

She stopped typing, turned and looked at him, their faces close.

"As wonderful as your hands feel on me, I'm not having sex with you. Not tonight."

"What?" he said, stepping back and holding his hands up in mock shocked surprise. "You think *that's* what I'm after?"

"Well, isn't it?"

"I wouldn't mind it," he said with a lecherous grin. "But c'mon, fifteen minutes? Give me more credit than that. The way we go at it, with our attention to the tantric side of things, we wouldn't even get through foreplay in fifteen minutes. I'm talkin' about a walk. C'mon, let's go up top and get some fresh air. It would do you good to get out and away from that computer."

She nudged her glasses up on top of her head and gave him a steady look. "You know I love you, right?"

"I do, but—"

"And you are aware of how tight our deadline is, aren't you?"

Hayden nodded.

"Well, then, let me work. Please. If you want to speed things along, fire up your laptop and write a chapter or two. After all, *you're* the established author," she said with a peevish edge. "You're the one everybody knows." She kissed him on his bushy beard, slid her glasses back in place, and went back to typing.

Nora was in her blinders-on, no-nonsense workaholic mode. He had never been with a woman so industrious, so goal oriented and scheduled. He was having difficulty dealing with it.

He sighed and went into the bedroom—the *boudoir* as Gilliam liked to call it (he probably referred to the kitchen as the *scullery* or the bathroom as the *en suite*). Hayden plopped down on the bed and flipped up the lid of his laptop. Nora was right. They *were* saddled with an outrageously close deadline. And she was also correct in that he was the celebrated *New York Times* bestselling author, albeit two decades ago—a lifetime in the fast-paced big publishing world.

He'd been contacted by his old literary agent, Henry Wycliff, from the William Morris Agency, who had negotiated a lucrative publishing deal with Penguin Random House. It was a take-it-immediately-or-else-it's-off-the-table offer. According to Wycliff, acquisition editors at Penguin Random House acted quickly and aggressively in a desire to beat out all competition and avoid a costly bidding war. Hayden didn't balk. He knew a sweet deal when he saw one. The contract gave them an insanely large advance coupled with a guaranteed royalty more than ten percent above the standard publishing retail sell-through rate. The big money being thrown at them told Hayden that Penguin Random House would put together an expensive promotional campaign and produce a large first print run in hardcover. Three weeks ago, well before their offer came in, when he first floated the idea of coauthoring a book with Nora, he'd told her with a straight face that a book coauthored by them would make them "rich beyond belief." But of course that was hollow speculation on his part. He had no idea what the New York book industry would make of them. It was a publishing pipe dream so absurd it made him laugh at himself. And he knew Nora thought him quite out of his skull, too. But then, the call came from Henry Wycliff, and his long-ago agent had procured the deal of all publishing deals. The one that turned his ridiculous dream into reality. Or at least it would once they delivered.

The original offer called for Hayden to be the sole author. But he wasn't going to do it without Nora. He told Wycliff he'd take the deal only if Nora Lemoyne was included as coauthor with equal billing and contractual rights. The publisher never balked. They knew all about Nora's scientific credentials and her key role in this second coming of the dinosaurs. Negotiations were handled online in a late-night back-and-forth that included so much coffee Hayden battled heartburn for days. All parties agreed to the revised terms of the contract and signed on the dotted line just before dawn two weeks ago.

Of course, he knew the reality behind the deal. It wasn't that he was a skilled writer or even vaguely remembered by the reading public who made two of his books bestsellers back in his young post-grad days. A new generation of authors was churning out books by the hundreds of thousands now, and his tomes were long out of print and forgotten, collecting dust in libraries and used bookstores. Henry Wycliff informed him there was talk within publishing circles about reprinting those editions, what with Hayden's reentry into the fame bubble. But that was just talk at this point, and he had learned that talk in the publishing business was a hollow currency. Until there was a signed contract, it was all just words blowing in the wind.

He refused to deceive himself about the demand for his writing. This was all about his and Nora's name recognition. Due to a quirky shift in the winds of fate, they had reluctantly attained celebrity status, which was the golden key to the city for big publishing houses. Fate had put them in the right place at the right time, allowing them to ride Bryan Gilliam's coattails to worldwide fame. Drawn to Gilliam's Guidepost shortly after one of the first egg-laden meteorites struck, they became household names despite their determined efforts to avoid the media. Those winds of destiny had blown in like an uncharted twister, shocking them both with the rapidity in which it all unfolded. Hayden didn't care much for the fame part of it. He didn't care to be center stage, standing in the glare of the spotlight like Bryan Gilliam. He felt awkward when recognized in public, and exhausted by the constant attention of strangers, especially reporters and journalists, who seemed to be everywhere. He recalled the apprehension he'd felt in his late twenties, on the road for a long book tour, promoting his first bestseller, *Ancient Life, Final Strife*. Every meet-and-greet event took a great effort for him to muster the courage needed to walk into those bookstores and face mobs of zealous readers wanting to get close to him. He was okay giving talks or reading from his works, but he'd never been comfortable signing books and hobnobbing with fans. He'd always felt like a fraud somehow. He was a scientist to his core, much happier remaining on the private side of his chosen profession. He preferred the solitude of research, testing, and data analysis to being in the public eye. That was one of the things he found most attractive about Nora. She also preferred to do good work quietly and let her achievements speak for themselves.

But he couldn't complain much about this newfound fame. Even if the publication of their book meant another dreaded publicity tour, which the contract called for, at least it would be with Nora. This strange experience over the past two months had brought

him a wonderful working partner and lover, living Cretaceous dinosaurs to study, and a rewarding book deal. Fate had been kind to
him, fame be damned.

Their contract called for a manuscript of a minimum of 75,000
words, illustrated with color photographs. They were contracted to
deliver a completed manuscript by the end of November. Just four
months away. And they had to deliver partials the end of each
month. Hayden knew from experience just how much work that
entailed.

The race was on.

Neither of them wanted to hand in a weak manuscript. Their
professionalism wouldn't allow it. And both of them inherently
knew that Nora was the better writer. She was the more efficient
organizer of complex material, more self-disciplined. Nora would
never boast about her skills, but Hayden recognized her genius. Her
reports to Smithsonian management were works of art, flowing with
an easy-to-read literary grace. She had the innate narrative gift that
transformed highly technical material into engaging prose that
could hook even the most disinterested reader. Her writing skills
had been a major factor in her landing the Smithsonian Institution
paleo expedition. He was surprised, to be quite honest, that she had
not already published a book or two. When he asked her about it,
she just humbly waved him off and refused to discuss it.

Even with Nora's obvious writing talent, it wasn't fair that she
should do all the heavy lifting. He should be contributing to some
of that 75,000-word workload. He should be doing more than just
hanging out at Gilliam's Glade recording the latest data and playing
househusband. He had to get started on something to help Nora out.

He thought he'd ease into writing mode by reviewing his note
files. Delay tactic? Probably. But he needed a launching point.
Something that would stimulate his scientific mind and push him
into action. Scrolling through, he realized they had compiled a
treasure trove of valuable information. They were learning some
fascinating things about these prehistoric creatures they could never
glean from bones and fossils. For one, their body temperatures
differed from most Earthbound animals. The three species of dino-

saurs living in captivity at Gilliam's Glade could not be categorized as reptiles as was the popular paleontological viewpoint. They were not cold-blooded. Nor were they warm-blooded like present-day mammals. The Dromaeosaurs, T-Rexes, and Triceratops were *mesotherms*, which meant their body temperatures fluctuated between those of cold-blooded reptiles (88 degrees F) and warm-blooded mammals (99 degrees F). They were able to change temperature based on their environment through unique metabolic processes. Very few modern species possessed this ability, with leatherback sea turtles, great white sharks, and tuna being the most prevalent. This mesotherm discovery finally put to rest the long-running dispute amongst paleontologists, zoologists, and paleo-biologists, about dinosaurs being either warm- or cold-blooded. These species were somewhere in between on any given day. Studies at the Glade revealed upward spikes in median body temps as the animals grew in size.

Blood samples taken from the captive dinos revealed many findings. All three species had large, nucleated red blood cells, giving them greater stores of hemoglobin than warm-blooded verte-brates. This hemoglobin abundance gave the creatures super oxygenated systems, and dovetailed with the dinosaurs' closest current day relatives—crocodiles and birds, especially ostriches and emus. Blood from these animals also showed inordinate amounts of collagen, a building block protein that strengthened their bones, muscles, tendons, and ligaments, and toughened their hides. And all blood samples showed antimicrobial and antiviral enzyme levels never before seen in humans, mammals, or reptiles. Hayden figured these differences in biology and serology held the key as to how these animals proliferated and prospered for millions of years. It was a given they were extremely adaptable animals with super immune systems.

These findings were certainly revelatory. But they also shot holes in one of Hayden's initial hypotheses. Early on, before testing of the hatchlings began in earnest, when the scientists were engaged in discussions of how this region of the northwestern United States would fare with the introduction of these seriously invasive new species, Hayden had conjectured that these dinosaurs would probably die off during the long frigid winter, when this area was blasted with snow and ice and subzero temperatures. He'd argued that their ancestors millions of years ago lived in warm, tropical climates with abundant plant life to sustain the herbivores, and a balance of plentiful prey for the carnivores. But now that he better understood the physiological makeup of these living specimens, Hayden had changed his thinking. These creatures were built to survive almost anything. Anything short of another massive asteroid impact extinction event. Their ability to fluctuate their body temperatures and their other fortified anatomical features would give them the protection necessary to survive the harshest of winter conditions. These animals had also shown a keen intelligence that would serve them well. They'd rely on their primal instincts, finding refuge in mountain caves, abandoned dwellings, and subterranean caverns to wait it out. He reasoned they could very well shut down their systems in a deep sleep state much in the way Earthbound animals hibernated. Hayden could picture that scenario playing out. The only question was sustenance. Would there be enough food for them to endure? They had high metabolic rates for quick growth that required great amounts of food intake. What if there wasn't enough food sources to get them through the long winter months? That led to an alternative scenario he'd pondered. The animals might have the innate ability to know that a drastic change in season was coming and migrate south, to Nevada, Utah, and Arizona, all the way down through Mexico to tropical regions in Central America. After all, the creatures' closest modern cousins—birds—were ruled by their seasonal migration instincts. But Hayden didn't think that was realistic on a large scale. As far as anyone knew, Triceratops was a migrating herd animal, but the carnivore theropods were not. Dromaeosaurus and Tyrannosaurus Rex tended to be territorial and not as far ranging.

And what about the animals being contained here at the Glade? The Dromaeosaur habitat was the only pen that had a structure to shield the animals from winter weather, and it wasn't fully enclosed. It was scant protection at best. And the T-Rexes and Triceratops would have no shelter from the harsh Montana winter weather. Would they be able to survive the harsh elements without cover? He entered a note as a reminder to discuss this situation with the other scientists and Bryan Gilliam.

He turned his attention to daily feeding procedures. The Triceratops—Glut and Grub (yes, that's what the government wildlife biologists had named them)—seemed to be doing well on their diet of wheat straw from a local farm, and assorted greenery supplied by federal government agricultural co-ops. As herbivores, they were content with the grains, plants, and vegetables dumped into their enclosure. But he wondered about the two T-Rexes and the half dozen Dromaeosaurs. They were carnivores, predators wired to stalk and kill their food. Hunting live prey had been burned into their DNA for millions of years. And yet, here in captivity, they had been fed a steady diet of processed beef and chicken byproduct. Bloody and moist, yes, but stationary and lifeless. So far they'd been devouring every last ounce of the 40-pound meat blocks the two Gilliam boys and ranch hands dropped over the fence. But Hayden wondered how long the carnivores would be content with that unvarying, inert meat diet. They were bulking up and getting bigger, maintaining good health while ingesting the meat cubes. But sooner or later, their dormant instincts would activate, and they would need to hunt. At the very least, the scientists overseeing their care would have to change their feed program to fresh kill carcasses, much in the way zoos fed fresh animal parts of cattle, sheep, rabbit, chicken, and horses to lions and tigers. Going to a fresh kill animal diet would also give dinosaurs in the Glade a muchly needed supply of bones to keep their teeth healthy and their jaws strong.

The creatures were growing alarmingly fast, as Hayden and the wildlife biologists and zoologists predicted, though raising wild, prehistoric animals in captivity presented many gray areas. The two T-Rexes now stood six feet tall and weighed more than 300 pounds, most of it hard muscle and heavy jaws. They were putting on five pounds a day on their meat byproduct diet. In another month, the scientists predicted they would reach seven feet in height and weigh in at 500 pounds, the size of mature grizzly bears. The Dromaeosaurs were no less voracious meat eaters but were lighter due to their hollow, birdlike bone structure. The six Dromaeosaurs at the Glade averaged four feet when standing erect and weighed only 60 pounds due to their extremely high metabolisms. But no one should underestimate the smallish Dromaeosaurs. Pound-for-pound, they were every bit as vicious as the Tyrannosaurs with their razor-sharp teeth and aggressive demeanor. The pair of Triceratops—Glut and Grub—had grown quickly, too. They were built like triple-horned tanks, both eight feet long and four feet tall as of this morning. Glut weighed in at 330 pounds while Grub tipped the scales at 320. Hayden was surprised animals could reach that size in just two months consuming only vegetation.

The appetites and growth of these dinosaurs presented challenges in the care and study of them. Keeping their enclosures clean and sanitary had become a difficult job. Turds the size of bowling balls littered the habitats. The areas had to be cleaned out every three days. The scientists and handlers collected voluminous piles of smelly excrement and checked for parasites and potential disease, then discarded it in the outlying forest. They worked in pairs, taking shifts on the dreaded *Shit Detail*. Adding to the complexity of sanitation, the animals had to be tranquillized every time someone entered their territory. One handler would work the pole syringe, sedating the creatures while the second watched his back, brandishing a high-powered stun gun. When they were assured the animals were completely under, they began the arduous and malodourous cleanup. It was dangerous, unpleasant work, but necessary. Hayden worried about the long-term effects of frequent anaesthetization on these animals, but Barrett Hailey seemed to have a good handle on proper tranq dosages.

The other, longer term problem, was that Gilliam's Glade wouldn't contain these creatures forever. Within six months, maybe less, other captivity arrangements would have to be made. Bryan Gilliam was under the naive impression that these paddocks would hold these beasts for many years, allowing him to profit from his dinosaur zoo fantasy. Gilliam thought the heavily fortified 15 foot high fences made of the toughest steel and shot through with electric current would keep them corralled. But Hayden and the other scientists knew the reality. Within a year, the T-Rexes and Triceratops would be large enough to bust down the fences. And a little electric shock wouldn't bother them at all. Within a year, the Dromaeosaurs would probably be able to leap over the enclosure fences. And either Bryan Gilliam wasn't aware, or refused to believe, but the Tyrannosaurus Rexes, would in ten years, if they lived that long, would be the size of a 12-story building and weigh seven tons. Another containment issue: all of these creatures needed more room to run. Gilliam's Glade was twenty-seven acres, divided into three habitats. Soon, they would need many times that space to ensure their survival. They would need thousands of acres in a federally protected park, cut off from civilization, like some of the national wildlife parks in African countries. Hayden and Nora had discussed this, and Nora had begun the process of contacting movers and shakers in the Department of the Interior, educating them on how best to protect these prehistoric wonders.

He could hear Nora clacking away on her keyboard in the office nook, getting real work done. Here he was, comfortably stretched out on the bed, reviewing his notes, stalling for time like a procrastinating slug. Guilt tugged at his conscience.

Time to get down to business, old man.

You can't let Lady Lemoyne show you up.

He created a new document file and stared at the blank page. And stared . . . and stared. His hands were poised over the keyboard, frozen. The blank screen was an ocean of whiteness. The blinking cursor mocked him with its insistence, challenging him to type something of worth.

What to write about?

A title seemed a good way to rev the writing muscles.

He typed:

A Treatise On Trapping Cretaceous Dinosaurs

No. Too scholarly. He needed something more snazzy. Something with pizzazz that would leap off the page. Where was Gilliam when you needed him? Hayden deleted his first attempt and tried:

Mother Meteorites Hatch Cretaceous Beasts

No. Too flowery. *Bryan Gilliam would love it, but it's not me.*
And it was way too broad. He needed to narrow the focus.

He deleted it and once again faced the blank screen. Stared.
Thought. Cracked his knuckles and stared some more. The white
space was intimidating. He felt pressure building behind his eyes,
the frustration building into a headache.

How the hell did I write three books twenty years ago?
Oh, yeah. Alcohol.

Well, there wouldn't be any firewater now to lubricate his
writing muscles. No Chivas Regal or Glenfiddich premium whisky
to overcome his authorial inhibitions. Not if he wanted to keep Nora
in his life.

But oh, how he ached for some bottled courage.

He decided to skip the title and just start in with his story from
the beginning. He typed:

On the day the meteorites struck carrying their strange cargo,
I was the lead paleontologist on the Smithsonian Paleo Expo at
our dig site in Choteau, Montana. I recall the excitement in our
camp a few days later when we got word of exotic creatures
hatching out of a downed meteorite an hour north of us on a ranch
in Heart Butte. Our expedition geologist, Dr. Gregory Dulowski,
was first to go check out the extraterrestrial boulder. He returned
with phenomenal video footage of large rock wedges flush with
egg nests and bizarre reptilian hatchlings running around. The
team lead, Dr. Nora Lemoyne, along with me and paleozoologist,
Dr. Franz Krause, were astounded by what we were seeing. The
next day we made the trip north to Gilliam's Guidepost ranch to
see things with our own eyes. As crazy as it sounds, we identified
the hatchlings as Dromaeosaurs, a carnivorous bipedal theropod
of the Late Cretaceous Period, extinct for more than 66 million
years. That trip changed mine and Dr. Lemoyne's lives inexorably,
shifting our area of scientific focus from paleontology to prehistoric
zoology. This area, along the Continental Divide of the Rockies,
will never be the same. Nor will the millions of Americans affected
by this inexplicable return of a very destructive invasive species, a
species that once ruled the Earth . . .

He stopped typing. Hayden thought he heard muffled shrieks

coming from the office nook. He glanced into the hall.

"You okay in there, Nora?"

She appeared in the doorway, glasses pushed up on top of her head. Her face was a washed-out pale white. She clutched her laptop close to her chest looking like she was about to topple over in a dead faint.

"Wha—what is it, babe? Are you sick?"

"There's been another attack, Hayden."

"What? More livestock? Elk? Bison? What?"

"No. *People*."

"Oh, Christ! How many? Where?"

"A strip mall in Boise. Shoppers. Fourteen dead and seventeen critically injured. Many probably won't make it."

"Tyrannosaurs?"

"Yeah, eyewitnesses counted at least eight of them. But our T-Rexes didn't act alone."

"Whaddaya mean?"

She moved to sit next to him on the bed, opened her laptop and angled the screen where he could see it. "Here, take a look."

Nora turned away as Hayden watched the chaotic scene play out on a shaky cellphone camera. Chilling screams. Warning shouts. People running in confusion, many disappearing into shops. Pushing and shoving. People falling. Crying out for help. The screen cleared before the camera jerked to another angle, the picture blur-ring momentarily before refocusing and picking up a woman being attacked and slammed to the ground by a large T-Rex, her shopping bags scattered across the sidewalk as the beast feasted on her. A quick cut to another Tyrannosaur pouncing on an older man, powerful jaws ripping flesh from his torso. The creature threw its head back and downed the chunk of meat in one frighteningly quick gulp, its demonic red eyes glaring at the camera, seeming to taunt the cellphone owner. Blood pooled on the walkway, painting the concrete a shiny crimson. These Tyrannosaurs looked quite a bit larger than the two they had in the Glade. The scene brought back disturbing memories of the Livingston rodeo. Nausea slammed him. Bile gushed into Hayden's throat. The bed seemed to move beneath him, as though he was on a raft in an angry sea. He took in several deep breaths attempting to ease his queasy stomach. Another jarring camera cut as the cellphone owner took off running, then stopped to capture two smaller animals working as a tag team to bring down a shrieking teenage girl. One went for her neck, the other her stomach. Hayden had a difficult time holding it together. He squinted, trying to make out what he was seeing.

"Dromaeosaurs?" he asked Nora, who remained turned away from him, refusing to look.

"Yes, I think so," she said to the wall.

He watched another twenty seconds of the carnage, then shut it off. "This is an important new development. T-Rexes and Dromaeosaurs feeding together. Both species are known to be territorial. It's not like either to share their feeding grounds."

Nora looked at him, disappointment shading her features. "That's it? That's all you have to say after watching people getting slaughtered in broad daylight? At a shopping mall? Are you not able to remove your scientist hat for just one minute and show some remorse for your fellow human beings?"

Hayden was surprised by her reaction. "Of *course* I feel for them, Nora. It's a terrible thing. I feel a deep sympathy for the victims as well as the survivors who had to witness it. For the friends and families of the people killed. You make it sound like I'm a monster with no empathy. Believe me, I *feel* plenty."

"Oh, God, I didn't mean . . . I don't think you're a monster, Hayden," she said weepily. She scooted closer to him and took his hand. "I guess I was just surprised to hear you put science before humanity."

"Yeah, probably not my best moment there, huh?"

"There's more," she said. "The Boise mall attack happened this morning. Just an hour ago, the Idaho and Montana governors issued a joint statement announcing that the Wildlife Services Division of the U.S. Department of Agriculture is offering a five thousand dollar bounty on every dinosaur carcass brought in. Effective immediately. Wildlife Services will also be on the hunt."

Hayden felt a venomous heat rise in him. "I hoped we could

avoid this. Every backwoods halfwit Davy Crockett wannabe with a gun will be stalking these creatures, not knowing a fucking thing about what they're getting into. A lot of hunters will die horrible deaths. Hunting these predators isn't like going after deer or bears or even big game animals in Africa." He sat and thought for a moment, trying to calm himself. "Besides, the government will hunt these dinosaurs to extinction. Now that they're here, we can't let them go extinct, Nora. We have to learn to coexist with them. We have to learn to live *with* them, not without them. It would be irresponsible of us to wipe them out again."

"Yes," she said, "I agree."

He pushed the laptop aside. "The Glade will be a prime target. I've got to go warn Bryan Gilliam."

He started to get up off the bed, but Nora pulled him back. "You didn't let me finish. The governors, speaking for the federal government, made the Gilliam ranch—the Glade—a protected zone. Anyone killing a dinosaur here will face stiff fines and possible jail time. So you see, Hayden. The feds don't want to completely eradicate these animals. They're spending lots of money keeping them here. They have their own scientists here working with us. The government has too much invested in this operation. They're just trying to protect the American people and save Montana and Idaho farmers and ranchers."

Hayden nodded. "Maybe so. But that isn't going to stop chemically unbalanced hunters from easy kills. Plugging a few of our creatures here at the Glade would be like shooting fish in a barrel. I've got to go see Gilliam. We've got to lock down the Guidepost."

Slaying the Dragons

July 25: Montana Fish Wildlife & Parks HQ
Missoula, Montana

A LARGE CROWD GATHERED AROUND the temporary stage at the Montana Fish Wildlife and Parks (MFWP) headquarters. Montanans had shown up in big numbers for this event, which had game hunters bringing in their dinosaur kills to collect government bounties. The affair had a ghoulish carnival sideshow feel to it. People within driving distance wanted a look at the prehistoric oddities on display. A never-ending parade of people took turns standing in front of the stage, taking selfies or having friends take photos of them with the mangled, lifeless dinosaurs strung up behind them. MFWP had done a thorough job of publicizing today's happening. State politicos wanted to gain the citizens' confidence that they were taking appropriate action to combat this invasion of deadly and destructive animals. Local media was well represented, with several minicam crews and photojournalists stationed around the perimeter.

Onstage, a podium bearing the Montana Fish Wildlife and Parks logo sat between two hunters and their quarry. To the left, a hunter wearing blood-spattered camo pants, an orange vest, and a Pine Mountain Hunting Lodge cap, stood between two dinosaur carcasses hung from gambrels on pulley hoists. He scanned the crowd, smiling proudly at cameras. A seven foot Tyrannosaurus Rex was strung up on his right, both eyes shot out and its gaping shovel mouth open, displaying powerful jaws and lethal teeth. To his left a Triceratops corpse swung in the breeze, its dead eyes glazed over, reflecting the sunlight like glassy red marbles. Two bloody stumps above its eyes and one on its snout were all that remained of the three horns the hunter had carved out of the mangled herbivore. The second hunter stood to the right, next to his two kills—a pair of Dromaeosaurs stretched out on aluminum racks, ragged blood-crusted holes in their sides resulting from shotgun blasts. Clouds of flies whizzed around the dead animals. A gamy smell of death and decay hung in the hot afternoon air. The more boisterous in the crowd shouted their appreciation at the two hunters, who acknowledged the shouts of encouragement with waves and thumbs-up gestures.

A Fish Wildlife and Parks spokesman dressed in a two-toned Western shirt with a bolo tie walked behind the podium and spoke, his microphone squealing with annoying feedback.

"Thank you all for coming today. My name is Jack Thomaston, Director of the Region Two Montana Fish Wildlife and Parks Services Division. We're here to honor these two brave men standing behind me. They have done a huge favor for Montana ranchers, farmers, and citizens. These men risked their lives to track and kill these beasts you see up here on the stage. No easy feat to bag these creatures, let me tell you. These fearsome animals have been more than just a nuisance, they have carved a path of death and destruction throughout western Montana and eastern Idaho. These pre-historic eating machines present a grave danger to our communities and they must be stopped. They *must* be eradicated to preserve the livelihoods of our farmers and ranchers, and to save human lives. Today, due to the phenomenal courage of our two esteemed big game hunters, Ty Rensdorf and William Stallings, the dinosaur population has been reduced by four. And we have received word from our counterparts in Boise just an hour ago that hunters in Idaho have brought in three kills..." Director Thomaston paused while the crowd cheered the news, then continued, "... It is my distinct pleasure and honor, on behalf of the U.S. Department of Agriculture Wildlife Services, to present checks to these two heroes in the amount of ten thousand dollars each for bringing in two trophies each in our Montana Ultimate Hunt program." He pulled two oversized cardboard checks from behind the podium.

"Gentlemen, if you'd join me please."

Jack Thomaston made a show of giving each hunter their check, shaking hands, and posing with them for photos. The crowd whistled and cheered. The host asked Ty Rensdorf what he intended to do with the Triceratops horns.

Rensdorf, fondling the horns in his gloved hands, responded in a deep baritone. "Oh, I plan to mount them on my den wall, next to my lion's head."

"You killed a lion?"

"Yessir. Two years back, on a hunt in Botswana. A black-maned lion. They're pretty rare cats. Cost me a bunch, but it was worth it. Them lions are beautiful animals."

And then the trouble started.

It began with a single voice out of the back, shouting "Murderers! Serial killers! You should be ashamed!"

Another angry voice: "Stop the slaughter! Dinosaurs deserve to live!"

Heads turned and necks craned to see where the commotion was coming from.

More heated shouts from the rear, a critiquing chorus now. A man on a bullhorn yelled, "We are People For the Ethical Treatment of Animals and we're here today to protest this barbaric Ultimate Hunt travesty. What we see up there on that stage is detestable. Dinosaurs are sentient beings. They deserve to live every bit as much as we do. They are God's creations, and we demand a stop to this unnecessary butchery..."

His words were swallowed up by a surge of opposing views:

"Shut the hell up, whack job!"

"How 'bout we kill you and string you up, motherfucker!"

"Crawl back in your hole, you slug!"

"Tell that to the people your reptile friends have killed!"

Hand-painted signs and placards popped up in back:

DINO MIGHT, NOT DINO DEATH
ULTIMATE HUNT = ULTIMATE SLAUGHTER
PETA SAYS NO TO THE ULTIMATE HUNT

The insults continued, back and forth. Many in the crowd turned to face the PETA interlopers. There was pushing and shoving, a few wild swings taken. Somebody tossed a clump of feces at the stage, landing short of the mark and splatting against a woman's back. More excrement bombs were thrown, and things quickly erupted into an all-out melee. Fists flew. PETA members used their hand-held signs as weapons, swinging them at attackers.

Director Jack Thomaston frantically called for security over the PA system. The four on-duty Montana Highway Patrol officers rushed into action, trying to restore order with their batons and taser guns.

The federal government's Wildlife Services Ultimate Hunt program was underway.

And the media captured every second of it.

The Sanctity of Life

July 27: Lolo National Forest Flyover
Northwest Montana

PETER LACROIX WAS HAPPY TO BE BACK at his old job, flying for the Montana Forest Service. His departure from Mount Bennett Air Force Base and release from Colonel Thaddeus Glick's ironfisted control hadn't been easy. Glick had raised hell, threatening him with a lawsuit for breach of contract, but Peter didn't care. He wasn't going to continue flying those ancient repurposed Army Sikorsky rattletraps that had taken the lives of his fellow pilots and two air guardsmen. The helicopter flight recorder had provided evidence of mechanical failure in the main gearbox that caused the tail rotor to fail. Proper maintenance would have prevented the tragedy. Peter's days of putting his life on the line for somebody like Glick were over.

Now he was back in the pilot's seat of a newer, safer Bell UH-1H Huey chopper, reunited with his navigator, first officer Martin Fulbright. They were flying a high altitude route of 10,000 feet over the Lolo National Forest north of Missoula, having just crossed over McLeod Peak. They were headed west, searching for potential fire hazard areas in the dense carpet of greenery rolling out below. They weren't far from Camels Hump where firewatcher George Dantley had nearly lost his life from a meteorite strike that took down his lookout tower.

Peter heard Fulbright in his headset. "We really could have used you a couple of weeks ago."

"You mean the Trail Creek fire?"

Fulbright nodded solemnly. "I'm not gonna mention any

names, but Command sent out a couple of rookie pilots to give them some real-time wildfire experience working with helitack crews. Their drop points were off, which almost got two of the smoke-jumpers killed. One of the birds flamed out and barely made it back to Missoula. Not a good scene at all. Needless to say, both pilot crews are grounded pending further flight training. Ralston was literally jumping for joy when he heard you were coming back. I think old Gary might have even peed his pants he was so excited."

Peter laughed. "Gary briefed me on the Trail Creek mess. In all fairness, those lightning strike fires can be tricky. Even for old codger vets like us."

"That might be true. But I've never seen anybody could handle a chopper the way you do, my friend. The way you get in and out of tight spots . . . your hovering skills . . . it's off the charts. I heard about that black box recovery you made on the side of that Idaho cliff. Not many pilots could pull that off."

"Yeah, well, I had a great crew with me. Unfortunately, the flight data recorder was the only thing we retrieved. We were too late to save the crew."

"You know, Pete. I never could wrap my head around you flying for the United States Air Force. Me, maybe. But not you. I just don't see you as a military type."

"You're right, I'm no GI Joe," Peter said, thinking about his final conversation with Glick. The colonel was taking a lot of heat over the Sikorsky crash, and rightly so. Glick's irate outburst at Peter told of a desperate man. Peter had become the civilian pilots' de facto leader. Glick knew that if he lost Peter, the other pilots would follow. And they did. Williams, Bartholomew, and Bing all quit the day after Peter left. Glick's standing with his Pentagon superiors had taken a huge hit. His Operation Hot Rocks had failed. A fatal helicopter crash had occurred under his watch. Drastic professional and legal actions were undoubtedly coming his way. Colonel Glick, once the golden boy of the U.S. Air Force, was now being viewed by the Pentagon brass as incompetent and not worthy of the promotion to Brigadier General he wanted so badly. As things stood, he was doomed to spend the remainder of his career as a colonel at Mount Bennett Air Force base in the middle of Nowhere, Idaho.

Couldn't happen to a nicer guy.

His escape from the Idaho Air Force base gave Peter a new lease on life. His days were a lot less stressful now. He was much more relaxed, back to flying routes familiar to him and doing the work he was trained to do. The work he *loved*. He could spend his off hours with Brin and the baby, though he thought it strange to be living in an underground bunker on a Montana ranch. That said, their suite was spacious and comfortable, surprisingly modern, and Brin was happier than Peter had seen her in quite some time. She seemed more self-confident and poised now that Bryan Gilliam had given her a leadership position in his Cretaceous Stone jewelry operation. And his being home every night seemed to bolster those positive changes in her.

Peter and his first officer flew over Interstate 90, passing over mountain pastureland when Fulbright, peering through binoculars, said, "I see four of them, Pete, congregating in a field, halfway up that hill, at about two o'clock," he said, pointing with his free hand. "It's those three-horned rhinoceros-looking things."

"Triceratops," Peter said, recalling news segments he'd seen, and conversations he'd had with his now next-door neighbor, the paleontologist, Hayden Fowler.

"Want me to call it in or do you want to do the honors?"

Peter looked to his right, squinting through the tinted Plexiglas windshield, seeing four tiny dark dots moving slowly through a scrubby highland grove. "No. Let's just leave them be."

"What? You know we're supposed—"

"Yes, I *know* what we're supposed to do, Marty. That doesn't make it right."

Fulbright shot Peter a stunned, openmouthed look. "Shit-fire, Lacroix! No wonder the Air Force had problems with you. I'm not takin' the hit if Missoula finds out."

"The only way they'll find out is if you tell them, Marty."

Fulbright stared at Peter for a long beat, then said, "Please don't tell me you're one of those tree-hugger PETA assholes."

"No, I'm not. But I do believe in the sanctity of life."

All life with the possible exception of Nashota Taleka.

His ne'er do well father-in-law remained behind bars in the Flathead tribal jail.

A cage is the right place for a hosebag like him.

Peter banked the chopper south, away from the Triceratops. Forestry air personnel had been issued a directive to call in dinosaur sightings so that USDA Wildlife Services hunters could fly in and gun the animals down with semiautomatic weapons. He didn't want any part of that.

Peter had been an animal lover as long as he could remember. He recalled a time as a young boy accompanying his father on a woodcock hunt in New Brunswick province. Pierre wanted to teach Peter gun safety, the finer points of hunting, and the joy of communing with nature. They bagged six of the small game birds that day, and Peter hated every minute of it. The shotgun blasts hurt his ears. The recoil of the 12-gauge bruised his shoulder. The gun smoke stung his eyes and made him sick to his stomach. He was overcome with grief when he saw those cute little birds with the long, needle-like bills lying lifeless in the mud, their bulbous bodies peppered by buckshot. The family dog, their lovable Wiley, a yellow Lab, surprised Peter with his tracking and retrieving skills. Peter cried when he saw Wiley trotting back to them with a dead bird in his mouth and a gleam in his eyes, like he was proud of his part in the killing. He didn't understand why his father derived so much pleasure from killing beautiful, defenseless birds, and why Wiley seemed so eager to participate in such a grisly exercise. It was Peter's first and only hunting outing with his dad. To his credit, Pierre—realizing his only son wasn't wired for the hunting life—began bonding with him on hockey rinks and soccer fields, where young Peter excelled. They never spoke of the upsetting hunting trip again, for which Peter was thankful. But that early childhood hunting trip traumatized his young self, and it carried over into his adulthood. To this day, Peter could not understand the allure of gunning down innocent animals.

Granted, these dinosaurs devastating the Continental Divide corridor were far from innocent. But still, they were God's creatures returned to Earth for some heretofore unknown and mystical reason. Peter thought they deserved our respect, not slaughter.

He chuckled to himself thinking about Marty Fulbright's associating him with PETA. Yes, Peter could certainly get behind some of their causes. But their extreme, militaristic nature seemed to be in direct conflict with those causes, and turned him off completely. PETA was ironically hypocritical in his opinion.

He had been following the clashes between bounty game hunters and animal protection groups the past three days. It was all over the news cycles. There had been trouble in Boise and Missoula as hunters brought in terribly mutilated carcasses in exchange for big money checks. In protest, members of PETA and the Animal Liberation Front (ALF), carried out vehement acts of opposition. So far, no one had died during these confrontations, but several had been seriously injured. Many were arrested on public nuisance, disorderly conduct, and vandalism charges. Peter discussed this issue with Hayden Fowler, his paleontologist neighbor in The Cellar, who was on a personal quest to get these dinosaur hunts stopped. Dr. Fowler's stance was that in the name of scientific study, we could not, in good faith, afford to wipe these creatures out. "To hunt these species to extinction a second time would be an affront to God and the natural world," the big scientist had told him. Hayden Fowler could be most persuasive, but Peter didn't need much persuading. He'd seen the sadistic, gruesome ways in which these poor creatures suffered. So Peter was very comfortable defying the Forest Servicemanagement edict that they report dinosaur sightings. They had plenty else to deal with—wildfires, rockfalls, landslides, snow ava-lanches in the winter, floods, lost or injured hikers. He was just fine leaving the tracking and killing of dinosaurs to others.

Peter heard a rush of static over his headset, followed by a greeting from Dispatch. A female voice.

"This is Heliport Command. Do you read me, Treetop-Five?"

Peter activated his mic. "Yes, we read you, Command. This is pilot Lacroix and first officer Fulbright. Is this Nancy Diehl? Over."

"Yes, it's me, Pete. Howdy, Marty. How are you guys doing? Over."

Fulbright answered. "We're free and easy, Nance. Hope you're well. Over."

"I am. Thanks for askin'. Over."

Peter said, "You have a hot spot for us? Do we need to change our route? Over."

"That's a negative, Treetop-Five. I'm contacting you with some good news that just came in. Over."

"Lord knows we could sure use a piece of good news right about now. What's cookin'? Over."

"The missing Idaho helicopter pilot, Russell Cavanaugh, was found this morning. Over."

Peter looked across the cockpit at Fulbright, a hopeful warmth blooming in his chest. "Is he still alive? Over."

"Yes, he is, amazing though it is. Mr. Cavanaugh is in rough shape but doctors believe he will make it. Over."

"Where'd they find him? Over."

"Twelve miles south of the crash site—between Big Creek and Thunder Mountain. He was airlifted to Saint Luke's Medical Center in Boise and is in intensive care. He's got broken ribs, a shattered collarbone, a collapsed lung, and a broken wrist. He's extremely dehydrated, but he's coherent and talking. Says he spent eight days in the wilderness, surviving on wild berries and nuts, cattail roots, wild onions, mushrooms, and river water. According to the news release, he claims he was pursued by a pair of Tyrannosaurs. He thanks God that his legs and feet were spared in the crash. Otherwise he would have ended up as dinosaur food. Those are his exact words. It's truly a miracle! Over."

"Wow! That's great news," Fulbright said.

Peter added, "Didn't his wife just have a baby? Over."

"Yes. A healthy boy. Their first child. Mother and son are on their way to the hospital as we speak. Mr. Cavanaugh is going to have a lengthy recovery time, but he looks like he's going to make it, and his new family will be together. Over."

"That's wonderful, Nancy," Peter said, remembering the quiet freckle-faced, red-headed, slender young pilot that he'd spent three weeks with at Mount Bennett AFB. The man was tougher than he looked. Peter wondered if he could have survived in the wilderness with critical injuries and a pair of Tyrannosaurs chasing him. He had his doubts. "You just made our day, Nancy. Over."

"We're feeling good about it, too. Fly easy and be safe, guys. We'll see you soon. Over and out, Tree-top-Five."

Peter smiled most of the way through the remainder of their route. Things were looking up.

Special Delivery

July 29: Gilliam's Glade
Heart Butte, Montana

THE GUIDEPOST WAS EERILY QUIET. A rare stillness blanketed the ranch, reminding Loretta of ghost towns she'd seen on late night Westerns. The only elements missing were saloon doors swinging in the whistling wind, tumbleweeds blowing across a deserted street, and spooky background music.

Loretta sat with Bryan at the top of the bleachers overlooking the Glade enclosures. They were alone, observing three of the Dromaeosaurs tussling with each other in their usual rough-and-tumble style of play. Loretta listened to their grunts, squawks, and squeals, watched them snap their powerful jaws and bite each other with those razor-sharp teeth, wondering how it was they didn't end up dead. They were indeed tough, durable animals—thick muscle-bound hides with dispositions to match.

She held an umbrella, shading her and Bryan from the blistering sun. Today marked the fifth straight day of above-ninety-degree weather, the hottest day so far in this heatwave summer. Between them sat a thermos of ice-cold lemonade. Loretta was enjoying this rare alone time with hubby. Lianne was back with the Enrights for a few days and the boys were up at the general store working with Apisi, loading the big, greasy meat blocks and wheat straw bales on the flatbed trailer for the afternoon feeding.

The Guidepost was deserted thanks to Bryan finally coming to his senses and shutting everything down. Just three days ago, this area was crawling with television news teams, scientists, and curiosity seekers, the governor's ban on large group assembly all but ignored. The flood of people coming and going had become unmanageable. They'd lost control and Loretta had become uncomfortable with all the strangers wandering around their property. She'd pleaded with Bryan for a couple of weeks to at least shut out the media, but he wouldn't hear of it. But then the new dinosaur bounty reward had been announced, bringing hundreds of hunters to Montana and Idaho. Hayden Fowler told Bryan that with big money payouts being offered for dinosaur kills, Gilliam's Glade could become a target. Bryan argued with Fowler, saying state government had declared Gilliam's Guidepost a safe zone, with heavy fines for trespassing and jail time for shooting a dinosaur on their property.

Loretta recalled Dr. Fowler's reaction: "Don't be so fucking naive, Gilliam. Believe me, many of these hunters would shoot their own mothers to collect the bounty cash. Shit, five grand a pop? I guarantee you that by calling out your ranch to the general public, the state government did you a huge disservice. You need a lot more security, my friend. And quickly."

Hayden Fowler had ridden Bryan hard, trying to convince him a lockdown was best for everyone involved. Loretta loved Bryan mightily, but her husband was a severely stubborn man. He'd objected strenuously, putting his foot down, saying a lockdown would end his television interviews, and that it would diminish the precious Gilliam brand he'd worked so hard to cultivate. Loretta and Hayden, along with Franz Krause, Barrett Hailey, and Nora Lemoyne, sat him down and tried to talk sense into him. Safety was the number one priority. No one wanted to see the Gilliam's Glade dinosaurs harmed. And certainly no one wanted armed confrontations at the Gilliam ranch. They'd told Bryan about the past week of dinosaur killings and the resulting violent clashes between pro-bounty supporters and animal rights activists. That information should have told him he was sitting on a powder keg of potential trouble. Bryan made a show of listening, but it was with a tin ear.

Finally, after several exasperating attempts to sell him on the idea, Loretta got him alone and tried a different approach. She had learned over her forty years that men were fairly simple creatures.

Cater to a man's ego and a woman could get pretty much anything she wanted. So, she played the ego card. She told him his popularity was unparalleled, that he was so much in demand that most television news teams would be happy to follow his lead. He could name an offsite location and the press would trip all over themselves getting there to interview him. She also played to another of his weaknesses—their children. What if something terrible should befall Lianne or Ethan or Paul? His precious Gilliam brand would not shine so brightly then, would it?

That did the trick. Bryan finally agreed to ban all media types and anyone not working for the Gilliams. Security had been beefed up, with round-the-clock armed guards posted at key points around the perimeter of the 1,285-acre ranch. All deliveries had to be checked and approved at the front gate. And both she and Bryan agreed that this would be a good time to close the general store for two weeks to further reduce daily traffic.

Loretta was grateful for the break. The noisy, frantic days of the past two months had nearly done her in. She liked this quieter Guidepost and the return to a semblance of sanity. She slept better knowing she wouldn't have to face a sea of reporters constantly shadowing her, shoving a microphone in her face, demanding her time and attention. She would have a two week reprieve from her general store responsibilities. There wouldn't be a never-ending deluge of strangers traipsing their property. She could relax. Catch up on her reading. Take long walks without being hassled by paparazzi and journalists and curiosity seekers with videocams looking to capture something outrageous to post on YouTube or Instagram. And Loretta vowed to get their horses back from the Enrights and do some riding with Lianne and the boys. Lianne had about driven her crazy with missing her horse, Beauregard.

Bryan's voice broke through the silence. "Sure wish we could open up the zoo, Lor."

Loretta looked at him, saw the longing on his face as he stared out over the Glade, eyes following the two Tyrannosaurs loping around their enclosure. "It'll happen when the time is right," she said in an attempt to console him, seeing disappointment in his blank stare, the defeat in his slumped posture. "And then it will be spectacular."

Long minutes of silence passed, Bryan continuing to stare into the distance. Finally he said, "You know, Hayden Fowler has told me a few times that my zoo—*our* zoo—couldn't be a long-term thing. He said these enclosures probably wouldn't hold these animals until winter, that they'd get big enough and smart enough to escape before then. He tells me that even if we can keep them confined that long, the Montana winter would probably kill them. He's always talking down to me, Lor. Telling me everything I'm doing wrong. Like I'm some hayseed farmer who doesn't know anything. He's one of those intellectual elitists that I despise. Real big man, with all his advanced college degrees and books he's published. Fowler's an arrogant bastard, Loretta. I can only imagine what that cretin is writing about us in that book of his. Why oh why are we comping him a free suite in The Cellar?"

Loretta ran her free hand up his arm. "He's done a lot for us, Bry. And he's knowledgeable about these animals," she said, lifting her chin at the habitats. "He's spent most of his life studying dinosaurs, specifically from the Cretaceous Period. He knows his stuff. You can't deny that."

"He knows bones and fossils . . . long *dead* dinosaurs," Bryan said angrily. "He's no zoologist or biologist. He can't bullshit me. He's just making stuff up about these creatures. They're wild guesses at best."

"His colleagues agree with his findings," she said. "Franz Krause is a world renowned paleozoologist and Barrett Hailey is a high-level government wildlife biologist. They're on the same page with Dr. Fowler."

"That's still no reason to treat me like I'm some mindless fool," he said in a thin, exasperated voice. "And did you know Fowler and that Lemoyne woman are lobbying to get the government to move our dinosaurs into a national park . . . someplace with thousands of acres, like the game preserves they have in Africa. I will *not* let them take our tourist attractions away."

"*Tourist attractions?* Bryan, listen to me. We don't own these dinosaurs. They're wild animals that need a great deal of room to roam. And you've seen how fast they grow. You didn't actually think this dinosaur zoo idea of yours would be a permanent thing, did you? C'mon, I know you're smarter than that."

Loretta realized immediately from his reaction that she'd hurt him, that he'd taken it as a personal attack. She looped her free hand around his back, pulled him closer. Kissed him on the cheek. "I'm sorry, hon. I didn't mean that the way it came out. It's just that if those animals out there belong to anyone, it's the federal government and the Smithsonian. They're paying us good money to keep those creatures on our land. They're paying to keep them fed and healthy. We're just landlords."

"That's true," he said, looking back out over the Glade. "But we have another nine-hundred acres of usable land. We could build much larger habitats for these guys, with barns in each for winter protection. There's no need to move them into a national park."

Loretta frowned. *Sometimes there's no getting through to him.*

"I admire the size and scope of your dreams, Bry. I'm definitely your dreamcatcher, honey. Always have been. But this is one dream you're gonna have to let go of. Trust me, dearest, when I say we don't want this hassle long term. At least, I don't. That's a migraine I can do without. I believe Dr. Fowler is a hundred percent right about the need to find these animals a new home."

Bryan looked at her, scanning her face. She locked eyes with him, nodded her head up and down, showing him the seriousness of her intent.

"Just be happy with the here and now," she said. "All of us have our health and we're raking in substantial cash. We're doing well, and Hayden Fowler—whom you call an elitist, arrogant bastard—and Nora Lemoyne made that happen for us. And your Cretaceous Stone jewelry operation is going great guns, too. We have so much to be thankful for, Bry. And most of it is due to your vision and hard work."

The bitterness pinching his face melted away. His eyes sparkled with respect and gratitude. "You're so right, honey. I've been way too wrapped up in myself since this whole thing started. I should be more grateful to Fowler. And to Nora Lemoyne. They *have* done a lot of good things for us." He kissed her, tenderly, deeply. Gave her a relaxed smile. "You're always the voice of reason, Lor, you know that?"

"Yes, I *do* know that," she said, tugging him closer, putting more heat into another kiss. When they broke apart, she said, "And since I'm the voice of reason, I want to run an idea by you, oh great visionary husband of mine."

He laughed. "Oh yeah? What's that?"

"You remember those big barbecue cookouts we used to have when the kids were younger? We'd dig a deep firepit and roast a pig and brisket and potatoes and ears of corn? We'd invite neighbors near and far for a big feast and drink cold keg beer."

"Of *course* I remember. Those were some good times. You're not sayin' you wanna do that again, are you?"

"Well, not that big a gathering. Just our new small family. Our *Cretaceous* family—us Gilliams, Livvy and Jimmy and Marnie, Peter and Brin Lacroix, Brin's mother, Apisi and Chogan and the Blackfeet working in the Cretaceous Cavern, the scientists, the Smithsonian and government folks who're staying at the inn. Maybe Mitena and the maids from the inn. How about it, Bry? I think it would be fun to bring everyone together."

He studied her. "You've given this a lot of thought."

"Well, this wild dinosaur experience has brought a lot of interesting people together . . . people from very different walks of life. With all that's going on, it's been too hectic for folks to get to know each other. Now that things are shut down for a couple of weeks, I think it would be one hell of a fun party. We need some kind of release valve. Now's the time."

"You know what? You just might be onto something, my gorgeous wife." He made a sour face. "But do we have to invite the scientists? They're such major league killjoys!"

Loretta took in his serious expression and felt disappointment. After the talk they'd just had, did he really still think Hayden Fowler was the enemy?

Then, unable to hold back any longer, he burst out with a

boisterous laugh. "Come on, honey. How big an asshole would I have to be to not invite the scientists? They are indeed killjoys, but they're *intriguing* killjoys."

"Wonderful! So, next week then?"

"Sure. You handle the food and I'll get the fire pit dug and prepped, get us a couple of kegs of that brown ale we both like. Pauley and Ethan can help me. You can get Lee to help with food prep . . ."

His cell phone buzzed. He pulled it from his pocket and glanced at the display. "It's Security at the front gate," he told her. "Tom Hennessey." He scooted away from Loretta and brought the phone to his ear. "Yeah, whaddaya got for me, T?"

"There's a delivery for you, Mr. Gilliam."

"From whom? What is it?"

"It's a panel van—Helena Auto Parts. The bill of lading shows four Duralast fuel injectors, a carton of shock absorbers, and two AC Delco Gold truck batteries."

Bryan gave Loretta a quizzical look. "I don't remember ordering any of that, Tom."

"It's addressed to your company, sir—Gilliam Mechanical Repairs. Date of the order is July twenty-fifth . . . four days ago. I checked the merchandise and it all looks legit."

"Okay. Send the driver down to the Glade. I'm here with Loretta."

"You got it, Mr. Gilliam."

"You do good work, T. Thanks for being thorough."

"We do our best, sir."

Loretta grabbed the thermos and followed Bryan down the bleacher steps. Four minutes later, she saw a white van with a red-and-black Helena Auto Parts crest emblazoned on the side, kicking up a dust trail as it puttered along the service road. The driver brought the truck to a stop twenty feet from the stands and climbed out. He was a young beefy guy, maybe late twenties, dressed in a pale green work uniform with the company logo stitched on the chest. He wore dark aviator shades under the bill of a ballcap. His bushy ponytail was pulled through the back of his hat and bounced as he approached. He clutched a manila envelope, moving warily past the dinosaurs snorting and growling at him from behind the chain-link fence.

"Mr. Bryan Richard Gilliam?" he asked, stopping three feet in front of them.

"Yes, that'd be me. I didn't order—"

"You've been served," the delivery driver said, thrusting the envelope at Bryan.

Stunned, Bryan took the envelope from him. "Huh? What the hell?" he said looking at the plain envelope, then raising his head to see the driver get back in the van and drive off.

A process server? Loretta thought.

She watched Bryan fumble open the envelope and pull out a few sheets of white paper. An official looking emblem of the United States government ran along the top.

"What is it, Bry?"

He didn't answer, his eyes moving side-to-side as he scanned the document, his expression shifting from curious to surprise to a red-faced rage.

"Bryan?"

"It's a cease and desist order." He read a little further, his face a dark mask of anger. "From the U.S. Treasury Department. The Inspector General's office. They're demanding we shut down the Cretaceous Stone operation. Says we're illegally engaging in interstate commerce, selling stolen government property, the property, of course, being the meteorite. They refer to some vague eminent domain statute that claims federal government ownership. They say we must return the remaining stock and pay the monies we've collected to date, including all taxes and shipping. Treasury agents will be calling next week to set up an appointment. They want to check our books and iron out final details," he said, shaking his head. "Oh, and we are to shut down our website, effective immediately. If we don't comply with all terms of the order, they will be forced to impose costly penalties, which could lead to them launching a civil suit against us." He looked up, shook the paperwork angrily. "They just can't leave that fucking meteorite business alone."

Loretta said, "You don't have much of the rock left, do you?"

"No. Just a couple of weeks' worth."

She came to him, took the papers from him and started reading. "I don't see how the federal government can make a claim on a rock that came from outer space."

"They think they own every goddamn thing, Lor."

"Aren't the Treasury and Department of the Interior under the same branch of government?"

"I think so, yeah."

"So wouldn't the Treasury Department know the Department of the Interior has been funding our dinosaur programs?"

"Oh, they know all right," Bryan said. "Uncle Sam giveth and Uncle Sam taketh away. I think they're trying to recoup some of those costs. I also think the feds aren't real happy with me publicly criticizing the government for their mistreatment of our Blackfoot friends."

She finished reading a section and looked up. "I believe this is just a scare tactic. No way a meteorite coming down in private pastureland falls under eminent domain laws."

He didn't acknowledge her comment. He was preoccupied with something else. "You know, I'll bet good money that Air Force colonel in Idaho had something to do with this. Pete Lacroix told me about him, the way that guy he reported to was such a ruthless asswipe. Pete told me the colonel went apeshit when he returned to base after his visit here with a greatly underweight load of meteorite rock. The colonel told him to get back in his chopper and return to pick up the rest. Pete refused, which only infuriated him more. I could see someone like that initiating a threat against us to save face, to save his military career. I ran into officers like that overseas."

"So you think this might be for real, Bry?"

"Oh, for sure it's real. The question is, what are our options. Come on, let's head back to the house. We need to find us a good lawyer. And fast."

The Author and the Cowgirl

August 1: Gilliam's Guidepost Cellar Suite
Heart Butte, Montana

NORA WAS IN A GOOD WRITING GROOVE. Her thoughts flowed faster than her fingers could transcribe them. Hayden called it *authorial quicksilver*, a magical spell that was manna from heaven for a writer.

Hayden had left for the Glade early this morning, giving her the solitude she needed to finish this critical chapter: an eyewitness account of her frightening ordeal at the Livingston Roundup. A month had gone by since they'd attended the rodeo from hell, and yet she'd been unable to document the experience until three days ago. She'd had some queasy moments working on this chapter. The dreadful images still lingered of marauding dinosaurs in the parking lot. Recalling the sights and sounds of that perilous night made her physically ill. But she toughed it out, knowing the only effective journalist was a fearless journalist.

There had been two more dinosaur attacks on humans the past three days. One in a populous Bozeman suburb, the other south of Ketchum, Idaho, an assault on a tour group near the Craters of the Moon National Monument. A total of 27 deaths and scores critically injured, with Tyrannosaurs responsible for all of the mayhem. The government bounty program seemed to be fighting a losing battle against the aggressive beasts. Every day hunters strung up their kills for public viewing and collected their cash rewards, but it didn't seem to put a dent in the dinosaur population. And animal rights groups continued to protest the killings with loud and forceful opposition. A number of game hunters had gone missing, just as Hayden had predicted. Nora didn't hold out much hope of their survival, but then again, that helicopter pilot had been rescued after he'd wandered more than a week in the Idaho wilderness, so anything was possible.

Hayden was finally chipping in, pulling his weight on the writing. Yesterday he'd given her two of his chapters for her to proofread. He'd appeared uncharacteristically insecure, like a college freshman handing in a writing assignment to his professor. He'd fidgeted nervously as she read through his work, obviously concerned about her reaction. As though *she* was the well-known author with three bestselling books and not him. Ultimately he had nothing to worry about. His chapters were superb, and he graciously accepted the few changes she suggested.

Earlier in the week Nora received a call from Greg Dulowski, who told her the Smithsonian expedition was winding down. The team was doing the final excavation work on the big discovery they'd made in Glacier National Park—a nearly intact skeleton of Troodon Formosus, the Late Cretaceous carnivore with a deadly venomous bite that immobilized its prey. Dulowski had told Nora of the find two weeks ago, and he excitedly gave her more details about it now.

"That's exciting, Greg," she said, feeling glum at not being there to celebrate with the team. *Her* team.

"I hear you and Hayden have made some big discoveries of your own," the geologist said. "Is it true you're writing a book with him?"

"It's true, yes. We got a book deal from Random House. Can you believe it? But I have to confess. The deadline pressure is getting to me, Greg. I'm not sure I can handle it."

"Oh, stop it, Nora. You'll do great. You excel at *everything*."

"Thanks. But I'm swimming in new waters here. Very deep waters. How about you? What are your plans after you close out the expedition?"

"We're shutting it down as we speak. I've sent the interns home. The rest of us are prepping the Troodon bones for shipment, which will take another three days. Then I'm heading to Washington for a

National Geographic cable TV special."

"Really? What's that about?"

"You mean Hayden didn't tell you about it?"

"No, he hasn't," she said, feeling hurt that her man had kept her out of the loop for some reason.

"Hmmm. Well, it's a symposium made up of a panel of experts to discuss this dinosaur invasion. The how, why, when, and where of the whole thing. Franz Krause has been invited along with a couple of renowned astrophysicists who have a rather interesting take on where those egg-bearing meteorites came from. Franz will be showing some of the video from the incubator hatchout and footage showing their growth cycles. I'll be showing some of the video clips I shot and describing the special qualities of the meteorites. Hayden was invited, too, but he turned them down. He told them he'd send them some video footage you and he had taken of juveniles in the wild. I'm surprised he didn't tell you about it."

"No," she said, feeling the burn of being left out. "He hasn't said a word to me about it. We've sort of been on separate paths since we started work on the book."

"Speaking of which, I can't wait to read it."

"I sure hope we nail it, Greg. I'm kind of nervous about it all. Congrats on your successful paleo expedition by the way."

"It's really *your* expedition, Nora."

"You're too kind. And you know for sure I'll be watching your TV special," she said, signing off with a suggestion they get together and catch up after the first of the year, when she was done working on the book. "Break a leg, Greg."

When she asked Hayden about the National Geographic symposium, he told her he didn't want to be a TV star.

"That's well and good, but you still should have told me about it," she said. "I felt like an idiot with Greg telling me something I should have known about."

"Well, you have to admit, Nora. We haven't exactly been connecting much lately."

"Don't even go there, Hayden Fowler! Getting invited to be on a National Geographic special is a huge deal. If you start keeping big things like that from me, then—"

"I didn't tell you out of respect for *you*. I didn't know how you would take it since you didn't get an invitation. I really have no interest in appearing on television, that's true. But it's more than that. I don't want to do anything without you, Nora. You and me, we belong together. I couldn't stand the thought of being away from you."

"Oh, don't hand me that third-rate romance drivel, Hayden! That might work on your hot young trophy girlfriends, but it doesn't fly with me."

"It's true. The way I see it, we're a team. We're coauthors. Cretaceous cozies. Romantic round heels. Soul mate sillies. Tantric sex twins . . ."

"Okay, okay, Hayden," she said, smiling, then bursting into a robust laugh. "Romantic round heels? Tantric sex twins? You're a real piece of work, you know that? You make it impossible for me to hate you for even a second."

"*There's* my girl," he'd said, giving her his best flirty grin. "You know, you're really gorgeous when you laugh. Your whole face lights up."

It was true that she couldn't stay mad at him. He had a boyish charm about him she found appealing. Addictive even. Nora had always held to the claim that a man who could make her laugh was a definite keeper. Hayden had a way of bringing out her deeply buried sense of humor. Her *nerdy* sense of humor. He also had— with his frank, direct talk—a natural feel for getting her past her inhibitions, getting her to open up. Truth be known, she was glad he had no interest in being a television star. She didn't want him to go to D.C. Nora had become accustomed to having him around. They'd been nearly inseparable the past two months, and having him gone for a few days, maybe a week, would be too much. She felt protected and secure with Hayden around. He made her feel whole. *Is that love?* She thought so.

Nora grabbed her empty mug and went to the kitchen to brew another pot of coffee. While there, she heard a soft rap on the door. She tilted her head, listening. A long silence, then the knocks came again. More forceful knocks that made her jump. She left the kitch-en alcove and walked through the living area, wondering who it could be. Visits in the middle of the afternoon were rare. Maybe it was Kachina, the dear older Kootenai woman staying in the suite across the hall. Or Bryan Gilliam looking for Hayden.

She went to the door and looked through the peephole. Saw nothing but the grayness of the dim hallway. Feeling a flash of anxiety, Nora called out, "Who is it?"

Through the door she heard the squeaky, high-pitched voice of a young girl. "Um . . . it's Lianne . . . Lianne Gilliam, ma'am."

Interesting. I wonder what she could possibly want with me.

Nora pulled the door open and looked down at the Gilliam girl, who was dressed in blue jeans, boots, and child's cowgirl hat. The front of her pink t-shirt showed a black silhouette of a prancing horse with the words *Just a Girl Who Loves Horses*. Tiny black hearts were interspersed around the graphic.

Nora gave her a big smile and bent down to meet her eye-to-eye. "Well aren't you just the most darling little thing, Lianne."

"My friends call me Lee," she said, doing a nervous hop-skip. "So do my brothers, even though they aren't my friends. They pick fights with me and call me names."

Nora laughed. "I know, Lee. Brothers are like that. Do you remember talking to me at your cousin Marnie's farm in Shelby?"

Lianne nodded shyly. "You were with that big man with the beard. You told me not to be afraid of those dinosaurs with the horns."

"That's right."

"My mama said you're a really nice lady."

"Well, that was a nice thing for your mother to say. I'm Nora."

"Yeah, I know."

"Would you like to come in for a minute, Lee?"

"Okay," she said, timidly entering the living area. "My daddy built this place with my Uncle Jimmy. Did you know that?"

She's just the cutest thing.

Nora closed the door. "Yes, I *do* know that, darling. Your father is a very smart man to be able to make something like this."

"Yeah, he is," she said, looking around the room, taking it all in. "Daddy also works on cars and tractors. Mama's smart, too."

"You're lucky to have parents who love you."

"Yeah, I am. And I love them, too. Except when they punish me. Then I don't like them so much."

"They're just looking out for you, Lianne." Nora glanced at her t-shirt. "So I take it you like horses, right?"

"I *love* horses. Especially my Beauregard. We had to take Beau and the other horses to stay with Uncle Jimmy and Aunt Livvy so they'll be safe from those awful dinosaurs. I really miss my Beau." Lianne appeared to consider something, then said, "Daddy said you are a scientist who knows everything about dinosaurs. Is that right?"

Nora offered a rueful smile. "Well, I don't know *everything* about them, but I know a lot."

The girl pulled her necklace out from under her t-shirt and showed Nora the polished black teardrop-shaped pendant. "Daddy gave me this necklace. His company makes 'em. It's from that meeteeyite that landed in our field. My daddy said this will stop those terrible ol' dinosaurs from hurting me cuz the meeteeyite is where they were born."

She is the sweetest little thing I've ever seen.

Nora smiled down at her. "I'm sure your daddy is right, Lee. Those bad old dinosaurs are sure to steer clear of you. Your necklace gives you special powers over them. Can I get you something to drink?"

"No thanks. I have to be going." She stuffed her necklace back under her shirt and reached around to her back pocket, pulled out a folded piece of paper. "My daddy wanted me to give you this. I have two more to give to people on this floor."

It was an invitation to a Gilliam barbecue party scheduled a week from today, August 8. Nora saw her and Hayden listed above the fancy script: *You're invited to the Gilliam Grill-a-Cue. Lots of tasty eats. Rockin' music. Beer by the barrel. RSVP by August 5.*

It looked like fun. A nice break from the writing marathon. Besides which, Lianne's parents were extending Hayden and her this suite of rooms here in The Cellar rent-free, so it wouldn't be proper to decline. Nora looked at Lianne and said, "Please tell your daddy that Mr. Fowler and I would be honored to come."

Lianne smiled. "Daddy will like that. Mama, too."

Nora opened the door to let the girl out. "It was nice meeting you, Lee. I hope you get your Beauregard back soon."

"Me too. Thanks, Ms. Nora."

Nora watched the girl skip down the hall to the Lacroix's next door. She wondered, not for the first time, whether she'd made a mistake in choosing career over children.

Threat Assessment

August 3: Gilliam's Guidepost
Heart Butte, Montana

BRYAN SAT AT THE KITCHEN TABLE, Loretta directly across from him. His cell phone was on speaker so they could both talk with the lawyer, Atlee Pinnaker from Davis, Morton, and Pinnaker Legal Associates in Missoula. Pinnaker's firm specialized in federal cases, both criminal and civil. Bryan had e-mailed the attorney a copy of the cease and desist order he'd been served in preparation for today's phone consultation.

"So is this a legitimate threat, Mr. Pinnaker?" Bryan said. "Is it something we need to worry about? Kinda seems outta the blue."

"Yes, it is indeed out of the blue. It is also legitimate in that it was issued by the United States Department of the Treasury. So it *is* official in that capacity and definitely a threat. But it doesn't have any teeth." Atlee Pinnaker spoke in a deep, confident baritone that Bryan was certain made juries sit up and take notice.

"No teeth? What do you mean by that," Loretta asked.

"Well, for one, cease and desist orders carry no weight and are not legally binding. They are merely a written request from one party to another to stop doing something, or to change behavior that the issuing party finds detrimental to them. The served party has no legal obligation to carry out the order. Cease and desist orders are often a preamble to a lawsuit, which is what this is."

Bryan shook his head. "Yeah, they're threatening us with a civil suit. Said they were going to send Treasury agents out here to review our books."

"Yes, I see that. This kind of thing occurs more often than I care to admit. It's all a big bluff, Mr. Gilliam. A scare tactic. Shameful really. The federal government doesn't have a legal leg to stand on with this eminent domain power they cite, and they know it. They use this kind of tactic on Native American reservations and urban gentrification areas. Are you and Mrs. Gilliam familiar with eminent domain laws?"

"No," Loretta said. "Can't say we are."

"Okay, they can be complex, and that's by design. Their aim is to scare citizens into giving up something of value—almost always land—and giving you pennies on the dollar for it. I'll give it to you in a nutshell. Eminent domain gives the government the right to expropriate private property and convert it into public use. The key words there are *private property*, with property meaning land, not objects on your private property. Also, the property must be taken for the express purpose of public use, which is not the case here. You are protected by the Fifth Amendment of the Constitution, which states that the government must provide just compensation to the property owners. Your meteorite does not fall under the definition of private property. Nowhere in this cease and desist order does it say anything about compensating you. And their demand that you pay them for all sales you have made thus far is ludicrous. Laughable really. They are not entitled to one red cent of monies you have collected from your product sales. I believe you told me in our initial phone conversation, Mr. Gilliam, that you turned over almost half of that rock to a government operation in Idaho. Am I remembering that correctly?"

"Well, it was maybe a third of the rock. But you're correct, yes. I did hand some of it over."

"Well, you weren't obligated to do so. In essence, they stole from you. This is a situation where you are well within your rights to bring a lawsuit against the U.S. Treasury Department to reclaim what is legally yours. You also have a solid case against them for harassment. I wouldn't advise going after them, however. Individual citizens rarely win against big government. I just wanted to ease your mind a bit about who is in the wrong here."

"I don't really want to sue anybody," Bryan said. "We just want to be free and clear of it. We don't want any Treasury agents sniffing around in our business."

"You won't see any agents, Mr. Gilliam. I'm sure of that. Their hook was this cease and desist order. If you don't fall for it, they aren't going to waste precious time and resources hitting you with a lawsuit to claim proceeds from your meteorite rock. I've seen this kind of thing play out dozens of times. You were smart to come to me for this."

"So we're okay, then?" Loretta asked.

"Yes. My advice is to ignore the order. Just continue on with your jewelry business. If they contact you or try to put pressure on you in any way, call me. We'll hit back with some scare tactics of our own. Threaten them with a harassment suit. I've won a bunch of those cases over the years."

Bryan leaned over the table. "We've only got another week, maybe ten days of meteorite rock left anyway. As good as our Cretaceous Stone operation is going, I sure would love to have back the portion they stole from us. But I have no stomach for lawsuits."

"I understand completely, Mr. Gilliam."

Loretta said, "Something you should know, Mr. Pinnaker. Another branch of the federal government—the Department of the Interior—is paying us to house and feed the dinosaurs we're holding in captivity. They, along with the Smithsonian Institution, paid to have the habitats built out and are reimbursing us for round-the-clock security. I sure would hate for them to pull that funding if we didn't comply."

"They're not going to pull any funding from you, Mrs. Gilliam. My advice is to hold tight and keep mum. Nothing would please them more than to see you react to their cease and desist order. They would get what they want without having to give up anything in return. I've prosecuted cases against the federal government for fifteen years, and I can assure you it's a huge bumbling bureaucracy. The right hand doesn't know the left exists. I feel almost certain that the Treasury Department has no clue of your working relationship with the Department of the Interior."

Loretta frowned. "So you're saying the U.S. government pulls scams against honest taxpaying citizens?"

Bryan smirked, thinking Loretta came off sounding naive.

"Yes, Mrs. Gilliam. That's exactly what I'm telling you. And they're not even intelligent scams. The bureaucrats in Washington aren't the brightest bulbs. In your case, they would have been much smarter to stay clear of the eminent domain reference in their cease and desist order. It obligates them to follow the laws put forth in the Fifth Amendment, which defeats their purpose entirely."

"That's good to hear," Bryan said. And I know exactly what you're saying about D.C. bureaucrats. I did two tours in Afghanistan. It's no secret to us Army grunts why we lost that war."

Atlee Pinnaker laughed. "Please pardon my momentary lack of professionalism, but in my time dealing with the feds I've learned the United States government is the biggest organized crime syndicate on the planet. Lucky for me and my career, many of the movers and shakers are mental midgets and incompetent bullies. Much more bark than bite. More brawn than brains."

Bryan and Loretta shared a hardy laugh.

"I've long thought that myself," Bryan said. "Thank you for meeting with us and sharing your expertise on this matter."

"My pleasure, Mr. Gilliam. You can call me anytime if you need further assistance."

"One other thing before you go, Mr. Pinnaker," Bryan said. "Do you have any idea who requested the cease and desist order? It was composed and signed by a Treasury attorney, but surely he wouldn't have been the initiator, would he?"

"No, he wouldn't. The original request would have come from outside the department. But, as opposed to lawsuits, where the plaintiff must disclose their identity, cease and desist orders are less transparent. More anonymous. I thought this particular case was peculiar when you first contacted me about it. The Treasury Department surely has better things to do than chase down meteorites. But to get them involved, I would say the original request had to come from someone high up in the government. Someone who carries some clout. Why do you ask?"

Bryan exchanged glances with Loretta before answering.

"Well, the helicopter pilot who flew out here to pick up the rocks told me his superior, an Air Force colonel in Idaho, threatened him with a lawsuit when he returned with much less meteorite rock than expected. I can't remember the colonel's name off the top of my head, but he threatened the pilot with more legal action when the chopper pilot quit the meteorite roundup operation. Could he be the one behind this?"

"An Air Force colonel would certainly have the sway to get the Treasury Department to act. And the fact that this colonel was heading up a meteorite collection operation would make that a very logical guess. However, the only way we could prove who's behind it is with the presentation of a formal lawsuit."

"Thanks, Mr. Pinnaker. That definitely answers my question."

They signed off with the lawyer. Loretta breathed a sigh of relief. "I still can't believe our own government would try to pull something like this on us, Bry. We aren't criminals."

"Doesn't surprise me much now that he explained it to us. You heard the man. They pull this kind of power play often. Oh, the stories I could tell you about the head games the military played on us grunts. It'd turn your stomach."

"What's happened to our country, Bry?"

"Believe me, Lor, there's not enough time in the day, week, or month to explain it."

Loretta shook her head in disgust. "Well, at least we found out we're not liable for any of this."

"Yeah. We dodged a bullet there."

"I told you our celebrity status might come to haunt us."

"Yes, you did. And you were right, Lor. If I had it to do all over again—"

"No need to go there, Bry," she said holding up her hand. "I need to go check on Lianne. She and Marnie have been too quiet the past few hours."

Bryan took the long walk out to The Cellar to do his daily progress check of their Cretaceous Stone jewelry operation. He was feeling ebullient after their meeting with the lawyer, and there was a bouncy spring in his step. Bryan wouldn't have to shut down his moneymaker. He wouldn't have to pay any fines. Life was good. A huge potential legal problem had been swept aside.

He was in the elevator on his way down to Cretaceous Cavern when his cellphone buzzed. He didn't recognize the number but decided to answer, thinking it could be another request for a television interview.

"Bryan Gilliam?" said a husky, deep voice.

"Yes?"

"You should be ashamed of yourself. Keeping those poor animals cooped up and profiting off of their misery. I've seen you on TV. You think you're God, comin' across all high and mighty. But you're no god, Bryan. You're like all the rest of the ugly human scum who mistreat the real God's creatures. You're just a piece of shit, an infected hemorrhoid . . ."

The elevator reached the third sublevel—Cretaceous Cavern. Bryan stood there listening to the caller continue to spew invective, each word stabbing him in the chest like an ice pick. "Who the hell is this?" he said when the caller took a breath.

"Who I am doesn't matter. It's who I represent you should be concerned about. We believe that animals should be free. Even pets. And especially wild animals. It's God's way. We're giving you three days from right now to release those poor animals you've got caged in that inhumane prehistoric zoo of yours. If you don't release them by August sixth, we're comin' to do it for you, Bryan. We'll do what you should've done two months ago. And we'll hunt you down and make you pay for your sins. You got it, motherfucker?"

Bryan was stunned. It was difficult to move his mouth. "Are you *threatening* me?" he said, the words tripping off his tongue awkwardly.

"Are you dense? Did I not make myself perfectly clear?"

"How'd you get my cell number?"

"You *are* dense! We live in the information age, Bryan ol' buddy. Not too hard to get in touch with folks when the motivation is there."

Bryan's fear turned to anger. "Listen to me, asshole. If I set those dinosaurs free, many people will die. Many more will be seriously injured."

"Well, that's for God to sort out, isn't it?"

"You won't get anywhere near those dinosaur habitats, douche-bag! I've got a battalion of hardcore security surrounding my property."

"You think that'll stop us? Dream on, Bryan."

"What's this organization you represent? You owe me that much, at least."

"You'll find out soon enough. You've got three days. If you don't release those creatures by the sixth, you'll see who we are up close and personal. Sayonara, Bryan."

Bryan heard a click. The bastard had disconnected.

He stood there in shock, disbelieving what had just transpired. He peered at his workers in the Cavern through the crisscrossed steel latticework of the freight elevator gate. He'd received a number of prank calls since this dinosaur thing had made him famous, but most of those calls came in on the family landline. Those had been easy to dismiss as frivolous nonsense from punks he knew had no intention of acting on it. None of them threatened him in any way. No demands that he take action on something. But this call had a much darker framework. A much more lethal possibility. It was a direct threat against him and his family.

It had him rattled.

He checked the display and punched the callback option. He'd give this jerkoff a piece of his mind. He held the phone to his ear. A recorded female voice stated: *We're sorry. This number is out of service. Please check with directory assistance to get a current number for the person you wish to contact.*

Bryan wanted to scream. The guy was using a spoofed caller ID number. There were FCC laws against defrauding people using this tactic. But how did he go about reporting such activity?

He stood there frozen in place, replaying the call in his mind. He was creeped out by the way the guy kept saying his name, all calm and collected. A cool and composed sociopath. Who in their right mind would want the Gilliam caged dinosaurs unleashed upon the public?

Three days.

He imagined the Dromaeosaurs, T-Rexes, and Triceratops released and running helter-skelter around Gilliam's Guidepost.

It was a terrifying vision.

Is this an idle threat or a grave danger?

Bryan's elated post-lawyer-meeting buoyancy had deflated. He remained in a daze when Apisi came to the elevator.

"Whatsamatter, boss?" the Blackfoot said through the wire mesh gate. "You look like you've seen a *Sta-au*."

Bryan focused on his ranch hand. *Sta-au* was Blackfoot for ghost.

"I haven't seen a ghost, Ap. But I think I just heard the voice of Satan!"

Eggs, Cycads, and Iridium
In Deep Space

August 4:
National Geographic Grosvenor Auditorium
Washington D.C.

GROSVENOR AUDITORIUM WAS STANDING room only. An electric hum of anticipation droned through the crowd awaiting the start of National Geographic's *The Return of Prehistoric Life* forum. The big media outlets were well represented, with a phalanx of reporters lined up in front of the stage with cameras and boom mics.

The conference aimed to analyze the reintroduction of late Mesozoic era Cretaceous Period dinosaurs to the northwestern United States. The known facts: three species—Dromaeosaurus, Tyrannosaurus Rex, and Ceratopsians—had hatched out of fifteen large meteorites coming down along the Continental Divide in western Montana and eastern Idaho. These species disappeared from that specific region more than 66 million years ago. The unknown? What transpired to bring about this rebirth of long extinct prehistoric life? How did the egg-laden meteorites form and where did they originate? How did the eggs survive the superheated entry into the Earth's atmosphere and endure the devastating meteorite impact to hatch out hordes of baby dinosaurs? A panel of top experts would be addressing these looming questions. Presentations were to be accompanied by film clips of the animals in the wild and in captivity. Animated graphics would also be utilized to illustrate theories and calculations.

Astrophysicist Dr. Corella Britton, a petite black woman with impressive qualifications, served as the moderator. She held a Ph.D. in Astronomy from the University of Michigan and had done an Astrophysics Fellowship at Goddard. During her time at Goddard, she worked as an assistant professor at Howard University, where in her lecture halls, she had learned to command a stage and lead complex technical discussions.

Dr. Britton stepped up to the microphone at the front of the stage. "Good evening ladies and gentlemen and fellow scientists." Her strong tenor belied her small stature. The house lights dimmed and the hall quieted. "Thank you all for coming tonight. It's my honor to welcome you to the National Geographic/Smithsonian Institution *Return of Prehistoric Life* symposium. Many of you know me, but for those who don't, my name is Dr. Corella Britton and I will be your host for this three hour panel discussion. Tonight we will search for answers to the many questions confronting us about the strange zoological phenomenon taking place in our western states. Serving on the panel behind me are five distinguished individuals from different scientific disciplines, ranging from geology to paleozoology to astronomy and astrophysics. Two of our guests have worked closely with the dinosaurs and another has had an up close personal encounter with them. And our two astrophysicists have some intriguing theories as to how this fascinating anomaly could have evolved.

"But before I introduce them, I'd like to share a few program notes. First, this discussion is being broadcast live on the National Geographic cable channel and will be picked up for later showing by our co-sponsors, the Smithsonian Institution. Tonight's talk is being recorded to be edited into a more comprehensive eight part television and internet special scheduled to air in October. So I must request that all cell phones be turned off and that you please refrain from talking during the presentations as a courtesy to our panelists and our television viewing audience. We will have a fifteen minute break at the ninety minute mark followed by an in-house audience Q and A session. I thank you all in advance for your cooperation."

Dr. Britton moved to the end of the presentation table. "Thank you, panel, for coming here tonight to share your expertise with us. I would like to start down at the end, with Dr. Gregory Dulowski, the panel geologist." She turned to address the crowd. "Dr. Dulowski holds a master's degree from MIT in Geology, Geochemistry, and Geobiology, and is a past president of the American Geosciences Institute. "May I call you Greg?"

"Yes, by all means."

"So let's start the discussion from the beginning, Greg, I understand you were one of the first people to see a downed meteorite, and perhaps *the* first to see hatchlings being birthed. Many Americans have seen the incredible video footage you shot of the smoking meteorite wedges and Dromaeosaur hatchlings. You even filmed another of our panelists—William Blazenhurst from the American Meteor Society—being attacked by one." Dr. Britton nodded at the meteor specialist.

"Yes, indeed," Blazenhurst said, leaning into his mic. "The little varmint tried to rip my leg off!"

A ripple of laughter spread through the audience. Dr. Britton gave Blazenhurst a compassionate smile.

The large presentation screen behind the panelist table activated with a video montage of Dr. Dulowski's Dromaeosaur hatchout clips. Dozens of the little reptilian-looking creatures scurried around the big black rock wedges, squeaking and chirping.

Dr. Britton turned back to the geologist. "So, Greg, why don't you tell us how it was you became involved and were able to capture this magnificent video footage."

"Sure. My pleasure, Dr. Britton." He tilted his head to the panelist sitting next to him. "My respected colleague sitting next to me here—Dr. Franz Krause—and I were working on a Smithsonian sponsored paleontology dig in Choteau, Montana when we got a call from a rancher sixty miles north in Heart Butte about a large meteorite striking their property. I'd never seen a meteorite as large as what was being described, so of course I was intrigued. Due to my responsibilities at the dig site, I wasn't able to get up there for a few days. When I arrived, I was given complete access by the ranchers, Bryan and Loretta Gilliam. As you can see in the video, the rock had broken into four large sections on impact. All told, the size of the stone was mind boggling, the composition of the meteorite even more so. And, of course, there were the embedded egg nests that were in the process of hatching out, with a terrible noxious smell and a gummy yolky substance puddled around the base. Mr. Blazenhurst was there when I arrived. He'd been called in as a meteorite specialist."

Blazenhurst spoke. "I've seen many meteorite samples over the years, but none as impressive as this one. It really had me baffled as to how something that large made it through the shield of Earth's heavy and forbidding atmosphere. Even before we saw its cargo of dinosaur eggs and hatchlings, I knew we were looking at something special. And that odor was potent. It was like inhaling raw sewage. We needed oxygen masks, but we didn't have them."

"We'll get to that smell in a moment," Dr. Britton said, looking back at the presentation screen. "We can see the perspective of how large the meteorite is from Mr. Gilliam standing next to one of the wedges. I believe you estimated that these wedges are segments from a six-foot-by-six-foot rock?"

"That's correct, yes."

She looked at Dr. Dulowski. "That is indeed a most unusual meteorite. And you mentioned the uncommon composition of the rock, Greg."

Dulowski nodded. "Yes. Most common meteorites are composed of ninety percent iron and nickel. However, these egg-bearing meteorites are siderolites, which contain stone and concentrations of heavy metals. Siderolites are very uncommon. But what makes these siderolites even more unusual is their metals composition. They contain only trace amounts of iron, which is peculiar. Instead, they are nearly seventy percent iridium, which is a rare, corrosion-resistant, silver-white heavy metal with a melting point of well over four thousand degrees Fahrenheit. The way the iridium is distributed throughout the stone suggests a protective firewall around the egg nests. Both Mr. Blazenhurst and myself agree that this heavy layer of iridium might possibly shield the eggs from frying during the extreme temperatures they encounter when entering the Earth's atmosphere. The iridium would also prevent the meteorites from burning down to the small shards that we see in most meteoroids that make it to the ground. Think of it as iridium being a heat shield that allows the meteorites to maintain their size and shape, and not burn to a crisp on their way down." The geologist looked down the length of the table at Blazenhurst. "Do I have it right so far, Bill?"

Blazenhurst nodded. "Yes, you're spot on, Greg."

Dulowski continued. "So that begs the question. Where did these huge concentrations of iridium come from? In our contemporary world, iridium is but a trace metal. It's one of the rarest precious metals in the Earth's crust, mined as a byproduct of platinum and palladium. To those of us who studied the geologic implications of the Cretaceous Period and the dinosaur extinction, iridium has special meaning. Near the end of the Cretaceous, in the late Mesozoic era, planet Earth was dusted with a layer of heavy metals, the most prevalent being iridium. There are two main hypotheses among geologists studying that prehistory as to how that iridium got there. One theory says that during the last million years of the Cretaceous, a great, simultaneous eruption of volcanic activity coupled with tectonic shifts in the Earth's plates caused massive amounts of hot magma to bubble to the surface. As the volcanic lava and magma mixed and cooled, various chemical reactions took place, and over time, formed great quantities of iridium and other heavy metals. A second, more popular school of thought is that massive iridium-filled asteroids impacted with Earth, causing a prehistoric nuclear winter, and consequently, a heavy layer of iridium coating Earth's surface. The only thing we know for sure is that both the dinosaurs and heavy concentrations of iridium disappeared simultaneously from Earth, sixty-six million years ago.

"My theory pulls from both of these hypotheses. I say that the volcanic activity and tectonic plate shifts happened first, generating deep strata of iridium on Earth's surface. This was followed by giant asteroids striking the planet, killing off the dinosaurs, hurling massive chunks of the Earth's surface into orbit. Newly laid egg nests got wrapped up tight in these iridium casings. In essence, this string of events launched new iridium asteroids filled with dinosaur egg clusters out into deep space. Over the millennia, these large asteroids broke apart into smaller meteoroids, but still maintained their egg pod centers. Think of the egg nests like a nucleus in a cell. But I'm a bit out of my knowledge zone discussing that part of it." He turned his head to glance at Dr. Franz Krause. "I'm not speaking out of school here, am I, Franz?"

"No, you're not. Your description is apt."

Dr. Britton said, "So you think those eggs remained in some kind of suspended state for sixty-six million years before returning to Earth?"

"Yes. That is my theory. *Our* theory . . ." Dulowski looked at Krause again, who nodded agreement. "I have discussed this in great detail with my respected colleagues up here on this panel. Franz, Bill Blazenhurst, your astrophysicists, Dr. Anthony Mallory and Dr. Walton Rayburn . . . we are all in agreement on that theory. They each have much more to add to that dialogue with their presentations. But before we leave the topic of the meteorites, I'd like to point out another characteristic about them that makes them totally unique. It will lend credence to my geological conclusions."

"Sure, please expound on that, Greg."

"My pleasure. The cores of the three meteorites Franz and I saw contain fronds of ancient ferns and palm-like plants wrapped around the nests. I understand from government geologists I have spoken with that this is common in all the meteorites they have inspected. I have some slides to show, if you could."

Dr. Britton signaled to the projection room at the back of the auditorium. "Please activate Dr. Dulowski's slide carousel."

The screen behind the panel changed from video to still photos. A series of images cycled through, showing meteorite wedges with greenery packed around hollow spaces where the dinosaur nests resided. Dulowski stood and used a laser pointer to accentuate his message.

"These are ancient cycads, last seen in the Late Cretaceous. You can see the leathery, glossy pinnate leaves. We would expect them to be petrified into plant fossils, but they are not. They're alive. A rich greenish-yellow. They look like fresh growth. Doctors Mallory and Rayburn will expound on how this could be possible later."

"Interesting, Greg," Dr. Britton said. "Can you explain to our audience who might not know, what do you mean by *pinnate* leaves?"

Franz Krause answered. "Pinnate means a leaf that is divided into individual leaflets, which are arranged symmetrically on either side of the main stalk. Pinnate leaves have a featherlike appearance."

"I see. What marks them as being ancient?"

The geologist indicated with his pointer. "The shape of these pinnate leaves and their makeup shows these plants to be ancient flora. We can see the feathery leaflets arranged in sets of symmetrical twins on each side of the branch. The rhizome—or stem—the fronds, and sporangia—which is the chemical reproductive structure—are all indicative of plant life long since vanished from Earth. We've seen fossils of these cycads in our paleontology work. Many Cretaceous species feathered their nests with this type of foliage. Some of my undergrad studies were in paleobotany, and I'm one-hundred percent sure these are primitive seed-bearing cycads from more than sixty-six-million years ago. They're a precursor to our modern day palmettos and ferns. A number of highly qualified botanists with whom I consulted agree. I'll leave the discussion of their role in how they dovetail with the eggs to Doctors Krause, Mallory, and Rayburn."

"Most interesting," Corella Britton said with an engaging smile. "But before we leave the geology conversation, what about the foul odor that wafted out of the rock after impact?"

"I've used up my time, so I'll hand it off now to Dr. Krause. The foul odor is from the eggs and the eggs are more his area of expertise."

Dr. Britton said, "That was a most enlightening presentation, Greg. Thank you." She turned to face the audience. "How about a big round of applause for Dr. Gregory Dulowski."

The crowd responded appreciatively. Dulowski nodded in acknowledgment and smiled for the cameras.

When the hall quieted, Corella Britton introduced the German scientist. "We are honored to hear next from paleozoologist Franz Krause. Dr. Krause has a Masters in Paleontology from the University of Bremen and a Ph.D. in Prehistoric Zoology from Humboldt University in Berlin. He is a Leibniz Prizewinner for his outstanding research in Biochemistry and is the author of more than one hundred articles published in top-flight scholarly journals." She turned to Krause. "The stage is yours, Dr. Krause."

"Thank you, Dr. Britton. Since I've been given the stinky task, I'll start by telling you the smell and the gooey substance we found glazing the meteorites is quite simply the result of broken eggs. So let's talk about the eggs. They are nature's most efficient birthing package, other than the human womb, of course." The German looked out over the crowd, to the back of the auditorium. "Could you AV folks please queue up my slides?"

The screen behind the panel lit up with a closeup of a nest of five large eggs with swirls of deep blue-green patterns.

"These are the five unhatched Dromaeosaur eggs Bryan Gilliam pulled from the meteorite, the eggs we later hatched in a chicken incubator. All five of those Dromaeosaurs are now living on the Gilliam ranch. Let's start with the shells. Our dinosaur eggs have thick, rugged leathery outer skins that are softer and more pliable than the hard shelled eggs of our birds and reptiles. These Dromaeosaur shells consist of calcium carbonate—same as our birds and reptiles—but also contain large amounts of albite to give the shells strength and vivid coloring. They also possess silicone compounds to give the eggs flexibility and pliability. This chemical compound admixture enables our dinosaur eggs to withstand and absorb great forces of impact without breakage or damage to the embryos.

"Next slide, please . . . The egg interior is an engineering marvel. Again, similar to bird and reptile eggs, our dino eggs contain a yolk sac and three membranes: the amnion, chorion, and allantois. All are critical in sustaining embryo growth. The amnion is a fluid-filled sac that surrounds and protects the embryo. The amnion in our Dromaeosaur eggs is four times thicker than that of bird and reptile eggs, to shield the larger embryo. The chorion facilitates gas exchange between the embryo and external environments. The allantois stores nitrogenous wastes produced by the embryo and facilitates respiration. And finally, the yolk sac transports nutrients to the embryo's circulatory system. The chorion and allantois are both larger since dinosaur embryos give off much more gas and nitrogen than do our contemporary birds or reptiles. When the eggs break open, the membrane gases mix with chemicals in the yolk—namely phosphorous, and pantothenic and aspartic acids—to produce that pungent odor. You don't get that chemical interaction in our terrestrial eggs, mainly due to the lower volume of phosphorus and acids. The gooey substance glazing the meteorite that Greg showed you is the yolk from both hatched and unhatched eggs. The yolky matter acts as a glue, holding the noxious smell for a week or more.

"Okay, now that I've bored you with my chemistry lesson, let's move on to something more fun. Let's take a look at the living animals. Guys," he said, signaling to the AV team in back, "please roll my video. I must mention here that the footage shot in the wild was supplied by my friends from the Smithsonian Paleo Expedition, Doctors Hayden Fowler and Nora Lemoyne." Krause waved at the TV camera transmitting this presentation live. "I'm sure you are watching, so from me and the world, a big thank you, Hayden and Nora, for your spectacular recordings."

Franz Krause spent the next forty minutes narrating videos and still shots, beginning with the baby Dromaeosaurs hatching out of the chicken incubator in the Gilliam barn. He walked the rapt audience through the animal's diets, feeding process, and growth rates, then took them through a day in the life, using video clips shot at Gilliam's Glade to show the creatures' behavior, communications, instincts, and habits. He described the buildout of Gilliam's Glade, with the many considerations that had to be taken into account to ensure the ongoing health of the animals and safety of the Gilliam family and their visitors. He explained the biology and anatomy of each of the three species—blood anomalies, pelt constitution, skeletal formation, teeth and claw properties, respiration rates, metabolism, eyesight, olfactory senses. He explained the Triceratops' unique bony frill and tri-horned plated head.

The paleozoologist followed his in-depth analysis with sensational footage of the animals in the wild . . . Four Triceratops trampling through a wheat field . . . Another pair of the herbivores rubbing their immature horns against the trunks of aspens, instinctively marking their territory . . . Two Tyrannosaurus Rexes fighting over a downed and gutted elk . . . A trio of Dromaeosaurs headbutting and growling at each other in their rough form of play. The audience oohed and aahed as they watched a Triceratops sprint through a barley field, trying to elude a couple of musclebound Tyrannosaurs hot on its tail, the T-Rexes bringing it down in a cloud of dust and feasting on it. The clip went on to show Hayden Fowler and federal wildlife biologist, Barrett Hailey, sedating both of the gorging T-Rexes with long range shots from their tranquilizer rifles. Krause reported the two Tyrannosaurs were brought back to the Gilliam ranch for study, and that the live specimens gave scientists extraordinary insight into the big carnivores, perhaps giving them information that might reduce future attacks on the human population. The last of the video loops showed Hayden Fowler following T-Rex tracks along Thurston Creek bordering the John Tully farm, to a decimated beaver dam, where Fowler discovered stripped clean beaver skeletons in the lodge and a drowned Tyrannosaurus Rex juvenile floating nearby. Dr. Krause thanked Nora Lemoyne for the excellent videography of the last two segments, and closed out his presentation. Much of this "wilderness" video had never been made available to the public, and the audience cheered enthusiastically, both for Dr. Krause's informative session and for the opportunity to see rare visuals.

Following a 20-minute break, Corella Britton called the symposium back to order. The humming crowd quieted as people returned to their seats. She introduced Dr. Anthony Mallory and Dr. Walton Rayburn, the two astrophysicists who together had derived a theory postulating how this return of Cretaceous dinosaurs could be possible. Both men were highly credentialed. Dr. Mallory earned a bachelor's degree in Astronomy, a masters in Space Science, and a doctorate in Astrophysics, doing his postgraduate study at UCLA. Mallory had worked on two of NASA's top astrophysics programs—*Cosmic Origins* and *Exoplanet Explorations*—for 17 years. Dr. Rayburn held a bachelor's in Computer Science, a masters in Physics, and a doctorate in Astrophysics, earning his Ph.D. at the University of Texas. He was a much-in-demand aerospace engineering consultant in the private sector for companies such as SpaceX, Firefly Aerospace, and Rocket Lab. Dr. Rayburn also hosted a popular weekly podcast called *Talk to the Starman*, where he had floated a few of the pair's controversial ideas concerning this dinosaur invasion. Both men had published widely in prestigious scientific journals and academic publications. Both were in their early fifties and were dressed casually in open-neck oxford shirts, khaki pants, and blue blazers.

"Hello, everyone," Dr. Mallory said in greeting. "Many of you might already be familiar with my colleague here, Dr. Walton Rayburn, from his very informative and entertaining podcast, *Talk to the Starman*. I'm nowhere as popular as my friend Walt, but any of you following NASA doings over the past couple of decades might know of my work. I have been active in deep space research, specifically dark matter, black holes, the Big Bang, and planets outside our solar system. So, you might be asking yourselves, what does any of that have to do with the reintroduction of Cretaceous Period dinosaurs to our American West? My answer is: quite a lot, actually.

"Walt and I have known our peers up here on this stage—Greg Dulowski, Franz Krause, and Bill Blazenhurst—for several years. They have done an excellent job in paving the way for our discussion. They told you about the heavy concentration of the rare metal iridium in the meteorites, and the ancient cycads wrapped around the nests. They gave a thorough overview of the dinosaur eggs. They provided many intriguing details about the creatures roaming Montana and Idaho. Greg even explained how the meteorites were formed, which Walton and I back one-hundred percent. So that leaves the big mystery of how the eggs remained in a suspended state and survived for sixty-six million years. What events transpired to enable that? What brought those egg-filled meteorites back into Earth's orbit and made them strike the precise geographical area from where they were propelled into deep space sixty-six million years ago?

"Think about this, folks. Dinosaurs ruled the Earth for one-hundred-and-sixty-six million years. And then, As Dr. Dulowski pointed out, a series of asteroid storms wiped them out completely. And now? After being extinct for millions of years, they have returned. How could that possibly be? Dr. Rayburn and I will try to lay it out for you as simply as we can. Please know that our findings are obviously speculative in nature. They are educated guesses at this point as the happenings we have witnessed over the past two months fall outside what our scientific tools and technology can prove conclusively. Nevertheless, Dr. Rayburn and I have pooled our combined fifty-plus years of education and research experience in astronomy and interstellar space to arrive at our hypothesis. We have also consulted with others—geologists, biologists, paleonto-logists, astronomers, and astrophysicists—who agree with the scenario we are about to present. Yes, it's true we have had our naysayers, especially on social media. We have had some very vocal opposition to our conclusions, but to this point, none have offered any viable alternatives." Dr. Mallory shielded his eyes from the glare of the stage lights and looked to the rear of the auditorium. "AV team, could you please start up our slide show?"

The houselights dimmed and the screen behind the panel lit up with a slide of the solar system.

"Thank you," Mallory said. "I'd like to turn things over to my partner in deep space, Dr. Walton Rayburn. Do you have answers to these questions, Walt?"

"Indeed I do. Thanks, Anthony." Dr. Rayburn rose from his seat and walked to the projection screen. "What you see here is our solar system. Many of you are intimately familiar with this view. Our star—the Sun—is the glue that holds the eight planets and the dwarf planet Pluto together. It does that by force of gravity. This system contains dozens of moons, and millions of asteroids, comets, and meteoroids. Our discussion today will take us out beyond this sys-tem into deep space, also known as interstellar space. Next slide, please . . ."

A diagram showed the Sun with the solar system planets in a straight line, showing distances between each planet, and the distance of each from the Sun. Interstellar space was depicted as starting beyond Neptune.

Dr. Rayburn continued, using the laser pointer. "Interstellar space is the region that begins where the Sun's heat, light, and magnetic fields stop affecting its environs. That point is called the *heliopause*. It's extremely cold and dark beyond this point, with temperatures at minus four-hundred-and-sixty degrees Fahrenheit. The only light out here is the dim light of distant stars. Our diagram shows the Kuiper Belt and Oort Cloud out here. Think of the Kuiper Belt as a scrapyard of icy objects remaining from the formation of our solar system. As you can see here, the Oort Cloud is much further out. It's a massive shell of billions of comets, which are accumulations of dust, rock, and ice. To put into perspective the distance from Earth to this area, NASA's Voyager One mission was launched in 1977 with the aim of studying interstellar space. It didn't cross the heliopause until 2012, a thirty-five year journey! It traveled through the Kuiper Belt but to this day still has not made it to the Oort Cloud. It has the distinction of being the first spacecraft to enter interstellar space, covering a distance of fourteen billion miles! Voyager One is an aerospace engineering marvel. It stopped taking photos thirty years ago, but it's still sending back valuable instrument readings." Rayburn paused for effect.

"I tell you this because this is where we believe those iridium, egg-filled asteroids went into a suspended sleep state for sixty-six million years. I'm sure most of you know about cryonics, the often challenged pseudoscience of freezing human body parts for later reanimation. Think of our dinosaur meteorites as deep space cryonics pods, delivering prehistoric eggs in stasis. The difference is, instead of freezing deceased human tissue and organs for reanimation, our dinosaur pods contain living animal embryos frozen in an inanimate state, just waiting for the right conditions to animate them. Quite difficult to comprehend, I know. But hear me out. It makes sense if you look at scientific principles. Interstellar space is forbiddingly cold. It is also void of oxygen, creating a vacuum that seals up objects and both light and dark matter. Our Earth-launched asteroids existed in this harsh environment for hundreds of thousands, perhaps *millions,* of years before being overwhelmed and sucked into matter having a stronger gravitational force. More on that in a minute.

"In this bitter cold vacuum, living organisms—especially egg embryos—could be preserved in a suspended state for extremely long periods. The plant life shrouding the egg nests—the prehistoric cycads—would also be preserved, staying green since the natural cryonic environment stops growth in its tracks and yet keeps living organisms alive. Therefore, the foliage would survive and would not need sunlight for photosynthesis to remain in its green state. The egg embryos would also not require oxygen while in this suspended state. Once the meteors enter the Earth's atmosphere and heat up, the plants come out of stasis and release the oxygen needed by the embryos. The thick shell of iridium prevents the eggs from over-heating. Of course, the impact is tremendous, but the iridium is distributed in such a way as to absorb much of the shock and bust the meteorites open in wedges, allowing the animals to hatch out."

He returned to the presenters' table and took his seat, glanced at Dr. Krause. "You're the paleobotanist, Franz. Did I hit pretty close to the target on this?"

"I couldn't have explained it better myself," Krause said.

Rayburn turned to Greg Dulowski. "And did I get the iridium explanation right?"

Dulowski gave him a thumbs-up. "Spot on, Walt."

Walton Rayburn looked back out over the audience. "And now we get to the most fascinating part of this discussion: Where exactly did our meteors hole up for the eternal duration, and what astro-physical event transpired to send the meteors to Earth? For that, I'm going to turn it back over to Dr. Mallory. This is more in his wheel-house. Take it away, Anthony."

Astrophysicist Mallory stood. "Thanks, Walt. Good job." He checked his watch, then glanced at Dr. Britton. "How much time do I have, Corella?"

"We've got about fifteen minutes before we'll open it up for questions."

"Okay. Before I get into the cause of the meteorite strikes, I'm going to talk a bit about wormholes. This is the part of our theory that is the most speculative. Dr. Rayburn mentioned matter having a strong gravitational force on our asteroids and sucking them in. AV team, could you please run our animation?"

The background screen showed a broad nightscape of stars and shooting comets, with several small tunnel-like tubes outlined in white. A flurry of glittery particles rotated around the entrance of each.

"Dark matter exists around wormholes in deep space, acting as a kind of gatekeeper, allowing wormholes to open and close, directing them to gobble up, or spit out, objects and matter having lesser gravitational pull. We sometimes refer to dark matter as *exotic* matter. Our animation clip here shows it as swirls of sparkly dust, but in reality, you can't see dark matter, even with NASA's powerful satellite scopes. The only way we know dark matter exists is by the way it affects the density and velocity of ordinary matter.

"Simply put, wormholes are tunnels between two far-reaching points in space caused by the extreme warping of the space-time continuum. Once an object enters a wormhole, be it an asteroid, comet, gas, or a cluster of matter, everything in the object becomes inactive. Growth freezes in living cells. Time stops. Space collapses inward. Distance is recalibrated. The trapped object exists in nothingness, until some gravitational event in the dark matter propels the object elsewhere. The tunnel-like structure of wormholes provides a shortcut passage to distant geolocations or even different times. Think of wormholes as similar to the portals you've seen in science fiction movies. So you might be asking, how are wormholes different from black holes? There's a big difference, actually. Both take in nearby masses and matter, and completely shut down the trapped objects' properties. But black holes do not relinquish their contents. Wormholes do, however.

"We believe our dinosaur asteroids that were catapulted from Earth sixty-six million years ago were parked in one or more of these wormholes for much of their absence. I know what many of you are thinking right about now . . . you're saying, Anthony, this is all a bunch of science fiction imagination. All of us sitting up here have heard that repeatedly. We've heard it ad nauseum on social media sites. We get a lot of pushback on our websites. Walt gets a lot of condemnation about it during his podcasts. But think of this. Even though much of this is theoretical at this point, one of the greatest geniuses who ever lived—Albert Einstein—predicted the existence of wormholes in his famous theory of general relativity in 1915. His beliefs about gravity within our solar system foretold of the bends in space and time and distance that wormholes produce. It's a theory that has stood for more than a hundred years and has become the fundamental principle of all modes of physics, most especially astrophysics and astronomy. It's quite possible that a million years inside a wormhole could be skewed and reduced to a week or a few months. And since wormholes theoretically create shortcuts across the universe, our egg-laden meteors could possibly travel the fourteen billion space miles in a matter of hours or days if the proper conditions occurred. Trust me, I know it's difficult to comprehend. We human beings base our spatial thinking and con- cept of time on our terrestrial experiences. Granted, much of this is heavily conjectural. But this scenario explains so much about this startling scientific anomaly that has reintroduced long extinct dino- saurs to our planet.

"So now we get to the big astronomical event that kicked off the cluster of these meteorites coming down in Idaho and Montana. A few weeks before the first strike, in mid-May, astronomers out west picked up an unusual flurry of meteor showers. Much larger in volume, and brighter and more vivid than what they see in early fall. Very uncommon for late spring. Some of you might have caught coverage of that on the news. We now know that activity was generated by comet storms in the Kuiper Belt, just beyond Neptune. These comets—we call them *sungrazers*—were knocked off course and collided with the Sun, producing massive solar flareups for a week or more. That kind of massive solar disturbance spews out tidal waves of radiation, x-rays, and gravitational fluctuations. At NASA, we heard from Navy and Air Force jet pilots telling us their instrument panels were producing strange readouts and their flight paths were compromised by unusual magnetic fields. Anyway, this extreme solar reaction created a vacuum in the Earth's atmosphere that sucked in our meteors, which caused the brilliant lightshow. It took another seventy-two hours for the meteorites to strike along the Continental Divide. We still have not determined how and why these meteorites targeted that area. We might not ever figure that part out. But for now, we believe we've got a pretty good handle on the rest of it.

"That's all I've got," Mallory said, leaning on his elbows and craning his neck to peer down the table at the other panelists. "Do any of you have anything to add?"

When they didn't, Dr. Britton stood and grabbed a handheld microphone. "Okay," she said, smiling. "This wraps up our presentation portion of the program. Thank you gentlemen, for your time and your thorough preparation. I'm sure our viewing audience would agree that your efforts have made this session extremely informative and enlightening. I'm now going to open up our forum for in-house questions." She moved down the stage steps to the auditorium floor, speaking into the remote mic. "By a show of hands, who has questions or comments for our panelists?"

Several arms raised. The first question—about life spans—went to Franz Krause. He answered that Tyrannosaurus Rexes and Triceratopses were thought to live twenty-five to thirty years while Dromaeosaurs probably would live half that long due to their much higher metabolisms. A second question was for Greg Dulowski. Based on meteorite egg breakage, how many dinosaurs did he think hatched out?

Dulowski scratched at his chin. "Keep in mind my assertions are limited to the three meteorites I inspected. This is sheer extrapolation here. Let's start with what we know for sure. A total of fifteen meteorites struck along the Continental Divide. The nests I examined were quite large, with anywhere from forty to sixty eggs in each nest. The breakage rate was around thirty percent. So if my math is correct, conservatively speaking, I'd say close to three-hundred animals hatched out. However, the numbers we have seen in the wild would suggest a higher number—possibly as many as four- to five-hundred. It's impossible to know with much certainty since not all of the meteorites have been located."

William Blazenhurst said, "Yeah, astronomers in our network were able to track how many came down. They recorded approximate strike locations, but finding them and retrieving them presented some difficult challenges. We're talking extremely remote areas."

Franz Krause chipped in. "Another factor that makes dinosaur counts difficult is the fact that these animals are cagey. They are adept at hiding. They're very evasive, except when coming out to feed."

Next came a comment from a stylishly attired man in his early thirties getting up from his seat in the back row. Dr. Britton held the mic in front of his face. "Yeah, this is for you two astrophysicists up there. With all due respect, your theories about wormholes and dark matter and the space-time continuum sound like sci-fi fantasy to me. I mean, come on, dinosaur eggs parking in deep space for sixty-six million years? Then remaining fertile and whole, actually hatching out after impacting Earth at great speed? Even if we believe the way the meteorites formed, which I *do not*, it's ludicrous! I've heard Q-Anon conspiracy theories that make more sense!"

Dr. Britton yanked the mic away from the man. "I must remind our audience members that we are to show our esteemed panelists the utmost respect. Comments like this are antagonistic and will not be tolerated."

Dr. Rayburn leaned into his mic. "It's okay, Corella. I applaud the young man's courage in getting up and stating his opinion. Science is a platform for information exchange and debate. You sound like an intelligent young man, and I'll be the first to agree with you that our notion of how this all went down comes off as quite bizarre. But let me ask you this. Do you believe the dinosaurs out west exist?"

"Well, yeah . . . I was out there a few weeks ago at the Gilliam ranch and saw them with my own eyes. But I don't believe for a second they came to us through meteorites. That defies all laws of physics and biology."

Walton Rayburn smirked. "So then, I suppose you have a theory about where the creatures came from? Please share it with us. We are always open to opposing points of view. We're good listeners."

The man hemmed and hawed, shuffled his feet. Dr. Britton wore an expression of impatience as she held the microphone for him. "No, I don't have any, um . . . *theories*," he said finally. "I'm still trying to piece it all together. It's just that your ideas strike me as preposterous."

William Blazenhurst spoke up. "All of us up here on this panel have seen at least a few of the meteorites. We've studied the egg-shell fragments and yolky goo. Greg and Franz and I witnessed a hatchout. Hell, one of the meteorite hatchlings bit me. All of us up here *know* how these dinosaurs came to us."

Anthony Mallory said, "And as far as our astrophysical and geological assumptions go, as I said earlier, yes, they are specula-tive and largely unprovable, but we chased down every possible scenario that would bring us Cretaceous-Paleogene extinction dino-saurs wrapped in meteorites. What we presented tonight checks all the boxes, crazy as it sounds. We don't have time to get into the details of other scenarios we examined, but none really tied it all together the way our concept does."

Dr. Corella Britton pulled the microphone away from the man, who looked like he had plenty more to say. "Okay, people. Our time is almost up, so maybe one more question?"

"Wait, Corella," Dr. Mallory said. "I would like to address the young man before we move on. Sir, you are absolutely right to question science. Every one of us sitting at this table questions science every day. It's a big part of what we do. It's what makes our professions so rewarding. Science is a tool we use to prove or disprove happenings in the natural world. And let's face it, much of the natural world is shrouded in mystery. There is still much we do not know about the Bermuda Triangle. The pyramids in Egypt. UFOs, or, as they are now known, unidentified aerial phenomena. The tides of the oceans . . . sections in the deepest trenches of our oceans never seen by humans. No telling what exists in those depths. We still have much to learn about hurricanes and tornados and the overall effects of climate change. When we apply the tool of scientific discovery to these things, we are trying to find answers to the how, why, when, and where questions. We apply scientific principles to see what floats and what doesn't. To separate fact from fiction. Are you a scientist by any chance, sir?"

"No, I'm not. I'm a realtor. I just have an interest in this. I'm a bit of a paleontology hobbyist. I've had an obsession with dinosaurs since I was a young boy old enough to read."

"Well, the fact that you traveled to the Gilliam ranch to see them in person tells me a lot. You have an intellectual curiosity. That's good. This country could use more like you."

The man blushed. "Well, um . . . thank you, sir," he said, giving Dr. Mallory a thumbs-up. "I will certainly take another look at your theories. They make more sense now that I think about it."

Dr. Britton checked her watch. "That's all we have time for this evening. I want to thank the scientists on our panel, the National Geographic staff—especially our sensational audio-visual crew—you folks here in our studio audience, and our cable viewers, for making this a wonderful educational experience. As I stated in the opening, segments of this broadcast will be edited into our television special to air in October. For more details, please go to our website. This has been a National Geographic/Smithsonian Institution production. Thank you and goodnight."

The house lights came up amid thunderous applause. The panelists retreated to a conference room for press interviews.

Dr. Corella Britton sighed with relief as she watched the crowd file out. A broad smile came to her lips as she overheard people chatting excitedly. Based on audience reaction, the symposium had been a huge success.

Insecurity

August 5: Gilliam's Glade
Heart Butte, Montana

SWEAT TRICKLED DOWN BRYAN'S BACK as he swung a pick-axe in a deep ditch fifty yards from the Glade enclosures. Paul and Ethan were in the trench beside him, digging out a long barbecue pit for Saturday's party. Grunts of exertion filled the air. Shovel-heads swished through dirt. The pickaxe pinged against solid rock. The loamy smell of freshly turned soil floated on the breeze. Small piles of dirt accumulated around the perimeter. Much of the hole already existed thanks to the big meteorite that had struck here two months ago. Bryan and the boys were merely transforming it into a functional cooking pit, large enough to grill for 40 people.

The Glade remained quiet. Most of the scientists had not yet returned from D.C., where they were attending the National Geographic conference. Bryan looked up to see the two T-Rexes standing near the fence, heads tilted in curiosity, observing them through the chain-link, their watchful crimson eyes alert, focused.

Paul stopped digging and pointed his shovel at the creatures. "Those things are really creepin' me out . . . the way they keep staring at us. Don't they have anything better to do?"

"They probably think we're diggin' their graves," Ethan said, tossing a shovelful of dirt.

Paul cast a wary eye at the carnivores. "I'd like to bury 'em, that's for sure."

"They're lookin' at you, bro," Ethan said, winking at him. "They're thinkin' what a tasty dinner you'd make."

"They'd come for you first," Paul said. "You're younger . . .

your flesh is more tender."

Bryan peered across the way at the Tyrannosaurs. Truth be known, Paul wasn't the only one here who was creeped out by the prehistoric oddities. Their predatory stares always ran a chill up his spine.

Ethan said, "I don't think they'd stop to consider choice cuts, Pauley Poo. Knowing how they attack the weakest in the pack, you'd be the first one they'd go after."

"Who you callin' weak, Mr. Puny boy? I could whip yer ass with one hand and you know it."

Ethan smirked. "We both know *exactly* what you whip with that one hand, Pauley."

Bryan smiled and went back to working the pick while his sons continued to trade insults in their familiar teen testosterone, one-upmanship exchange. Finally, after several quips about male anatomy sizes, he said, "All right, guys. That's enough. We've got a lot of work to do, so let's get back to it."

Paul leaned on his shovel. "Well, well, well," he said. "The great mime finally speaks."

"Mime?" Bryan said. "What're you talkin' about?"

"You've been really quiet the last two days, Pops. It's not like you. What gives?"

Bryan slung the pickaxe up on his shoulder and stared at his oldest son, not really seeing him. His thoughts were elsewhere. He'd received a second call this morning from the eco-terrorist, once again demanding he set the dinosaurs free. The caller had left a long demented, vitriolic voice mail. The message was even more intimidating than his first contact. Much more direct and explicit, as in: *We will kill you if you don't comply!* Bryan had listened to it repeatedly through the day, wondering what to do about it. Thinking this second call had elevated things to a genuine, dangerous level.

"Nothing *gives,* Pauley," he said, doing his best to act naturally and keep his voice level. "Aren't I allowed to be quiet once in a while?"

"It's just weird, is all. Normally you're a motormouth, Dad. But you haven't said two words yesterday 'n today."

"*Motormouth*? Thanks a bunch, pal."

"I don't mean it in a bad way. You're usually chatty. Friendly. Haven't seen that the past coupla days. It's like you lost your best friend or sumpthin."

"Yeah, Dad," Ethan said. "Even Lee is aware, and she never notices much of anything. Lianne told me this morning she hoped you weren't sick."

"I'm not sick and I haven't lost my best friend," Bryan said testily. "There's just a lot goin' on right now, boys."

That first threatening phone call had him tucked up inside his own head the past two days. His paranoid instincts had taken over. He'd gotten little sleep the past 48 hours, choosing to spend much of the past two nights sitting on the front porch with a half case of Coors and his shotgun. And now, this morning's second call from this eco-terrorist asshole had him completely preoccupied and over the edge. Even still, he thought he'd been doing a good job hiding it. Looking at the expectant expressions on his two sons' faces told him he hadn't fooled them whatsoever. *And Lianne, too?* It sometimes startled him how much his children picked up.

Paul glanced at the Glade again. "Why are we havin' this barbecue out here so close to those beasts?"

"Well, because this is where the meteorite struck and those animals in the Glade were what brought together most of the people coming to our party. Your mother and I thought it would be appropriate. Not to mention we've got a sound system out here to play music and seats for people to sit while they eat. You always wanted to play DJ Mix-A-Lot, Pauley. Here's your chance. Just don't play any of that rap or hip-hop stuff. This isn't the crowd for that."

Paul made a sour face. "Well, I'm not playing that middle of the road crap like Michael Bublé or John Legend, that's for sure."

"That's not what I'm sayin' and I think you know that."

"Dad just wants to show off his zoo," Ethan said to Paul.

"I believe you're onto somethin' little bro," Paul said, high-fiving Ethan. "I still think this cookout would be better back at the house. Easier than hauling all the food and drinks out here, don't ya think, Pops?"

Bryan was about to respond when he noticed the white Vigilant Eye Security & Investigation pickup approaching on the east meadow road. He followed the truck's progress as it neared. He slammed the pick into the ground and hopped up out of the ditch, slapped the dirt from his gloves. Waited on the truck as it pulled off the dirt road and rumbled down the embankment into the meadow. The giant blue eye on the side of the truck—the centerpiece of the Missoula security firm's logo—looked three-dimensional in the bright afternoon sun.

Tom Hennessey, head of the Gilliam security detail, pulled up and shut off the ignition. Got out and walked toward Bryan, wiping at his brow with a handkerchief, his holstered sidearm bouncing against his hip.

He smiled as he greeted them. "Hey, Mr. Gilliam . . . howdy, boys. You guys diggin' a tunnel to China?"

Bryan wondered what this visit was about. "Hey, Tom. What brings you out this way?"

"Well, I tried your cell, but it went straight to voice mail."

"Yeah, I left my phone up at the house. What's up?"

"I looked into your request for additional security, and—"

"Uh, wait a second, T," Bryan said, taking a quick glance back at his sons. "Let's go over to the bleachers and talk, okay?"

"Sure enough, Mr. Gilliam."

They settled in on the bottom row of the bleachers nearest the Dromaeosaur habitat, where three of the animals had moved up against the fence to check them out. One of them growled and bared his teeth.

Hennessey said, "Long as I've been here on this detail I can't get over how scary those things are. Odd looking creatures, I must say. Sure would hate to have to tangle with one of 'em."

"Yeah, me, too. They're a great attraction, though. Just wish I could open up the zoo for the public."

"Shouldn't be long now. The sightings in the wild have slowed way down. By the way, I saw the National Geographic special last night. Mr. Dulowski and Mr. Krause did a great job. You were mentioned a few times. Lots of good video from your ranch. Did you watch it?"

"Sure did. The whole family saw it."

"Forgive me fer bein' nosy, Mr. Gilliam, but I've always wondered, what does it feel like to be famous?"

Bryan thought about the crackpots he'd heard from, all the hateful social media posts from nameless bullies. The two intimidating phone calls that had him so distressed. He was inclined to say that being a celebrity sucked swamp water. Instead he said, "It has its moments."

"I'm sure it does," Hennessey said with a fawning smile.

"So what about my security request, Tom?"

"Well, I'm afraid I don't have good news on that front. My contact at the State Department told me we've already exceeded the budget twofold and that I'm to reduce the security staff from our seven round-the-clock armed guards to two . . ."

"*What*? That's insane! Two guards will only cover the front gate with maybe one taking hourly rounds. That won't work, Tom. Surely you—"

"I know, I know, Mr. Gilliam," Hennessey said, holding up a hand to cut Bryan off. "I hate it every bit as much as you do. It gouges Vigilant Eye's bottom line quite a bit. But the State Department is payin' the freight on this and they have the final word. My guy says Gilliam's Guidepost doesn't need as much protection now that the dinosaur threat is winding down. Tomorrow I have to send most of my people back to Missoula. I'm sorry. I know it's not what you wanted, but—"

"Your *guy*—that tightwad bureaucrat fed—has never even been to Montana, let alone my ranch. How the hell would he know how much protection is needed here? And you know my request for more security doesn't have anything to do with dinosaurs in the wild. I need protection for the ten animals I've got here in captivity."

Hennessey looked away, fidgeted with a loose thread on his black uniform pants. "Look, in addition to me pulling fulltime shifts here, I'll give you my two best people at all times. That's the best I can do. Surely you can understand that my hands are tied on this."

Bryan felt revulsion coursing through him. Everything was

going to shit. He was disappointed in Tom Hennessey for not nego-tiating harder. He was pissed off at the government penny-pincher who controlled the purse strings. He wondered if this cutting off security funding had anything to do with the meteorite cease and desist order they were ignoring.

What next? Cutting off funding for the feed program?

"Okay," Bryan said, standing, feeling a deep ache in his bones from the stress and sleep deprivation of the past few days, a soreness in his shoulders from swinging the pickaxe. "I appreciate the good work you and your company has done for us, Tom. Please do keep us staffed with your two best and brightest at all times."

"Will do, Mr. Gilliam."

As they walked back to Hennessey's truck, Bryan felt depleted. Carved out and empty. Afraid. Fearful of what might be ahead. He wondered, not for the first time, whether to tell Loretta about the phone calls and the direct threat. He thought maybe they should call off the party. Tomorrow was the sixth. The day the caller demanded action.

He'd give it another day. See if anything happened tomorrow when he didn't set loose the animals.

No use upsetting the family if I don't need to. They've been through so much already.

Front Porch Warrior

August 6: Gilliam's Guidepost
Heart Butte, Montana

LORETTA AWOKE FROM AN EROTIC DREAM that had her in bed with Brad Pitt. A liquid heat surged through her; a flash flood of runaway hormones. She reached across the bed, hands searching for Bryan. Nothing but a cool expanse of mattress there.

She sighed.

Third night in a row he's pulled his insomniac routine.

She yawned, stretched, checked the clock on her nightstand. 4:12 AM. She scanned the dim bedroom through bleary eyes. No sign that Bryan had ever come to bed.

He had been acting strange the past few days, unusually quiet and withdrawn, as if he was a victim in that body snatcher horror flick, where ordinary people are replicated into emotionless automatons. At first she thought it might be the government cease and desist order and lawsuit threat. But the attorney had cleared that up. They weren't liable for any of that. So what was eating at him, then?

Time to get to the bottom of this, Loretta.

She sat up, yawned. Swung around and dropped her feet to the floor. Sleepily went to the closet, put on her terrycloth robe and slippers. Shuffled down the hall quietly so as not to wake the kids. She negotiated her way down the dark tunnel of the stairwell, clinging tightly to the rail, entering the shadowy living room. A cluster of empty Coors bottles on the coffee table reflected pinpoints of moonlight. The yeasty fruity scent of stale beer tickled her nose, and she held back a sneeze.

She opened the door with a loud squeak and walked out onto

the front porch, the cool early-morning air waking her up. At the far end of the porch, Bryan slouched in the oak Adirondack rocker, a thin blanket draped over his shoulders, beer in one hand, his rifle flat across the chair arms. Boxes of ammunition sat on the floor by his feet next to more empty beer bottles. She pulled the collar of her robe tighter around her neck and went to him. He gave her a quick glance, then looked away, raised the bottle to his mouth and drank.

"Looks like you're prepared for Armageddon," she said, her voice piercing in the dead quiet. She took a seat in the chair next to him. "What gives, Bry?"

He was silent for a long while, staring out beyond the inn and general store to the front gate a half-mile away, where a streetlamp spotlighted a lone security vehicle. She didn't think he was going to respond and was about to speak again when he mumbled, "Nothin' gives. Just can't sleep."

"Are you fearful of a dinosaur attack?"

He didn't answer. Just finished off his beer then grabbed a fresh one out of a cooler on the far side of his chair. Twisted off the cap.

Loretta persisted. "You know, dear, Pauley told me about you wanting to beef up security. He told me he was there today when Tom Hennessey turned you down. Said they actually were going to reduce the staff. What's that all about?"

Bryan turned to her. "Our son needs to learn to mind his own business, Lor."

"This *is* Pauley's business, Bryan. It's *all* of our business. We're a family in case you've forgotten. Paul and Ethan both came to me. They were scared. For you . . . for them. For all of us. Askin' for more security when the Guidepost is guarded tighter than Fort Knox? It upset the boys. So I wanna know what gives with that request for more protection?"

Another swig of beer. The thousand-yard stare. As if she wasn't even there.

"Not gonna talk to me, huh? If I'm being honest, I'm kinda pissed off that you haven't confided in me. I've been sleeping in a cold empty bed the last three nights while you sit out here armed to the teeth . . . getting drunk. You're like your old paranoid self.

Reminds me of when you and Jimmy got back from overseas, when you were all screwed up from that horrible war. I'm not gonna go through that with you again, Bryan. So let's have it. What are you holdin' back from me?"

He turned his head and looked at her. Something dark and foreboding passed through her as she saw the fear in his eyes.

She reached over and caressed his leg under the blanket. "What is it? Talk to me, Bry. Please."

He opened his mouth to say something, then held back.

"Come on, I'm here for you, baby."

He brought his arm out from underneath the blanket. Pointed toward the front gate. "See that security truck out there?"

"Yeah. What about it?"

"In just a few hours, that'll be all the protection we'll have. Hennessey told me the feds have decided we're over budget. They're cutting back from seven round-the-clock guards to two. No way a pair of rental cops can protect a twelve-hundred-acre ranch."

"Well, you can kind of understand their point, Bry. It *has* been a bit of overkill. We haven't had any problems, even after the dinosaur bounty program went into effect."

He spoke as if he hadn't heard her. "Later today I'll get the boys to help me patrol the perimeter. I'm gonna try and enlist Jimmy and—"

"Paul and Ethan will do no such thing," she said adamantly. "I will *not* have our sons put in harm's way again. Tell me what's going on with you, dear. Why the sudden request for more security when we haven't had any trouble?"

He shook his head as though fed up, looked back out over the property. Brought the bottle to his mouth and drank. Wiped his mouth with the blanket. Finally he said, "I screwed up, Loretta. I should've told you, but . . ." He continued to shake his head sullenly.

"Told me what?" she said, not liking where this was headed.

"I, um . . . I got a disturbing call three days ago. Some asswipe from one of those animal protection groups. He, uh . . . he threatened me. Demanded I set free our dinosaurs . . . said they were God's wild animals and they deserved to run free. Told me if I didn't release them by a certain date his bunch would come and do it for me. He also implied that if I didn't do it, I would suffer. Christ, Lor. This is bad," he said, his voice trembling, his eyes misting up. "*Real bad!*"

Loretta sat back, thinking. "We've received threatening calls before. Why is this one shaking you up?"

"Because those other calls were obviously pranks . . . people having their fun callin' us names with no serious intent or demands behind them. This one was deadly serious. This guy is with some dangerous environmental terrorist group, like that bunch goin' after the dinosaur hunters. He's a hard case, Loretta. I got the impression there would be definite action taken if I didn't go along."

"What deadline did he give you?"

"Um . . . well, today. The sixth."

"Today? He only gave you three days?"

"Yeah, he was a pushy bastard. I could tell he's used to having people jump through hoops for him."

"You got his number, I'm assuming?"

"Yeah. I called it back immediately only to get a recorded message. An out-of-service number. The guy is sophisticated enough to spoof me with a fake caller ID. I'm tellin' you, this dude is an unhinged lunatic. He definitely means business."

Never seen Bryan this spooked.

"Did he call back during the last three days?"

He stared straight ahead without responding. Loretta's heart sank as she listened to him sniffle, saw the tears wetting his cheeks.

"Bryan?"

He nodded slowly. "Yeah. Yesterday morning."

"Jesus! Did he call from the same spoofed number?"

"No. Different number, but also spoofed. Also out of service."

"And how did that conversation go?"

"There was no conversation. I didn't pick up. He left a voice mail."

"Same guy?"

"Yeah."

"You have that recording?"

Bryan looked at her like she was crazy. "Of *course* I have it. I'm not gonna delete a—"

"Let's hear it!"

As Bryan fumbled under the blanket for his phone, Loretta got a serious case of the heebie-jeebies. This was indeed problematic, a threat to the entire family and guests staying at the Guidepost. She so much wanted to slap him right now, chastise him for keeping this from her. She despised him in that moment for putting the family in jeopardy.

They listened to the playback of the voice mail, the man's voice menacing in the early morning darkness:

"Hello again, Bryan. Tick, tick, tick . . . the clock pushes forward. It's been forty eight hours and I see you have taken no action. You taunt me with your delay. I don't like to be taunted, Bryan. You have another twenty-four hours to set your caged dinosaurs free. You will be very sorry if we have to come and do your dirty work for you. We will track you and your family down and kill you for the disgusting animal abusers you are. We will burn the buildings of incarceration. Gilliam's Guidepost will be left a smoldering heap of ashes when we are through . . ."

The frightening message went on for another two minutes. Nausea slammed Loretta. The guy was definitely deranged. He was threatening not only Bryan, but the entire Gilliam family for their part in "contributing to the unlawful incarceration of wild animals who have every right to experience freedom of movement the way humans do." A real, off-his-rocker whack job. And his threats were direct death threats. There was no mistaking that. Enough there to get local law enforcement involved. Maybe even the FBI.

The man is definitely a psycho. He's also an idiot for leaving a voice mail.

The message ended. Bryan and Loretta sat in stunned silence for several minutes.

Loretta took a deep breath and said, "You're not thinking of releasing the dinosaurs, are you?"

"Hell no! Are you crazed? That would be mass murder."

"So what *is* your plan? Play front porch warrior and pick off these terrorists one by one when they show up?"

"If I have to, yeah."

Loretta stared at him in disbelief. This otherwise bright and industrious man she had loved for twenty years was slipping into his ridiculous vigilante mode. Pure machismo insanity. She wanted to remind him that this was the very thing she feared happening two months ago when the national spotlight began shining on the Gilliam family and the creatures that hatched out of that stupid meteorite. Back when media throngs and crazies started showing up.

"That is absolutely *not* what you're gonna do, Bryan Richard Gilliam!" she said, surprising him with her strident tone. "Here's what we're gonna do. We're gonna contact Blackfeet Nation Law Enforcement and the Browning Police, and send them both a copy of this voice mail. We're gonna tell 'em we need help, pronto, that we could soon be under attack. Hell, if they can't—or won't—help, I'll call in the National Guard if I have to. Those animals in the Glade are a national treasure, regardless of what many people think, myself included sometimes. For the benefit of science, we can't lose them. Not to mention that setting them free will kill hundreds of people. That's for certain . . ."

She gave him an exasperated side glance and said, "Our family is my whole world, Bryan. And I believe it's your entire world as well. At least I used to think so."

She stood and grabbed the beer out of Bryan's hand. "I'm going to put on a pot of coffee. We need to get you sobered up. We have a lot of work to do, dearest husband of mine. You look up those police numbers and when I get back, we'll make the calls."

Loretta turned to go back in the house. When she got to the door, she said, "You know, I wish that fucking meteorite never came down on our property. It's been nothing but a black curse on us."

The Pit Boss
and the Pied Piper

August 8: Gilliam's Glade
Heart Butte, Montana

RECRUITING ADDITIONAL SECURITY on short notice proved
to be difficult. The Blackfeet Law Enforcement Service had just
gone through layoffs due to budget cutbacks, and could only spare
one fulltime patrolman. The Browning Police couldn't afford much
more; just one daytime officer and another covering the graveyard
shift. Bryan knew this meager supplement to the Vigilant Eye
Security guards (two-guard patrols changing out every 12 hours)
would only cover half the Guidepost, at best. Loretta contacted the
FBI field office in Billings and played the damning voice mail to
them over the phone. A jaded female desk jockey put her off, telling
her there wasn't much they could do. There just wasn't enough there
to put valuable agency resources on it, she'd said. Loretta persisted,
telling her this could be a life or death situation. The administrator
sounded like she couldn't wait to get off the phone, telling Loretta
to send them a copy of the voice mail and they would see what they
could do. More than 48 hours later and still no word from them.
Loretta was frustrated and upset, but Bryan hadn't really expected
any different response.

Bryan thought it to be fateful good luck that they had not needed
any security the past three days. The sixth—the deadline set for
Bryan to release the dinosaurs—had come and gone without incident. He and Loretta had gone about their daily routines that day,
both amped up on high anxiety, doing their best to hide their worries

from the children and guests. Yesterday, the seventh, had been equally quiet. Bryan thought he might be going mad several times playing the waiting game, his runaway angst giving him chest pains and nausea so intense he had to retreat to the house a couple of times. He was sure yesterday would be the day the terrorists would strike. But strangely, there had been no crazed animal lovers getting past the slapdash security detail. No trespassers setting free the dinosaurs. No eco-terrorists storming the grounds laying waste to the Guidepost. No menacing phone calls. And now, today, midafternoon on the day of the barbecue, there had still been no contact from the man who had threatened Bryan and promised to take no prisoners.

Is it too soon to assume we're safe now?

Will we ever really feel safe again?

Mother Nature had cooperated on this day of the cookout. Cloudless powder blue sky, low humidity, temperature in the low eighties rather than the sticky, ninety-degree weather they'd been suffering through much of the summer.

Bryan wanted desperately to believe those two frightening phone calls had been a clever bluff to coax him into doing something supremely stupid, something this nefarious animal rights bunch wanted done so they could take credit for it without having to invest anything themselves. He wanted so much to trust that he could finally relax and let his guard down. But the prolonged silence only put him more on edge. He was exhausted from the lack of sleep, the prodigious amount of alcohol he'd consumed, the constant worry. He'd had a bad feeling brewing in his gut through the morning and early afternoon, and he'd worn a path to and from the lookout posts around the property, getting up-to-the-minute security reports at each location. The cops' bored reactions told him they regarded his overwrought paranoia as unnecessary, and even a bit comical. Their casual attitudes angered Bryan. He wished they would adopt a more serious outlook instead of acting like they'd lucked into some cushy assignment. There were too many vulnerable points of entry around the perimeter for his liking.

Now nearing four o'clock, he stood in the east meadow tending to the fire pit, only slightly comforted by the knowledge he was prepared with his own brand of security should it come to that. His shotgun was loaded and ready for action in the cab of his truck parked a few steps away. His Smith & Wesson 500 revolver—a potent handheld cannon—was tucked in the glovebox. His scoped Remington Sendero deer rifle sat in the gunrack. He'd be ready should anybody get past the thin line of perimeter security.

Wearing his floppy white chef's hat—monogrammed with *Chef Gilliam*—and an apron with the legend *Pit Boss Extraordinaire* embroidered across the flank of a plump hog, he poked the long barbecue tongs through the grate, stirring up the charred hickory chips. Intense heat rose in waves, and he felt the warmth across his face. He'd been up before dawn, slathering the meats—beef brisket, two whole suckling pigs, and a 12-pound turkey—with his own special rub of olive oil, salt, garlic powder, and paprika. At daylight, he'd come out here to start smoking the foil-wrapped beef brisket. He'd returned at ten this morning to rack and roast the two suckling pigs. At noon, he'd added the turkey to the mix. The slow-cook meats were almost ready. Time to throw on the chicken and toss in the corn, carrots, onions, and potatoes. It promised to be a mouth-watering feast. It had been years since Bryan had smoked meats in a fire pit like this, and he'd forgotten how much he enjoyed large scale barbecuing.

He stirred the coals, inhaling the sweet savory scent of roasting meat and burning hickory. His thoughts took a morbid turn, realizing that if he'd been standing in this precise spot two and a half months ago, he'd be dead, obliterated by the huge meteorite that had carved out much of this barbecue pit. He recalled the thunderous explosion he'd heard that day, the ground trembling with the impact, the intensity like that of a plane crash or sonic boom. Strange how that singular event had altered the course of their lives. Stranger still is what came after.

He stole a glance at the dinosaur habitats, saw the bizarre looking creatures lounging behind the electrified fence. Spied his sign painted in a flashy blood-red Medieval script:

GILLIAM'S GLADE PREHISTORIC ZOO

Strange indeed!

The guests began arriving, pulling his attention away from the Glade. Paul started up the music. "Heat Waves" by Glass Animals blasted across the pasture. Partygoers drove down the service road into the grassy bowl of the meadow, parking their vehicles and walking down the slope to gather around the keg Loretta had just tapped near the habitat enclosures. The adults drifted between the beer keg and the picnic tables behind the bleachers, picking at the spread of appetizers Loretta and Lianne had laid out. The young people pulled cans of soda out of coolers. He saw Brinshou Lacroix pushing a stroller. Brin's mother walked beside her. Her face was nearly healed now. Ranch hands Apisi and Chogan shared a laugh as they munched on veggies. Franz Krause was involved in a serious discussion with a couple of the government biologists. Mitena, the inn's front desk clerk, accompanied her two young boys. Jimmy and Olivia Enright were engaged in conversation with Loretta near the beer barrel, Jimmy with the ever-present cigarette dangling from his lips. Lianne and Marnie Enright threw a frisbee back and forth in the open field. Ethan tossed a football with a few of the Blackfoot worker's sons. Bryan spotted Nuna, Tahki, Koko, and Nadie, his Cretaceous Stone jewelers, arriving simultaneously in three cars, their significant others and children piling out behind them. He watched Barrett Hailey get out of his car and accompany Hayden Fowler and Nora Lemoyne down the hill to join the festivities. Bryan had seen Hailey around quite a bit in recent days, but the two paleontologists had been keeping a low profile, working on their book.

This promised to be one great party.

He hoped and prayed there wouldn't be trouble.

As he tended to the grilling, Bryan observed his wife from a distance, seeing her throw her head back and laugh at something Livvy Enright said. Loretta was still peeved at him for keeping the two threatening phone calls from her. She hadn't displayed her anger in any openly demonstrative way, but rather through sarcastic quips and exasperated, impatient looks. Her snide comments and body language said it all: she was supremely disappointed in him.

He couldn't really blame her. Bryan was embarrassed by how badly he'd botched things, even though his intentions were good. He was only trying to avoid paralyzing the entire family with fear. After that first call, he really thought he was doing the right thing, shouldering the danger himself and shielding Loretta and the kids from worry. Wasn't that what a husband and father was supposed to do? Protect his family? But now, he realized he'd been shortsighted. He'd been a complete idiot. Not only did he keep the phoned threats from his wife, he hadn't even bothered to contact the authorities. He'd just hoped the whole thing would magically disappear.

The last person he wanted to hurt was Loretta Enright Gilliam, the love of his life—his *dreamcatcher,* as she liked to tell him. And yet, he had done just that—hurt her by keeping her distanced from the truth. He had kept a secret from her that could possibly result in dire consequences. He'd apologized profusely, but her demeanor told him her disappointment in him wasn't going away any time soon. And to make matters worse, he suggested they cancel the cookout, just to be safe. Loretta wouldn't hear of it. Today's barbecue was her idea and no eco-terrorist threat was going to derail it, no matter how badly her husband had screwed things up.

What the hell is wrong with you, Gilliam?

His self-chastising was interrupted by a faint thumping sound. At first he thought it was an offbeat snare drum in the music Paul was playing. But as the sound increased, he realized it was the muffled chuffing of helicopter blades whipping the air. He scanned the sky, picking up the silhouette of the chopper outlined against the backdrop of the snow-capped Rockies. As the craft neared the ranch, Bryan could make out the Montana State Forest emblem across the fuselage. He stopped tending the grill pit and followed the flight of the chopper. The chuffing was loud now, punching through the Ed Sheeran song playing over the sound system. The big whirlybird came in low over the east meadow, the downdraft fanning the prairie grass and kicking up tiny spirals of dust. The children pointed up at the copter, laughing and shouting gleefully. The adult guests paused their conversations to raise their heads in unison, gazing at the descending chopper. The helicopter made a final, sweeping turn and set down near Bryan's truck. The engine shut down and the rotor blades came to a full stop.

A small group of excited kids, including Lianne and Marnie Enright, rushed the aircraft, wanting a closer look at the fascinating flying machine.

Peter Lacroix stepped down from the cockpit dressed in his yellow polo shirt—the Montana DNRC Forest Servicepatch on the breast—khaki pants, and black boots. He peered out from under the bill of a blue Toronto Maple Leafs ball cap.

"Howdy, Bryan," he said, approaching, winding his way through the group of children, a slight limp hobbling his gait. "Looks like you're preparing quite a feast there."

"Yeah," Bryan said, going to meet him and fist bumping with him. "We've got a little of everything on the menu today . . . a meaty banquet of smoked delights."

Lacroix eyed Bryan's outfit, looking him up and down, saying, "It looks like the master chef—excuse me, *pit boss extraordinaire*—has done this a few times."

Bryan laughed. He genuinely liked this affable guy. "Yeah, this ensemble puts me in the meat smoking frame of mind," he said, looking around the pilot and over the kids, at the helicopter with its closed doors. "You flyin' solo today?"

"Yep. It's the height of fire season, so I'm on call for second shift." He glimpsed the vehicles parked in the meadow and the people gathered near the Glade. "Hope I don't have to cut out on you early. Looks like this is going to be fun. I thought I could contribute something to the party by giving the kids helicopter rides."

The comment raised the children's excitement level up a notch, Bryan hearing shouts of "Cool!" and "Take me first, I'm going first! No, *I'm* gonna be first!"

Bryan shared a laugh with Peter, and spoke to the pilot over the clamor of the youngsters. "Your wife and mother-in-law are over at the picnic tables with your baby girl. She's a little darlin' by the way."

Peter squinted in that direction, trying to keep his balance as several Blackfoot boys gathered around him, pushing and shoving, jostling him, wanting desperately to be first in line for a flight in the chopper. "C'mon, guys, let's be cool here," he said to the overly aggressive boys. To Bryan, he said, "Thanks. Kimi's the light of our life. I want to thank you again for all you and Loretta have done for us. It's really generous of you to put us up here in The Cellar. You've made a new woman out of Brin."

"Don't mention it, Pete. Lor and I love having you folks around. It's the least I can do for the guy who jumpstarted my meteorite jewelry business."

"Yeah, there *is* that." Lacroix gave Bryan a guarded side-eye that suggested his guilt in the meteorite transaction. "Brin tells me it's going quite well."

"Oh, it's been going gangbusters. So good in fact that the federal government threatened us with a lawsuit."

"Really? For what?"

"Stealing government property."

"The meteorite?"

Bryan nodded. "Some eminent domain bullshit. It was bogus. I believe your colonel friend was behind it."

"Who? Glick?"

"Yeah. I can't prove it, but I'm pretty sure it was him."

"Sounds like Glick, for sure."

"I know he's threatened you, Pete."

"Yeah, a couple of times. But nothing ever came of it."

Bryan poked through the coals. A hissing cloud of smoke rose from the pit. He coughed and waved the smoke away, said, "I wish I kept all of that damned rock."

Lacroix gave him a lazy grin. "I probably would have let you keep it all. Just to get under that old buzzard's skin."

Bryan laughed.

The pilot turned away, saying over his shoulder, "My wife and daughter await. Good chatting with you, Bryan."

Peter pushed through the throng of boys. "Okay, kids," he said, "Pilot Pete will begin the helicopter rides after he gets something to eat. We'll draw straws to see who goes first, okay?"

There was a whispery sigh of disappointment. The children had little patience. They wanted Pilot Pete to accommodate their flying wishes *now*, not later.

Bryan watched Peter Lacroix walk to the picnic tables, a pack of high-strung kids trailing close behind. The scene put him in mind of the Pied Piper.

Baby Steps

August 8: Gilliam's Glade
Heart Butte, Montana

PETER APPROACHED THE PICNIC TABLES where the adults munched on appetizers and drank beer from red plastic cups. Conversations stopped. Several partyers waved to acknowledge his arrival while others mumbled quick greetings.

Hayden Fowler addressed him with a wide grin. "Mighty impressive handling of that whirlybird there, Pete, ol' boy. You deserve the rotor-head rebel award for that dramatic entrance."

Peter was acquainted with Dr. Fowler and his lady friend, Dr. Lemoyne. They had been his next door neighbors in The Cellar for the past three weeks, but his relationship with them was limited to brief conversations in the hallway. He didn't know them well, but Peter suspected that Fowler might not be too pleased with Kimi's crying at all hours. Fowler possessed a gruff, snappish side that leaned toward arrogance, and Peter couldn't decide if the paleontologist's comment held sarcasm or sincerity. The big man's bulk and boorish demeanor made Peter uncomfortable much of the time.

He forced a grin and tipped his cap in the scientist's direction. "Hey, Hayden. Can't say I'm familiar with that award."

The half-dozen children behind him started in with their boisterous pestering. They wanted their rides *now*.

Loretta Gilliam said, "Looks like you've attracted a serious fan club."

He laughed, scanning the bright, expectant faces of the kids moving in around him. "That's what I get for offering amusement park rides."

"When're you takin' me and Nora up?" Fowler again. "You

promised me a week ago, Pilot Pete."

"I haven't forgotten you, Hayden. I'll take—"

"Don't listen to him, Peter," Nora Lemoyne cut in. "Hayden's just another impatient child suffering from arrested development."

Fowler smiled, taking the ribbing in stride. "You can see why I love this woman so much, right?" He pulled Nora close and kissed her cheek. She beamed at him and leaned her head against his shoulder.

That's quite a strange relationship they have, Peter thought, saying to Fowler, "I'll take you and Dr. Lemoyne up after I give the kids their rides."

Peter walked away, joining Brin who was walking Kimi near the bleachers. He kissed his wife and rubbed Kimi's head, the group of kids—his *fan club*—tagging along behind him. Kimi looked up at her daddy and gave him a bright-eyed smile, then giggled as she chanted "Doe-dah! Doe-dah! Doe-dah!" which made Peter's heart soar. Then, Kimi saw the children and went into her shell. Intimidated, she ducked behind Brin, clutching at her pants leg, bashfully peeking around her mother at the rowdy kids.

Peter told the kids it would be at least an hour before he started with the chopper rides, and for them to grab some food or go back to their playing. He'd call them when he was ready to fly. Reluctantly the kids obeyed, running off, shouting out unbridled cries of youthful happiness. Peter watched them scatter, wondering if his Kimi would grow up to be loud and annoying like them.

Not if I can help it!

Kimi's growth amazed Peter. It seemed like he'd go off to work in the morning, returning home in the evenings to find an entirely new miniature human being waiting for him. A little more than two months ago, when the dinosaurs returned, Peter and Brin had been concerned that Kimi was still nonverbal at 16 months. But then, three weeks ago, just after they'd moved into The Cellar here at the Guidepost, she started babbling, and soon after, began attempting to form real words. Her speech was limited to single-word utterances. But she was trying, and that thrilled Peter. She called Brin *Momo* and Brin's mother, *Gwanny*. She said *teepee* when she wanted to watch TV and *foo* when she was hungry. Kimi's attempts at basic communication was a continuing source of entertainment for Peter and Brin. They laughed and clapped, encouraging their daughter, helping her sound out words, all the while caught up in the excitement of watching their baby grow into her own little person. And last week Kimi had graduated from crawling to taking her first steps, albeit assisted. Day after day, Kimi became more vocal about being let out of her crib and stroller, wanting to stretch her stubby little legs and strut her independence.

It was all good stuff to Peter, this raising a child, though he knew it mostly fell on Brin, especially during the time he'd been away in Idaho. Since he'd been back he'd taken over nighttime baby duties to give Brin the rest she needed and deserved. It was his turn to suffer through sleep deprived nights calming his crying daughter. His turn to change out the reeking diapers. His responsibility to feed Kimi her three AM bottle. Peter didn't mind. To him, raising a child was rewarding and life affirming. He loved being a doting parent, loved being a father.

"Let's get away from these pens," Brin said, pointing at the Glade habitats. "Those creatures make Kimi nervous. I don't care much for them either. Let's walk out in the open field, okay?"

As if on cue, one of the Tyrannosaurs charged the fence and roared at them. Kimi shrieked and jumped back behind Brin, eyes wide with terror, small shoulders shaking as she cried.

Peter turned her away from the Glade and shielded her from the animals, which were screeching loudly at them now. He leaned down and spoke calmly to her, consoling her, telling her there was no way the animals could hurt her since they were caged behind a strong electrified fence. Brin made goofy faces at her, trying to get her to laugh. Her mother's ridiculous facial expressions stopped Kimi's sobs. The baby broke out a big smile, which quickly turned into the giggles. When she was more relaxed, Peter grasped her shoulder and Brin took her hand to guide her out into the meadow. Kimi took plodding, unsure steps, pointing at things and babbling incoherently as she went.

They walked, the music playing over the PA echoing across the pasture. Peter recognized the tune: "Joy of My Life" by Chris Stapleton. The mellow song and upbeat lyrics matched his ebullient mood. He glanced at Brin, and thought the words could have been written just for him, describing his feelings for his wife.

"You know, I've been thinking, babe," he said to Brin as Kimi stooped to pluck a handful of dandelions. "I think it's about time we gave her a little brother. Don't you?"

Brin stopped her forward progress and stared at Peter, her dark eyes questioning. "Are you being serious right now, Petey?"

"Of *course* I'm serious. Our little girl here is going to need a sibling to play with."

She pulled Kimi up by her hand and started walking again. "We haven't really discussed this," she said, tugging a reluctant Kimi along. "And after next week, when the jewelry work runs out here, we'll be back home in Missoula with only your income to support us. Another pregnancy? Another mouth to feed? I just don't know, honey."

"But we *have* talked about it, Brin. You've told me many times you hated being an only child, that you didn't want that for us. You've said you always dreamed of having a big family. I thought you'd be happy with this."

"We can't afford another child right now," she said. We're barely making ends meet now. And I'm not crazy about spending another nine months with a budding child in my womb. Not so soon. I still have a few years of child bearing ahead of me, Petey. Let's not rush things."

Her response knocked Peter for a loop, though he tried not to show it. Her reaction was the exact opposite of what he expected. They walked in silence for a ways, a babbling Kimi between them, Peter searching for appropriate words.

"You're mad at me, aren't you?" she said finally.

"No, not mad. Just surprised. I love you, Brin, and I want to make a big family with you. I want the same thing you've been saying you wanted."

She reached across and grabbed his hand, her touch sparking something deep inside him. "I love you so much, Petey. You have to believe that. Those weeks you were gone nearly killed me. But I'm just not ready for another child right now. And *we're* not ready financially. Someday, yes. But not now. You'll wait for me, won't you?"

Peter felt the burning stab of disappointment like a knife to his chest. He wanted to refute her logic but realized it was pointless. She had made up her mind and nothing he said would change it. And so they would wait. They'd enjoy raising Kimi. They would love each other and continue building a life together.

When he finally found his voice, he said, "I'd wait a thousand years for you, Brin. I'm fine with whatever you want, sweetie. I always have been."

Smoked Meats and Science Friction

August 8: Gilliam's Glade
Heart Butte, Montana

HAYDEN WIPED THE BARBECUE SAUCE from his beard with a napkin and dumped his plastic plate in the trash bin. He felt bloated from the meal, but it was a pleasing fullness. Some of the best beef brisket he'd ever tasted. The glazed ham was delicious as well. It was all so flavorsome he'd even gobbled down a large portion of pulled chicken. Hayden had laughed at Bryan Gilliam, who looked ridiculous running around in that idiotic chef outfit of his, but the man certainly knew how to barbecue with the best of them.

Hayden sipped his lemonade and scanned the meadow, where the kids played tag and threw a frisbee. The younger Gilliam boy rode a four-wheel ATV through the field, whooping and hollering and pumping his fist as he jounced over small hillocks. A group of kids waiting their turn for a helicopter ride cheered him on.

Hayden followed the chopper that droned overhead, circling the Guidepost in slow, lazy arcs. Gilliam—his chef's hat looking like a giant marshmallow fastened to the top of his head—stood over the fire pit, smoke spiraling from the trench, engulfing him like swirling gray fingers. The Gilliam son they called Pauley sat up in the tower overlooking the Glade habitats, playing DJ. The kid had amped up the music, increasing the volume and tempo as the guests became more inebriated. The tunes were much more to Hayden's liking now. Much better than that soft, middle of the road crap the boy was playing earlier. The big PA speakers now shook with heavy metal.

Most of it Hayden recognized: Metallica, Guns N' Roses, AC/DC, Red Hot Chili Peppers, Rammstein.

He strummed air guitar in time to the music and did his best lead guitarist moves back to his seat where Nora, Franz Krause, Barrett Hailey, Loretta Gilliam, and Jimmy and Olivia Enright sat finishing their meals. Hayden was feeling good, really enjoying himself. Great food. Decent company. Stimulating conversation. He had been against this shindig at first, thinking it would be difficult for him to be around people who were drinking. But Nora had pushed him, saying they owed the Gilliams for their generous hospitality. And she said she would make sure he didn't fall off the wagon and surrender to his old alcoholic ways. So he'd reluctantly come along, planning to duck out after chowing down. But Bryan Gilliam's mouthwatering dishes and being with Nora in a pleasant social gathering had him in a positive frame of mind. This was certainly a welcome break from work on the book. Parking his ass at the keyboard for hours at a time and writing was getting to him. And anything to get Nora out of The Cellar was a good thing.

As he reclaimed his seat next to Nora, she said, "Franz was just thanking us for letting him use our video footage at the National Geo conference."

Hayden nodded at Krause. "You're welcome. The world needs to see that stuff." He gestured toward the habitats. "People need to see that these incredible animals are much more than man-eaters and crop destroyers. They ruled this planet for a hundred-and-sixty-six million years! That's a hell of a lot longer than we humans can ever hope to be around."

Nora shook her head, said, "You're letting your misanthropic side show, darling."

"Oh, come on, sweetness," he said testily. "It's plain to see. I'm nothing if not pragmatic. The human race is too clueless and self-absorbed to survive for millions of years." He looked across the table at Krause, wanting to get off the thing Nora loved most to needle him about. "Anyway, Franz, I thought you did a bang-up job as a panelist. You used our film and images to good effect."

"Thank you, kind sir," Krause said, his Germanic inflection

sounding like *Zank you, kind zir.* "Yours and Nora's photography captured the essence of these animals. Your videos especially brought a new perspective to our prehistoric friends. Your work created a lot of positive buzz at the convention."

Nora said, "That's wonderful. We appreciate you giving us a shout-out during the broadcast, Franz."

"It was very well deserved. Gregory thanks you, too. I think he was the real star of the show. He got discussions rolling in the right direction. He set the tone for the evening."

"I thought Dulowski would be here today," Barrett Hailey said.

"Dr. Dulowski was on the invite list," Loretta Gilliam said. "You talked with him, didn't you, Nora?"

"Yes, I did. Unfortunately Greg said he wouldn't be able to make it. He stayed back east after the conference to be with his wife and kids in New Jersey. He hadn't seen them since he came out here to work the expedition."

Hayden said, "Greg has the ability to break down complex scientific concepts into layman's terms that everyday folks can understand." He looked at Nora. "My gorgeous writing partner has that same skill. Nora's a wizard with the written word. She can make the driest, most convoluted source material exciting and accessible. I might have the publishing cred, but she's the real deal. She has the authorial gift. Not me."

Nora blushed and gently slapped the top of his hand. "Stop it, Hayden. You're embarrassing me."

"How's the book coming along, Dr. Lemoyne?" Olivia Enright inquired from the far end of the table.

"Please, call me Nora. It's going okay, I guess. We're grinding it out. At least we haven't missed any deadlines yet."

"She's being her usual humble self," Hayden said. "Our publisher is ecstatic over what we've delivered so far. They're thrilled with the book."

Krause said, "Well, I'm certainly looking forward to its publication. I'm interested in reading what both of you have been through with this thing. You have been closer to this dinosaur repopulation than anybody." The German tipped his cup in the direction of the habitats. "I imagine it was thrilling to track and capture those animals in the wild."

"It was," Barrett Hailey said. "My team helped Hayden and Nora bring down the pair of Tyrannosaurs. It was exciting. A real mind-blowing experience."

Krause looked at Nora. "A lot of people we talked with were disappointed that you and Hayden weren't able to make it to the conference."

Nora glanced at Hayden, said, "We're sorry we missed it, but we have very demanding deadlines to meet."

Jimmy Enright pointed his cigarette at the Glade enclosures. "Will you look at that! The animals are all riled up. Looks like they're on amphetamines or sumpthin'."

Heads turned to look. The creatures were exhibiting strange behavior. Hayden noticed it earlier, when they first sat down to eat. The Dromaeosaurs persisted in sprinting willy-nilly, up and down the length of their pen, kicking up chunks of sod as their clawed feet dug into the turf. The Tyrannosaurs were rattling the fences with aggressive tail slaps and head butts, the electric coils buzzing with the contact, the animals squealing from the shocks. The Triceratopses had knocked over their water trough and were rooting around in the mud, snorting and grunting like big, agitated hogs. Hayden had never seen this kind of hyperactivity from these animals.

"I think it's the loud music that's got them excited," Loretta Gilliam said, standing. "My son gets carried away with his music sometimes. I'll go tell Pauley to tone it down."

"You can do that if you want, Mrs. Gilliam," Krause said, "but I'm pretty sure it's the smell of the roasting meat that has them worked up. These carnivorous 'saurs possess acute olfactory senses. Every whiff of that barbecue smoke is a strong stimulant . . . like a jolt of speed to them . . . the promise of a tasty meal. I don't know why the Triceratops are acting that way, but I suspect they are reacting to the behavior of the meat eaters and mimicking them."

Loretta stood at the head of the table, frowning. "Perhaps I should tell my husband to shut down the fire pit, then?"

"Too late for that, Loretta," Nora said. "I think the best thing to do is feed them."

Loretta nodded and raised her arm to look at her watch. "The animals missed their regular afternoon feeding session. I'll get the boys and Apisi to feed them before nightfall."

"Nora's right," Hayden said. "Some of those big beef slabs and a few bales of hay should satisfy 'em . . . take the edge off."

Hayden watched Loretta round up her sons. A few minutes later the music cut off. He heard the buzzing from the electric fences and the grunting-snorting-shrieking of the dinos more clearly now.

Jimmy Enright lit up a cigarette and stared at the rough activity taking place in the enclosures. Frown lines etched his forehead. "I sure hope that fence is strong enough to hold 'em," he said. "It'd sure be a hell of a mess if they escaped."

"Don't worry about it, Enright," Hayden said. "They aren't big enough to bring down that fence. Not yet, anyway. A couple of months from now, however . . ." He left the sentence hanging, causing the others at the table to gawk at him apprehensively. "Oh don't give me that look, people. Nora and I have been trying to find homes for them in a national park. Gilliam doesn't want to hear it, but they can't stay here a whole lot longer."

"I agree," Barrett Hailey said. "Have you had any luck?"

"Not yet. There's been opposition, as you might imagine."

Hayden took a sip of his lemonade, then said to Krause, "I'm glad the symposium went well. I'm a little bummed that we weren't able to make it to D.C. We enjoyed watching you and Dulowski do your thing. You both were great. But I sure can't say the same for those two astrophysicists that presented with you, Franz. A lot of their talk was . . . I don't know . . . *fuzzy*. Clouded in doublespeak. I mean, I'm an overeducated scientist—just a bone and fossil scientist, granted—but even I had a difficult time following a lot of it. Wormholes? Dark matter? The space-time continuum? Collapsing space? Distance recalibration? I mean, I understand gravitational events due to solar disturbances might have caused the meteor showers, and hence, our meteorites. I get that. But after that they lost me. I have to agree with the skeptics in the audience. It sounded like a lot of sci-fi fantasy to me."

Franz Krause gave Hayden a stern look. "It's definitely *not* science fiction, Hayden. While in D.C. I spent a good deal of time with Dr. Mallory and Dr. Rayburn, and, to a lesser extent, the moderator Dr. Corella Britton. The three of them worked hard to arrive at their theory of dinosaur repopulation. Through our many offline discussions, they convinced Gregory and me—and even Bill Blazenhurst—of its validity. Yes, much of it is speculative, and very difficult for the human mind to grasp. But when you break it all down into smaller segments, it begins to make sense. The physics of it. The biological factors involved. The shrinkage of time and space. You might recall that Gregory and I came up with a similar theory early on, though it was barebones . . . not as complete or sophisticated as the views of the astrophysicists."

Hayden just couldn't buy into it. Not completely. He was surprised someone like Dr. Franz Krause, a brilliant scientist of international renown, a man whom he admired and respected for his logical, analytical mind, *did* believe it.

"I don't know, Franz. I think that if—"

"We've all *seen* the dinosaurs," Krause continued, cutting Hayden off. "We've *seen* the meteorites that delivered the eggs to us. We've *seen* the eggs hatch out. That's the reality of it. There's no disputing those facts. Something big happened in the natural world to cause it, and to my way of thinking, my astrophysicist friends have the best explanation for it. Since we're talking about interstellar space, the only way to illuminate it is through hypothetical scenarios based on established scientific principles. I wish we had definitive, airtight methods to prove it, but we don't. Dr. Rayburn has been challenging listeners of his podcast to come forth with alternative theories, but so far no one has. Dr. Mallory has put forth a similar challenge to the scientific community. Same thing. No one has offered anything that comes close to the technical credibility of the Mallory-Rayburn-Britton Theory of Terrestrial Cretaceous Rebirth, as it has come to be known. Most top astrophysicists and astronomers believe their theory to be plausible. The general scientific consensus is that it's rock solid."

Hayden shook his head. "Well, like I said, I'm just a bone and fossil guy, so what do I know? I'm Earthbound. You start talking intergalactic space and I'm way out of my comfort zone."

He noticed Peter Lacroix approach the table with a broad smile. This time he didn't have a group of kids trailing in his wake.

"Okay, guys, your turn," Lacroix said, tipping his cap at Hayden and Nora. "Are you ready to fly the beautiful skies of Gilliam's Guidepost with me?"

Breaking Out the Bulls

August 8: Gilliam's Glade
Heart Butte, Montana

BRYAN HAD FINISHED COOKING FOR THE DAY and sat, finally getting his chance to eat. The brisket was tender and lean, his beer ice cold and sudsy. He was exhausted and grungy, his skin greasy from the barbecue smoke, but the food and drink were slowly reviving him. Loretta sat across from him, picking at her grilled chicken salad. It was just the two of them at the table, the other adults having migrated to the beer keg and wine table. The kids played in the meadow; Ethan had organized a softball game that included all but the youngest of the children. With the music shut down, Bryan could hear the *thwack* of the bat slapping the ball and excited shouts as a Blackfoot boy ran the bases.

"Isn't it about time for the boys to feed the animals?" he asked Loretta between bites of brisket.

"They're waiting for Apisi and Chogan to load the trailer. We just received a new shipment of meat blocks and wheat straw."

Bryan felt his phone vibrating in his shirt pocket and set his knife and fork down, pulled it out and checked the display. Made a face.

Loretta looked up from her salad, tense. "Who is it?"

"Peter Lacroix," he said, the surprise evident in his voice. "I thought he was up in the chopper giving Fowler and Nora a ride."

He answered the call. "Hey, Pete. What gives? Aren't you giving our guests the aerial tour of the Guidepost."

"I am. We're flying over your southern border and I have to ask you, Bryan. Are you having work done out here?"

The sound of the rotors cut through Peter's words. Bryan felt a disconcerting tug in his gut. "No. Why are you asking?"

"Well, a truck pulling a flatbed trailer with two big bulldozers just drove up the tractor path and parked. Three offroad vehicles are behind it—looks like a Land Rover and two Jeep Wranglers. I count nine men that I can see. Some of them are carrying rifles. They don't look like any construction crew I've ever seen."

"Say *what?*" Bryan said, giving Loretta a startled look across the table. "Did you say armed men and *bulldozers?*"

"Yep. They're offloading the dozers now. It's crazy . . . wait a minute . . . I'm gonna circle back around . . ." Bryan waited, phone to his ear, hearing the rotors thwapping out a sharp cadence. After a painfully long pause, Peter spoke. "One of the bulldozers just flattened the fence. Rode right over it. Took two of the posts with it. The other dozer's following close behind. Looks like they're headed your way."

A pair of bulldozers? Men with guns? Christ!
They're finally making their move!

Panic speared Bryan in the stomach. He stood and moved away from the table, vertigo making his head swim. This group had done their homework. They had studied the Guidepost layout thoroughly. The southern corner of the property was the furthest distance from the Glade and was marked by the most susceptible, dilapidated fencing. The dirt tractor path gave vehicles easy access in from Birch Creek Road.

He heard Peter say, "They're aware of us now. A few of them are pointing up at us."

Bryan's heart pumped furiously. He could feel his pulse pounding in his head. "Hightail it out of there, Pete!" he screamed. "Those men are dangerous!"

Peter said. "Who the hell are these guys, Bryan? I can't believe it. They're actually taking potshots at us."

"It's an animal rights bunch. They're here to set our animals free," Bryan shouted, hyperventilating, the adrenaline surge making him dizzy.

"*What?*"

"Yeah. They're a bunch of lunatics! Just get out! Get away, get away, get away!"

"Roger that. I'm heading back to the Glade now."

"No, Pete. *Do not* come back here. It's not safe. Fly to The Cellar. I believe there's enough clearance to land out there. Then you and Fowler and Nora go to your suites and stay there. This is serious. It's gonna get ugly."

"Screw that! My wife and daughter are there. Brin's mother, too. I'm not gonna abandon my family . . . no way! We'll be back in a few."

Peter ended the call.

Bryan gawked at his silent phone, picturing a bad end with the helicopter returning to the Glade. His thoughts were in a jumble. He tried to anticipate how much time he had. Had difficulty computing things in his feverish mind.

Loretta stared at him, her face frozen in fear and disbelief.

He tucked the phone in his pocket and ran to his pickup, grabbed the two rifles and the Smith and Wesson revolver from the glovebox. Trotted back to the picnic table and tossed his keys to Loretta, yelling, "Take the truck! Grab the kids and get up to the house, Lor," he said, breathless. "Lock all the doors and stay there."

Loretta looked at the keys in her hands, then at the rifles strapped over his shoulder. "Damnit, Bryan! I'm not gonna let you run off and play superhero. No way! You're gonna get yourself killed."

"We don't have time to argue about this, Loretta. Get the kids and go to the house. *Now*! I'll be there soon."

Loretta gave him a long, damning look. "You'd *better* get there soon," she huffed before sprinting into the meadow to collect Lianne and the boys.

Her reaction stung him, but there was precious little time to waste. He raced for the observation tower where the sound system was located, planning to broadcast a Mayday warning. The wooden tower overlooking the Glade habitats would give him a better vantage point of the trespassers coming in from the south and a more direct line of fire.

He stopped at the base of the tower and leaned his rifles against the steps, watching Loretta frantically gesturing to the guests, hearing her shouts to parents to get their children and head back up the hill to the barns.

Chaos ensued.

People stumbled and bumped into each other, confused as to what was happening.

Bryan returned his focus to the task at hand, speed dialing security at the front gate. No one picked up. He tried a second time. Same result.

Shit! Where are you, Tom Hennessey? Where is my security?

He strapped his rifles over his shoulder and started up the tower steps. The sound of gunshots coming from the direction of the front gate stopped him in his tracks.

Is a second wave trying to bust in through the front?

Is my security detail in a shootout with them?

Flashbacks from his firefights with the Taliban unspooled in his head.

His legs rubbery, he climbed the remaining stairs to the top, entering the small room where he faced a board of knobs and switches that controlled the sound system, Glade spotlights, and electric fences. From this elevation, he had good visibility overlooking the habitats and surrounding fields.

A sudden jolt shook him. The tower floor trembled, knocking him up against the console board.

Below him, the Tyrannosaurs slammed into the fence with brute force.

The Dromaeosaurs ran in circles, taking running leaps at the fence, squealing as sparks flew from the hot wires.

The Triceratops used their horns and stumpy front legs, trying to dig under the fence.

Bryan's prehistoric zoo animals were completely unhinged.

Looking out beyond the enclosures, he spotted a white Land Rover leading the pair of bulldozers up over the rise, approaching slowly across the scrubby field. He wished he had binoculars. From this distance—maybe 700 yards—it was difficult to make out details, but he thought he detected men with rifles hugging the sides of both bulldozers.

His hands shook and his fingers were jittery as he punched the three numbers into his cellphone.

"*9-1-1. What's your emergency?*"

"HELP! We're under siege!"

Wounded Bird

August 8: Gilliam's Guidepost Flyover
Heart Butte, Montana

NORA FELT THE TERROR IN HER BONES. She clung to Hayden with a death grip. A bunch of rednecks riding bulldozers were shooting at them from below!

Peter Lacroix, a scowl on his face, worked the controls with angry deliberation, lifting the chopper out of shooting range. He was tense, his usual carefree personality absent.

Nora gazed at the pock marks marring the two small Plexiglas panels in the floor near the foot pedals. Peter had informed them they were vertical reference windows, used as a visual landing aid and an eye on the skids. Fortunately the bullets hadn't penetrated the glass, but she considered whether a well-placed shot couldn't bring them down in a violent death spiral. She shivered with the thought. She hoped and prayed Peter Lacroix had the skill and composure to get them to safety.

Nora felt for him. His aircraft had been shot up. His wife, baby daughter, and mother-in-law were in jeopardy back at the Glade. He was holding up well considering.

She peered out the side window. A white SUV bounced over the rutted pasture, leading the two lumbering bulldozers. Gunmen rode the side running boards of the dozers.

She leaned into Hayden, speaking close to his ear to be heard over the chopper's loud drone. "What are you thinking?"

His breath was warm in her ear. "I was afraid something like this might happen—a bunch of pointy headed morons thinking they're doing the world a favor. I warned Gilliam about this weeks ago, but he didn't listen. Or didn't care. Some of these animal protection groups are really hardcore. Terrorists, actually. You can see how violent their ways are. It's sad. It's *dangerous*, and quite frankly, despicable."

"You think they're going to get away with it, Hayden? You think they'll succeed?"

"Hell no! These halfwits are gonna pay a steep price. They've damaged government property, not to mention endangering lives. They're already guilty of assault with deadly weapons. There's criminal trespass involved. If they succeed in taking down the habitat fencing, they're facing serious vandalism charges. And if they let loose even one of those dinosaurs, the feds will come down on them hard. Those animals are valuable scientific assets, protected by government statutes."

"We're in trouble, aren't we?"

"Don't worry, sweets," he said. "We'll get through this." He pulled her close and massaged her shoulder.

Within three minutes they were swooping in over the Glade. Nora saw the confusion on the ground, the bedlam of people running for their vehicles, cars moving along the dirt road leading out of the meadow. She saw the dinosaurs running haphazardly in their pens, the Dromaeosaurs attempting to scale the fence.

Peter Lacroix's voice in the speakers startled her. "Holy shit! What the hell is *that*?"

Nora leaned forward, getting a look through the cockpit bubble, seeing what Peter was seeing. Smoke and fire in the distance, beyond the Glade habitats. Could it be? Oh, god, no! Gilliam's Guidepost was engulfed in flames. It looked like every building on the homestead was burning—the family house, the inn, the general store, the barns and horse stables. The ridge was lit up in a hazy yellowish-orange like a scene from a war zone.

Hayden leaned over. "You can add arson to their list of charges. These cretins will be going away for a long time."

"Dear god, I hope no one is trapped in those buildings," she said, trying to keep the distress she was feeling out of her voice.

"I believe most were still at the barbecue when we left."

"I hope you're right," she said, hearing Peter calling his wife on his cell, asking where she and the baby were, and whether Brin's mother was with them. Brinshou told him they were all in the car getting ready to head up the hill to the utility barn.

"No, no, no!" Peter shouted. "The Gilliam compound is on fire. It's not safe to go there. Tell everyone you can, Brin, and stay right where you are. I'm coming to get you, babe. Don't leave, do you hear me? I'll be there to pick you up in a few minutes."

"Okay, Petey. Please hurry! It's crazy here! Kimi's really upset and I can't calm her down. Mother's a wreck, too."

Peter disconnected and made a radio call to his superiors in Missoula. His words were rushed and anxious. "Dispatch, this is Pilot Lacroix in Treetop-Five, reporting a massive fire at the Gilliam Guidepost ranch in Heart Butte. All onsite structures are burning and fire is moving toward the edge of heavily forested area. Arson is suspected so accelerants might be in play. Need emergency wildfire crews here ASAP. Over."

Nora felt a crushing bleakness. Silently she prayed for the Gilliam family and their party guests. She also prayed Peter would get them back to the east meadow before the bulldozers and homicidal gunmen stormed in.

But then where do we go?

Gunfire in the Glade

August 8: Gilliam's Glade
Heart Butte, Montana

BRYAN BROKE OUT THE SOUTH-FACING WINDOW of the Glade tower and sighted the approaching vehicles through his rifle-scope. The invaders were 500 yards out, moving slowly. The heavy crawler bulldozers lumbered over the uneven field, the Land Rover out front providing a shield. He couldn't tell how many rode in the SUV due to the dark tinted windows. At least three gunmen rode on the dozers.

Still too far away to get off an accurate shot. He'd let them get closer before opening up on them. His ammunition was limited and he couldn't afford to waste any on low percentage shots.

Just then he detected a shivery movement in his peripheral vision to his right. He turned. Could not believe what he was seeing. Their family house burned. Flames leaped high into the dusky sky, painting the ridge a sickly shade of yellow. Smoke billowed from the adjacent structures—the inn, the store, barns, stables—funnels of ashy fire circling, twisting, spiraling from the roofs and windows.

An icy dread raced down his spine. Surely his eyes deceived him. The scene made no logical sense. *These assholes wouldn't go that far, would they?* And then he came to the stark realization that they would. It was happening in real time. The reality of it hit him. He'd been so focused on the invading bulldozer army he'd missed it. They were attacking from two sides.

Bryan thought he would be sick. A crushing hollowness emp-tied out his soul. He felt a sense of extreme violation as he watched his family residence burn in the distance. Quickly, his despair bloomed into a vengeful rage.

I spent the better part of my life building the Guidepost, only to see it destroyed by this gang of thugs. It's not enough for them to set free my dinosaurs. These psychos want to take everything.

The bastards!

I'll kill every last one of them!

And then his fevered mind cleared, remembering he'd given his keys to Loretta and told her to take the kids to the house. She might not be able to see the fire from where they were down on the ground. He spun to his left and scanned the east meadow, searching for his truck. Saw it advancing up the slope to the pasture road, the back of Loretta's and the kids' heads visible through the rear window. He pulled out his cell phone and called her.

"Lor, those monsters have torched our home," he said in a breathless rush. "You can't go there!"

"I know. Brin just told us. Her husband saw it from the air. It's awful, Bry," she said, her voice shaky. "I don't understand why someone would do this."

"I don't either, but—"

"We're headed for The Cellar. It's quite a traffic jam."

"I see that. Drive through the fields if you have to. Just get there and stay there!"

"Please come down off that tower and join us, Bryan. Don't be a hero."

He turned and eyed the oncoming bulldozers. Closer now. He shuddered as he took in the size of the dozers—enormous construction crawlers with enclosed cabs and running boards along the sides where the gunners rode. Big blades up front. Expensive machinery. This bunch was well financed.

"I love you, Lor. But this is something I have to do. Get down into The Cellar and don't come out. I'll be there soon."

He ended the call after hearing her say "I love you, too, baby. *Please* don't be a fool."

He was about to return the phone to his shirt pocket when he noticed the voice mail message icon flashing on the display. He opened it and listened, keeping an eye on the advancing terrorists.

Same voice that had threatened him twice before:

"You let your guard down, Bryan. And you ignored our wishes. We do not take kindly to being snubbed. For that you will pay dearly. We—the stewards of the Animal Emancipation Faction— are here to do what we so graciously gave you the chance to do yourself. Today will go down in history as one of the great acts of animal liberation. We are here to free the dinosaurs from your inhumane prehistoric zoo. We are here to kill everyone involved with the incarceration and mistreatment of these fine animals. That includes the scientists who have inflicted their barbaric medical tests on them. And especially you, Bryan, and your family, who have used them for fame and profit. They are God's creatures and were born to run wild, not to be prisoners in your pathetic zoo. We are here to destroy everything connected with your evil operation, Gilliam. Today will be the day that the world learns of the Animal Emancipation Faction. Long live the AEF! And Goodbye, Bryan Gilliam."

The convoy was nearing the fence on the far side of the habitats. Close enough now.

With shock and furious indignation, Bryan jammed the phone in his shirt pocket and turned back to the Glade enclosures. Took aim with his Remington Sendero.

He was distracted momentarily by the *thwap-thwap-thwap* of the Forest Service helicopter flying overhead, coming in low, preparing to touch down in the east meadow. A couple of the gunners riding the dozers raised their rifles and fired on the chopper. Peter Lacroix expertly maneuvered the copter out of range. The gunners continued to shoot skyward, exposing themselves to Bryan, giving him excellent clearance to make killing shots.

Bryan seethed with anger as he fired on the operator of the lead bulldozer. The direct hit did nothing more than spider-web the windshield. *Damn! Bulletproof glass!*

He drew a bead on a gunner riding the nearest crawler, knocking him off with a shot to the chest. Another shot took off the side of the second gunner's face, a trail of bloody brain matter spraying across the cracked dozer windshield. He swung his rifle to the right and took a shot at the Land Rover. The windshield shattered and the SUV veered wildly to the right.

A direct hit on the driver.

You will not take my home, goddamnit!

He bent to one knee and reloaded, hands shaking.

The crawlers kept coming, striking the fence on the far side of the Tyrannosaurus Rex habitat in tandem, bringing down the chain-link in a screeching clatter.

The vehicles motored into the Tyrannosaurus Rex enclosure.

One of the Tyrannosaurs rushed out over the downed fence and took off running into the east meadow. The other T-Rex remained in the habitat, eyeing the human intruders, circling one of the bull-dozers, aggressively charging it and lunging at a gunner. The six foot beast swiftly plucked the gunner off the side of the dozer, whipping its head side to side with the screaming man securely clamped in its powerful jaws. The Tyrannosaur hesitated for a long moment, searching the habitat with its alert crimson eyes, then slammed the gunner's body to the turf and ripped him apart with its rows of deadly teeth. One more look around, then the creature dipped its massive head and feasted, repeatedly raising its head to gobble down the gunner's bloody torso, arms, legs, and head.

The AEF gunmen opened up a scorched earth assault on the tower. Bryan ducked under the console as bullets peppered the walls. Wood splinters sprayed around him. The window behind him blew out, chips of safety glass raining down on him. He popped up and fired, hitting the last remaining dozer gunman in the shoulder, the blast knocking him to the ground. Bryan saw he was wounded but still alive, and was about to shoot him again when he saw the Tyrannosaur pounce on him, ripping him limb from limb, gulping down body parts in three head-jerking swallows. The animal then proceeded to devour the bodies of the other two dead AEF gunmen in similar fashion.

Bryan ducked more return fire, then popped up, taking a shot then ducking again. The Land Rover now followed the bulldozers through the Glade. Most of the SUV's windshield was gone, exposing the wounded driver and two other men. Bryan rose and shot, scoring a direct hit on the driver, finishing him off. The Land Rover came to a stop. The other two men jumped out and stooped behind the stalled SUV, firing at the tower.

Bryan was delirious with rage, adrenaline coursing through him like a turbulent river. He watched the bulldozers hit the Dromaeosaur habitat fence with force, the heavy blades pushing it inward, the massive treads (track grousers) crushing the solid steel posts and rolling up and over the chain-link with a screeching crunch. The shorted-out electric circuitry popped and sizzled on the ground. The Dromaeosaurs leaped over the downed fence and scattered, three of them running to the picnic tables where food items had been left. The other three followed the Tyrannosaur out into the east meadow.

Bryan heard screams coming from the meadow. He turned in time to see a few party stragglers sprinting for their lives. A Dromaeosaur brought down a man he could not identify, slamming him up against a parked car, gutting him with its hind claws. The man's dying shrieks resonated across the meadow, mournful and unsettling. Another Dromaeosaur leaped on what looked like Mitena— the young Blackfoot woman who worked the front desk at the inn— tearing into her midsection with its powerful jaws. He was shocked at how terrifyingly quick and vicious the undersized Dromaeosaurs were. He looked on as the escaped Tyrannosaurus Rex dismembered the body of another woman on the ground, the animal ripping bloody strips of flesh from the corpse. A terrible tableau. This grisly scene was the most disturbing thing he'd witnessed since the depravity of his tours in Afghanistan. His friends were being annihilated by prehistoric carnivores. Just an hour ago his guests were eating his barbecue and having a good time. And now . . . ?

He began to weep, his shoulders shaking with each sob.

How did we ever get to this point?

Bryan felt his beef brisket coming up. He dropped down on the floor and vomited a great gush of half-digested barbecue.

He lay there, gasping for air, the bitter taste of bile in his mouth. His arms and legs were heavy. The stench of his puke increased his nausea.

Such a waste. None of this had to happen. Nobody had to die.

He was overwhelmed by a daunting despair. He lay on the floor, curled in a fetal position, trying to tamp down his queasiness. He listened to the pings and ricochets of bullets plinking the steel floor beneath him.

All of this is on me. I'm responsible for this shootout. I'm to blame for the deaths of my party guests.

The window to his left shattered. He tucked his head as glass chips rained down on him. The all-out assault on the observation tower continued for several eternal minutes.

Bryan considered his slim odds for survival.

I'm trapped up here. There's no safe way down.

He lay there, enveloped in his overwhelming melancholy, listening to the shooting barrage. He tried his old VA shrink's positivity mantras, but none of Dr. Richardson's methods clicked. The good doctor's elevator analogy did him no good now; he felt like he was at the bottom level of hell.

I am doomed to die here in this shot-up tower.

Maybe this is the end I deserve.

He listened to the rumbling of the bulldozers and the groan of motorized vehicles on the move. The thought struck him of how selfish it was of him to consider dying up here. That would be the easy way out. He had three children who needed him and a wife who loved him despite his many flaws. He got himself into this mess and had dragged his family into it as well. He knew damn well he should be with them right now. He had to find a way out of this somehow. He owed that much to his family.

The shooting came to an abrupt end.

Shouts cut through the stillness. Familiar voices.

Jimmy Enright?

Bryan heard two more distinct voices. Blackfoot words. Unmistakably his ranch hands, Apisi and Chogan.

He heard Jimmy Enright again, cussing a blue streak.

Bryan carefully lifted himself from the floor, peeked over the shattered console down into the Glade.

The shooting started up again.

Jimmy had pulled his Jeep in from the meadow and crouched

behind it, firing off rifle rounds at the bulldozers that had circled back around after freeing the Triceratops.

Apisi and Chogan were on the flatbed trailer of the dinosaur feed truck, behind the meat blocks, exchanging fire with the Land Rover gunners. Apisi and Chogan cried out with each shot, their *yee-ha* shrieks adding an eerie soundtrack to the firefight. Bryan recognized their shouts as Blackfoot war cries, the two ranch hands emulating battleground vocalizations from their great ancestors.

God bless 'em. Jimmy too. They're my saviors. Be careful, guys. Don't want to lose any of you.

Keeping low and out of the line of fire, Bryan shook his head. It was all too bizarre. His home of eighteen years burning. Bulldozers on the attack. Dinosaurs loose and hunting human prey. Indian war whoops. Gunfight in the Glade.

Utter insanity.

The two dozer operators shut down the crawlers and picked up rifles. They stepped down out of the cabs and ducked behind the big blades to support the two shooters from the SUV in the gunfight, exchanging fire with Jimmy Enright in the middle of what had been the T-Rex habitat.

With the trespassers' attention focused on Jimmy, Apisi, and Chogan, Bryan saw an opportunity to escape. He shouldered his shotgun and grabbed his Remington rifle, shoved the revolver in his waistband. Started down the steps, keeping an attentive eye on the action in the Glade.

As he creeped down the steps he saw Jimmy take out a bulldozer rifleman and Apisi nail one of the Land Rover shooters.

And then Bryan saw a T-Rex, moving stealthily through the sycamore trees lining the east side of the habitats. The beast was crouched in hunting mode, circling around behind Jimmy, stalking him.

"Oh no you don't! Not on my watch!" Bryan said aloud, taking aim on the creature, trying to get a clear shot at the animal as it moved between the trees, then broke into the clearing charging Jimmy's back.

A split second before he pulled the trigger, Bryan felt a bullet rip through his left shoulder, spinning him around, causing his shot to sail high and wide of the Tyrannosaur. A second bullet caught him in the gut. He toppled over the railing, falling fifteen feet, hitting the hard turf awkwardly.

Stunned, he lay spread-eagled at the base of the tower, unable to move. He was disoriented and confused. His head throbbed. Excruciating pain gripped him. An alarming amount of blood pooled beside him. His shoulder was on fire. Every attempt at movement was agony. He peered at his left leg, shocked to see the unnatural way his calf was twisted around. Definitely some broken bones.

The pre-dusk sun dimmed.

Sounds diminished.

His senses were shutting down. His world was going dark.

You've been such a fool, Bryan ol' buddy. Survived two bloody tours in Afghanistan and this is how you're going to die?

A penetrating cold seeped through him. A deep-freeze chill. He couldn't stop shivering.

He heard sirens in the distance, faint but clear.

Please hurry . . .

The last thing Bryan Gilliam saw before blacking out was the Tyrannosaurus Rex dragging what was left of Jimmy Enright's body into the trees.

Refugees

August 8: The East Meadow
Gilliam's Guidepost
Heart Butte, Montana

PETER HAD JUST LANDED THE HELICOPTER at the far end of the meadow. Brinshou ran for it, toting Kimi in her backpack carrier. The extra weight strapped to her back slowed her progress, as did her mother Kachina, whom Brin pulled along by her hand.

Gunshots boomed in the Glade.

Shrill screams and desperate cries for help behind them.

Kimi wailed frantically.

Brin ran on rubbery legs. Her heart raced triple time. She gasped for air, her lungs burning. Sweat drenched her blouse. She thought she would lose it at any moment, but knew she had to keep them moving. To stop meant sure peril.

It seemed the harder and faster she ran the further away Peter's helicopter got, like she was running in place in one of those dreams of frustration she'd had so often.

Things had unraveled so fast. Shortly after Peter called her from the air notifying her that the Gilliam ranch was on fire, Brin had heard gunshots and seen those big bulldozers knock down the habitat fences. She and Kachina had watched from the picnic tables as many of the freed dinosaurs streaked into the meadow, on the attack. They'd seen the government scientist, Barrett Hailey, chased down and dismembered, chunks of his flesh stripped from bones and swallowed in several swift gulps.

Brin was shocked senseless at the swift violence of it.

Her shock had quickly given way to self-preservation. Her flight response kicked in. They'd left everything in the picnic area and made a run for it.

"We're going to die," Kachina yelled as they sprinted through the grassy pasture.

Brin didn't need her mother's frightful anguish. The baby's bawling didn't help her frame of mind either. Brin was plenty scared herself, thinking that any second those men setting the fires and shooting up the Glade would turn their attention to them. And then there were those fearsome carnivores.

Brin picked up her pace.

"We're going to be fine, Mother," she gasped to Kachina, hoping she sounded confident. "Just stay with me. Try and keep up and don't let go!"

They ran.

They neared the parked helicopter. The downwash from the overhead rotor fanned warm air in her face. Brin shoved her mother up into the chopper and jumped in, sliding the door closed behind her. One of the creatures took a running leap from fifteen feet away and smacked into the side of the craft with a resounding thud.

Kachina screamed and jumped back, falling to the floor. Brin shrieked. Kimi howled an ear-piercing cry.

The noise increased in the cabin as Peter revved the engine and kicked the rotors into high gear. Brin watched her husband work the pitch stick and tamp the foot pedals. She felt it in her stomach as the chopper lifted. Listened to Peter communicating with dispatch, announcing an estimated time of arrival.

Nora Lemoyne said, "Are you ladies okay?"

Brin nodded, attending to Kimi while trying to catch her breath.

"Those Dromaeosaurs are extremely aggressive," Nora said. "Pound for pound, they're every bit as vicious as the T-Rexes."

"Yeah," Hayden Fowler agreed. "In another two months they'll be able to take the sides off this helicopter."

"Are you okay, Petey?" Brin said, touching his shoulder.

"I'm fine, and so are my passengers. You've got the best pilot in America at the controls. No need to worry, babe," Peter said. "I'm taking us to a safe place."

"Where? The Cellar?"

"Hell no! This place is a war zone. We're flyin' back to Missoula."

"Home?"

"Gotta get this wounded bird back to the heliport. After that we'll go home."

She reached across the seat and grabbed her mother's trembling hand. Kachina looked haunted, devastated. Brin squeezed her hand and mouthed the words, "We're okay now."

She questioned whether she was trying to convince her mother or herself. Brin hated flying in these loud death traps, even if being flown by the best pilot in America.

She squinted out the window into the low-lying sun as they flew over the Gilliam ranch. The pair of Dromaeosaurs that had been chasing them dashed through the field below. Brin took in the wreckage of the Glade and the big yellow bulldozers inside, the tangle of downed chain-link fence. They flew west, over the fires raging across the Gilliam compound, Peter maneuvering the chopper around twisting black spirals of smoke.

As they headed west to Missoula, Brin thought sadly: *Petey was right. Gilliam's Guidepost is indeed a war zone.*

She bowed her head and said a silent prayer for the Gilliam family. She hoped the Great Spirit was listening.

Lianne's Talisman

August 8: Gilliam's Glade
Heart Butte, Montana

LORETTA'S HANDS SHOOK AS SHE GRIPPED the wheel. She saw the Dromaeosaurs darting between cars up ahead and braked. The pickup jerked to an abrupt stop.

Troubled, she looked across the seat at the kids. Lianne, Ethan, and Paul sat rigid, silent, stunned expressions marking their young faces. They had seen so much.

Too much.

Exasperated, she let loose a string of curses and beat on the wheel. She would have to take them through the old mining field, which was littered with rocks and rusted barbwire.

"You said potty words, Mama." Lianne's voice sounded thin and scared.

"I know, Lee. I'm sorry," Loretta said, knowing she had to keep it together for the sake of her children. Especially Lianne. "Mommy shouldn't have said that, sweetie." She leaned forward and looked up through the windshield, spotted Peter Lacroix's helicopter overhead whipping through the smoke-hazed air.

"You look scared, Mama."

"I'm just tired, baby."

Completely drained and in shock is more like it. A hundred years of therapy won't erase what we've been through.

"Look at those things," Paul said, coming out of his daze, pointing at the quick moving Dromaeosaurs. "Man, they really freak me out."

They freaked Loretta out, too. They had to be four feet tall now.

She remembered when they were small hatchlings, able to be contained in 30-gallon aquarium tanks. That had been just a couple of months ago. They had an agility to their movements that terrified her, and they had incredible spring in their legs. She had watched the creatures attempt to scale the fence when the terrorists attacked, getting as high as ten feet before the electrodes zapped them back into the enclosure. And those teeth! Like a mouth full of razor-blades.

Loretta was frazzled, teetering on the edge of a nervous breakdown. She still couldn't quite grasp what had happened to bring their barbecue party to a crashing, violent halt. This morning she'd discussed the eco-terrorist threat with Bryan, and it seemed as though they might have had luck on their side—48 hours beyond the terrorists' deadline and no sign of them. The party would go on as planned. Both of them had been pleased. Relieved even. Now, a mere eight hours after that conversation, she heard gunshots cracking in the Glade and ghoulish screams for help echoing across the meadow. Dinosaurs were running amok. She was crippled with worry over Bryan, fearing her husband had become lost in his machismo vigilante mindset and gotten himself hurt. Or worse. Loretta was still miffed at him for his part in putting their family at risk, but she certainly didn't want any harm to come to him. She found herself caught between worry, forgiveness, and reproachful anger. Not a good place to be. And their party guests who had been attacked by marauding dinosaurs?

Quite simply, *madness*.

All she could do now was protect her children. Get them to safety.

"Hang on, guys," she said, yanking the wheel sharply to the right, steering them off the dirt road and down into the field. The pickup bounced over the uneven terrain, the kids whipping from side to side. The suspension groaned with each jolt. Small rocks pelted the undercarriage. Loretta white-knuckled the wheel, keeping the speed down, praying they wouldn't blow a tire or bottom out.

Ethan spoke in a jittery voice. "Dad knew about those attackers, didn't he?"

It caught Loretta by surprise, but it shouldn't have. Ethan was sensitive, always quick to pick up on Bryan's and her moods. "Why do you say that?"

"Because he's been acting weird all week. Like he's waiting for something bad to happen. It's not like him at all."

"Not the right time to discuss this, Ethan," Loretta said, trying to concentrate on her driving, wishing her younger son hadn't brought up Bryan in front of Lianne.

"Is Daddy okay, Mama?"

Loretta could feel her daughter shaking next to her. The poor girl was panicked. It ripped a hole in Loretta's heart. "I'm sure he's fine, sweetie. He's going to meet us in—"

"Mom! Look out!" Paul yelled, head turned, looking out the passenger window.

Loretta picked up a streaking grayish blur a split second before it hit the truck with a terrible force. The pickup tilted to the left, and she fought the wheel trying to keep the truck upright.

Lianne and the boys screamed in unison. Bodies slid into Loretta, shoving her against the driver's side door.

She looked to her right to see a Dromaeosaur running beside the truck, keeping pace, turning its head to peer into the cab, drool dripping from its wide shovel mouth.

Loretta swung the wheel sharply to the left, away from the animal. The truck hit a small mound and hurtled four feet off the ground, sending them airborne for an endless minute, coming down with a jarring blow. She felt her teeth clunk together on impact.

"You guys okay?" she said, tasting blood on her tongue. There was no answer.

She hit the accelerator hard, increasing their speed, trying to outrun the beast, the truck juddering over the washboard ground. She tracked the sprinting beast in the sideview mirror.

It was right there, on their flank, keeping up its spirited chase.

Another powerful bump to the rear of the pickup.

The truck swayed to one side. Loretta tugged the wheel to straighten their course. Uneasy, she glanced in the rearview mirror, seeing the Dromaeosaur leap up into the truck bed. She could hear the creature's claws scrabbling across the cargo bed floor.

The kids shrieked in horror, their screams deafening in the enclosed cab.

The creature attempted to get at them through the rear window, repeatedly smashing its broad snout against the glass. Slobbery saliva dribbled down the pane. Oversized teeth scraped the glass. Loretta could hear groans and snarls that competed with the racing engine. *Hopefully that glass will hold up.*

Ethan and Paul slumped down in their seats, heads turned, gazing at the crazed animal in the rear window through fear-widened eyes.

To Loretta's surprise, Lianne jumped up on the seat and turned around to face the creature. She pulled her meteorite necklace out from under her shirt and placed the glittery black stone up against the glass.

"Get lost, you nasty dinosaur!" she cried.

Paul watched her. "What the hell're you doing, Lee?"

Lianne kept her focus on the Dromaeosaur, her hand steady on the meteorite pendant as the beast trained its malevolent red eyes on her through the rear window. "Daddy told me this necklace would protect me from the dinosaurs. He said they wouldn't hurt me if I showed 'em this rock."

"You're a dumbass," Paul snapped. "That's just somethin' Dad told you to help you sleep at night. It's not true."

"Is *so*!" she barked, bravely holding her ground as the beast upped the intensity of its attacks against the glass. "Daddy said it and I believe him."

"Pauley's right, Lee," Ethan said. "It's stupid."

"It's *not* stupid! Shut up, Ethan!"

"Sit back down, Lee," Loretta cried. "I'm gonna try and lose him."

"But Mama—"

"Don't *But Mama* me, young lady! Sit down right now!"

Lianne obeyed with a wounded sigh. She tucked the stone pendant back under her shirt.

"Hold on, kids. This could get a little dicey."

Loretta jerked the wheel left-right-left-right, hard, attempting to throw the Dromaeosaur out of the cargo bed. The animal lost its balance and skidded across the floor, crashing into the wall, then slid back into the opposite wall as Loretta continued her jerky steering.

Another quick pull to the right, too hard this time. She felt her stomach leave her as the truck flipped on its side, slewing across the rocky plain before rolling over twice.

Up became down, and down became up again in a disorienting tumble.

Screams filled the cab. Loretta banged her head against the dash, caught in the tumultuous tangle of bodies and arms and legs.

The truck came to a stop on its roof, the radiator spewing steam, the engine idling. Loretta was dazed. Her neck hurt. She tasted more blood in her mouth. She breathed in gasoline and burnt radiator fluid. Dust swirled through the cab. Her head was jammed up firmly against the ceiling, turned awkwardly toward the driver's-side window, leaving her staring out at an upside down world.

She heard Paul groan in pain and go into a coughing jag, the sounds distant, as if coming from the far side of the field.

Loretta opened her mouth to ask if everyone was okay, but she couldn't find her voice. Couldn't form any words. All that came out were breathy hoarse barks.

She heard Ethan's voice, raspy and throaty, the words thick on his tongue. "So much for your magic necklace, Lee."

No response from Lianne.

A wave of dizziness washed over Loretta.

And then she passed out.

Sifting Through the Embers

August 10: Gilliam's Guidepost
Heart Butte, Montana

THE STRUCTURES IN THE MAIN COMPOUND still smoldered 48 hours after the catastrophic events two days ago. The inn, general store, and Gilliam farmhouse had been decimated, burnt down to their concrete foundations. The horse stables and two barns—though severely damaged—were the only buildings still standing. The stench of charred wood and ash hung over the Guidepost. Drifting smoke tinted the air a hazy gray, dimming the sunlight. The once bustling Gilliam estate now lay in silent ruin. Bryan and Loretta Gilliam's beloved home resembled a scarred, shadowy battlefield, a post-apocalyptic ghost ranch.

The east meadow and Gilliam's Glade was also devastated. A handful of abandoned cars and pickup trucks dotted the meadow. Most of the Glade habitat fencing had been flattened. Two industrial Caterpillar bulldozers sat side by side, their blades draped in snarls of chain-link, their front grilles dinged with bullet holes. A shot-up Land Rover SUV sat nearby, its windshield completely gone, glass shards sprinkled over the hood, tires blown out. The red cedar observation tower was badly splintered, but intact and standing tall. A few discarded ball caps and t-shirts were strewn across rows of the aluminum viewing stands. Plastic containers and empty Coca-Cola bottles sat atop the picnic tables. A couple of baseball gloves lay in the dirt. The dinosaurs were gone, with the exception of the lone Dromaeosaur lying dead in an adjacent field, crushed beneath the Gilliams' overturned pickup truck. Turkey vultures circled overhead, their sharp eyes searching the grounds for carrion.

The press had rolled in early this afternoon, with most major media outlets represented. Upon arrival, broadcast crews were informed by law enforcement that the Gilliam home compound was off limits due to hazardous conditions and ongoing fire inspections. They were also told that the Glade was a no-entry zone, having been cordoned off as a crime scene. Several of the national network bigwigs put up a stink, saying they were being deprived of access, that they couldn't possibly report the story accurately to their viewers without entry into those areas. It became heated and after a couple of altercations, the police were forced into making arrest threats to get the New York suits to finally back off. Several networks with big budgets at their disposal elected to get aerial footage of the two prohibited areas.

So the on-air personalities and their AV teams congregated in the rock-strewn field on the western side of the east meadow where the crashed pickup truck with the dead Dromaeosaur pinned beneath it made a striking backdrop for evening news segments.

Lawrence Nyland, an NBC field correspondent, stood poised in front of the overturned truck, far enough away that his videocam tech could get the Dromaeosaur's bloody maw and mangled body in the frame. Nyland spoke loudly to be heard over the other journalists who were also filming their reports from around the pickup truck.

"I'm standing in a fallow field at Gilliam's Guidepost ranch in Heart Butte, Montana, where tragedy struck two days ago. It was here that a lethal attack was carried out by the Animal Emancipation Faction, best known as the AEF. If you've been following our story you'll know that two months ago, a meteorite carrying dinosaur eggs struck here, hatching out a long extinct Late Cretaceous Period species known as Dromaeosaurus. This ranch is where three different genera of Cretaceous dinosaurs were being held in captivity. This property had become ground zero for paleo-zoological studies, where many top scientists from around the globe came together to learn more about the creatures that went extinct more than sixty-six million years ago. Those valuable prehistoric research specimens are no longer here, thanks to the AEF, an animal rights extremist group that is an offshoot of the Animal Liberation Front. AEF is known by the FBI to be a well-funded and dangerous domestic terrorist operation hellbent on their cause. The group's mission statement preaches that all animals should be free of imprisonment and servitude to humans. The bunch that struck here two days ago, however, took things well beyond freeing the research dinosaurs.

"Investigators are still trying to piece together exactly what happened, but we have it on good authority that as many as fifteen AEF members stormed the ranch, using big industrial bulldozers to knock down fences to free the animals, torching buildings, and murdering innocent people who got in their way. At least six people lost their lives to the rampaging Dromaeosaurs and Tyrannosaurus Rexes that escaped. The latest official reports say sixteen dead—many of them AEF members—seven hospitalized, and at least three missing. Four arrests were made the evening of the attack, all members of the Animal Emancipation Faction. The bevy of charges brought against the four included criminal trespass, reckless endangerment, arson, felony vandalism, aggravated assault, assault with a deadly weapon, and deliberate homicide.

"I'm sorry to have to report that the Gilliam family lost everything. Their home, their motel, and their general store were all torched and burned to the ground. We're not permitted into that area due to post-fire safety concerns, but most of the buildings on their property are now piles of ash on concrete slabs. It was a sad, tragic day for the Gilliams. Behind me . . ." Nyland stepped aside, giving viewers a clearer sightline, "you can see the overturned truck and the dead Dromaeosaur pinned underneath. We're told four members of the Gilliam family were in this vehicle, trying to flee the mayhem when the truck rolled over, killing the animal. At least two of the Gilliams in that crash were transported to Blackfeet Community Hospital in Browning. The family patriarch, Bryan Gilliam, is also at that medical facility, in intensive care after suffering gunshot wounds while trying to defend his ranch. His condition, and those of his family members is not known at this time.

"The leader of this AEF terrorist attack is Leonard Sheridan, a forty-nine year old Caucasian from Bend, Oregon, a man well known to the FBI. He is being held at Crossroads Correctional

Center in Shelby, an hour east of here, awaiting his bail bond hearing. Sheridan has a long history of scrapes with the law, the most recent a domestic spousal battery charge in Oregon. This morning Leonard Sheridan issued a public statement from his cell. Remarkably he showed no remorse for his actions, instead boasting of a great achievement. This is what he had to say . . ."

The reporter pulled an index card from his shirt pocket, dropping his head to read:

"The storming of the Gilliam ranch marked a huge victory for our organization and animal lovers everywhere. The dinosaurs being caged at Gilliam's Glade were tortured and forced to live in cramped quarters. Their treatment was inhumane. They were subjected to all sorts of painful examinations and experiments. They had to consume diets of waste meat byproducts and stale, throw-away wheat straw. They weren't allowed to hunt for live prey or eat the vegetation of their choice as their natural instincts dictate. In short, those dinosaurs were prisoners, incarcerated in what for them was surely hell. We of the Animal Emancipation Faction liberated those poor, mistreated creatures. They now run free, as is God's wish. My only regret is that we didn't kill more of the people responsible for their neglect, maltreatment, and exploitation. Long live the AEF! You will be hearing more from us in the future."

The reporter stuffed the index card in his pocket and looked up at the camera, droopy eyelids and downturned mouth expressing sadness. He paused for dramatic effect before saying, "August eighth will not soon be forgotten in these parts. This is Lawrence Nyland for NBC News, reporting live from Heart Butte, Montana. Back to you in New York, Lester."

Father's Day

August 12: St. Patrick Hospital
Missoula, Montana

THE POLYETHYLENE NECK BRACE pinched Loretta's neck and limited her movement. She was exhausted, sitting on the hard sofa in the St. Patrick ICU waiting room, tugging at the restrictive cervical collar, her head throbbing despite the Aleve she gobbled down an hour ago. She had been treated at Blackfeet Community Hospital along with Paul and Bryan. Her MRI showed no sign of vertebrae damage or spinal cord compression. The diagnosis was a severely strained neck. Though battered and bruised, she felt lucky.

Paul had not been as lucky. He had fractured his clavicle and broken his right arm in the rollover crash. A thick cast sheathed his right forearm and a sling pinned his arm to his body. He sat across from her in an easy chair, slouching down and laying back to ease the pressure on his damaged shoulder.

Loretta and Paul were released from the community hospital two days ago, but elected to stay in Browning with Bryan, who remained in critical condition. His vital signs had stabilized yesterday, allowing him to be airlifted here to St. Patrick early this morning. Loretta was grateful to the Indian physicians who performed two high-stress emergency surgeries on Bryan. Their urgency and expert surgical skills had definitely saved his life. But she knew the intensive care staff at St. Patrick was more experienced and much better equipped to handle the aftercare of gunshot victims than were the doctors at the much smaller Blackfeet clinic. Loretta and Paul were permitted to ride with Bryan in the medevac chopper but had not been able to see him since drop-off and hospital admission.

Bryan had taken three bullets, rupturing his spleen and puncturing his large intestine. One slug narrowly missed his heart, nipping his left lung. He had clung precariously to life through the first 48 hours as surgeons worked to stop the hemorrhaging and stitch up his spleen. His fall from the Glade tower added to his suffering—four cracked ribs, a broken wrist, shattered tibia and fibula, and a concussion. His condition was complicated at best. It was touch and go during those first long hours in the community hospital. Loretta had done a lot of soul searching and round-the-clock praying. Only the Percocet she'd been given in the Blackfeet clinic allowed her to catch a few hours of fitful sleep.

Amazingly, Lianne and Ethan had emerged from the truck crash unscathed, padded as they were between Loretta and Paul when the pickup rolled over. They had arrived here this afternoon to see their father for the first time since the shootout. Apisi had been a lifesaver, driving them down from Browning—a long 200-mile jaunt over winding two-lanes through the Flathead National Forest. Cranky from the long car trip and bored with the wait to see their father, Lianne and Ethan were out of control, sniping at one another, running around the waiting area, their voices loud, burning off pent-up energy. At first, the few people in the room smiled at the kids' antics, but those smiles soon turned to annoyed, impatient glares at Loretta. She rose from the sofa, her movement stiff and mechanical. She grabbed Lianne and Ethan by their elbows, pulling them back to the sofa.

Her voice was a demanding whisper. "You two settle down right now! I'm too tired for this nonsense. You're embarrassing me." She looked at Ethan. "You're old enough to know better, young man."

"I'm old enough, too, Mama," Lianne whined.

"Yes, you are, Lee," Loretta said, brushing a shock of hair off her daughter's forehead. "So let's be good now, okay? For your father. Can you do that for me?"

Lianne nodded shyly. Ethan looked away, saying nothing.

Paul sat observing his younger siblings, shaking his head, a stern frown on his face. He gave Loretta a sympathetic smile.

She thought it could have been so much worse. Especially after seeing photos of the wrecked truck. It had been pure luck that the pickup had tumbled, killing the pursuing Dromaeosaur. If that old Ford pickup had remained upright, it was a good bet none of them would be sitting here now.

But had they been lucky? When she thought of the bigger picture she wanted to weep. Their home had been destroyed, everything lost. Some of their friends died on their property that awful afternoon. Loretta's brother Jimmy was still missing with no official word on his whereabouts. Olivia Enright had been hysterical with worry over her husband. She was convinced Jimmy was dead. Bryan had mumbled something about Jimmy coming to his rescue in the Glade, about having his back and helping him fight the AEF intruders. But then he slurred something about seeing Jimmy getting snatched up by a Tyrannosaurus Rex and dragged into the woods. Bryan had been drifting in and out of consciousness and was doped up on morphine when he said it, so Loretta didn't completely trust his testimony. However, the fact remained, Jimmy Enright was still missing after four days. Investigators had found no trace of him. The possibility that Loretta's brother had been devoured by one of the escaped beasts became more real with each passing hour. She was as devastated as Livvy by the thought of losing Jimmy.

And then there was Bryan, who remained in the ICU, desperately clinging to life. Even though he was more verbal now and his vital signs had stabilized, he was still in bad shape. Loretta wondered how her two youngest children would react to seeing their father in his current state. Bryan's mother was due in from Texas later tonight, and his condition would be difficult enough for her to deal with, let alone Ethan and Lianne.

Loretta had been vacillating between two extreme emotions concerning her husband—biting anger and pitying empathy. She had despised Bryan for his constant need for attention, for his reckless quest for celebrity that had dragged their family into this insanity. She had cursed him for his machismo vigilante ways, had verbally attacked him for his failure to contact authorities after the first threatening phone call. But now that she had seen him lying in that hospital bed, seriously wounded and reduced to his most vulnerable self, she felt an immense amount of compassion for him. Shame swelled within her. How could she have ever hated her husband? Doubted him? A man like him who stands up for his Blackfoot friends? An independent thinker, always working to help his family get ahead? He was a dreamer who had seen his dreams crushed and snuffed out. A good father and provider, her mate for half her life. Her best friend and trusted confidant, a caring and tenderhearted lover. Together they had built something extraordinary at Gilliam's Guidepost. A home. A family. A way of life. And as wrongheaded as he'd been, she understood now that he had only been trying to defend his home—*their* home. He'd been trying to protect his family the only way he knew how.

She thought about her sister-in-law Olivia, who, in all probability had lost her husband. Livvy was distraught without her Jimmy. And little Marnie was suffering just as much without her father. They were holed up at home in Shelby, mother and daughter mired in the grieving process, waiting for the dreaded phone call from authorities. Hoping against all odds for something else. Wishing for a miracle.

It made Loretta think about life without Bryan Gilliam. She couldn't really conceive of it. She stole looks at Lianne and Ethan and Paul. Couldn't picture her kids fatherless. Couldn't imagine being a single mother raising three children and trying to maintain a thousand-acre ranch. The thought was overwhelming. Terrifying. She found herself revisiting all the good times she had shared with Bryan over the years—purchasing the Guidepost . . . the early carefree, romantic days of their relationship filled with an abundance of youthful dreams and the excitement of the future . . . their wedding day . . . the hilarious but sobering quirks of trying to become legitimate ranchers . . . the births of each of their children, Lianne coming late as a blessed "accident" . . . building the inn and general store businesses . . . attending the boys' baseball games.

She and Bryan had shared so many beautiful memories.

Strange how a meteorite striking our property changed the trajectory of our lives so drastically. Almost overnight.

Her contemplation was broken by a sonorous male voice.

"Mrs. Gilliam?"

She looked up to see a fiftyish man with a pale complexion and silver hair standing in front of her. He wore a white lab coat and a stethoscope draped around his neck. His nametag read:

EMILE FLETCHER, M.D.

PULMONARY INTENSIVE CARE

"Your husband is awake and asking for you. You and your kids can see him now. But I must ask that you keep it brief. No more than five or ten minutes. He's had a rough go of it."

Loretta got to her feet. "I understand, Doctor. Thank you."

Dr. Fletcher led them out of the waiting area and down a wide hallway into a darkened room with banks of computerized medical equipment grouped around an elevated bed. Monitors displayed bright numbers and graphs. A hissing sound filled the small area. Intermittent beeps came from the stack of machines. A strong, tangy antiseptic smell filled the room.

Paul stepped up to the bed. "How're you feelin', Pops?"

"Good, Pauley," Bryan wheezed.

Loretta noticed Lianne and Ethan standing well away from the bed, both registering shock at seeing their tough, usually energetic father laid up in bed in a hospital gown, face pale and sweaty, plastic tubing and wires dangling from his gaunt body.

Having seen his father in the Blackfeet clinic before and after the surgeries, Paul was undaunted by Bryan's haggard appearance. "Look what I got," he said, trying to hide the pain caused by moving his damaged shoulder to push out his arm cast. "Me and Mom are a real sight aren't we? But hey, at least we slayed that hell dragon. Stomped that ornery bastard flat."

Bryan smiled, his bleary eyes brightening. He reached out, ran a finger along the edge of the cast.

"I don't think I'll be swinging a bat anytime soon, though," Paul continued. "And I hate to tell you this, Dad, but your truck is totaled."

A barely perceptible smile from Bryan. "That's okay, Pauley," he said, his voice a strained whisper. His eyes swept the room. "I'm just glad you're all okay."

Loretta turned to look behind her, where Lianne and Ethan were hiding. "Anything you two want to say to your father? You certainly weren't this bashful in the waiting room."

Ethan stared down at the floor but Lianne came forward.

"I've really missed you, Daddy."

"I missed you, too, peanut."

"Are you gonna be okay?"

Bryan nodded, his eyes glistening with tears.

Lianne pulled her necklace pendant out from under her shirt. "My meeteeyite necklace didn't work the way it was supposed to, Daddy. I tried, but it didn't scare off that creepy ol' dinosaur the way you said it would."

"Whaddaya mean? That Dromaeosaur is dead. I'd say the necklace worked just fine, Lee."

Lianne, momentarily confused, looked from the glittery black pendant in her hand to Bryan, then back to the pendant. "Well, if you say so," she said finally. "I just know I still love it, Daddy, because you made it specially for me. I will always wear it. Even when there aren't any of those bad dinosaurs around." She went to the edge of the bed and draped her arms across her father the best she could. "I love you, Daddy. Please get better."

"Love you, too, sweetheart."

Lianne pulled herself up on the edge of the bed and planted a kiss on her father's forehead.

Loretta could not hold back the tears any longer. Everything they had been through came crashing down on her and she had to take a seat. She pulled tissues out of her purse, sniffling as she dabbed at her face. Her neck ached under the brace.

"Are you okay, Mom?" Ethan said, going to her, putting a hand on her shoulder.

"I'll be fine in a minute," she said, embarrassed by her emotional display, trying to collect herself.

A meteorite and a menagerie of dinosaurs led us to this place. How strange the twists and turns life takes.

Dr. Fletcher entered the ICU. "Everyone all right in here?"

"Yeah, we're okay," Paul said. "My mother has just been

through a lot."

"You all have, son," the doctor said, looking at Loretta with concern. "Would you like me to get a nurse to take a look at you, Mrs. Gilliam?"

The attention made her uncomfortable. She waved him off. "No, I'm fine, really. But thank you."

Dr. Fletcher said, "Well, I think it might be best to let Mr. Gilliam get some rest now. Do you all have a place to stay?"

"Not yet. I'm planning to get us a hotel room nearby."

"The Marriott Residence Inn is within walking distance. It's nice and we get a big discount there. I'll have Polly at the main desk get you set up with a discount, if you'd like."

"Yes, that sounds good. Thank you so much, Doctor."

Paul, Ethan, and Lianne followed Dr. Fletcher out of the ICU. Loretta stayed behind, going to the bed. She leaned over and kissed Bryan, her neck brace making it awkward. She was shocked at how frail and depleted he looked up close.

"I'm so relieved you're conscious and talking again, hon," she said, her face close to his. "Do you remember anything about your stay in the Blackfeet clinic?"

"No. I only remember a sting in my gut and a burning pain in my chest, then falling off the tower. Everything after that is a hazy dream."

"Do you remember Pauley and me coming with you on the helicopter transport this morning?"

"A little. I was pretty doped up. The one thing I do remember is wondering why Pete Lacroix wasn't piloting the chopper."

She smiled down at him, stroked his cheek. "I'm really glad you're back among the living. You scared the bejeezus out of me."

"I scared the bejeezus out of *myself*."

Loretta's neck throbbed. She straightened, stood back from the bed, glancing at the readouts on the bedside monitors. The colored lights and numbers were medical hieroglyphics to her. A mystery.

"It was nice seeing the kids," he rasped as he reached for her hand, pulling her closer. "It's great seeing you, too, Lor . . . being able to talk with you. I've missed that pretty face and long silky hair. That's quite a brace you've got there. Your neck okay?"

"Just a minor sprain."

Bryan scrutinized her, the doubt in his eyes saying he didn't believe her.

She said, "The kids have been a handful without you, Bry. All the questions . . . their anxieties. About you. About Jimmy. I need you back in the saddle helping me with them."

"I'll be there soon, I promise, Lor."

"Was that true what you said about Jimmy? That you saw a Tyrannosaur drag him off into the woods?"

Bryan's face changed, taking on a darker cast. He nodded slowly. "Yeah. It was one of the last things I saw before I got shot. Jesus, Loretta, your brother came to help me and I watched him die! It will haunt me forever," he blurted through soft sobs. "I *know* I could have saved him . . . if only I acted quicker . . ."

His words reached deep inside her and squeezed her heart. Even though they were all aware Jimmy being gone was a real probability, hearing it here overwhelmed her. Loretta cried along with Bryan. She moved in close, wrapping her arms around him, kissing him. Though she was hurting, she consoled him, telling him there was nothing he could have done, that it was out of his control.

They wept softly for several long minutes before Loretta dried her eyes and regained a semblance of self-control. She wanted to lighten the mood and move on to something more pleasant, so she brought up Lianne.

"You should have seen Lee trying to scare that Dromaeosaur off, Bry. She stood up on that seat, brave as could be, and flashed that meteorite stone at it. The whole time the beast was trying to get at her—at *us*—through the rear window. But she stood her ground. You would have been proud of her. Lee believed you about the power of that pendant. She put all her faith in you. She tried to protect us with the courage you invested in her."

"And now she knows I'm a liar," Bryan said.

"No, she doesn't think that at all. Lianne loves you. She thinks you're the best daddy on the entire planet."

"Well, maybe . . . I don't know. One thing I do know is that

Ethan . . . well, he acted like he was mad at me. Maybe even afraid of me. My son just kept staring at me. Like I was a circus sideshow act or something."

"You were almost killed in a gunfight, Bry. That's a lot for a fourteen-year-old to process. Hell, it's a lot for *me* to process."

"Look, I know I took chances I shouldn't have," he said, the weepiness coming on again. "I admit I was a fool."

"You haven't been a fool, darlin'. You defended your castle. You're to be commended for that. It's really a noble and courageous thing you did. But that's all water under the bridge now. You just need to get well so we can all be together again."

Tears flowed, plopping on his gown. "I love you so much it hurts, Loretta."

"You've got enough hurtin' going on without hurtin' some more." She leaned over and wiped his eyes with a tissue. "I love you, too, Bry. I'm your dreamcatcher, remember?"

"I do," he murmured, squeezing her hand. "I *really* do."

"Listen to the doctors and nurses. Rest up and get well for us."

She kissed him goodbye. He was smiling as she left the ICU.

8 months later . . .

Bestselling Authors

April 11: Baird Auditorium
Smithsonian National Museum of Natural History
Washington, D.C.

THEY WERE ONSTAGE AT BAIRD AUDITORIUM on the final stop of their book tour. Hayden and Nora stood behind side-by-side podiums, giving their spiel to the packed house. Hayden was exhausted, this being their sixteenth event in three weeks. They'd visited a dozen cities and been through too many airports. They'd driven rental cars of every make and model, and been shuttled from one event to another by literary escorts. They'd made love and slept in a wide variety of hotel beds. He and Nora had made promotional television and radio appearances along with the bookstore meet-and-greets. Most days had been twelve-hour marathons of endless faces and names. But Hayden had to hand it to their publisher, Random House. They had treated him and Nora like royalty, rolling out the red carpet, giving them first class travel accommodations and a generous expense account that allowed them to dine at the best restaurants.

Most of their book signing appearances had been at the big-box corporate chains and large independent bookstores, with a few libraries sprinkled in. Baird Auditorium—located under the Smithsonian National Museum of Natural History Rotunda—was by far the nicest venue on the tour. The spacious room was stunning in its elegance, with its luxurious seating and stylish domed ceiling of original 1910 Guastavino tiles presenting a glimmering mosaic overhead. The place was filled to capacity—all 530 seats filled—

the event having been sold out for weeks. Rumor had it that at least twice that many had been turned away.

Hayden and Nora were following their usual author talk routine, with Hayden leading off, warming up the crowds with his off-the-cuff, folksy yarns about chasing prehistoric beasts, and Nora following, reading selected passages from the book. This one-two punch had been effective since the book launch in Los Angeles. Hayden could only shake his head when he thought back to the launch party in L.A. three weeks ago, the publisher's expensive promotional bash that included inflatable dinosaurs, glittery black balloons painted to resemble cracked meteorites, and cheese and crackers shaped like little Triceratops and T-Rexes. A little over-the-top tacky in his opinion, but hey, whatever sold books was fine with him.

Their book, *Cretaceous Stones: The Return of Prehistoric Life to Earth*, had climbed the *New York Times* Bestseller List rapidly since its release. *Cretaceous Stones* now sat at number three on the hardcover nonfiction list and was expected to hit the top spot on the overall list next week. Their appearances had drawn big crowds from the beginning, thanks to rave reviews in *Publishers Weekly, Kirkus Reviews,* and *Booklist*, and a big-dollar marketing campaign from the publisher. A large printing of 8,000 advance review copies generated more than a thousand five-star Amazon reader reviews. The public clamored for *Cretaceous Stones* and a chance to catch the pair of engaging paleontologist authors who told exciting tales of tracking and capturing dangerous and exotic dinosaurs.

As Nora read from the book about their rousing capture of the two Tyrannosaurus Rexes at the Montana barley farm, Hayden eyed the hardcover copies stacked on tables in front of the stage. Several Smithsonian employees sat to one side, a cash drawer and credit card machine in front of them, ready to sell books to the attendees once the presentation ended. Another table contained promotional posters propped up on easels showing the *Cretaceous Stones* cover—an artist's rendering of a meteor-streaked night sky over the Gilliams' meadow with fire spreading around a crashed meteorite and Dromaeosaur juveniles scurrying about. It was a striking, eye-catching image that Hayden and Nora both loved at first sight. The publisher had done a fine job with it, and Hayden figured the flashy cover art alone sold a lot of copies.

Julia Jackson, the Smithsonian Events Director, told Hayden the demand was so great they had more than a thousand books for them to sign. He and Nora had signed 1,200 copies in New York City last night, and his hand was already in an arthritic state. But he wasn't complaining.

Life was good.

He and Nora were riding a wave of publishing nirvana.

As Nora continued reading, he looked out over the crowd and found himself appreciating that Random House had pushed them to get their book out first, before a stream of other dinosaur memoirs flooded the market. Geologist Greg Dulowski had received a lucrative deal. His book had received a great deal of pre-publication buzz in the trades, as had the book being tri-authored by Anthony Mallory, Walton Rayburn, and Corella Britton, the astrophysicists who conceived the controversial MRB Theory of Terrestrial Cretaceous Rebirth. Paleozoologist Franz Krause was also reportedly working on a big-buzz book. The publishing world was also expecting works from William Blazenhurst of the American Meteor Society, several Idaho astronomers, a Montana wheat farmer, and a slew of first-hand witnesses to dinosaur attacks on humans. Publishers were eager to cash in on this dinosaur renaissance, going to great lengths to land stories from people who'd had direct contact with the prehistoric animals. Publishing money was flowing.

But not everyone was cashing in on the publishing gold mine. Bryan and Loretta Gilliam had been offered multiple book deals, but they declined them all, preferring to stay out of the public eye. They wanted no part in rejoining the media circus that imprisoned them last summer. Hayden couldn't blame them. That poor bastard Bryan had suffered greatly. All the Gilliams had paid a huge price. They'd lost their home. They'd lost dear friends. They'd lost family in Jimmy Enright. Hayden liked Jimmy. Thought he was a good man who died in a most horrific, nearly unimaginable fashion. Hayden was also saddened by the loss of wildlife biologist Barrett

Hailey, whose estate had turned down publishing offers out of respect for the late scientist. Normally Hayden didn't much care for government types, finding most of them to be bureaucratic bores. But Barrett was different. Hayden had enjoyed working with him and would miss him. Others declining publishing offers: Great Falls Boy Scout leaders Wayne Fahlman and Dennis Miaway, who were under court order not to speak publicly about the attack on their troop while their civil lawsuits were still in process, and Russell Cavanaugh, the Idaho Forest Service pilot who survived a helicopter crash and spent a week in the wilderness eluding hungry Tyrannosaurs. Cavanaugh had signed a binding nondisclosure agreement with the U.S. Air Force, for whom he was working at the time of the crash, and could not legally discuss the details of his catastrophe.

Nora finished her readings to enthusiastic applause. Julia Jackson put out the call for audience questions.

The first question came from a young woman with a serious expression, bottle-blonde shoulder-length hair, and electric blue wire rimmed glasses.

"Hi. First let me say I enjoyed your book very much. It reads like an exciting thriller."

Hayden grinned. "Thank you so much. Most of the credit goes to my partner here. I tell Nora all the time she missed her calling. She would make a terrific novelist."

"I pay him well to say these things," Nora said, poker-faced, generating a swell of laughter.

Hayden addressed the young woman. "Do you have a question for us?"

"Yes. As far as I'm aware there have been no official sightings of dinosaurs since the tragedy at the Gilliam ranch, and there have been no further attacks on people since that horrible day. Do you think these creatures are gone for good?"

Hayden shook his head. "Absolutely not. Quite the contrary. They just bedded down to ride out the harsh winter. There are thousands of square miles of uninhabited wilds along the Continental Divide in Montana and Idaho, with hundreds of deep caves.

Much of it is uncharted badlands. We believe they have retreated into that vast wilderness. These animals possess a keen intelligence and are quite adaptable. We think they learned quickly that humans present a strong threat to them. That alone has curtailed attacks on people. But it's the weather mostly that has sent them into hiding, with subzero temperatures, blizzards and ice storms hitting that area of the country from late October through March. That said, Nora and I spotted a few of them after that awful day at the Gilliam ranch. Granted they were quick glimpses. But we did see the aftermath of their destruction last September and early October, when we were called out to investigate livestock slaughters and crop decimation."

"Why didn't we hear about that on the news?" the young woman asked.

Nora answered. "I don't know. I have long since given up on trying to figure out how the national media picks their news stories. We visited two cattle ranches in southern Idaho and three wheat farms in western Montana. Like Hayden said, we got brief looks at a couple of dinos, even got video and photos—a T-Rex at one of the ranches, a Triceratops at a farm. We saw plenty of devastation up close. We weren't able to get those reports in the book, but you can find information about them online." She glanced at Hayden expectantly. "Maybe our next book?"

"Oh, so there *will* be a sequel to *Cretaceous Stones*?" the woman asked, a hopeful lilt in her voice.

Hayden nodded. "Yes, our publisher has contracted us to do a follow-up. The deal was just finalized two days ago."

"Awesome! I'm looking forward to it," the blonde said, taking her seat.

A sixtyish man with snow white hair spilling over his shoulders and a fluffy Santa Claus beard to match was next. "In your book you write that you fully expected the dinosaurs to migrate to the deep southwestern United States when winter set in. As far as anyone knows that hasn't happened. Do you have any conclusions on that?"

"Great question," Hayden said. "You're right, sir. There hasn't been any evidence of southerly migration. I have to admit it surprises me. I thought for sure they would instinctually move to a warmer climate more suitable to their physiology. The fact that no dinos have been seen in southern California, Arizona, or New Mexico through the winter tells me they're still in Montana and Idaho. Nora and I have a theory about that, some of which is in the book. The Cretaceous-Paleogene extinction event happened sixty-six million years ago. Just prior to that mass extinction, the species we have seen from the meteorite hatchouts were all prevalent in what is now northwestern Montana, Idaho, and southern Canada. As most of you know, an enormous asteroid struck the Yucatan Peninsula, wiping out the Dromaeosaurs, Tyrannosaurs, Tricera-topses, and Ankylosaurs that proliferated in great numbers along what is now the Continental Divide. For some mysterious reason, our meteorites returned them to the same geographical area. A strange irony. We think the reason these species are reluctant to leave the area is due to an ancient, deeply-rooted location sensibility telling them they have returned home. This primordial conscious-ness is strong, informing them they are back inhabiting the land that is theirs. Kind of like a biological GPS that guides them, if you will. Crazy? Yes. But it's one explanation for them staying put through the long bitter winter."

"Interesting," the snowy-haired man said. "But how do you know there are any dinosaurs still alive? The government bounty program killed off a large number of them, as did farmers and ranch-ers. And I would think many of them couldn't make it through the winter. Maybe they're all dead and gone."

Nora said, "The bounty program only took down a couple dozen animals. That's a small percentage of the estimated four-hundred-plus dinosaurs that hatched out. Also, if what you say is true, the fine folks at the Smithsonian wouldn't keep Hayden and me on the payroll as dinosaur trackers. We fully expect to see dinosaur activity as the weather warms up. *Where* they emerge is the big question."

"That's right, Nora," Hayden said. "I'll add to that. Astrono-mers tracked fifteen meteorites coming down out of that meteor shower in late May last year. We have evidence that most if not all of them contained Cretaceous dino eggs. The figure you mentioned is in the ballpark. Based on the egg nests we saw in the Gilliam meteorite, and those the government trackers located, our best educated guess is that somewhere between four- and five-hundred animals hatched out. The numbers killed by hunters and ranchers wouldn't put a dent in that number. And after studying these animals closely over a six-week period, we know how durable they are. They're crafty survivors. I have no doubt they could survive the elements through the long winter. We'll see them again soon, I guarantee it."

Another question from a young man wearing a Washington Nationals t-shirt, ripped blue jeans, and Air Jordan sneakers. "Doctor Fowler, I've been reading online that you don't believe the Mallory-Rayburn-Britton Theory concerning the origin of the dinosaur meteorites. With all due respect, sir, if you don't believe the MRB Theory, what is your explanation for where those meteorites came from?"

Hayden had heard this one a couple of times on the tour and had a ready answer. He stroked his beard in contemplation before saying, "You should know, if you don't already, that the internet is a gossipy public forum that doesn't always deal in fact or truth. I never said I didn't believe in the theory. I said I didn't *understand* much of it. Those astrophysicists are brilliant people. Their expertise is interstellar space. Mine is Cretaceous dinosaurs. I'll let them tackle egg-laden meteorite origin concepts. It's all a little too *out there* for me, if you'll pardon the bad pun. I'll stick with the zoology and biology of these animals and leave the *where they came from* analysis to them."

A tall black man wearing a brown felt fedora spoke next. "The chapter in your book where you detail your night at the Livingston rodeo was heartbreaking, but very well written. You put me right there in the middle of that madness. Scared the hell outta me, to be honest. You folks seem to have a knack for being where these dinosaurs show up. It's uncanny how often you're right there where the action is. How do you explain it?"

"We're dinosaur magnets," Nora said with a tongue-in-cheek smirk, bringing scattered laughs from the crowd. "Seriously, we were at the Livingston Roundup tragedy because I had never been to a rodeo and it was high on my bucket list. Hayden was sweet to remember that and he surprised me with tickets. Had we known what we were in for that night, we would have stayed well away. We were also at the Gilliam Guidepost calamity, but only because we were living there at the time, working on our book. Thankfully, we missed other big attacks . . . the Tully ranch livestock slaughter . . . the Boy Scout massacre . . . the Boise strip mall assault . . . a few others."

Hayden sensed Nora starting to get emotional and he stepped in. "Nora and I share a running joke that we are dinosaur magnets. You're right. We *do* seem to have a gift for being where the dinosaurs are, or have been. It might seem predestined. But the reality of that night at the rodeo was biology, not destiny. The predators on the hunt that night—the Dromaeosaurs and Tyrannosaurus Rexes—have borderline supernatural olfactory senses. We believe they can smell their prey up to five miles away. With the rodeo site spilling over with bulls and calves and horses, and thousands of human bodies, it was an attractive feeding ground for these creatures. And we believe the Fourth fireworks show might have attracted them to Livingston as well. Our being in attendance had nothing to do with them showing up. And I'm completely with Nora on this—I *never* want to witness something like that again."

A middle-aged man in a dark blue three-piece suit stood and spoke in an articulate, self-assured tone. "I enjoyed your book very much. One of the earlier questioners had it right. It reads like a propulsive thriller. Your last chapter in particular is electrifying and terrifying, with all the shooting going on and the bulldozers knocking down the habitat fences . . . the dinosaurs escaping. How much of that was written from your personal experience that day and were you ever afraid of losing your lives?"

Hayden showed a sad smile. "It was certainly frightening being in a helicopter that was under fire. I now have a whole new respect for our brave soldiers who go through that experience. I mean, seeing bullets crack the Plexiglas and hearing the strikes against the steel undercarriage would terrify anyone. One well-placed shot hitting the fuel line could have brought us down in an explosive crash. But as fearful as both Nora and I were, our friends on the ground went through much worse. We flew over it and the carnage was unthinkable. I can't imagine the terror they felt."

Nora said, "To answer your question, we interviewed a half dozen people who were on the ground when it all went to hell. I think you'll agree with me, Hayden, that they were the most difficult interviews we did for the book." Hayden dipped his head forward in agreement.

"I mean, people were dying down there," Nora continued. "There was gunfire everywhere and fires were burning out of control. I felt guilty flying over it, felt cowardly and shameful in a lot of ways. We should have been down there with them. I even felt like an imposter for writing about something we weren't a part of. But we wanted to capture the realism of the moment for our readers."

Julia Jackson said, "We have time for one more question. Our authors have a lot of books to sign so we need to wrap things up."

A nicely dressed woman in the front row waved her hand and stood. "I have to ask. What are the Gilliams like?"

"I'm glad you brought up the Gilliams," Nora said. We owe them a debt of gratitude for their hospitality. The Gilliams are really good people. Very sweet and friendly folks. Giving and caring. They accommodated us scientists and government officials through last summer, letting us all stay at their ranch for free. They sacrificed their privacy for us. They gave us access to all of their facilities so we could conduct our research. Bryan Gilliam allowed us the full use of one of his barns to hatch baby Dromaeosaurs in a chicken incubator and study the animals, and later worked with us to build the outdoor habitats. The two boys—Paul and Ethan—were a huge help in our dinosaur feeding program. And their youngest, their daughter Lianne, is such a little darling. She gave us all inspiration. Through all the chaos and stress, Bryan and Loretta and their kids went out of their way for us. Hayden and I are very appreciative. It's really tragic what happened to them. They got something they never asked for or could have predicted. They deserved a much better fate. We're lucky to still have Bryan. Hayden and I have developed a long-distance friendship with the Gilliams. They deserve to be honored here, so thank you for your question."

Julia Jackson stepped to the edge of the stage. "Okay, that's all we have time for today. How about a big round of applause for our wonderful authors." She paused for the lively response, then said, "Thank you all for being a great audience. Okay, we'll start the signing line down in front. Doctor Fowler has graciously agreed to sign copies of his previous books if you have them, but please, no photographs. We have lots of books to be signed and we want to keep the line moving."

As Hayden moved offstage and took his seat at the signing table, his right hand ached in anticipation.

* * *

Two hours later, they sat in the back of the chauffeured limousine headed to their hotel. Hayden leaned in close to Nora and said, "Well, we pulled it off, my fellow scribe."

"We sure did. That was one of the better events. The audience was really invested."

"Yeah, that always helps. But I can't say I'm disappointed the tour's over. I could sleep for a week."

"You and me both."

Hayden was drained, but he felt his excitement bubbling up as he thought about the surprise he had for her.

"You have officially earned the title of bestselling author," he said. "You deserve a special celebration, Nora."

"Celebration?" she said warily. "What do you have in mind?"

"You mean other than jumping your bones later?"

She let out a soft laugh. "You are unflinchingly crude, Hayden Fowler. No filter whatsoever."

"Aw, you love it, and you know it." He kissed her face, whispered in her ear. "Why wait for the hotel? We could do the horizontal cha-cha right here."

"I'm not an exhibitionist. The driver has a clear view of us."

"I'm sure he's seen worse in his line of work."

"Aren't you the romantic one," she said with a sarcastic edge.

"Actually I *am*. I think you might find this romantic." He reached inside his suit jacket and pulled out an envelope, handed it to her.

"What's this?"

"Go ahead. Open it."

Nora tore open the envelope and peered inside. "Plane tickets? On Delta?" She dug the pair of tickets out and examined them. "Minneapolis-St. Paul to Paris? Paris, France?" She looked at him, eyes wide behind her glasses, shining like a pair of polished emeralds.

"What other Paris is there?"

"Well, let's see. There's Paris Wisconsin, near where I grew up. There's Paris Texas, Paris Illinois—"

"Don't be ridiculous, Nora. The tickets say Charles de Gaulle Airport. Of *course* it's Paris France."

"Are you kidding, Hayden? Please don't let this be one of your practical jokes."

"No joke, sweetie. Only the best for my hardworking coauthor. Not to mention, the hottest woman on the planet."

"I can't believe this! You're such a sweet man," she said, clutching the tickets to her chest.

"I also booked us a suite at the San Régis in the heart of the Champs Elysées district. We're gonna have a week we'll never forget."

"Oh my god! You remembered me talking about this while we were on the dig."

"I remember *everything* you say, Nora. Everything you *do*."

"Wait," she said, giving him a skeptical look. "This isn't another of your marriage proposals, is it?"

"Wow! That's some gratitude, woman!"

She tilted her head, said, "I'm sorry, Hayden. It's just—"

"It has nothing to do with marriage, sweetheart. I've come to grips with your stance on that institution. And I've told you before I don't need a big expensive wedding and some legal license to announce my love for you. The fact that you gave up your house in Wisconsin and came to Eden Prairie to live with me is good enough. *Plenty* good."

She gazed at him for an endless moment. "You're an amazing man, Hayden."

"I've been told that a few times."

"And you have an ego the size of Montana."

"You're not very original, Nora. I've been told that before, too."

She looked at the tickets again. "I—I'm tongue-tied. It's such an unexpected surprise. I don't know what to say right now."

"Just tell me you love me. That'll make me happy."

"Oh, Hayden . . . I *do* love you! I love you! I love you!"

She climbed into his lap and was all over him, kissing and hugging him, running her fingers through his hair and beard.

Hayden's pulse quickened. His face was on fire. He felt himself getting hard. He pushed her back on the bench seat, snaking his left hand up under her blouse and fondling her thigh with his right.

Nora let out a breathy moan and proceeded to show him just how much she loved him.

The chauffeur observed them in the rearview mirror with more than a passing interest.

Family and Friends

April 25: The Lacroix Residence
Missoula, Montana

"ARE YOU OKAY IN THERE, BABE?" Peter stood outside the master bathroom, speaking through the closed door. Brin had been in there half an hour, and she wasn't one to devote a lot of time to applying makeup or messing with her hair.

"I'm fine," she replied. "Just putting on my pretty face. I'll be out in a minute."

Peter scratched at his chin. Brin didn't sound fine. Her voice was thin. Stressed.

He said, "No need to get all dolled up, honey. It's just Georgie and his girlfriend."

"I know, I *know*," she said, impatient, irritated.

He stood by the door and listened. Heard water running in the sink, the toilet flush. He heard something else. Was she crying? Peter was concerned. She hadn't been herself the past week or two, more quiet and distracted than usual. He had tried getting to the heart of it with her, but she repeatedly cut him off with snippy responses.

He went to the bed and stretched out, put his hands behind his head. Stared at the ceiling. Things had been so good with Brin until recently. She had been happy-go-lucky after getting past the terrors they'd experienced at the Gilliam ranch. And after working for Bryan Gilliam the demand for her handcrafted jewelry exploded. Orders started coming in faster than she could keep up. Her business went from part-time, in-home hobby to offsite commercial mass production, requiring Brin to add staff and move to a larger work-space.

Peter fondly recalled them hunting for retail space together. They closed on a 3,000-square-foot storefront in downtown Missoula in early October, located on Madison Street near the Double-Tree Hilton, across the Clark Fork River from the university. They turned the space into a small, walk-in boutique shop. Brin hired three experienced jewelers—Luana, a fellow Kootenai, and Koko and Nuna, two Blackfoot women who had worked with Brin in Cretaceous Cavern at the Gilliam ranch. He remembered the pure joy that lit up Brin's face the day her shop opened. It had been a bitter cold, blustery morning the week before Thanksgiving. She had gazed up at the lighted storefront sign—*Brinshou's Baubles & Jewelry*—expressing a mixture of wonder and disbelief. She had been elated. Happy. Proud.

He heard Kachina's gleeful laughter coming from the living room, with Kimi's infectious giggle intermingled. Peter smiled. His baby daughter and Kachina had hit it off right away. Kimi loved her *gwanny* and Kachina cherished her *little flower.* Brin's mother had been living with them for the nine months they'd been back in Missoula. Kachina had been a lifesaver, taking over childcare duties through the week, letting Peter and Brin work their demanding schedules without worry. It was a beneficial arrangement for everyone, though Kachina had felt some guilt early on, as her husband, Nashota, put pressure on her to return to the rez. According to Nash, Kachina needed to come home and perform her "wifely duties." Peter wasn't about to let his much-loved mother-in-law bend to Nash's brutally possessive will. The man was an abusive, misogynist racist. It had been touch-and-go the first couple of months, with Nash showing up a couple of times, loud and angry and demanding. But as Peter figured would eventually happen, Nash's anger issues finally got him fired from his longtime casino job, landing him back behind bars. He was currently being held in Lake County Jail, serving a two-year sentence for assault. One less thing for Peter to worry about.

The bathroom door opened and Brin stepped out, her face glazed with tears.

Her appearance startled him. "What's wrong, babe?" he said,

going to her and taking her into his arms.

"Oh, Petey," she sniveled. "I don't know how this happened."

"How *what* happened?"

"I missed my period this month. Here, look for yourself," she said through sniffles, handing him a home pregnancy test stick.

"What am I looking at here?" he said, glancing at the stick. "I don't know how to read these things."

"Two lines . . . it means I'm pregnant."

"*What*? You sound disappointed. That's absolutely fantastic news," he said, supporting her as she sat on the bed.

"For you, maybe. Oh, damnit, Petey, I'm . . . I'm so confused. I don't know if I'm crying tears of joy or sadness."

"Why would you be sad? It's a beautiful thing. Kimi needs a sibling . . . a playmate. This is glorious news!"

But she wasn't having it. "Not so glorious to me. *I'm* the one who has to carry the baby for nine months. I don't look forward to that awful morning sickness again . . . overwhelming food cravings . . . the backaches and feeling bloated as a whale. It took me six months to get over my postpartum depression after having Kimi. Not to mention my jewelry business is going great and I'm afraid I might lose that."

Brin continued with the waterworks. Peter plucked a couple of tissues from the night table. "Are you sure this test is accurate?" he said, dabbing at her eyes.

"I'm *pregnant*, Peter," she said tersely. "I got the same result last week."

He was losing patience with her but he had to find a way to get this on a positive path. "Listen to me, Brin. We're gonna have another little Lacroix running around here. And you know I'll always be there to help you through. Your mother's here with us, too. She's a huge help. You won't be alone in this. And your business certainly won't suffer for it. You've got some talented people working for you, and you'll still be able to work as much as you want to."

Her sobs suddenly turned to intense hiccupping, which started both of them laughing.

"You sound like a bullfrog. Brinny the bullfrog."

"Don't <hiccup> make fun <hiccup> of me," she said, giggling.

Her hiccups increased in intensity, which set off howls of laughter.

"I've heard that standing on your head and reciting the Pledge of Allegiance will stop hiccups."

"Stop it, Petey."

He grinned at her and stood. "I'll go get you some water."

He went to the bathroom, returning with a paper cup. Brin drank the water in a couple of swift gulps. Soon her hiccups subsided.

She turned to him, her bloodshot eyes softening. "Thanks, honey. I don't know what's gotten into me. I sound like a self-absorbed, hormonal bitch." She wiped her eyes with her wrist. "You're right. I should be thankful for my supportive family . . . for the gift of another child. Sorry I acted like an ass, Petey."

He was about to tell her he understood and she had no reason to apologize when the doorbell chimed. "Our guests are here. Why don't you wash your face and I'll go greet them."

"Okay." She pulled him close and kissed him. "We're gonna have a baby, Petey. You're right . . . it *is* a glorious thing."

He watched Brin walk to the bathroom, her coal-black hair cascading down her back. He sat there for a brief moment, tasting her kiss on his lips, thinking how lucky he was to be sharing his life with such a beautiful woman.

Peter rose from the bed and went through the living room, where Kachina was reading to Kimi on the couch—a story about magical cats. He opened the front door. His young friend George Dantley smiled at him, clutching a bottle of champagne. An attractive young blonde stood next to him, dressed fashionably in a blue-and-white floral blouse, white flared jeans, and white sneakers.

"Hey, old man," George said with a grin. "I'd like you to meet Emma. She's definitely my better half."

Peter looked at the girl. Georgie had told him Emma was entering her senior year at Montana U, but she looked so much younger than that, more like high school age. She had a fresh-scrubbed pale complexion with a splash of freckles across a pert upturned nose, prominent cheekbones, and full lips that outlined a self-conscious, toothy smile.

"Nice to meet you, Emma," Peter said, taking her hand in a gentle shake. "Georgie's been bragging on you so much I feel like I already know you."

"He's told me a lot of good things about you, too," she said in a breathy whisper. "Like how you saved his life last year."

Peter smiled. "Well, Georgie has a tendency to embellish things, Emma."

George turned to Emma. "See what I told you? Pete's humble to a fault."

They were all smiles walking into the house. Peter introduced George and Emma to Kachina. Kimi ran to George and threw her arms around his leg. "Unca Jaw! Unca Jaw!" Kimi cried out the name she had called him since George started visiting after his long rehabilitation.

George took a knee and hugged Kimi with his free arm. "How's my little sweet pea doin'?"

"Good. Play with me, Unca Jaw."

"She's adorable," Emma said. "How old is she?"

Peter said, "Just turned two in February. She loves her Uncle George," he said, putting air quotes around *Uncle*.

"Tell you what, sweetums," George said to Kimi, "I'll play with you after we visit with your daddy."

"Okay. Gwanny's reading me a cat story."

George smiled at the littlest Lacroix and got to his feet.

Peter pointed to the bottle of champagne. "What's with the bubbly?"

"It's to toast my new job. I start work with the Forest Service next month, after graduation. You and I are gonna be coworkers, old man."

"Hey, that's fantastic! I'm so happy for you, buddy. Where will you be starting out?"

"Right here in Missoula. It's a desk job for the first six months, with lots of classroom training. After that, it depends on where they need me. But most likely, I'll be staying in Missoula. After I complete my training and pass the fitness requirements test, I'll be a certified conservation ranger. And they've promised me I won't have to climb back up in one of those evil fire lookout towers."

Peter nodded and smiled impishly. "Understood about the lookout tower, but you might have trouble with the physical exam, Georgie. You're a bit on the thin, frail side. Conservation officers tend to be more—shall we say—stout and *manly*?" Peter grinned and touched him on the elbow to show he was kidding.

Emma, unfamiliar with the friendly needling that went on between them, felt the need to defend George. "Oh, I think he is *plenty* manly, Mr. Lacroix," she said taking George's arm.

Peter said, "We're all adults here, Emma. You can call me Peter or Pete."

"Yeah," George said, "Calling him Mr. Lacroix reminds Pete of how old he really is."

"I guess I deserve that," Peter said. To George he said, "Seriously, you're going to love working with us. We have a great bunch there." He turned to Emma. "I hear you'll be a senior next year. What are you studying?"

"I'm in the Forestry program like George," she said brightly. "We met in an Environmental Policy and Planning class. I was kinda shy around him at first. I mean, he was famous after that meteorite took down his tower. And I felt sorry for him after what he'd been through." She gave George a warm smile.

Peter thought George was doing pretty well nearly a year after the accident. He still showed some scarring on one side of his face, but he was moving well and his hair had grown back. Still, he couldn't resist taking a poke at his young friend.

Peter said to Emma. "You should have seen your boyfriend the beginning of September, when we went to the Washington Huskies game. I thought I was gonna have to carry him into the stadium."

"Dream on, old man. You couldn't lift me on your best day."

"I'll remind you, Georgie, that I'm only thirty-seven."

"Yeah, but all those body checks you took on the ice have really taken a toll."

Peter laughed. "Funny guy, aren't you, Dantley," he said, patting him on the shoulder. "C'mon, lets break out the bubbly. Brin and I have some exciting news, too."

"Oh yeah? Do tell."

"We're pregnant!"

"*What?*" Kachina gasped from the couch.

"It's true," Peter said.

Kachina frowned at him. "Why am I always the last to know these things?"

"You're not, Kachina. It was just made official twenty minutes ago."

"Congratulations, Pete!" George said, throwing his arms around Peter's shoulders, embracing him. "Where is that beautiful wife of yours? We need to celebrate."

"She'll be out soon."

Kimi tugged on George's pantleg, "Can you play with me now, Unca Jaw?"

The Moon Rises
Over the Guidepost

May 28: Gilliam's Guidepost
Heart Butte, Montana

TODAY MARKED THE ONE-YEAR ANNIVERSARY of *The Big Boom*. Bryan sat on the front porch of their newly built farmhouse in his padded patio chair, thinking about the day the meteorite struck. The day everything changed.

He dug a bottle of Coors out of his cooler, twisted off the cap. Took a swig and pulled the hood up on his sweatshirt to ward off the chilly afternoon breeze. Scanned the premises. He hardly recognized the Guidepost these days. So much had changed over the past year. The 12-room inn was gone. So was Loretta's general store. They decided not to rebuild those commercial buildings since they no longer needed the income from those businesses. They had received a large insurance payout for settlement of losses incurred last August, and Bryan's Cretaceous Stone jewelry operation had generated a robust savings account. There was also the forthcoming criminal lawsuit they were bringing against the AEF, spearheaded by their attorney, Atlee Pinnaker, who assured them it was a slam-dunk case that would bring them a substantial payout. Bryan and Loretta were now semi-retired private citizens, with the emphasis on *private*.

They had donated a portion of the insurance money to the four Blackfoot families who had lost loved ones on that tragic day last summer. Much of the remainder of the insurance money went to rebuilding the house, barns, and horse stables (the horses were back from the Enright ranch after a long absence, which pleased Lianne immensely). They hired a Blackfoot firm to clean up the east meadow and the remains of the dinosaur habitats. The crew hauled away the observation tower, enclosure fences, bleachers, and picnic tables, returning the meadow to its previous pastoral beauty. The three foot deep, charred meteorite strike pit was all that remained of last summer's bizarre events.

Bryan had the giant wooden sign that had adorned the zoo's entrance moved to the utility barn where he did his mechanic work, and nailed to the crossbeam over the double doors. He thought the sign—*GILLIAM'S GLADE PREHISTORIC ZOO*—with its blood-red medieval script, was fitting, seeing how ancient he felt these days (after his near-fatal shooting and fall, Bryan, now 43, often felt twenty years older).

Construction on their new house had been completed six weeks ago. He and Loretta were pleased with the work. Their cramped, timeworn two-story farmhouse had been replaced with a split-level upgrade. This new version was bright and airy with hardwood floors throughout. It had a cozy den with a wide fireplace. A contemporary kitchen with custom cabinetry, Brazilian granite countertops, and modern appliances. Classy wood block furniture and custom window treatments. An enclosed patio in the rear facing the barns. Attached three-car garage. A deep front porch where he now sat.

The place felt comfortable. Familiar. Like he had returned home after a long absence.

While waiting for construction to be completed, the Gilliams lived in The Cellar, the only structure on the ranch not destroyed by fire. Bryan didn't mind living out there in the subterranean dwelling, but ultimately he was glad to be back in a traditional, above-ground house. The Cellar painfully reminded him of his late brother-in-law, Jimmy Enright. He and Jimmy had built the place together, one nail and two-by-four and drywall panel at a time. Two years they'd spent, working together to convert the old zinc mine into a living space, dedicating all their free time to the project. Bryan recalled hearing his brother-from-another-mother call out "*Hey, Gilly*" in his raspy, cigarette-parched voice, followed by an off-color joke. They shared many laughs over the years, and had been there for each other through some hard times, too. And now, more than nine months after Jimmy's violent end, Bryan could not erase the disturbingly grisly image of his brother-in-law being ripped apart and devoured by a Tyrannosaurus Rex.

Loretta took her brother's death hard. But at least she hadn't had to witness it. A memorial service was held for Jimmy at Hostetler's Funeral Home in Browning, with a large Blackfeet Nation contingency showing up to pay their respects. Jimmy was loved by many on the reservation, and the day had been a sometimes somber, but ultimately happy, celebration of Jimmy's way-too-short life. Of course, Bryan couldn't make the memorial service. He was busy fighting for his own life. He remembered how crushed he'd been, lying in that hospital bed, that he couldn't attend. He'd also missed the funerals that preceded Jimmy's memorial. So many fine people taken on that ill-fated August afternoon of the Gilliam barbecue. Nine partygoers that included the government wildlife biologist, Barrett Hailey, a man Bryan had come to like and respect. A solid week of funerals. Also taken that day were the Vigilant Eye Security & Investigation head, Tom Hennessey, and two of his employees. The three men had been murdered at their guard posts by AEF gunmen.

Bryan spent that first month in St. Patrick Hospital, followed by three months of grueling outpatient physical therapy. He still had aches and pains, and suffered from occasional migraine headaches that felt like a hatchet cleaving the top of his skull. His shoulder ached most days. A jagged scar across his midsection was a painful reminder of the work the surgeons had done to remove bullets from his spleen and large intestine. There were days when he felt so weak it was a struggle to move. His walking was laborious; he had to use a cane to get around due to the bones in his left calf not healing properly. His doctors told him surgery to reset the bones could possibly fix that, but Bryan didn't want to go back under the knife again anytime soon.

Brinshou Lacroix had gifted him with an oak walking cane, which Bryan treasured. He considered it a classic work of art. She had mounted a knob of meteorite stone on top of the staff with tiny dinosaur claws poking out of a crevice. Brin had also set a pair of small garnet gemstones in the crack above the claws, giving it the appearance of dinosaur eyes peering out. Bryan hated to be thought of as handicapped, but he sure cherished that cane.

Those interminable days in the hospital when he was floating in and out of consciousness, drifting between life and death, he experienced vivid dreams. Most were joyful reminiscences. Precious life memories. One dream in particular that seemed to be on a replay loop saw Bryan and his late older brother Bobby playing cowboys and Indians in the vacant lot behind their childhood home in Lubbock, Texas. Bobby was eleven or twelve, Bryan nine. Bryan had always preferred to be the Indian, which was okay with Bobby, who thought of all Indians as evil, primitive savages. Bryan wore a headdress of colorful feathers, and brandished a rubber tomahawk and toy rifle. Bobby wore a cowboy hat, a sheriff's badge, and plastic six shooters on both hips in leather holsters. It was simultaneously hilarious and sad, a sentimental dream of an innocent time in his life.

Bryan had almost forgotten those carefree days of his childhood, but the repeating dream brought it all rushing back, including the one big difference of opinion that generated more than a few fights between the two Gilliam brothers. Bobby was blindly contemptuous of Indians, which infuriated Bryan. Even at that young age, Bryan had held a genuine empathy for Native Americans. The mistreatment of indigenous peoples had been one of his hot buttons for as long as he could remember. He recalled checking out library books on the history of American Indian tribes as early as eight years old, reading them with intense focus when he should have been doing his homework. He despised the TV shows and movies that portrayed cowboys as the heroic good guys and Indians as barbaric savages who were hungry for paleface scalps. Bobby bought into those Hollywood depictions, but Bryan knew better. Nothing but white elitist puffery as far as he was concerned. Bryan loved his brother—the hospital dreams certainly reinforced that love—but they disagreed vehemently on that point. As they grew older, Bryan suspicioned that Bobby had racist leanings. Bryan could never understand where his brother's blind hatred came from. They certainly were not raised that way. But that one issue aside, Bryan held a lot of affection for his older brother in his heart, and looked up to him in most respects. He would give anything to have Bobby alive today. The cancer took him at age 32 just after Bryan's 30th birthday.

Thinking about the recurring dream of cowboys and Indians on that Texas sandlot pulled his thoughts to the shootout in the Glade. He had killed three men that day, wounded a fourth man who was then eaten by a Tyrannosaurus Rex. He felt no guilt or remorse over the killings. The long-repressed soldier in him came out that day. Those AEF assholes deserved to die. They were responsible for the deaths of Jimmy Enright and a number of his and Loretta's friends. They were sociopathic terrorists. Arsonists who burned his ranch to the ground. And they had tried their damnedest to kill him. Bryan figured if they liked fire so much, he was justified in sending them directly to hell where they could enjoy the flames eternally.

He had been unconscious and knocking on death's door when the FBI SWAT teams stormed the ranch to put a quick end to the bloody confrontation. He was thankful for the lives the feds ultimately saved, but he was still angry about the FBI's refusal to provide his family with protection prior to the barbecue. Loretta had called the FBI field office in Billings, playing them the threatening voice mail from Leonard Sheridan, and they just blew her off like she was some crackpot rancher's wife. Bryan would forever point the blame finger at the FBI for the number of people who died that awful day.

While he lay in his hospital bed fighting to remain in this world, the authorities had done their due diligence investigating the crime scene. Agents from the Blackfeet Law Enforcement Service, Montana DCI (Division of Criminal Investigation), the FBI, and the Montana State Fire Marshal's office spent weeks combing the property and interviewing witnesses. They collected mountains of evidence, which led to a unanimous conclusion: the Animal Emancipation Faction interlopers who stormed Gilliam's Guidepost had acted maliciously and criminally in a premeditated manner, and were found guilty of a laundry list of charges. Multiple criminal counts were levied against the surviving AEF attackers and against the organization itself—criminal trespass and endangerment, aggravated assault with a weapon, deliberate homicide, and first degree arson. Authorities collected more than enough hard evidence showing that the Gilliam ranch had been under hostile attack. Meanwhile, self-defense stand-your-ground laws protected Bryan, Apisi, and Chogan from prosecution.

Atlee Pinnaker, the Gilliams' attorney, had spent months trying to convince Bryan and Loretta to bring personal lawsuits against Leonard Sheridan and the AEF organization. The Missoula lawyer was persistent in his attempts to persuade them that they had a golden opportunity to win a large settlement. The evidence was overwhelmingly in their favor. The AEF had deep pockets, he'd said. And the AEF's claim that the participants in the August 8 invasion were rogue operatives doing their own thing and not working under their direction did not hold water. Especially when investigators discovered the two big bulldozers used in the attack had been purchased by the AEF organization and were legally registered to them. So why not go for it? They had nothing to lose and everything to gain, Pinnaker had repeated at least twice a week.

Initially, Loretta was open to the idea, but Bryan was hesitant. Yes, he'd been violated. Yes, he'd suffered mightily—the *family* had suffered. And yes, he *did* want to exact revenge on Leonard Sheridan. However, he had no desire to return to the glare of the national media spotlight. A bigtime lawsuit like that would definitely put them back in the nightly news. But Pinnaker kept working on him, telling him they could easily win this thing and it would be a slam dunk. A *big money* slam dunk. Finally, three weeks ago, Bryan saw the light. He felt they *should* be justly compensated for damages incurred, for all the pain and suffering he and his family had been through. And he and Loretta had decided to split any settlement with the Blackfoot families who also lost so much that day. So what if the media hounds started coming around again. Bryan had a first-rate security firm providing round-the-clock security now. Grudgingly, he finally agreed to move forward with the twin lawsuits. Last week, Pinnaker started preliminary paper-work to bring legal actions against Leonard Sheridan and the Animal Emancipation Faction.

Bryan wasn't alone in his struggle to overcome the devastating events of last August. All of the Gilliams needed healing help. When Bryan had recovered physically to the point where he could travel, he joined Loretta and the kids in family counseling sessions with Dr. Helen Krickstad, the clinical psychologist who had worked wonders with Lianne last year. Twice a week the Gilliams would make the half-hour drive to Browning for heart-to-heart talks with the therapist, each discussing their innermost thoughts about the tragic events of last summer, and their problems dealing with the aftermath. The sessions had been extremely helpful. Especially for the kids. Dr. Krickstad had a way with children. She possessed a calming, self-assured nature that got Lianne, Ethan, and Paul to open up, to recognize and acknowledge their fears, and to accept her solutions for recovery. She got Lianne to overcome her trepida-tion of bad men with guns. She helped Ethan understand that the high pedestal he'd placed his father on just wasn't reasonable, that Bryan was a good man who loved his children dearly, but was fallible, like all human beings. She worked with Paul to get him past his panic attacks. And Dr. Krickstad worked with all three young Gilliams, getting them to regain their trust in Bryan and Loretta again, and curbing the kids' fears of losing their parents through a violent act.

Bryan heard a rumbling out on Badger Creek Road. Paul was getting home from school. Bryan had bought his oldest son a used (*very* used) Ford F-250 pickup for his 17th birthday in March. The run-down clunker was nearly as old as Paul and on its last wheels, but Pauley didn't care. The oil-burning beater was his ticket to teen independence. No more riding the school bus. He now had wheels to take his new girlfriend—Sinopa, an olive-skinned Blackfoot beauty—out on dates. But most importantly to Paul, the truck was the perfect vehicle for hauling his band's equipment to gigs.

Initially Bryan had been disappointed when Paul decided to give up baseball this season. Paul blamed it on the shoulder injury he'd suffered in the rollover crash. Said he couldn't swing the bat with authority due to the pain. The follow-through motion hurt too much, he'd said. So he'd given up the national pastime in favor of his new passion—playing music. Loretta bought him an electric guitar—a cheap Mexican Fender Stratocaster knockoff—and a small amplifier, and enrolled him in twice-a-week lessons in Browning. Bryan had been skeptical at first, thinking the boy would not stick with it. But Pauley surprised him. He took to the instrument immediately, seeming to have a natural flair for it. He practiced every free moment, and amazed Bryan and Loretta with how fast he progressed. It was like he'd been a guitar virtuoso in a previous life. Bryan built him a rehearsal space in the utility barn, a small stage adorned with the PA speakers from the Glade observation tower wired to a new 16-channel soundboard. Pauley was in heaven out there. Soon, he was inviting schoolmates over to jam with him. They produced a lot of raucous noise at first, but by late January, a band started to come together—Pauley on guitar and lead vocals, and two of his Blackfoot friends, Kit Reeder on bass and backup vocals, and Hass Oxendine (better known as Ox) on drums. They went by the name *Moonrise* and had recently started booking gigs at school parties. Bryan also got them bookings at VFW halls in Browning and Cut Bank using his veteran connections. Bryan loved to sit in on their practices and hear the songs come together. Kit and Ox were good kids and positive influences on Paul. And the music kept the three of them focused and away from the drug scene that was pervasive on the rez.

Ethan, nearing his fifteenth birthday, was the star shortstop of his American Legion team, which helped Bryan get over his disappointment in Paul walking away from baseball. Ethan underwent a weight training program over the winter and had bulked up. The off-season physical conditioning improved his fielding and turned him into a power hitter. And Ethan seemed to play better without his big brother casting a shadow over him. Bryan and Loretta enjoyed going to his games, and even Lianne liked watching her brother play, though Bryan suspected his daughter was mostly interested in the cotton candy they sold at Ethan's games.

Paul turned off Badger Creek Road and pulled through the front gate, the security guard on duty waving him through. He drove up the gravel drive, a cloud of exhaust streaming out the tailpipe like a smoky tail, the motor backfiring a couple of times. Bryan smiled as he saw Sinopa ("Please call me Sin") sitting close to Paul in the cab. Kit and Ox rode in the rear bed, safeguarding a large bass amplifier. They drove around to the back of the house, to the rehearsal barn, all of them waving at Bryan as they passed.

A few minutes later, Loretta joined him on the porch. "You okay, Bry?"

He shifted in his chair to look at her. She had recently cut her long brown hair short and looked more beautiful than ever. The change in hairstyle enhanced the caramel hue of her eyes and made her look younger somehow.

"Yeah, all's well, sweets. Just thinkin' is all."

She took a seat in the rocker next to him. "I get worried when you start thinking this much." She eyed the empty Coors bottles. "You like drinkin' alone?"

"Are you putting me down or wanting to join me?"

"Well . . . I'm not putting you down," she said, smiling.

He reached down and grabbed a beer, twisted off the cap and handed her the chilled bottle.

Loretta took a gurgling swallow. "Ah, that hits the spot." She gave him a sideways peek. "You've been out here thinking through four beers. Must be a lot on your mind. What's up?"

"Just reflecting on what we've been through. It's been a year since that meteorite came down."

"Yes, one year exactly. I'm aware of that, Bry."

"I was just thinking about how lucky we've been."

"We *have* been lucky. It could have been so much worse." She took another drink, shook her head. "I mean, my heart breaks every time I think about Jimmy . . . about friends who died at *our* cookout. It's just too much to comprehend at times."

"I know, Lor. Oh *god* how I know!"

They sat quietly, drinking. Finally Loretta said, "I dream about him, you know."

"Who?"

"Jimmy. I miss him terribly, Bryan. He comes to me in these dreams and it's like he's real, still alive. And then I wake up and, man oh man . . . it's just not fair."

"I understand. I dream about my brother, too, Lor."

"Who, Bobby? But that's been what? Eight or nine years?"

"Twelve." He looked at her. "I don't think we ever completely get over losing a sibling."

Loretta lowered her head, started peeling the Coors label off the bottle. "I really feel for Olivia and Marnie. They're still having a rough go of it."

Bryan nodded. "I know. Livvy's got a lot on her plate. I wish there was more I could do for them, but I'm just not physically up to the task these days."

They drank in silence, gazing out across the front of their property to the entrance gate and the sporadic traffic on Badger Creek Road. Finally, Loretta said, "I love this peace and quiet, honey. It's so much better than the madness we went through last summer. It's calming . . . solace for the soul."

"Well put, Lor," Bryan said, taking a drink.

"I've been thinking about those dinosaurs. Do you think they're still around?"

"Hayden Fowler seems to think so. Says they've been hibernating through the winter. Nora, agrees with him. If anybody has a handle on that situation, it's those two."

"Well I hope they're wrong. I couldn't take another summer like last year."

"This summer will be different," he said. "We aren't zookeepers anymore."

They sat quietly for a few minutes. Then Bryan said, "You know, I had an interesting conversation with Pauley a few days ago. He told me he dreamed of his band becoming rich and famous. I didn't wanna burst his bubble so I just said, 'Be careful what you wish for, son.' When he gave me a confused look I told him that fame is an ugly mistress. It was obvious he didn't understand, so I told him, 'Just look at what happened to me . . . to *our family*.' He just laughed and said, 'Well, that's different, Pops. Those terrorists *hated* us. Moonrise will enjoy the *good* kind of fame, where everybody loves us and spends lots of money on our records.' Our boy has some big aspirations, Loretta."

"It's just teenage naivete, Bry. The kids all need to pursue their dreams, the same way we did. They need to discover the hard life lessons themselves and learn from their mistakes."

"Yeah," Bryan said glumly, "I'm still learning, myself."

She reached out for him. "We all are. The learning never ends."

The music started up in the barn, Moonrise playing a cover of a Fastball song that Bryan loved. They listened for a minute, then he said, "Who knew our boy could shred a guitar like that."

"Who knew he could *sing*," Loretta said.

Bryan let out a raspy chuckle. "Our kids are a mystery . . . until they're not."

She laughed. "Very profound, Bry. You get philosophical when you drink, dear hubby of mine."

"It's better than bein' angry."

"Amen to that."

He finished off his beer and stood, the effort bringing a stab of pain to his leg. He grimaced and grabbed his cane, then Loretta's hand. "Come on, sweets. Lianne won't be home for another hour. Let's head out to the barn and catch a set of Moonrise classics. They're gonna be famous, y'know."

"Don't I know it," she said with a giggle as he pulled her up out of the rocker.

Bryan hobbled alongside Loretta, leaning on his cane as they slowly made their way around the house to the rehearsal space. He loved this ranch, with its grasslands rolling out to the snow-capped peaks of the Rockies. The fresh, clean country air and big sky overhead. It was picture-postcard perfection. He could never guess now that this beautiful land had been desecrated in a most appalling fashion last summer.

As they walked, hand in hand, he reflected on what the past year had taught him. He realized now that fame can be an ugly mistress. Celebrity is fleeting and fickle. Once the dinosaurs were gone and the Guidepost destroyed, the news media stopped paying attention. Bryan and his family were no longer interesting to them. Back then he'd felt like a jilted lover. He should have seen it coming. He'd been a fool to allow TV reporters to play him for their ratings games. Hayden and Nora and some of the other scientists were playing the fame game now. Celebrityhood was theirs for the taking for all he cared.

He knew now there was nothing more important than his family.

Family is what mattered.

They entered the rehearsal barn. His son stood on the makeshift stage, singing and playing his heart out, Kit and Ox enthusiastically pounding it out behind him. Sin lounged in the shadows, clapping and singing along. She knew all the lyrics.

Bryan squeezed Loretta's hand and smiled at her. Kissed her cheek. She smiled back at him and kissed him on the mouth, deeply, eagerly, her exuberance knocking him off balance. He lost his grip on his cane and it fell to the floor. Laughing, she grabbed his arm, preventing him from falling, Bryan giving her an embarrassed grin as he struggled to remain on his feet.

She wrapped her arms around him and held on. He felt the warm rush of love and deep gratitude flow through her embrace.

When Bryan regained his composure, he bent and retrieved his walking cane. Lifted it and flamboyantly waved it in time to the music, using the stout oak staff like a conductor's baton. Paul smiled at him as he sang, shaking his head at his father's silliness. Kit and Ox nodded their approval as they played on.

The music and his mood lifted Bryan up. He had arrived at the top floor of Dr. Elias Richardson's metaphorical elevator. The world looked good from this vantage point.

It's great to be alive, for life is a beautiful thing!

Acknowledgements

No author does it alone . . .

Huge thanks to my early-draft reviewers: Michael Bailey, Monica Burnette, Cheryl Dennis, Jane Grant, Steve Grant, Sherry Haney, Michael Watkins, and Patricia Yoder . . . they made this crazy tale so much better with their honest and thorough feedback.

Also a shout-out to the Robinsons (Doug, Diane, and Charles) of Eagle Eye Book Shop in Decatur, Georgia for their support. They were the first bookstore to stock my books. Thank you for believing in me early on.

A big thanks to David and Julie Shockley for their generosity and hospitality in hosting two of my more successful book signings at Julie's Barbershop in Acworth, Georgia. You guys rock!

Cheers to Becky Conway of McKay's Books in Nashville. Thanks for giving me your extra special Tennessee promotion. Keep bangin' on that bass, rocker girl!

Much appreciation goes to Carole Mauge-Lewis for another fantastic book cover. This is number four for me, and they just keep getting better.

And last, but certainly not least, my most heartfelt thanks go to my loyal readers who keep my imagination churning and the stories coming. I couldn't do it without you.

Jeff Dennis
August, 2022

About the Author

Jeff Dennis is the former editor-in-chief/publisher of the award-winning speculative fiction magazine, *Random Realities*. He is the author of six novels and a short story collection.

jeffdennisauthor.com

jeff@jeffdennisauthor.com